Also by Timm Muth

Mountain Biking North Carolina

Disciple of the Flames

Timm Muth

Moonshine Press • Franklin, North Carolina

Published by:
Moonshine Press
522 Allison-Watts Rd.
Franklin, NC 28734

International Standard Book Number : 978-0-9904548-0-9

Enormous thanks to my first teacher, Sifu John "Doomsday" Scott, for setting me on the Path. And thanks to my aikido sensei, Ned Danieley, for showing me that the Path has many Turns. A big thanks to Tyler Cook at Moonshine Press for shepherding me through the process of getting this story out. Thanks to Charles and Ellen Snodgrass of Deep Creek Arts for the awesome graphics work, as always. And thanks to iron artists Tripp Jarvis and Melissa VanSandt for helping me with casting the flames. Thanks to all my friends and family who have read various snippets over the years, and encouraged me to continue. Thank you to the Creator for blessing me with a overactive imagination. And most of all, thanks to my darling Pie, for refusing to allow me to leave this tale on a shelf somewhere collecting dust.

This is for all the young boys who were once told: "You're too small to do anything. Just accept it."

Reject all those lies and doubt, and find your own Path. It is waiting for you.

Dramatis Personae

Arak mel'Ulbreth; A Flame Dancer; senior student renown for vicious fighting style and attitude; native of the Camdian Peninsula.

Baron Umbek; A territorial title holder, grudgingly subject to the Eldorn King in Lorring.

Belerand Longshin; A Sylvan elf; ranger and leader of the elves of the Dawnwoods

Chaka; A Flame Master; guard in the Council chambers

Cheyka r; A Flame Dancer; a senior student in the Order.

Dal'q n'Ritti; Maternal leader of a major tribe of the Scarab people.

Darn; A human boy from the tiny village of Warden Woods; inducted into the Disciples of the Flames.

Eillena; A gifted Acolyte student; friend of Darn; native of the Chak'ran Isles and former slave; known as Sharphands within the Order.

Elias; A Flame Master; Warmark of the Order; leads Agni's Disciples into battle, and makes strategic decisions during times of war.

Gell'rin Springleaf; Elven huntress of renown skill; niece of Belerand Longshin.

Jehred; Captain of the City Watch; formerly a seasoned campaigner in the king's army; brother to Loon.

Jorge; Darns father; a herder of burdock.

K'tarr; A Flame Master; renown for his empty-hand defenses against weapons.

Karlonos; Chancellor of Shiningrock Council; known for his fearless and ruthless politics.

Katrinn; A fables and talented mistress of the pleasure arts.

King Ælfred; Ancient king of the Western Lands, the only one to claim dwarvish bloodlines as well as human.

Kirt Smithson (Stumptooth); Krolluck's son; involved in loathsome underworld trade like his father.

Krolluck; A blacksmith of very questionable character; known for involvement in the city's underworld and slave trade.

Loon; Jehred's brother; friend to Darn; huge young man with the muscles of a blacksmith and the mind of a child.

Makheim; a Green Robe, a True Healer, who resided in Warden Woods. He tutored and sheltered Darn at times when the boy was young.

Mardon; Darn's oldest brother; sergeant in the King's Guard, serving in Lorring.

Rekki; A Flame Master; guard in the Council chambers.

S'skyla; The Avatar of the Desert; Queen of Sand; a terrifying sand demon of legend.

Sandali; A well-known city merchant; Loon's landlord for his shack.

Saura; A Flame Master; current Grandmaster of the Order; leader, legal representative, and ultimate authority over the Disciples of the Flames.

Sott; Proprietor of Sott's Inn, a dockside drinking establishment of questionable renown.

Tobani; A Flame Master; Headmaster of Training; Eillena's mentor; a former galley slave from the Bandaran Isles.

Tyrin; Former Shiningrock Lord Marshall; taught the secrets of the soulfire by Lord Agni; Firstmaster of the Disciples of the Flames.

Vin'Dall; Current Lord Marshall of Shiningrock.

Chapter One
Master Elias

"Har! Whatsamatta, Pud? Not lairned t' walk yet?"

Darn raised his head and blinked the tears from his eyes. A hulking boy with filthy knotted hair and black rotten stumps for teeth stood over him, grinning nastily. Darn blew the mud from his nose and looked about: four other boys stood crowded around him, all as dirty and mean-looking as the first.

"Haps yer feet got tangled 'n yer little dress thar," the ugly youth said, as he smirked and elbowed one of his compatriots in the ribs. "Er haps ya should be more careful whar ya steps!" The rest of the motley gang broke into fresh squalls of laughter, as Darn looked down and discovered a rope snare looped around his foot.

Pah! Knew I wasn't as clumsy as that, Darn reassured himself. The thought took a little bit of the sting out of the situation.

"Tis not a dress, tis a kilt," Darn answered flatly, as he regained his feet and kicked the noose away. "And all of the men of my village wear them." He glanced briefly at the band of boys surrounding him: even the smallest of them topped him by a full head, and outweighed him by at least half again. Darn detested being played for a fool, and he could feel something hot begin to smolder in the pit of his stomach. But the boy had also taken enough beatings in his young life to know that he didn't want one here and now, and that's what he was likely facing if he let loose with his tongue. Biting back any further retort, Darn turned and bolted, trying to squeeze between the two boys closest to him. But as he'd almost known would happen, Darn was grabbed from both sides before he could escape, and roughly brought back to stand before the stumptoothed leader of the group.

"Naw, but don' rush away! Dress er not, thinks me heard a jingle in yer purse. So cumalong chums, an' bring our new friend." Stumptooth ducked into a crooked alleyway, and Darn was trundled along behind. Now hidden from the prying eyes of curious passers-bys, Darn could feel the air about the group thicken with the ill vapors of a more serious menace.

"Now we'll see whatcha got thar. An' mebbe if yer good, we'll take ya out back o' th' stalls, an' teach ya what we do wi' them that wear dresses!" Stumptooth flashed an awful smile, and reached out to clumsily pat Darn's cheek.

Darn made an instant and terrifying guess at the abhorrent lessons his captor was planning. With no thought for what might come after, Darn snapped his head to the side, biting quick and vicious as a daggertooth weasel, sinking his teeth deep into the meat at the base of Stumptooth's thumb.

The wounded boy howled in pain and yanked his hand away, tearing loose a ragged chunk of flesh in the process. Stumptooth's eyes nearly bulged from their sockets, and he sucked in a great whooping gasp to loose another cry. Instead, it came out as a mewling squeak when Darn's foot connected solidly with his crotch. Then Stumptooth slumped to the ground, holding his ruined jewels.

While the remaining boys began to beat him – as he'd surely known they would – Darn thought distractedly of one of old Makheim's favorite sayings: *Every sunny day hides a thunderstorm somewhere.* As this day had dawned, Darn has pronounced it the finest in his life. Perhaps now the young lad could give his teacher's words a bit more personal understanding.

***

Earlier that same day, as the third bell of the morning rang out clear and shining, Darn had realized with sudden, magic delight that he was utterly and wonderfully lost. As he strayed aimlessly through the aisleways of the marketplace, Darn felt a bit shaken by the assault on his senses. It felt much the same as that time he'd eaten a handful of the wild stumblegrass that grew among the boulders of his father's northern pasture. The intoxicating breath of the city swirled about him: the tantalizing smells of simmering meat and fresh-baked pastries, of perfumes and incense and exotic spices; the call and clamor of a thousand voices, speaking, cursing, shouting, squawking, roaring, screeching, and crying together; and extraordinary sights such as he'd never dreamed of, that bewildered, delighted, and at times even frightened him. Why, passing down just one aisle alone, Darn had petted a two-headed goat, purchased a deliciously-messy sweetmeat, and even seen a man swallow a handful of nails, only to then pull them one-by-one from his nose. Darn had also paid two copper droma to watch a pit fight between a gang of six or seven metal-spurred roosters, and what looked to be an extremely large and voracious toad. The warty beast was choking down its last feathered adversary when Darn had finally turned to leave.

The young boy congratulated himself upon his early morning performance, when he'd drug his feet and hung his head and made such a sullen pest of himself that his father had finally relented in frustration, releasing him from his chores to wander free for a time.

Surely, such wonders should not be denied me, simply so that

9

I may shovel another load of manure at the pens for Da, he mused to himself. *Let* him *be stabbed in the arse by an ornery nania every time he bends over!*

So many miracles and sights to see, and the Lady alone knew what marvels waited within the scores of pavilions still left to be explored! Since he had no idea which way to turn next, Darn simply surrendered himself to the crowd and drifted along wherever its current would take him. And as with most streams of traffic in the old port city of Shiningrock, eventually this one emptied into the sea of chaos that its citizens simply called the Bazaar.

Like the Spring flowers that were soon to follow, the tents and pavilions of the merchants and tradesmen had bloomed to life in the unanticipated sunlight of an early winter thaw, covering the broad cobbled avenues in the heart of Shiningrock with a dazzling patchwork cloak of a thousand brilliant hues. The sudden birth of the Bazaar every Spring followed no set plan or order. Each year it quickly and inevitably drew into a confounding maze of twisting passages walled by silk curtains, rough-cloth tents, wooden corrals, and trinket-covered blankets, with paths and walkways and dead ends that changed and shifted more often than the treacherous sandbars that lurked outside the harbor.

Those merchants with enough influence or strength-of-arms claimed the most visible and highly-trafficked spots for themselves. Those without were gradually pushed farther and farther back into the ill-lit and garbage-strewn alleyways, where both the wares and the clientele tended towards a darker nature. The easy availability of unwholesome commodities added a bit more dark fame to the city's already tarnished reputation. The allure also ensured that there were plenty of foreign corpses to provide raw materials for the vats of Popellous the Gluemaker. Most travelers to the great citadel, however, were content to pursue their needs in the open air of the Bazaar proper, where the mail-shirted members of the City Watch kept careful eye and rewarded unskillful pickpockets with strokes from their iron-bound quarterstaves.

Along the streets bordering the Bazaar, Darn watched perplexed as holy clerics of the commerce god, Fostus, blessed transactions and rubbed elbows with Nemian prostitutes. Each of the groups collecting alms for their necessary services, the boy assumed, and each saving souls in their own particular fashion.

An arrogant Sidhe nobleman roughly knocked Darn from his path, and the young boy stuck out his tongue and waggled his fingers in a deliciously rude gesture at the elegantly-cloaked figure. But when the Sidhe turned suddenly and cast a baleful eye his way, Darn cursed his folly and darted back into the safety of the crowd,. The High Elves were quick to anger and harsh in their punishments, and even such a childish indiscretion could have earned Darn a spell-induced stutter or a new-found craving for burdock droppings.

A thorny phalanx of the King's Leopard Guards suddenly turned onto the Avenue of Temples, driving the foot-traffic aside with oaths and pike-hafts and the occasional lash of a horseman's whip. The soldiers had nearly completed their tiresome chore of escorting the Royal Chancellor of the Exchequer from the palace in Lorring to the ruling-hall of Shiningrock's council, and they were in no mood to be either pious or polite about it. Darn found himself caught up in the crowd, crushed between the hips of two large, rather pungent washerwomen. Darn struggled against the matrons to no avail, finally resorting to a well-placed pinch to release him from his fleshy confines. Once free, he slipped unnoticed into the shelter beneath a baker's cart.

As Darn sat in his makeshift sanctuary and waited impatiently for the crowd to disburse, his eye caught the movement of the garrison soldiers as they paced along the sandstone battlements high above.

What an honor! Darn thought. How it must feel to wear the City's colors and be entrusted with Her safety! He imagined the weight of the heavy mail hauberks, the reassuring slap of a sword and the rough comfort of a spear haft in hand, keeping out an eye for Klemish spies or a troop of Tharian mercenaries out for trouble. Then reality dashed the boy's daydreams aside, as Darn watched the soldiers gesture to the crowd and laugh, and realized that they were much more alert for signs of the next comely country lass or Balmoran professional lady, than for any enemy of the city-state.

A sudden grumbling from his stomach alerted Darn to the fact that several rather excruciatingly wonderful smells were drifting down into his hiding place from above. After enduring a full moment's nod towards caution, he slipped a thin hand out from under the cart's cloth skirt and reached up to search for the source of the alluring aromas. As his questing fingers alighted on a certain promising stickiness, Darn smiled and licked his lips in secret delight – a conjuring that nearly cost him the tip of his tongue. For at that same moment, Darn's wrist was roughly seized and jerked sharply upwards, dealing his head a severe thump on the cart's bottom.

The pasty-faced baker drug Darn from his hideout, shaking

him as a terrier would a rat, all the while shouting for the City Watch. But before any more than a handful of faces had turned their way, Darn kicked the doughmaker hard in the shin, leaving the man hopping and cursing in a cloud of flour dust as the young thief disappeared into the laughing crowd, gobbling his stolen prize even as he dodged and ran.

No one in the Bazaar glanced twice at Darn, just another dirty boy wearing the simple kilt and homespun shirt of the northern woodland tribes. He was a small child, so slightly built that only the rounded tops of his ears and his wide-set hazel eyes prevented him from being mistaken for one of elven blood. Most would have guessed the lad to have seen only eight or nine winters, when in truth the past Sowing Moon had been the twelfth anniversary of his first breath. His hair gleamed a silky white-gold – a hue generally reserved only for innocent toddlers and toothless, leather-faced fishermen – and wisps of straw stuck out from the tousled mess, reminders of another night spent sleeping in the pens with his father's animals. The boy was unshod and happy to be that way, for he hated the coarse, ill-tanned, hide boots he was forced to wear in the winter, and he eagerly waited for the snows to melt each Spring and grant him another eight moons to feel the grass and mud between his toes. Even this early in the year, the calluses on Darn's feet were as tough as any boot sole, and his skin was already stained a deep burnished bronze from his toil in the fields and pastures.

The avenue that Darn followed eventually emptied into a huge circular courtyard, filled to overflowing with jugglers, musicians, and hawkers of various goods. He ignored most of the vendors and entertainers, for he'd seen their likes in the traveling troupes which sometimes visited his home in Warden Woods. But Darn stared like a slack-jawed fool at the exotic people and extraordinary creatures that also wandered among the crowd. The boy gawked openly at the tailed noblemen of Monkey Island, though he knew he deserved a thump for his rudeness. Several warriors of the Scarab People sat nearby on their hairy-faced droes, resplendent in their silken turbans and upturned mustaches, with their great curved swords by their sides. Darn watched the massive scaled form of a Carpathian stone troll saunter slowly through the midst of the crowd, a path clearing before it as it went. Then a sharp prick in the rump sent Darn stepping quickly aside as a high-born lady led a diminutive bearded unicorn by on a silver leash; the delicate-looking creatures were known to be fierce protectors of their virginal mistresses, and the deadly ivory horn they sported was warning enough for any but the most foolhardy of cutpurses and kidnappers.

Across the avenue gathered a group of what Darn guessed must be Kalthmus dwarves, far from their homes in the frozen mountains to the north. Each of the short dour figures wore the forked and braided beards that marked their clans. As they bellowed a raucous drinking song and crashed their tankards together, one of the group waved about a gleaming double-headed battleaxe to direct their chorus. Darn noticed a distinct lack of fellow patrons around the dwarves' table, and determined to include himself in their absence.

The tinkling chime of tiny bells captured Darn's attention and delivered it to an incredibly voluptuous young woman who passed nearby: dark-haired and sloe-eyed, she wore violet silk pantaloons slit from ankle to hip and a tight-fitting bodice of tanned snake leather. She paused, noticing Darn's interest, and turned to give him a better view of her "wares". Completely ensnared, Darn let his eyes travel slowly up the woman's magnificent form, pausing for a breathless moment where her bosoms fought to escape from their snakeskin tethers. And when he looked into her exquisite and fine-boned face, the inky depths of her kohl-lined eyes drank him in. Darn stood spellbound, entranced by the woman's exotic beauty. Then her lips pulled back in a smile, and an arm-length of ichor-dripping tongue slithered out past a double row of pointed yellow teeth to grace Darn's cheek with a slimy amorous caress. Darn jerked backwards in speechless horror, tripped over his own feet, and ended with an ignoble landing on his rear. The Nemian harlot loosed a bubbling girlish laugh at Darn's distress, and blew him a kiss before she turned and strolled away, hips swinging seductively as she continued on her hunt for a true buyer of her particular goods and talents.

Darn fought to regain his composure and balance, and glanced side-to-side to see if any had noticed his folly. But in the Bazaar, no one paid another rag-tag young lad the least bit of attention – except for a young Sidhe girl who smiled and winked at him before being snatched away by her mother. Darn felt a sudden tug upon his sleeve, and whirled about to find a small half-blind desert gnome beside him who launched into a tale of personal woe and despair. The leather-faced little man tried desperately to convince Darn to purchase the "rare and dangerous sand leopard" that he held on a leash. Darn eyed the sorrowful creature warily: it looked more like a common fuzzy rockcat, with a bad haircut and painted-on spots. He said as much, and received a curse and a barely-dodged wad of phlegm for his honesty.

Hmm, perhaps truth and courtesy should be guarded here as well as my purse, and used as sparingly as my coins, Darn reasoned. *So much for being friendly.*

Just then, the second afternoon bell sang out, reminding Darn that the day was quickly draining away and his freedom with it. Three thoughts raced through is mind, nipping at each others' heels: he must soon return to the nania pens and his own mundane existence. Yet the remaining five droma in his purse burned to be spent; and he had yet to eat a true dinner. So with the clarity of mind and inalterable purpose particular to boys his age, Darn hurriedly set out to find the absolute best place in which to fill his ever-empty twelve year-old belly.

The crowd flowed about the young boy as he walked along, his eyes searching this way and that for the roasting fenlock that his nose told him was nearby. He turned a weathered, corner down a smaller avenue, and as the scent grew stronger his growling stomach urged his spindly legs on faster. The open doorway of *The Boar and Hound* up ahead belched out a dark savory cloud, and he was running even as his mouth began to water. After a scant three steps, though, between one breath and the next, Darn found himself transported from upright and striding towards dinner, to face-down in the mud, his nose cruelly squashed and full of goo. The painful surprise, along with thoughts of the thrashing he'd get for muddying his best kilt, brought tears to his flushing cheeks.

As he had looked up from the mud into the faces of his tormentors, Darn knew that a thunderstorm had indeed arrived to dash away his sunny morning. Yet the darkening clouds heralded

16

much more than only an unpleasant rousting by the local bullyboys. Though he knew it not, the winds of a new fate had begun to blow through Darn's life. And the roads they revealed would begin a journey to last Darn's lifetime.

***

After much retching and tears, Stumptooth shakily regained his feet, a strained smile on his face and a sharp gleam of insanity growing steadily in the depths of his eyes. Darn still hung between two of Stumptooth's comrades, but now sported a bloody nose, a split lip, a collection of bruised ribs, and an eye swelling shut: painful payment for the single blow Darn had struck. But still, the look of astonishment on Stumptooth's face as he fell to the ground was well worth the price, Darn thought.

"Oh, that was smart, boyo!" Stumptooth hissed in a spray of spittle. "Now I'm gonna make sure ya belongs inna dress." Grinning wickedly, the hulking boy pulled a rusty blade of iron from the top of one boot and advanced slowly towards his captive.

"Hold 'im tight now, boys! Grab 'is legs thar, Willi. An' Del, do sumthin 'bout them bedamned fangs of 'is!" The gang leader ran a thumb over the edge of his knife and laughed with loathsome delight. "Taint as sharp as it oughta be. Guess I'll havta take m' time wi' this one!"

Thoughts of parley were tossed aside as Darn's body made an instinctive and heroic effort at keeping all of its attendant parts together. Though his mind knew he had no chance of escape against those who held him, his limbs thrashed and kicked with a life of their own until it was all the other four could do to keep their holds upon him. One his captors managed to loop a dirty scrap of rag over

17

Darn's mouth to guard against his bite and to prevent him from crying out for help – not that any aid would come, not in this town.

The leader's decayed grin grew wider as his blade slid under the edge of Darn's kilt, and his foul breath wafted in the terrified boy's face.

"Say goodbye t' it, Pud," Stumptooth whispered darkly, a rancid thread of saliva drooling from one corner of his gap-toothed smile.

Darn squeezed his eyes shut as he fought and twisted to avoid the cold kiss of the blade. A silent sob shook his chest as he mumbled a desperate prayer to any deity that cared to listen. And apparently, remarkably, Someone did care. For in answer to his plea, Darn felt the hand on his kilt suddenly snatched away, and heard Stumptooth utter a tremendous *"Oomph!"* Darn opened his eyes just in time to witness his tormenter fly through the air as if launched from a catapult. And despite his terror moments before, Darn grinned a bloody smile as he watched Stumptooth crash into the alley wall amidst the brittle crunch of crumbling plaster and broken bones. Then Darn turned back to discover the source of his salvation.

A rather small man clad in scarlet silk robes stood before the group of boys, oddly perched on one leg, his other foot slowly lowering to the ground. He took a step forward, looked at each of Darn's captors in turn, then shook his head in disgust. Too quickly to follow, the man's hands shot forward and with his pointer fingers he tapped the two closest boys each on the inside of the elbow, then again in the small hollow between neck and shoulder. The hooligans screamed as if impaled by red-hot needles, then turned and ran down the alleyway, the arms the stranger had touched hanging useless at their sides. The remaining two bullies released Darn straightway, and in an flash they had followed their companions up the trash-strewn lane, pausing only long enough to collect their fallen leader.

Darn picked himself up off the ground, and rubbed at the lump already forming where he'd been dropped on his head. He turned to where a fuzzy vision of his rescuer stood and shook his head to clear it before he spoke.

"Th-th-thank ye, sir. They intended to …" The young boy choked at the thought of the horror he'd just barely escaped, and he cursed himself silently as tears welled at the edges of his eyes.

"Bah, twas nothing, boy. Riff-raff and ruffians, I say!" The stranger busied himself brushing unseen flecks of dirt from the crimson habit he wore, pointedly ignoring the tears that Darn wiped hurriedly away. "Could have handled them yourself, had they been more your size," he said with an odd assurance, as he ran an embroidered silk scarf across his hairless skull. "That, or had you been carrying a healthy length of oak with which to insert a decent measure of respect into their thick skulls," he finished. Then the man laughed as he returned his scarf to a hidden pocket and straightened his robes.

Darn's savior was far paler than could be accounted for by a normal winter pallor, and together with the bright red of his beard, it named the island kingdom of Heshui as his birthplace. The heavy golden torc and earrings, along with the silk robes the man wore, would have made him appear a bit effete, had it not been for the ragged scar that snaked underneath the circlet and disappeared up into his beard. An aura of power seemed to envelope the man, filling even his simplest motions with an elegant and deadly grace. Though the robed stranger stood a full head less than most grown men, somehow Darn knew that no one ever looked down upon this particular diminutive fellow – at least not twice. The pale man looked up, suddenly aware of Darn's scrutiny, and his odd, blazing cobalt eyes clearly mirrored the broad smile on his face.

"Splendid response, by the way: that snap of the teeth. Looked for a moment as if you'd chosen an odd appointment for your midday meal!" The man gave a twisted smile. "Should have tried for the fingers though; I've found them only a bit tougher than those stale breadsticks they sell in the Bazaar. And you could have kept one as a memento of your adventure!" He laughed deep and loud then, and the gold hoops in his ears flashed brightly in a stray beam of sunlight.

Darn decided instantly that he liked this bald man with the bushy red beard and wild winging eyebrows, who thought that one's near-castration was a funny sort of thing. The young boy smiled back crookedly and willed himself to relax.

"But in any case, you did quite well, my boy," the man continued. "Didn't cry out or beg, just fought as best you could, even though you could smell Death coming. That declares a courage, a fire, that many a grown man would be proud to lay honest claim to." He turned and began to walk back towards the open avenue. "Come, let us quit this pig sty, for the stench could ruin a man's appetite for days. I've taste for an ale, and from the looks of it you could sorely use a platter of roast and a wash basin – not necessarily in that order, eh?" The crimson-clad stranger began to whistle a fair rendition of *The Lovely Ladies of Lorring* as he walked away, and Darn's empty stomach grumbled a harmony as he hurried to keep up.

"How are ye named, boy?" the stranger inquired as they moved up the alley.

"D-darn, sir. D-darn of Warden Woods," the boy answered meekly.

"Well, D-darn," the robed man chuckled. "I am Elias – Master Elias, if you would be so good. I do admit to a measure of vanity on the matter." A lovely merchant's wife, round and sweet, smiled shyly at Elias as they walked by, and he blew her a kiss.

"So tell me, my lad, what brings a young boy from the emerald glades of Warden Woods down to this tarnished old harlot we call Shiningrock?"

"I travel with my father, Master Elias," Darn explained. "He wanted to sell our harvest of burdock wool and a few good milking nania at the auctions. But *I* wanted to see the city."

It was the dream of easy gold that had lured Darn's father, Jorge, here from their home in the north, the boy explained. The burdock wool that their flocks grew was fine and fleecy this year, and promised to command a high price at auction. Though Emus the Trader had offered a fair enough price for all their wool back in Warden Woods, Jorge had reasoned – as he had unceasingly reminded Darn on their week-long trek south – that by selling it himself, he could double or perhaps even triple his profits.

In truth, Darn expected his father to forfeit the greatest portion of their money to the sharp-minded traders, or lose it all to a quick-handed gambler or a light-fingered whore. But the money made no difference to Darn: all he cared about was the chance to see Shiningrock, the magnificent city of which his brother Mardon had told his so many tales. Darn had pleaded and cajoled his father unceasingly for the chance to be allowed on this trip. He'd even picked early green-spears and bribed one of his sisters to bake a spring pie – one of his father's favorites. But it was Darn's luck and perseverance that had finally won him the right to make the journey. For when a prized burdock lamb turned up missing and all the farmhands gave up searching at dusk, it was Darn who had stayed out till midnight and discovered the youngling romping in a moonlit glen with a pair of mischievous wood sprites. Darn had convinced the sprites to give up their wooly companion in exchange for some crumbs of cookie Darn found in his pocket. Afterwards, his father could hardly deny him the reward of making the trip to Shiningrock. So Darn had withdrawn half the coppers he had hidden away in the depths of his straw mattress and waited impatiently for the day of the trip to arrive.

"I had wished to see the Bazaar," the boy finished. "Da told me to go, but to have care." He paused, and lines of worry laid familiar tracks across a face far too young for such markings. "I've not done well so far. He'll birth a burdock himself when he sees my kilt and hears my tale. I am most sure he will not wish to hear my excuses."

Elias waved away Darn's concern.

"Then most certainly, I shall have to accompany you back to your father," the scarlet-clad man remarked cheerfully, "and verify the truth of your words." He patted the young boy reassuringly on the shoulder. "Think no more on the matter. But allow me instead to be your guide to our *fair* city, and keep you on some of her *fairer* streets even as we track down our dinner." Elias lifted a blood-orange from a vendor's cart as they walked by, and handed it to his

22

young companion. The merchant began to shout his protest, but a single glance at Elias' robe seemed to cast a pall over the spindly old man. The grey-bearded fellow nodded a nervous bow of apology and turned back to his cart, even as Elias and Darn continued on their way.

The master proved to be a knowledgeable and talkative guide, as the pair wandered through the crowded walkways. The city of Shiningrock, Elias told Darn, bore her renown for many reasons: for her famous stone wharves and her infamous waterfront bars and brothels; for her daunting walls of sandstone four strides thick, carved out of and into the precipice on which the citadel stood; for the stark white needle of the council building, pointing an arrogant accusation at the sky; and for the bleaching bones of Klemish invaders and warships piled at the base of the cliffs, testament to the city's impregnability and to the might of her defenders.

To many people, Shiningrock's buff-colored walls and deep protected harbor were as welcome and familiar a site as the Endless Marshes were to the snow geese who summered there. To those who plied their trades on the world's waters, Shiningrock was a flashy bauble on the cloth of the sea: gaudy enough to draw the attention of all, despite her cheap setting and numerous flaws. But to the common folk – the farmers and craftworkers and herdsmen, who traveled for days or weeks to sell their meager goods in the Bazaar – to those people, Shiningrock was a child's bedtime tale made true, a place to find a balm for many of life's woes and bring at least one dab of magic into an otherwise weary, leather-stained existence.

By the time that the Blossom Moon had carelessly strewn her colors and fragrances across the orchards and gardens of the

Eldorn Kingdom, the port of Shiningrock fairly bristled with the masts of ships. The renown city herself, squatting like some titanic stone sentry on the sandstone cliffs above the harbor, swelled to bursting with the influx of sea-fairing foreigners and cart-drawn countryfolk. Every importer, exporter, and black-marketeer worthy of the name began their season at the ancient city-port: Etruscan rug merchants, prepared to dismiss offhandedly any who would balk at the price of their intricate tapestries, and equally ready to haggle over a single copper's increase in the price of good burdock wool; jewelers from fabled Parthus, bearing elegant fantasies of spun gold and fire-opals; and of course, the grain merchants and renown brewmasters of Hovill, leading wagons stacked high with barrels of their celebrated amber libations. And within the walled estates west of the city proper, pirate captains from the Chak'ran Isles haggled with certain wealthy citizens over the current price of *shisha* or Roc'coran slaves or stolen Camdian jade. Adding to the crush, each of these traders in turn brought their own entourage of servants and guards and hired hands. Then close on their heels, like the camp followers of a besieging army, came the pickpockets and cutpurses, the whores and hired-swords, all clamoring to get their fair share. For here in Shiningrock, it was said, a never-ending stream of silver and gold passed from hand to hand and round again, and one had only to find a way to dip into that tinkling flow to ensure a life of opulence and ease.

The short bald man and shorter barefooted boy passed an Etruscan rug merchant who stood in the doorway of a beautiful tent fashioned of turquoise silk and silver brocade and screeched oaths towards the open stall of a weapon smithy that faced him across the aisle. The forge belched thick twisting tendrils of sooty smoke into the sky, and the sparks that rode the ebon trails more often than not settled back down over the tents of the smith's neighbors. Several soldiers in the brown-iron hauberks of the City Watch listened half-heartedly to the merchant's complaints, and warily eyed the oaken-thewed armorer as he hammered the soul of a sword into a piece of ruby-red steel. As one, the guards silently agreed to ignore the merchant's insistent demands to relocate the blacksmith, and turned their attention to less adventurous endeavors elsewhere, leaving the Etruscan to shriek without an audience.

Darn paused for a moment to stare at a wretched grey-haired crone who squatted on a pallet of dirty straw next to the rug merchant's tent. The gnarled old woman muttered lowly as she breathed in the greasy sulphurous vapors that rose from a small iron brazier on the fire before her. She seemed to stare into some unseen space beyond the smoke, occasionally raising a twisted claw in a warding gesture. Darn wondered briefly why the cursing Etruscan didn't complain about the filthy hag and demand for her removal as well, for surely her presence must be a fly in the ointment of his business. Then the merchant stepped forward out of the shadow of his tent, and Darn could see the hideous mass of bristly purple warts that hung from his nose and chin like clusters of sour putrid grapes. Obviously, the Etruscan trader didn't think it prudent to try to have the old witchwoman moved a second time.

The shadows crept slowly longer as Darn and Elias moved through the city streets. And as they walked along, the boy's head swung back and forth furiously, determined not to miss a single marvel. They passed a small square filled with magicians of questionable abilities, who sold charms and philters, promising love or wealth or beauty to their patrons. Around the next corner, curiosity slowed Darn's steps as they passed an odd group of younglings like himself: humans, elves, even a grossly-huge Cherramite. They smiled to him and beckoned as Darn walked by. But even as Elias' hand steadied Darn on their path, the crack of a whip and a moan of pain or perhaps even pleasure leaked from the ratty felt tent behind the group. Darn wasn't sure if he completely understood what transpired behind the tent walls, but he was sure it was a question better left unanswered.

Elias laughed darkly and flipped a coin to a comely elf maid who lounged with supple grace against one of the tent supports; she just smiled sleepily in answer. Then a few steps farther on, Elias made a sudden turn into a narrow alleyway, hurrying his steps so that Darn must trot to keep pace.

"The tavern you spoke of lies this way?" Darn asked warily, suddenly uncomfortable with their new surroundings. The hair on his neck rose, and Darn felt a sudden rush of warmth into his stomach. His trust in his new companion was beginning to waver.

"No," Elias answered quickly, looking side-to-side as they moved down the alley. "But we have gained several new companions on our journey – ones whose company I'd not have as public knowledge."

Elias spun in sudden swirl of crimson silk, pushing Darn to one side. Four men – or semblance of men – had stepped from the street to bar the alley's exit. The two immense figures at the rear of the group were half again taller than their cohorts, covered by pelts of coarse purplish fur, with gangly arms that hung down past their knees. From stories he'd heard from his older brother, Darn guessed that the pair of creatures were *thungari*: primitive beastmen from the jungles of Yot, their slanted yellow eyes and porcine snouts lending them a cruel but not stupid caste. One of the thungari's human companions stood lightly off to the side, with a dully-gleaming, flat-bladed dagger in each hand and the ravenous look of a weasel about him.

The last member of the motley group stepped forward out of the shadows, much shorter than any of the other three. But while his bandy legs looked barely able to support him, the swarthy fellow was as wide across the shoulders as the *thungari* that followed him, possessing powerfully-muscled arms and a face full of dark intent. In one of his blackened hands he swung a massive iron hammer, the menacing tool of his trade. Lice swarmed through the man's grease-clotted beard. He made no introduction, but when he opened his mouth to speak, any questions surrounding his identity were swiftly dispatched.

"M'boy sez ya broke 'is arm!" the soot-faced smith grumbled through a maw of crumbling rotten teeth. "Sez 'im an' 'is friends were playin' wi' th' tree-rat there, an' ya stepped in t' make trouble!"

"Tree-rat, am I?" Darn's temper flared at the insult to his woodland people, and he stepped up beside Elias. "And just how would ye care to wear a broken crown, Lord Bright Smile? I shall …" Darn cut short his tirade as Elias' hand – strangely warm to the touch – dropped to his shoulder and warned him to silence.

"Little miscreants got less than they deserved, actually," Elias casually replied, smiling mischievously as if he enjoyed the exchange. "And if you are the one who taught them to 'play' in such a manner, then you may be in need of some schooling yourself."

"Izzat so?" Stumptooth's father growled in a voice like breaking stones. "Well, 'haps I'll be teachin' ya how t' wear a grave shroud, 'stead o' dem fancy silks yer kind likes so much!" The great hammer stopped its aimless swinging and the dark smith started forward.

Elias stood still as the man advanced upon him, refusing to even lift a hand in defense. But Darn sensed an invisible stirring about the unimposing scarlet-clad master: a haziness in the air around him like that above a hard-packed road in midsummer. Without turning, Elias placed a hand on Darn's chest – a hand that burned like a sun-baked stone – and gave him a gentle push back down the alley.

"Run, boy!" Elias said quietly from one corner of his mouth. Then the master smiled all the wider, as the angry smith stepped close and raised the blackened hammer for a skull-crushing blow.

Darn fled several steps, then skidded to a halt as a vivid picture flashed through his mind: a vision of himself, lying in a filthy alleyway with dark blood pooling at his groin. Abandonment seemed like poor payment for rescue from such ruin. In the span of a heartbeat, Darn made a decision that would forever alter his fate. The boy stooped to pick up two egg-sized stones from the ground, and pulled free the thin leather strap that cinched his tunic. Then he turned back to the brawl with his teeth bared.

Remarkably, Master Elias still stood in the same spot, and now a derisive grin stretched across his face as he suffered the smith's attack. Three times, Darn watched in disbelief as the scarlet-robed master flickered slightly to one side or the other, allowing the smith's hammer only a teasing kiss of his garments. And Elias laughed scornfully each time as his attacker stumbled off balance.

The enraged smith, though, found no humor in the situation. Instead, he bellowed his frustration and swung his scarred iron hammer with a murderous vengeance. And with each missed stroke, the man turned darker with rage, till he looked akin to the purple-skinned thungari behind him. After a series of wild, desperate swings, Stumptooth's father was forced to pause for a moment, heaving for breath.

Elias stepped forward, placed his hands on his hips, and brayed his laughter into the smith's face.

"Oh, so tired already? Perhaps we could find a tiny tinker's hammer for you to swing. Or would a bouquet of forget-me-nots pain thee less?"

The smith's face blackened with fury, and his eyes rolled wildly. Then his lips peeled back from the jagged stubs of his teeth, and the great muscles of his arms knotted with strain as he leapt forward suddenly with a triumphant howl, swinging an unexpected crippling blow at Elias' legs.

Darn tried to shut his eyes, horribly sure of his friend's imminent demise, for no one could survive such a blow. But one of the boy's eyes only squinted near closed. And the miraculous sight it found brought both eyes wide open again.

Master Elias floated gracefully above the ground, his vermillion robes billowing out like a cloud shot through by the setting sun. As the deadly hammer cut beneath him in a lethal arc, Elias began to twist in mid-air. Then his right leg flashed out and around like Death's own scythe, and his heel slammed squarely into his foe's skull just above the ear.

A single blow, and it was over in an instant. The smith's greasy head nearly shot from his shoulders, and his body followed to crash bonelessly to the ground. As the smith fell, a wad of crushed brown cloth dropped unnoticed from his belt into the mud. But Darn had little time to wonder if the smith was alive or dead, for Elias had already progressed to more entertaining pursuit.

The crimson stranger fairly danced a jig back and forth before the shaggy thungari, taunting the fearsome creatures with insults and curses, beckoning them to step forward. The thungari shifted uncertainly, befuddled by the loss of their leader. Then Master Elias snatched a half-eaten earthapple from a nearby pile of garbage, took aim, and struck one of the immense brutes square in the snout. Even an ignorant beastman could bear no more insult, and with a deafening roar the thungari charged, great taloned hands raking downward with death in their grip.

Elias darted about like a hummingbird – or even more so, like a flickering flame – as he met the man-beast's ferocious attack. His arms and legs flew in a storm of scarlet fury, seeming to strike the thungari from every angle at once. And with every blow that he landed, Elias only seemed to become more enflamed and impassioned, increasing the speed and power with which the next strike was unleashed.

The thungari lashed out with its lethal claws in return, but touched nothing more than the hem of Elias' robe. The creature began to collapse under the unceasing onslaught, unable to land a single strike of its own. To its knees, the beastman dropped. Then further, to the ground, as Master Elias landed a short chopping elbow strike like a bolt of fiery lightning directly between the slanted yellow eyes. The shaggy brute fell face down in the filthy alleyway and moved no more.

Elias spun quickly to face the remaining thungari, a roguish grin on his face. But a crashing wave of pained disbelief washed his smile away, as the hilt of a dagger suddenly appeared jutting from his left shoulder. His arm fell useless, and as Elias fought through the pain and shock, he tried to slide back away from the beast facing him. But the remaining thungari now held the taste of victory in its jaws, and it moved without caution to block Elias' escape.

Darn looked on in horror, unsure how to help, as his new friend twisted and danced to avoid the thungari's attack. But when Darn glanced past his wounded savior, his gaze fell upon the forgotten weasel-faced man. A bloodthirsty smile full of sharp teeth graced the man's face, and another dagger was ready in hand. Ruby-red fury colored Darn's vision at the sight, and the boy snugged a stone into the pouch of his sling and began to whirl it around his head.

Finally, Elias stumbled and the thungari seized advantage, leaping upon the master in a berserking fury. Thick powerful claws ripped downward, and though Elias somehow managed to slip past the first two strikes, the third blow tore into his back and shoulders, staining his robes an even darker shade of crimson.

Too enthralled by its own bloodlust to be wary, the ill-formed brute snatched its prey high into the air, holding the diminutive master by the neck and leg. As it prepared to dash out the brains of the puny human who had injured its littermate, the thungari beast roared in triumph, and thought eagerly of the grisly victory feast it would soon enjoy.

31

Elias, however, had no intention of providing a raw repast for his shaggy adversary. As the thungari lifted him skyward, Elias reached down and dug his fingers into the creature's arm, searching for a nerve bundle buried there. The man-beast answered with a snarl of sudden pain, and it released Elias' throat in unwilling response. The robed master dangled by one leg for half a heartbeat, then arched his body like a snake's, whipping his torso upright before the creature could react. Then with an earsplitting cry, Elias stabbed a clawing hand straight into the thungari's glaring topaz eyes.

With a shriek of agony, the beast dropped its prey and clutched at its ruined visage. Elias twisted in mid-air, landing on his feet. He slid forward gracefully, despite his injury, and his left foot whipped out to strike and shatter one of the thungari's knees. Then Elias stepped back from the writhing, howling madness of the crippled man-beast, and smiled in pained satisfaction.

A trio of sounds came from behind the master: a dull thud, a low moan, and a heavy liquid *splat*. The scarlet-clad warrior spun about, ready to continue his assault upon any and all who would try him, wounded or not. Then just as quickly, Elias relaxed and looked down in amused surprise at the last of his attackers. The weasel-faced man now lay prone in the mud, a tremendous bloody knot rising on the thug's forehead, and the remaining dagger flung across the lane.

Elias turned to look back down the alley, and found Darn standing warily a hand of paces away, a leather sling still spinning a lazy circle by the boy's side.

"Aha!" Elias shouted in triumph and delight, dancing to his young companion's side. "Splendid cast, my boy! By Lord Agni's

Holy Flames, a truer throw has never been made!" He clapped Darn on the back several times, and ungently nudged the oblivious bladesman with his foot. "Well done, I say! Dropped this swine like the dung-eating backstabber that he is!" Elias continued to caper about and shout. Then he paused, as if he'd forgotten something. Frowning grimly, Elias reached back and pull the slim dagger from his shoulder. Then with no apparent remorse, he knelt down and buried the blade to the hilt in the chest of the weasel-faced man who'd thrown it. The master checked his handiwork, nodded in satisfaction, then stood and resumed his rather festive celebration.

Darn couldn't understand his friend's strange euphoria. The boy felt almost certain that he was about to throw up, and he could quite possibly require a change of underclothes. But Darn couldn't keep himself from laughing as Elias danced among their fallen attackers, giving one or the other a swift kick now and then and calling them foul and imaginative names.

Something caught his eye, and Darn noticed an odd shape crushed into the mud near the fallen smith's body. He looked closer, and abruptly recognized the leaf-and-vine pattern of his mother's embroidery. The boy chewed at his lip as he retrieved the small leather purse from the muck: it was torn down one side and, of course, emptied of its contents. It was the only real gift he had left from his mother, and its ruin filled Darn with an almost unbearable pain. He sniffed back a flood of tears and shook his head angrily. When he looked up once more, his eyes fell on the huddled form of Stumptooth's father, still sprawled in the garbage, eyes showing white and legs widespread. A moment later, Darn stood glaring down at the smith's motionless body.

"Tree-rat, is it?" Darn asked his unconscious foe. "Well, what is good for the piglet, shall be good for the boar!" Darn reared back and kicked the smith in the groin as hard as his spindly legs were able. He turned to walk away, then thought better of it and spun back to deliver a second kick. Then he smiled and nodded to himself and dashed off to join Elias, where he danced and laughed and kicked with a determined regularity.

Chapter Two
The First Step

"*Buuurrr-rrrawwkkk!*"

Elias pushed himself away from the table boards, confidently leaned back in his rough-sawn, rickety chair, and patted his stomach in contentment.

"Aah, a good heart-felt belch does wonders to settle one's bowels and aide the digestion." Elias smiled across the scarred and burnt table at his young companion. "And alongside that, it is one of the few manly pleasure which cannot be denied us."

Darn tried to smile knowingly, but in truth he had only the vaguest idea what the "manly pleasures" might be. He did know, though, that his belly was full to bursting, and that was pleasure enough. The roasted fenlock was the best he'd ever eaten, and even the jacks of dark bitter ale that Elias had handed him seemed rather tasty after the first two.

Darned leaned back in imitation of his new friend, and tried determinedly to work up a belch of his own. *His* seat, however, had seen use as an ill-wielded bludgeon in a brawl the night before – and as a Kalthmus dwarf's head is far tougher than any piece of wood, the battered stool simply would not concede any more abuse. The chair's rear legs gave way with a dry splintery snap, and Darn found himself deposited suddenly and unceremoniously onto his thinly-fleshed flanks.

Elias made a valiant attempt to retain both his dignity and his most recent swallow of ale, though his face matched the crimson of his robe. But the sight of Darn's legs waving helplessly in the air proved more powerful than even a master's control, and Elias sprayed a mouthful of brew across the table and over his somewhat-stunned young companion. This sight fertilized a handful of close-lipped snickers already being passed around the room, which bloomed into full-blown howls of laughter. Elias added his own guffaws to the fray, once he stopped choking. Darn joined in laughing as he got up from the floor, and even Gordmon the dour-faced innkeeper cracked a rare smile.

The rough-hewn door of the inn slammed back on its leather hinges without warning, slitting the throat of the laughter in the room, leaving only Elias' slowly dying chuckles. Three men dressed in the burnished scale-mail of the King's Guard strode inside. After a moment, one of the guardsmen spotted Elias and Darn in the corner, and pointed them out to his superior. The squad commander – a captain by the purple cord knotted around his upper arm – stalked up to the pair and planted himself squarely before them.

"Well, Master Elias, back in town fer more adventure, I see. Or's this jest a trip fer some sweetleaf an' ale?" The captain's scowl belied the lightness of his words. This was a man, Darn thought, who'd been born with a scowl on his face. His eyes were hard, impenetrable, as black and closed as the bottom of a well. And though the curls that hung from beneath his bronze half-helm had faded to iron gray, they lent the soldier an air of discipline and measure. His arms still bulged with thick knotted cords of muscle, and the scars that covered them bore testament to campaigns both hard won and occasionally lost. Next to him, the younger guardsmen seemed like costumed imposters, and the force of the captain's anger filled the room.

Remembering Master Elias' equally volatile spirit, Darn began a furtive search for a place to hide.

"Now, Captain Jehred," Elias answered politely, "as a citizen of Shiningrock, I am entitled to go where I please, for what I please. But in answer to your question, I am, in fact, here for leaf and ale . . . and for some of this fine fenlock as well!" He picked up a knuckled haunch and waved it about. "Perhaps you would care to join our repast? A bellyful of food and a few tankards of Boar's Fine Red Ale would surely help to ease the burden of your station." Elias replied in a friendly tone, and smiled brightly all the while he spoke. But Darn could sense a fire hidden beneath the master's words.

"I have no time fer games er ale," Captain Jehred spat. "I'm charged t' investigate th' murder of an honest citizen, an' th' grievous assault upon his three companions!"

"Well, Ladies Above and Lords Below!" Elias mocked. "Shiningrock finally manages to produce an honest citizen, and saints-be-damned if someone doesn't proceed to kill him. Tragic, that's what it is. This used to be such a refined and charming town." Elias brought his chair back to the floor with a crash, and the soldiers under Captain Jehred's command jumped like old women in a thunder storm. "Now, what is it, truly, that I can do for you this evening, Captain?" Elias raised an eyebrow in question, adding an unspoken, sarcastic lilt to his words. He continued to sip at his ale, seemingly unperturbed by the anger and attention that whirled about him.

The seething captain stepped forward, his face darkening as the temper within him strove to break its bonds.

"I want t' know why ev'ry time some o' Agni's Children show

up in my sector o' th' city – especially if they're accompanied by a certain bald-headed master – reports o' beatings an' such like t' triple, an' dead bodies pile up half as high as th' west wall!" Jehred took another step, and his hands clenched unconsciously. "I want t' know where ya were 'round th' second bell, an' why I can see bandages padded unnerneath yer robe there!" Then abruptly, the captain lost some crucial keystone of control, for his left hand strayed to the hilt of his sword and his right fist pounded down on the table before him. "An' I want t' know what I can do t' keep yer accursed smile an' shinin' head from my sight!!" he bellowed.

The captain cursed his temper, but these *Flame Master*s were most times more than he could stomach, parading around in their bright silks and gold like court harlots, basking in their glory as 'Saviors of the City'. Meanwhile, true soldiers such as himself – those who had kept the Eldorn Kingdom free from Klemish domination for over three generations now – were rewarded by being sent to this backwater to keep the King's Peace. And then to be commanded by the Chancellor to handle simple garrison duty! Jehred ground his teeth and tried with all his will to wish a heart attack upon the small robed man still seated before him.

Elias' smile broadened as he drew fading circles in a puddle of spilt ale.

"Well Captain," Elias replied cheerfully, untouched by the soldier's wrath, "perhaps I can provide you with answers to the questions which obviously distress you so." He counted slowly on his fingers, as if explaining to a child. "Firstly, some of our 'honest citizens' die because they haven't the good manners or simple common sense to keep their hands to themselves; it is no more than that. Secondly, I've spent this day gifting my young friend here with a tour of our fair city. And as for my arm, I injured it in … ahh … practice earlier today. Lastly," the master ticked off his final point, and his hand closed casually into a fist, "in order to never lay eyes on me again, simply pull free that sword you're grasping so tightly." Elias sipped at his drink and spoke in a light bantering tone, as if chatting about the weather or the results of the recent bundhar races. But no one who heard him speak could fail to glimpse the fell message that lay hidden behind the sheer veil of his words.

Jehred stiffened at the challenge, and the soldiers behind him paled visibly. Then the captain heard a quiet deadly hiss, and realized with horrible surprise that his sword was already halfway drawn in a back-handed slashing grip. It required a conscious effort for Jehred to halt the motion, and his arm ached from the strain. He glared balefully at the small bearded man, who smiled like Jehred's simpleton brother and who dared, *dared* to mock a captain of the King's Guard before his own men!

Jehred cursed Elias' entire Order. He cursed the Chancellor and the citizens – nay, the *vermin* – that his Honor had called 'special cooperators of the Council' and charged Jehred to protect. Then he cursed himself for a coward, as he exhaled his rage with a strained sigh and dropped his sword back into its scabbard. Proud and hot-headed as he was, Jehred was anything but a fool – and only a fool pulled steel on a Red Robe, particularly *this* Red Robe. Jehred had once seen Elias cut three Tharian mercenaries to literal ribbons using only a small, keen-edged table knife – *Tharian* swordsmen at that, the finest hired blades that gold could command! And during the last Klemish siege, the bald-pated master had given full demonstration of his extraordinary fighting abilities against a host of foes. Jehred felt no desire to pit his own skills against those of the smiling little man seated before him, for the outcome of such a contest was as sure as death itself.

"Forgive my insult, Elias." Jehred forced his words through clenched teeth and straightened slowly, allowing his hands to fall by his sides. "I am simply tasked with keeping th' peace, such as it is," he remarked, irony and anger evident in his voice. "'Tis my duty, nothing more."

Elias' smile changed from mocking, to one of pained understanding.

"And a heavy burden that duty is, good Captain," Elias replied quietly. "One that I shall never envy you." Elias took a long pull from his tankard, then stared into the depths of his ale as he continued. "I have no quarrel with you, Jehred. I only wish to finish my meal in peace, rather than answer such dull questions. May we not instead, enlighten my young friend here with tales from our glorious pasts?"

Captain Jehred shook his head slowly, almost painfully. He began to speak several times, but each time he seemed to reject his words. Then, with a visible effort, he chose an appropriate reply.

"My commander, Lord Marshal Vin'Dall..."

"... is a fat, pompous, long-winded buffoon, who hasn't spent enough time in the field to know which end of the sword to grasp," Elias finished for him.

The silence in the room was as brittle as glass, threatening to crash into shards at the next sound or movement. Then a deep grumbling seemed to come from the corners of the room. And when Captain Jehred bared his teeth, Darn realized that the grizzled veteran was chuckling.

"Aye, that he is, Elias," Jehred answered with a sarcastic grin. "And from th' stories I hear, he hasn't hardly any idea how to handle his own sword, much less something that bites. The Lady Chelsae has him wrapped up so tight round 'er finger, that if she wishes fer a golden egg, he squats on th' floor an' starts cluckin." Jehred's slight smile lingered for a moment more, then died under the crush of his duty.

"Unfortunately, Krolluck th' Smith has th' ear o' th' Chancellor, and he cried that he an' his boys were roughed up by a Red Robe. Chancellor Karlonos had a private word with Lord Marshal Vin'Dall, an' next I know, I'm ordered t' stump th' Bazaar district an' look fer any Disciple what might have 'bumped' into Krolluck. Yer th' only member of yer Order that was seen in th' area, so needs I must question you."

Elias took a long slow drink, working the malty ale around in his mouth with obvious satisfaction, savoring it thoroughly. When he replied, all trace of malice was gone from his voice, but for a moment the master's eyes blazed like coals. "As for Krolluck the black-hearted smith: *if* he was disciplined by one of my Order, I am quite sure that it was well deserved. Tell him to thank his petty little gods that he still draws breath, and to pray that he never repeats the mistake."

Jehred nodded once, knowing that he'd get no better apology or explanation. His investigation of the mayhem in the Bazaar ended at this point, for those of Elias' station were unofficially above punishment – or even reproach – for any actions or judgments they saw fit to enforce.

To hell with Krolluck and the Chancellor both, Jehred thought to himself. *I'll not endanger my men or m'self arguing with a Red Robe over some worthless dead street cur.*

"Good day then, Elias." Jehred motioned his men to follow as he turned towards the door. Then he paused and spoke back over his shoulder:

"Take care this evening, esteemed Master. And try t' be gentle, should ya find need t' instruct some of th' citizenry in th' arts of proper etiquette .... we do need a few left fer tax time, remember." He smiled without humor and continued out the inn's doorway. Both of Jehred's subordinates looked almost sick with relief, and they crowded each other in the doorway in their haste to leave.

Elias sighed and shook his head as he eased back into his chair. He dug a small clay pipe from a pocket hidden inside his robes, and began to methodically fill it from an embroidered pouch of sweetleaf and other herbs.

"Jehred's a good man, mind you," Elias remarked to Darn. "Takes himself and his station much too seriously, I should say, but a good man all told. He fought quite bravely at the Siege of the Dark Sun." Elias drifted off into his own thoughts for a moment, and absently reached into the hearth beside him, selecting a small blazing coal with which to light his pipe.

Darn stared mutely at the tiny jets of flame he could see dancing between Elias' fingers before they were sucked down into the bowl of the pipe. Some studious part of Darn's mind registered the fact that no smell of burning flesh assaulted the room, and no howls of pain echoed off the walls. But still, the boy's eyes carried the fact that his strange new friend held a burning hot ember the size of a walnut pinched delicately between thumb and forefinger, with no apparent distress.

Elias casually puffed until the pipe was well lit, then tossed the still-smoldering ember back into the fire. "Yes, yes, the Siege of the Dark Sun. Now truly, that was a glorious battle! I remem . . . Why, what troubles you, young one?" Elias broke off, as he noticed the shocked look on Darn's face.

"Thy...thy fingers, Elias! They were not burned, though I could see the flames as clearly as those still in the hearth!" The boy swallowed hard, choking down the fear he felt. But his curiosity would not allow to allow him to retreat at this point. "Are...are ye a wizard, to bend the elements to thy will, as well as a great warrior?" Darn sputtered in confusion and embarrassment and – as he'd only ever admit to himself – a healthy dose of fear. The small magicks that his elven friends had taught him dealt only with healing and growing and the life of green things. The working of fire they disdained, hinting that such spells of destruction belonged to the Dark One and his minions.

"A wizard! Hah!" Elias' laughter pierced the quiet comfortable buzz of the tavern's conversations, leaving a gaping hole in its passing that the other patrons seemed reluctant to fill. "I am no demon-porking spellweaver, nor have any business with Goldath or Dàmon or any of the flesh eating lords of the Dark – their kind is a blot on the world. Nay, I've been called many a name in my day, young one, but wizard was never one of them." He chuckled once or twice more, and dabbed at the corner of his eye. "No, Darn," he replied at last, "it is only that I am a Disciple of the Flames, so such a small fire had no reason to cause me harm." He smiled as if this were explanation enough, and reached for his tankard.

Darn's frown deepened even further, creases of ale-fortified concentration marking his brow. "Forgive me, Elias, but I do not understand," he puzzled. "How could such a thing be, lest ye were a wizard?"

"Why, because I am one of Lord Agni's Flame Masters!" Elias replied airily, waving his arms wide and performing a mock bow from his chair. He paused for a long moment, waiting for his words to take effect. Then slowly, his jaunty smile dissolved in a thin wash of foolishness, as none of his drama brought even a glint of understanding to his young friend's eyes. Elias asked slowly, almost in disbelief: "Have ye never heard tale of our Order?"

Despite his caution, the ale had loosened Darn's tongue, and he leapt to answer.

"No disrespect intended, sir, but I know nothing of Flame Masters or being a companion to fire. I know only that I have seen no man perform the feats that I have seen of thee today: float upon the air as if thou had claimed wings to wear; beat a thungari down with thy bare hands; pick up hot coals as if they were river stones! No – perhaps such miracles are common here, but in Warden Woods, I have never seen the like."

"You know nothing of the Disciples of the Flames?" Elias asked, obviously astonished. Before the boy could answer, Elias continued, seemingly unaware that his words were spoken aloud.

"Surely even the woodland rabble, even one as young and naive as this must have heard tales? Why, such lack of renown is an affront to our very Order! This is unacceptable – Saura and I must surely speak of the matter!" Elias finally remembered his company, and bit down hard on his cheek for penance as he watched Darn redden with shame.

Fool! the master chided himself. *The boy's innocence is no fault of his own.* Elias bore his own embarrassment poorly, as he reached across the table to pat the young herdsman's son on the arm. The motion felt clumsy and awkward, an experience the master had not suffered in a score of years.

"Please accept my apologies, Darn. I must one day learn to taste the rudeness of my words before offering them to another." Elias sat back and felt an uncomfortable tightness in his chest for a moment. Then he passed it off as indigestion, and waved again for the serving girl to refill their jacks of ale.

As the girl approached, Elias traced her form with a practiced eye. He'd have guessed her to have seen no more than sixteen summers, though she deftly fended off the hands of drunken patrons and cursed with the tired familiarity of a career tavern wench. Elias appreciated such traits in a woman. He smiled as he watched her walk away, then turned his attention back to his companion.

"Now then, my young friend, allow me to relieve you of the weight of your ignorance." Elias puffed on his pipe for a bit, then casually glanced over at the next table. The three merchants seated there – whom up till now had been eavesdropping in a less-than-discreet fashion – suddenly found subjects of extreme and immediate interest in the bottoms of their mugs. The scarlet-clad master allowed a small grin to curl around his pipe stem as he continued with Darn's education.

"The first of our Order was Lord Marshall Tyrin, who lived during the waning years of the Great Famine. For refusing to set his swords against the starving populous, Tyrin was sentenced by a corrupt Council to die in the desert. And when he was placed outside the Gate of Bones, Tyrin neither begged nor bargained, but marched straight into the Land of Ashes, searching for his death. It is written that he walked for three days and nights before he fell." Elias leaned across the table, and Darn sat there moon-eyed, hanging on his every word.

"In those days, they had cast aside the Old Gods, and no one cared or remembered that Holy Lord Agni, the spirit of the sun, watched everything from His chariot in the sky. Lord Agni applauded Tyrin's courage and was moved by the soldier's sense of justice. So much, in fact, that moments before the vultures began their feast, Lord Agni bore Tyrin to a deep cave and healed him of his mortality. Tyrin was stripped bare, they say, of all fleshy confines by the Sunrider's fiery breath, and pared down to his core: the pure and simple soul of a warrior."

Elias snatched up his jack and took several quick gulps, then slammed the jack back down, too excited to savor his drink, as the end of the tale was burning to be told.

"The scrolls say that Lord Agni then granted Tyrin a gift of unimaginable power. Lord Agni taught our Firstmaster to wield the soulfire within himself, to drive his body past all mortal limitations, to endure any pain, to forge himself into a weapon deadlier than any blade or bolt."

"Years passed, and the Council became more corrupt, and the people starved. But then one day – one glorious day! – our Firstmaster Tyrin returned to Shiningrock. They say that Tyrin cut through the Council's guardsmen like a firestorm through a wheat field! And the vengeance he gifted upon those who had banished him to the Land of Ashes was like a cleansing fire, burning the stench of corruption from our fair city for generations." Elias stopped suddenly, then blew a puff of smoke from his nose, an angry bull-like gesture. "Were such things so easily accomplished now," he murmured, only half beneath his breath.

Now Elias took his time to enjoy his ale, leaving the rest of the story waiting. He guessed that his young friend had little patience, and he enjoyed baiting the boy.

"Then what, Elias?" Darn nearly shouted, emboldened by the ales he'd had himself. "That can't be all! My questions have still not been answered!" The boy went so far as to grab his scarlet-robed mentor by the sleeve, an action that caused several of their neighbors to blanch and move their chairs further away. But Elias only smiled and gently plucked his robe free from his youthful companion's grasp.

The master sat back and he stroked his whiskers in what he felt must surely be a scholarly fashion, as he warmed to his own tale. "After the city was redeemed," he continued, "Tyrin reclaimed his former estate, and renamed it the *Pyre*. He said that Lord Agni had placed upon him the joyous burden of bearing His Three Sacred Flames, those of Honor, Justice, and Battle. For only a man of Honor may ensure that Justice prevails. And in a violent world such as our own, Battle is the tool we must wield to uphold that Justice."

"So to any who pledged to uphold Agni's Sacred Flames, Tyrin taught a new manner of fighting, a way that combined the strength of one's limbs and the fire of one's soul." Elias tapped his chest with the stem of his pipe. "And like any fine blade, we are forged with the hottest of flames: our soulfire, the essence of the warrior within."

Elias' voice had risen with the telling, and more than a few eyes dropped away when he paused for a smoke and glanced around the room.

"Since that time, nearly eight centuries ago, our home has been here in Shiningrock, next to the Land of Ashes from which we are born. However, members of our Order can be found in every major city of the Eldorn Kingdom, and scattered across half the known world. Aye, and they may be found simply wandering the countryside, acting as counselors and defenders for those deserving of mercy, or judge, jury, and executioner for those who are not. We do not sell ourselves, and we vow to forgo conquest. Though there are times when one of our Order may lend their talents as councilor or arbitrator to some backwoods baron or northern earl. But other than to ourselves and our strictures, we hold allegiance to no king or councilman, bishop or duke. We are servants of the Law, drawing answers for the crimes of great or the small, ensuring that at least some measure of Justice and Honor is born across the land."

Elias drained the last few drops of ale from his jack, then set it aside with a sigh. "That, my lad, is the most accurate accounting of the Order as you're ever likely to hear. Alas, it is also one of the most boring." Elias lifted his feet up onto the table, leaned back and drew on his pipe, frowning as he realized belatedly that its fire was spent. He pulled a thin, odd-shaped stiletto from his sleeve and began to scrape the ashes from the bowl, as he continued.

"I myself prefer several of the other versions regarding our beginnings." Elias chuckled darkly, and smiled in a less than wholesome manner. "Some say that the Disciples are descended from the unholy union of a certain Lord Marshall and a sand demon. Others charge that we're all bastard children of Lord Agni Himself. Both tales, I believe, have their own merit." After a pause, the scarlet-robed master leaned forward and lowered his voice to a conspiratory whisper.

"I must admit, the idea of coupling with one of those murderous, soul-sucking bitches fills me with an uneasy mixture of revulsion and fascination. But, such is my own particular perversity, I imagine." Elias grinned widely, then leaned back and returned to cleaning his pipe.

Darn nodded seriously, despite the fact that he had only the barest comprehension of Elias' ramblings, this talk of gods and death and rebirth and mating with demons. Darn found his thoughts unfocused, following stray paths of reasoning until they dissolved or doubled back on themselves. He drew his brows together in an effort at reflective thought, but only managed to go cross-eyed and nearly fall from his chair.

"Tis time, I believe, for us to retire from this fine establishment, young Darn," Elias remarked as he stood, secreting his blade and pipe back into the hidden recesses of his robe. "Come. I shall see you back to your father's stables. The night has cloaked about us as we talked, and this city provides few safe pathways even in the daylight." Elias tossed a few copper droma on the table to pay for their meal. Then he turned and deftly flipped a silver tracham piece down the gaping blouse of the serving maid who had brought their ale and other staples. The young woman gasped in surprise and looked down into her well-displayed if meagerly-endowed treasure chest. The leering, gap-toothed smile she tossed back made Elias wince just a bit, but he was never one to decline an open invitation. His plans for the evening suddenly seemed much less boring than previously anticipated.

"Yes, to the stables with you, my boy. Then, I am afraid that we must part company, young friend, for I've classes to teach, and, umm," he glanced to where the server stood with a saucy smile on her face, "business to attend to later." Elias gathered his pipe, his pouch, and his slightly-addled young companion, then headed towards the door, swerving in his path to permit a quick squeeze of the server's well-rounded flanks in passing.

Darn moved unsteadily on his feet, and tried to free his mind of the cobwebs which the ale had spun there. *I would best find my wits and be quick about it*, he said to himself, *or Da will surely help me find them with a crack of his staff 'cross my arse!* He giggled at the thought, though he knew it wouldn't be funny at all, then followed Elias back into the street, marking a course nearly as straight as a hound's leg.

***

Jorge the burdock herder glared loudly from beneath his single, great, black-furred eyebrow, anger and disgust boiling upon his face like an evil-smelling stew. He glanced from his youngest son, who stood with his kilt torn and muddied, to the fancy-dressed city-dweller who'd brought the boy back here to the burdock pens. Bitterness settled into familiar lines on the brawny herdsman's face, filling its creases with something even older and more telling than the dirt that already clung there. Unruly locks of dung-colored hair strayed in front of his eyes, and he swept them aside roughly, cursing in a tired, thoughtless manner. Though he'd once been a proud-bearing man, the weight of his crude and simple existence had left Jorge bent and twisted. His nose hooked sharply to the left, pointing the way his lazy eye was wont to drift – as they both had ever since a young bullock had kicked him in the face. His shoulders hunched forward and his head drew down between them, as if anticipating the next crushing blow that destiny should bring. The sun had left its brand on him, stripping away the bronzed flesh of his youth, leaving the blotched, leather mask of an old man in its passing. Leather too, were his hands, coarse and crude as rough-sawn timber – and holding no sweeter a caress, as Darn well knew. Jorge's kilt and tunic, and skin where it showed, were stained with the filth and stench of the animals he tended – as his soul was forever stained by the bitterness and anger than suffused his life.

"Beg yer pard'n fer th' trouble, sirrah," Jorge offered. "But ya should've left th' worthless pup ta th' street cur who 'ad 'im. Least it would've saved me th' grain an' earthapples I'll have ta feed 'im this winter." A burdock wandered up and tried to rub its woolly head against the herder's leg, which earned the poor creature an ill-deserved kick in the flanks. The thick-headed ewe bleated in pain and surprise, then blundered away, leaving behind a steaming monument to her unjust treatment.

Jorge shifted his gaze back to the battered young boy, and the sight of the child was like another foul bubble bursting in his guts, one filled with shame and embarrassment.

"Couldntcha e'en run away this time?" he asked, not waiting for an answer. The grimy burdock herder rumbled deep in his throat, then spat to one side. "I s'pose ya lost yer coin too? Boy, yer not worth a tenth o' th' trouble ya causes me." Jorge's hands still

51

ached from shoveling out the stalls, something which *this* miserable excuse for a son should have been back in time to do. Rancid black thoughts drifted through Jorge's mind, leaving only slight trails of shame and remorse in their passing.

Should've let 'im die wi' th' bleedin' cough when 'is mother did, Jorge growled to himself. *'Stead, I'm left wi' no one t' cook er warm m' bed, 'nother mouth t' feed, an' a weak calf too small t' e'er be more'n a hindrance on th' farm. Gods, but I am truly a cursed man!"*

The simple herdsman shrugged as he accepted the cruelty and despair of his world, shouldering another load of sins like a sack filled with serpents. Without further preamble, Jorge struck his son hard along the face with the back of one callused hand, then watched flat-faced as the boy slowly struggled back to his feet, blood dripping steadily from the split and torn lips he'd just earned.

"Ya can pick herbs from th' woods t' pay fer th' cost offa new kilt," Jorge said dully. "An' I'll take that lil hoard o' copper ya got hidd'n 'neath yer cot, t' pay *me* fer yer chores that I had t' do. Now go split th' nania from th' rest o' th' herd, an' feed 'em that spoilt kibbig I scrounged up; they been waitin' long nuff t' eat. Once yer finished, pack up th' wool we didna sell. We be leavin fer th' Woods in th' morn."

The big man turned to walk away, but paused when he realized that the boy hadn't scurried off to the appointed tasks. Jorge looked down into Darn's battered face, and was taken back: a balefire of anger burned there, rather than the look of a whipped mongrel that Jorge was accustomed to seeing. An incandescent spark seemed to leap at him from the boy's eyes, and Jorge stumbled over his own feet as he took a hasty step backward. He caught his balance quickly, cursing both the brat's impertinence and his own cowardice. A moment later, Jorge answered Darn's challenge with the only solution his simple mind could offer: the man's horny hand swung out again – this time knotted tightly in a fist – to rock Darn's head back like a broken doll's and knock the whelp to the dung-covered floor of the pen. Then the lumbering herdsman stepped to where his son lay and drew back his foot.

Darn lay curled up in the mud, pain from the blow screaming inside his head. But an unfamiliar voice shouted to him over the pain.

"Move, Boy!! Now!"

Without thinking, Darn obeyed. And an instant before the heavy boot would have staved in his ribs, Darn rolled to one side and slapped his father's foot as it passed. Jorge's leg shot by awkwardly, out of control, and in comical slowness the herder slipped in a fresh pile of manure and crashed down to join his son in the muck.

Jorge's teeth snapped hard together, and he nearly choked on the crimson flood of pain pouring from his bitten tongue. Rage and confusion chased each other inside the herder's lumpish mind. He'd spent a lifetime dealing with his livestock, his late wife, various farm hands, and Darn's older brothers: all save his eldest, Mardon, had accepted his orders and punishments in silence and obedience. Then who was this mewling brat to avoid his just punishment, and to raise a hand against his own father, who'd fed and protected him these past years? Jorge's rage quickly outran his confusion, and it flared up inside his head like wild black fire, bringing Jorge scrabbling to his feet with an inarguable hunger for murder in his heart. He looked around desperately for a moment, then snatched up a solid length of broken fence railing that lay nearby. He started towards the boy – but again was given pause by the sight which met him: his youngest son, the weakling pup of his litter, stood with teeth bared in defiance and a stone snugged in the pouch of his sling. Jorge stood dumbfounded for several heartbeats. Then the ebony flames of his rage roared up even higher and burned all else from his mind. The big farmer took two slow steps forward and reared back with his club, and Darn's sling began to sing in answer. But a low still voice – like Death's own raspy whisper – batted aside the wildfire that danced and gibbered inside Jorge's head, and instead froze the herder's blood to ruby ice.

"Lay so much as a single, filthy finger upon the small one again, and I promise you that I shall tear open your worthless throat and *piss* down it until you die."

The tendons in Jorge's neck creaked as he turned to look at the red-robed stranger, who perched daintily upon a bale of burdock wool a hand of paces away. Jorge could feel the wood bite into his palms as he clenched his club tighter, and he snarled and turned towards the little man. But when he looked into the elemental fury trapped within the stranger's eyes, the blood drained from the herder's face. The ebony rage that had capered inside his head suddenly melted, forming an oily puddle of fear that trickled down his spine and soaked through his guts.

Elias hopped down lightly from where he sat and walked towards Darn's spellbound father.

"That small boy has more heart than you have ever *dreamed* of, you ill-graced, shit-besmeared, burdock-porking wastrel!" The master's voice grew louder with each step, and his hands trembled as they fought his control. "This is no mindless beast or addle-brained sodhopper for you to bend to your will as is your wont. This is a boy with a *soulfire*, do you understand? With heart and flame enough to scatter your wretched ashes to the wind, should he so choose!"

Jorge took an unbidden step backward as the small, fiery-cloaked man – whose head barely reached Jorge's chest – planted squarely before the thick-framed herdsman and somehow seemed to tower over him. Smoldering coals seemed to burn within the stranger's eyes, and a thick palpable wave of heat and loathing rolled off the man, rocking Jorge back a second step. The herder felt several small streams of sweat spring to life, plotting new courses through the landscape of grime on his face and arms, and the sour stink of fear began to mingle with the musk and tang of the burdock pens.

"Your fate is not the boy's!" Elias spat with distaste. "Do not try to consign him to it, for the fire captive inside him may not be quenched!" "Your flame was never given the care, the guidance needed to grow, country man, and so it wavered and died. What life you ever had is over, and death alone will be your final relief. You have no Honor, and no one will mourn or even remember you once your body feeds the worms." The master's tone then softened a measure, but gained an inexorable edge, turning from cold pig iron to hot hammered steel.

"Allow the boy to leave with me now, and some small part of you may still know the meaning of glory." Elias' face held no compassion for the herder's fate – only disgust and contempt and some small measure of pity.

Jorge struggled to interpret the robed man's dark words. But the only idea that swam clear of Jorge's muddied thoughts was that this stranger wished to take Darn away, and empty Jorge's pockets of the meager coin which the worthless boy contributed. Jorge's anger at losing a few more coppers won a brief respite over his fear, and he bellowed a response before his caution could contain him.

"E's mine, sirrah! *I* raised 'im, an' *I* fed 'im, an' *I* clothed 'im! 'E works fer wot 'e gets, an' pays one way er t' other, jest like th' rest. I canna' afford ta lose 'im, an' pay a man ta stand in 'is stead!" The black fire struggled to take life inside his head once more, and Jorge disregarded the way the small man had melted his bones just moments earlier. "Ye'll not take 'im! I'll... I'll call th' city guards, I will! Or I'll call me boys, an' we'll stop ya! But 'e belongs ta me, till..."

Elias' lips curled back in a feral snarl, and Jorge was too much the fool to realize his danger. Faster than eyes could follow, the master's right hand blurred forward, like the blinding strike of a crimson sha-viper.

Jorge blinked stupidly at the iron-callused fist that suddenly appeared quivering at the end of his nose. The wind of its passage ruffled Jorge's unkempt hair, and blew a tiny scrap of memory through the vast empty halls of his mind. He stumbled to catch the errant thought; but once he had it, Jorge would have gladly traded what little he owned in the world to have left the remembrance unfound.

The scarlet robe ... The scarred hands ... The heat of his anger ... The flames in his eyes ... Oh sweet Lady Elandril protect me!!

Jorge's eyes sprung wide in terror, even the wandering one showing white all around, as he realized at last exactly who and what he faced. The understanding raced through his mind like a fire-maddened beast, half-thoughts of escape or pardon whirling in the eddies as it passed. Jorge recalled the tavern lies and fireside tales he'd heard tell of unholy, red-robed warriors. Remembered also the shattered remains of Olden Ulafson and his cousin Yuri after they'd rousted some crimson-cloaked traveler along the edge of the Woods, as they were wont to do when the hunting turned poor. Jorge clutched frantically for some means of salvation – finding none, he could only void into his pants and gibber with fear.

Elias strove to restrain his hand, which shook like an eager hound, anxious to complete the blow to the herder's face. Slowly – so very slowly – the master willed his clenched fist to open, and a single gold solari dropped into the mud and manure at Jorge's feet, shining there like a piece of the sun.

"*That* will pay for several more farm hands, for you to whip and kick and curse as you like." Elias bared his teeth as he spoke. "Though if you still wish to call for your boys, do so now and I shall gladly send the lot of you back to your hovels wrapped in grave shrouds!"

Jorge served no reply to the challenge, for the gleaming goldpiece had stolen all other thoughts from him. He stared down in stupid wonder at the dung-smudged coin, unable to hold the truth of it, but afraid to disbelieve his eyes. In a liquid amber voice, the coin demanded to be retrieved from the muck of the pen, to be polished and cherished, and yes, even worshipped. Jorge hastened to obey the treasure's command, but a fist knotted painfully in his matted beard first, breaking his trance and yanking his head sharply downward. Jorge found himself staring into a pair of soulless blue eyes – eyes that brimmed with such fury that the twin gates of Nek'ru's third frozen hell could have held no more promise of pain.

"The boy is free from your hand, and your word, from this

day forward," Elias said slowly, intently. , "He may accompany me or not, or even choose to stay beneath your roof. But *hear me well Herdsman!*" Elias shook Jorge's head for emphasis. "And engrave my words as a promise on your very soul: should you ever touch this boy again without his wont, I shall come for you in your sleep, wherever you may be. And then, my friend, you will awaken into a nightmare that you would plead for death to deliver you from!" Elias released his hold suddenly, and the big man staggered back, wisps of smoke rising from his singed beard. The diminutive flame master glared hatefully for a long moment, allowing no mistake of the truth of his words. Then Elias spat at Jorge's feet and turned his back, disdaining concern for the herder's reprisal. He walked quietly to where Darn stood, and looked solemnly down at the boy's battered face.

"I make no claims upon you myself, young friend." Elias' voice was now quiet, almost gentle – a sudden and somewhat suspicious eye in the midst of his recent tempest. "You may come with me to the Pyre, where I can promise you at least enough food to drive the hunger from your belly and a warm bed for a time. But perhaps – *perhaps*, mind you – you may there earn the privilege off seeing the glory and fiery resplendence of your own soulfire!"

The master's face screwed up in a sour grimace, as he glanced with undisguised contempt to where Jorge knelt, cradling the solari like a babe.

"You may, of course, return to your home with this pathetic hulk who fathered you. Or," Elias continued, smiling benignly, "I can gift you with my blessings and what coins I possess. After that, you may follow whate'er path you elect."

Elias paused for a moment, then surprised himself by reaching out to gently wipe a trickle of blood from the boy's chin. For a moment, the master reflected.

Odd – thought I had cast such sentiments aside long ago. Yet there's no denying the boy reminds me of myself. Uncomfortable with such musings, Elias shrugged and pushed them away.

"I have given you the ability to choose, Darn – that and nothing more." Elias squatted down on his heels to look the boy in the eye, ignoring the stains to his robe. "But know this, Darn: you do indeed possess a most potent soulfire. To what heights it may be fanned, only Lord Agni may say. But I see the flames within you, aching to be fed. And that fire is capable of such glorious and magnificent feats that in a thousand winters I could never fully describe it to you, nor would you ever believe my words!" Elias straightened slowly and shook his head, the hoops in his ears flashing silently in the firelight.

"I have spoken enough." He drew a small leather purse from his belt, one tooled with wavering flames and dancing script, and closed Darn's hand about it. "Show this to any captain in the harbor and mention my name, and he will grant you fair and safe passage to wherever you may."

Elias visibly brightened as he continued. "But if the Flames call to you, if you wish to fear no man's hand, if you have the courage to face the fiery beast roaring inside of you, then come to me at the Pyre! And together we shall tame that vast conflagration, and set it burning to a greater purpose!" Elias smoothed his robed, and visibly fought to reign in his enthusiasm. "Look for the beacon-fire on the hill, north-west of the city, the only one that sits alone," he said. "Come to the Pyre, give my name at the gates, and someone shall see to your needs."

Elias clapped his hand softly on the boy's shoulder. "Otherwise, fare thee well, my young friend. And keep your sling ready by your side, for the world outside of Warden Woods is ever a devious and dangerous place." Elias turned in a sudden whirl of scarlet silk, and in three steps Darn's mysterious, crimson-robed savior had faded into the shadows' grasp.

Darn measured the weight of the purse in his hand, and heard the watery chime of coins much finer than copper.

Enough here to spend the rest of my days as a lord back in Warden Woods, he guessed as he smiled to himself. Then Darn glanced to where his father sat, and felt disgust churn in his stomach. The herder still squatted in the muck of the pens, oblivious to his own stench and filth, having eyes only for the gold in his hand.

A watered, faded memory of his mother drifted through Darn's thoughts, and he almost smiled. Then a sharp blade forged of grief twisted grimly in his soul. Mum had passed long ago, taking all the love and comfort with her. His brother Mardon had left a few years later to join the King's Guard. And his sisters had no time for Darn, busy as they were with their own families. There was no true home for him back in Warden Woods: only a moldy mattress, some meager food, and the hollow emptiness that haunted the place.

Darn's decision was made between one heartbeat and the next. He paused, carving a memory of this day, this evening, this very moment, deep into his mind, so as to forbid any future doubts or question of his choice. Then he turned to walk away into the dark unseen future of the night, never noticing the tears he left behind.

Chapter Three
The Pyre

Darn stood forlornly before the iron-bound gates of the walled estate, and shivered within the grasp of his cold, sodden clothes. The sky had opened shortly after he'd stalked from his father's camp, and the torrent of gods' tears had been his only companion as he wove his way through Shiningrock. Though he cursed the rain weakly, some dim part of Darn's mind recognized it as a blessing from the White Lady, for the torrential downpour turned the streets into rivers of mud and made an impenetrable curtain of the night. And without such shelter, Darn would surely have fallen prey to the city's nocturnal predators: slavers, and far, far worse, who stalked the streets and dark alleyways, searching for the weak, the young, and any else who would provide easy sustenance for their abhorrent appetites. But on such a night as this, even the most baleful of fiends shunned the open avenues, resigning themselves to remain indoors and practice their malefic arts on those unfortunates already in their possession. And so Darn traveled silently through the empty city streets, unseen and unharmed.

Almost by pure chance, Darn had located one of the small, western gates that let out onto the foothills behind the city, slipping past the dozing watchman like a shadow in the rain. He stumbled along in the dark, almost asleep at times, drawn like a moth by the blazing signal fire he could see on a distant hilltop, capering high into the night sky. Darn puzzled for a moment over how the flames were kept alive, for surely no mortal fire could survive the sky's onslaught. But the fires had shone ever brightly over the head of the sleeping city, guiding Darn to this bastioned manorhouse where Elias had promised him warm food and dry lodging – that, and perhaps something much more, something both alluring and perilous, like the poison-thorned branches of a blissberry bush.

A handful of fortified mansions squatted among the rolling hills that stretched north and west of the city proper: some only a candlemark's walk from the base of the city walls, and others at the very feet of the encircling Rendrac peaks. Most of these estates were owned by the city's larger trade guilds, or by reclusive citizens who possessed enough gold to protect their privacy with walls and fences and private militia. One of the manses was whispered to be frequented by a certain Crimian pirate lord. And the spires and courtyards of the elegant, indigo-walled manor just north of town were forever graced by the beautiful men and women who toiled under the guidance of Madam Zoë and catered to those with a taste for earthly pleasures.

Each private holding was guarded by a heavy wrought-iron fence or a high wooden palisade: protection enough against the wolves that wandered down from the mountains in the heart of winter, or from their two-legged cousins who occasionally ventured out from their dens in the city. But the fortified manor-house at which Darn sought refuge had been built by a former Lord Marshall, and so it possessed forbidding walls of smoothed black stone that stood nearly three times a man's height. The Pyre, as Elias had named it, was nothing less than a modest, battlemented citadel: its walls would repel anything short of a full-scale siege, and its copper-roofed storehouses and deep protected wells ensured that those within its safekeeping would not easily be starved into submission.

A thickset gate of heavy goldenoak timbers laughed openly at any who would try its strength, and within the short rounded towers on either side of it waited heavy crossbows, ready to add further injury to insult. Behind the gate, a trestled walkway stretched over the courtyard to the inner bailey, and any uninvited guests who attempted the crossing would find a less-than-welcome greeting in the spike-filled pit below. And at the walkway's end, the sharp, iron maw of a portcullis waited patiently to crush any surviving trespassers.

Though its formidable defenses might suggest otherwise, the mournful cry of battle horns had not been sounded outside the Pyre's walls in over two centuries. Since its present occupants had taken up residence, both Klemish invaders and robber barons alike made all attempts to give this particular stronghold a wide berth, for the Disciples of the Flames were known to take very personal offense to assaults against their home. The last would-be conqueror to lay siege against the Pyre itself – Prince Valstok di Kontorr, the thirteenth Klemish warlord – had been unmanned and sent back to his father in disgrace, riding an ass-drawn wagon filled with the heads and hands of his entire regiment of elite personal guards. None other, not even the grieving Klemish king himself, had dared to come against the Flame Masters' abode in open combat since then.

Darn stared intently at the dark forbidding portal, hoping to pierce it with his desire alone. But the gates stood unmoved, deaf to his silent cry for entrance, while the steady rain worked to wash away his crumbling resolve. His clothes were nothing more than soaking rags by now, and the cold that descended with the darkness on these early Spring nights made him ache to the very marrow of his young bones. He sighed deeply, almost despairingly, and the heavy purse of coins at his side seem more attractive with each passing moment. But then Elias' words of praise drifted like a ghost through his mind, bringing Darn to curse his own cowardice and to pinch himself hard on the thigh in penance.

Wrapping what courage he still possessed about him, Darn stepped forward and knocked upon a narrow guardhouse door that crouched in the wall beside one tower. He waited unanswered for a count of ten. Then a great wracking cough shook his thin frame, reminding him that a night spent outside in such weather could mean death, as it had for his mother. The thought seemed to shake loose the languor that dulled his thoughts and courage, and he stepped to the door again to pound harder, his growing indignant ire fueled by a dousing of fear.

A tiny watch-window set in the door creaked slowly open in answer, and a boy three or four years Darn's senior looked out through the bars.

"If yer a beggar, you'll leave here with naught but the rags ya wear," the boy snapped, blind to Darn's shivering. "If ya bring word from th' Lord Marshall or Chancellor Karlonos, be quick about it, for my dinner gets cold."

"M-m-master Elias t-told m-me to c-come here for a d-dry p-p-place to s-s-sleep," Darn chattered. He shook uncontrollably now, and his fingers were nearly too numb with cold to grip his cloak closed any longer.

The older boy raised a lantern to the window and eyed Darn suspiciously. "What would Elias want with the likes of you?" He barked out a laugh. "A drowned sewer-rat, and half-starved at that!"

A warm pulse of anger began to beat through Darn's veins. "He t-told me himself, n-n-not three bells past," Darn nearly shouted. His cracked and swollen lips – parting gifts from his father – split open again, and the trickles of blood which ran down his chin added fuel to the fire within him. "G-go find him and ask him thyself, if ye believe me not. B-b-but let me in from this rain, f-for he p-promised me shelter!"

The watch-window snapped shut, leaving Darn to face the night alone once again. He began to sink in upon himself in despair, melting slowly into the mud that now reached to his ankles. Then he heard the sounds of a heavy bar being lifted, and the small, thick-timbered door grated as it swung inward.

The doorkeeper stepped forward, wearing a white acolyte's robe and a smile on his face like a rotten pear full of hornets. He hung his lantern from a peg, then folded his arms and stood to block the doorway.

"Step forward then, little rat! If ya want in badly enough, just get by me and yer dry for the night." The smile on the boy's face dripped putrid nectar. "Come now," he motioned. "If ya wish t' pass these doors, ya have t' prove yer worth."

Darn eyed the older boy warily. The acolyte had the smooth, sooty skin of a Camdian, and a thick mane of coal-black hair. Like most of his people, he possessed fine, clean features and dark, penetrating eyes – a handsome countenance that many a young lass had surely succumbed to. And yet the sneer that claimed squatter's rights on the boy's face gave unspoken testimony to the obsidian core of his soul. Tall and lean, with whipcords of muscle outlined by his thin tunic, the door's guardian looked quite capable of defending his charge, and more than eager to do so.

Darn slipped a hand inside his cloak, clutching for his sling. But his heart shrank when he touched the leather band, for it was soaked by the rain and would never throw true. Hopelessness crept slowly up his back to whisper dark words in his ear, but Darn shrugged the ill-speaking imp away, taking heart from Elias' earlier comments. He took two faltering steps forward, fists clenched at his side, and concentrated on nothing but his anger, his hurt, and the fire in his soul which fed off of them both. The tall acolyte smiled at Darn's approach and shifted lazily into a fighting stance.

The rain-soaked lad stopped a few paces from the open doorway and its warder. His thin frame still trembled, but no longer from the rain or cold – for now a much more formidable element possessed him. Darn tightened every muscle, every fiber, every cord of his being, and when the strain reached his face and his dark eyes fairly bulged from their sockets, he released the tethers on his rage, and it poured from him with the raging fury of a desert whirlwind.

"LET ME IN, YOU SNOT-SUCKING, MAGGOT-FACED, INBRED SON OF A TWO-COPPER WHORE!!"

The raw power and spirit of Darn's shout forced the acolyte back several steps. The older boy gaped dumbfounded for a long moment, his ears ringing from the explosion of Darn's anger. Then understanding brought a carmine flush to his dusky face, and the doorkeeper growled deep in his throat, like a wolf scenting some unknown and untried rival. He raised his fists and smiled almost sweetly in malicious anticipation as he stepped out from the doorway.

A soft, low voice slipped from the darkness beyond the older boy's shoulder:

"I believe that the young man would very much like to come in, Arak."

Though quiet, almost subdued, the voice held a sense of hidden power, like a bare wisp of smoke rising from a mountaintop.

The acolyte glanced behind him and began to gnaw his lip nervously.

"But Grandmaster Saura," the boy whined, "he claims Master Elias sent him." He flicked a dismissive hand in Darn's direction. "What could the Master possible want with such a worthless country mongrel? Not worth a moldy crust of bread, he is! Why, anyone could see .... AAAIIEEEEEE!!" The acolyte screeched in sudden pain and clapped a hand to his face, while a runnel of crimson leaked from between his fingers. A flash of quicksilver darted back into the shadows.

The faceless voice spoke again, no longer soft nor subdued, but gaining fearsome strength like a quick-rising firestorm.

"*Anyone* could see, Arak ..."

A thin, metal staff snaked out of the darkness, quicker than Darn could follow, quicker than a flash of pain, and a scarlet line drew itself across the acolyte's bare shins, punctuating the statement.

"... that *you* should not question a *master's* decision." Several more fiery tracks appeared along Arak's shielding forearms. "And even the *blind* could see that you could use some fresh *lessons* in the matter of *courtesy*!" The discipline and anger of this last word was echoed by the biting staff, which slapped across Arak's back so swiftly it parted clothing and flesh as neatly as a blade.

Arak slowly lowered his arms, revealing a long, bloody welt that crossed his cheek and closed his left eye, a companion to

67

the crimson traces gracing his arms and legs. From his open eye, unrefined hatred stabbed outward like a crudely-wrought spear of rough iron. Then the older boy bowed his head and turned fully to face the source of his pain.

"Forgive me, Grandmaster Saura. It is not my station yet to judge," the acolyte said low and grudgingly, biting off the words as if they burned his tongue.

"Nor may it ever be your station, impetuous young fool!" answered the darkness. "Stupidity earns no forgiveness here Arak: only punishment." The shadows fell back into silence, and Arak fought unsuccessfully not to cringe, waiting for the staff to sing out again. A vindictive smile stretched across Darn's face at the sight of Arak's discomfiture. And though it made his torn lips bleed, Darn thought the sight to be well worth the pain.

Only the wind broke the silence, swirling about Darn's ankles and giving voice to its misery. Then the unseen speaker continued. "Find your way to Master Era, if that doesn't prove too arduous a task, Arak. Tell him that your fondest wish is to shovel coal for his forge for the next three days. I am sure that *he* will be *quite* forgiving."

The acolyte's gaze flickered to Darn for only an instant, but it carried long anthems of rancor and revenge within it. Then he turned and darted back through the doorway, leaving Darn alone to face the forbidding voice of the shadows.

A wizened old man clad in the long, crimson robe of a master stepped forward into the glow of the lantern, the slim staff which had shown Arak its bite held delicately in his hand. The venerable master looked as gnarled and twisted as a briar root. But despite the snowy locks of hair which hung past his shoulders, the elderly warrior moved with a sure and powerful grace, reminding Darn of the ancient, tawny panthers that hunted the deep forests near Warden Woods. The old man's eyes reflected the lantern light like chips of jasper, and Darn shivered under their gaze. Then the ghost of a smile wrinkled the leathery face, and the master beckoned Darn inside.

"Come in, lad, come in. The rain brings life, but it can take it just as well." He held out a thin-boned hand skinned with parchment, and Darn knew without question that it held trust and security in its grasp. Darn made to enter, but either fatigue or the mud underfoot betrayed his step, for he slipped and began to fall. The same frail-seeming hand darted forward, quick as thought, and a grip of iron closed on Darn's wrist, saving him from an unpleasant landing. At the touch, Darn could feel some indefinable primal force coursing just beneath the old man's skin: call it heat or fire, but neither exactly fit the true nature of its power. In any case, Darn guessed that to cross such a force was a wish for misery or worse. He shuddered, and allowed the elderly master to draw him inside.

Grandmaster Saura led Darn through the doorway, then turned back o shut out the rain and wind. He directed the boy to turn the handles of a small windlass mounted on the wall, and a heavy beam of ironwood snugged down tightly across the door. Darn turned back and squinted in the torchlight. The small, stone-walled guardroom was a stark and barren place, furnished with only a table and a pair of rough stools. Darn glanced upward, then took an unconscious step back from the murder holes that stared down at him from the ceiling. *Not the most welcome place I have ever chanced to visit,* he thought briefly. But it was both warm and dry, and together with the half-eaten meal that sat on the table, it felt like sanctuary.

"One of Elias' chosen, eh?" the white-haired master asked. "Well, he is seldom wrong in these matters, regardless of his other shortcomings. Come." He spun about with a grace that would have brought jealous tears from the Holy Dancers of Eshatti, and led the way through an arched doorway into an adjoining hall.

Darn lifted a barely-gnawed marshfowl leg from the table as he passed, and slipped it quietly inside his cloak. The boy never saw the smile which tugged at the old man's lips and gathered wrinkled creases at the corner of his eyes.

They walked quietly down the hallway for a short distance, then turned and climbed a torch-lit stairway. Darn was considering a taste of his stolen prize when the master's voice stepped lightly through the silence.

"Elias should have been here to greet you himself, and spare you such an ungracious welcome. Though Lord Agni knows, the bones of the city themselves should have woken to your call." Darn blushed deeply, and Grandmaster Saura patted his head gently and chuckled. "Do not be ashamed, little one, for a great voice is evidence of great fire. Many take long to learn such lessons – and some fail it all together. Be proud of what you have taught yourself, for now you have one less step to travel in the path ahead."

The two walked along several dark hallways that jagged left and right, up and down, in no apparent order or reason. They ascended a long flight of stone stairs, and Darn became uncomfortably aware that the only noise to mark their passing was the soggy slap of his own steps. He leaned his weight to the outside edges of his feet, as he did when stalking rock conies in the meadows back home. Grandmaster Saura might have smiled at the resulting silence, though Darn was never sure, for the rest of his thoughts were stolen away as they turned a sharp corner and were brought to a halt by a thick wooden door that leaked bloody torchlight and the muted sound of voices from its edges. Darn turned to speak, but the master held up a hand. Even in the weak torch light, Darn could see the thick plates of calluses that covered the old man's palm. That, and the impatient tapping of the bloodthirsty, metal staff reminded Darn that this most certainly was not a man to interrupt. With a supreme effort, the boy bit back the buzzing hive of questions that waited impatiently behind his lips.

"This way leads through the great hall of our Pyre," Master Saura answered Darn's unspoken thoughts, "to what we call the Forge. Here, we take plainly-fashioned lumps of humanity – such as yourself – and hammer them to fit the mold of a warrior. We shall see later if you are worth our effort. But for now, warm clothes and hot food are what you need most. Come." He opened the door and led Darn inside. And in that one single step, the boy crossed over the threshold of a new life, and the one he had known before was forever lost to him.

***

What Darn noticed first were the flames: round and about, the hall seemed cloaked in flames. Torches bloomed from sconces along every wall, like blazing yellow flowers in their own fiery springtime. Three huge, star-shaped copper braziers hung from the hall's ridgebeam, artfully constructed so that a flame sprang from each point, drinking hungrily from the oil within. And at the far end of the vast room, an immense open hearth sat like a fat, voracious dragon, happily consuming any and all fuel that could be found to feed her. Grandmaster Saura had named the hall *the Forge*, and rightly so, for the room was as stifling as an afternoon in full summer, and Darn could feel steam rising from his wet clothes.

The great hall was easily the largest enclosed space that Darn had ever set foot inside. The Elders' lodge, back in Warden Woods, would not have filled so much as a corner of the magnificent chamber. Massive wooden timbers stretched skyward to support the distant, arched ceiling, all gilded with a patina of torch soot. The flooring stones gleamed a glossy black, polished by centuries of bare feet. Elaborate tapestries covered most of the paneled walls, commemorating famous battles of Eldorn history. In one, Darn was sure he recognized old High King Ælfred from a story his brother Mardon had told him long ago. Ælfred, with the forked yellow beard of his distant dwarvish kin and his great black-iron spear, *Throduar*, was forever woven into immortal combat against the infamous troll-king, Sha'sha'doom.

A flash of light from the far wall drew Darn's eyes, and every grain of his attention was gathered in a single glance. Three magnificent, stylized flames were rendered there, above the blazing hearth fire, the tallest stretching halfway to the distant ceiling. The one on the left looked to be fashioned of beaten brass, and the one on the right shone with the moonlit gleam of polished silver. But the flame that blossomed from the center of the group gleamed and pulsed in the firelight, its amber depths collecting all the torchlight in the room and reflecting it back with a rich, fluid grace. It was sculpted of pure gold, enough to fill the coffers of an emperor's treasure room.

Grandmaster Saura followed Darn's enraptured stare, and nodded in agreement. "Yes, they are indeed beautiful: Lord Agni's Sacred Flames, those of Battle, Justice, and Honor." The old man closed his eyes and seemed to bask in their glow. "It is said Lord Agni forged them Himself in the crucible of the sun, and brought them here that we may never forget."

Darn was simply overwhelmed by the fortune that the rendered flames represented, never mind who forged them! The largest sum of money he'd ever seen before was a double-hand of silver pieces that Fat Cholly the Innkeeper had paid for a wagonload of potent Hovill brew. Darn was also surprised to see that the bottom of the golden flame was an easy reach from the floor, offering itself to any passerby with a quick hand. But even knowing as little as he did, Darn guessed that no thief in the world, no robber baron or barbarian raider or even upstart king would dare come any closer to this treasure than in his dreams. Indeed, these priceless monuments could be no safer if they were locked in the King's treasure room in Courdeless. For Agni's Flames symbolized the essence, the very soul of his Disciples. And all who lived by His strictures would gladly use their own guts for garrotes, before allowing their Lord's holy symbols to be sullied by the hands of an unbeliever.

A sudden, strident shout drew Darn's attention downward, and the sights that met him as he looked over the railing cast all thoughts of gold and tapestries forever from his mind. For there on the floor below, the unnamed desires which haunted Darn's dreams were finally given life and substance.

A hundred or more young students sweated and strained

across the flooring stones, each striving to attain mastery of their art. Here, by a row of arched doorways, a small group waited their turn as a handful of their number blocked and kicked at wooden-limbed training dummies. There, at the base of the stairs, another band watched in stunned silence as two masters leapt and whirled and struck at each other with long batons: the staccato clack of the sticks setting a counterpoint to the harsh breathing and guttural shouts of the combatants. On the opposite side of the hall, white-robed novices practiced simple kicks and blows against hemp-wrapped poles, while crimson-sashed adepts threw multiple strikes and launched devastating flying kicks against heavy bags of sand. And filling the center of the floor, a crowd of exhausted acolytes performed the same basic strike again and again to the call of a scarlet-clad master, while several of the senior students stalked among them, dealing out harsh words and stinging blows to any they deemed sluggards.

Upon the raised dais before the roaring hearth, two students stood in fighting positions with lead hands touching, clad only in their loincloths. Each bore some type of scar on the flesh of his chest. One of a dozen fiery-cloaked masters nearby uttered a short, piercing cry, and the two opponents blurred into motion. To Darn's eyes, it seemed like each of the two dealt and received dozens of blows in the space of a single heartbeat. Their limbs licked out towards each other like hungry tongues of flame, striking with elbow, palm, fingertip and fist, knee, heel, and blade of foot. Most of the blows were met with lightning-quick parries, or avoided with a subtle twist of the body or slight bob of the head. But several strikes slipped by their intended defenses to land with terrible thudding impacts, and more than one left a splash of crimson behind to mark its passing.

One of the fighters seemed to momentarily fail, and his opponent began to dance in a circle about him, blows falling even faster than before. A clawing attack to the face was barely blocked before it took out an eye, but the palm-heel strike which followed it landed squarely upon the student's jaw, breaking it with an awful crack that Darn could hear from across the hall. The wounded fighter, face awash with pain, attempted to protect himself and slide away from his adversary. But the injury seemed to have weakened his defenses even further, and two vicious front kicks snapped hard into his stomach, driving the wind from his lungs and the strength from his legs.

The injured combatant's knees began to buckle, and his opponent spun in a tight circle, right fist lashing out and around as swift and deadly as a slung stone, striking home upon the boy's temple. The stunned fighter's eyes rolled back in his head, and he slumped bonelessly to the floor. Even then, the attack continued; Darn watched in horror as the victor leapt high into the air, preparing to deliver a skull-crushing stomp to his lifeless opponent.

"Enough!" cried one of the masters. The fighter effortlessly altered his flight in mid-stoop, choosing instead to land lightly beside his fallen foe. The master dismissed him with a simple nod, without a word of compliment or condemnation. The student had apparently expected nothing more, for the intricate bow he made before his teachers held only respect and gratitude within its flowing, graceful motions. Once finished, he turned to gather his unconscious fellow up in his arms, then marched victoriously from the dais. Two new combatants immediately took their places, and prepared to do battle.

"H-he is not dead, is he Master?" Darn stammered. He felt somewhat ashamed, even a bit afraid, to reveal his apprehension here in this hall of warriors. But the brutal manner of the contest he had just witnessed – with no quarter sought and none offered – disturbed him in a manner which he could not name, but feared all the same.

"No, my son." Grandmaster Saura shook his head and smiled, almost sadly. "His shame may cause him to wish for death, but for now he endures. His true test shall fall upon him in the morning, when he must begin to quest inside himself for the key which eludes him yet. He must accept his failure, learn from it, and never surrender to it again. That, or choose the coward's escape, and end his life by his own hand." Saura glanced down at Darn's shocked expression, and a chuckle escaped his lips. "Oh, do not judge me, my young friend, till you have walked my path." He waved a hand towards the dais. "You think me harsh. Yet the truth is that the one we watched fall has learned far more than the victor. He realizes now that the prize he seeks may never be his own, for he fears the fire within himself still. He has yet not learned to embrace its power, to surrender to it, to bathe in the purity of the primal flames and free himself from the shackles of his humanity." Saura's eyes blazed like hot coals as he spoke, and Darn took what he hoped was a casual-seeming step backward.

And I thought Master Elias seemed intense! Darn mused. *I hope to never know the penalty for failing to meet this old man's wishes.*

"The other one, the victor of this match, has in truth won nothing," the old master continued. "He was well aware that he was the superior fighter, and sought only to bolster his own ego. A lesson in humility will soon be visited upon him by one who is his better. In this way, he too may have an opportunity for advanced training."

Darn turned back to the railing, and he was filled with an uneasy mixture of awe and fear. Never had he seen men move with such blinding speed and ruinous power. Oh, he had watched from the safety of the woods while his father and the other men of Warden Woods had fought with the occasional band of Klemish raiders. He'd even been allowed to attend the King's Tournament in Lorring two Springs past to watch his older brother Mardon fight in the mêlée. But the knights and squires and other fighters there, with their greatswords and maces and heavy plate armor, they seemed now like thick-witted cattle compared to the warriors training in the hall below, Darn thought to himself. *Why, even the youngest acolytes below move with such speed that I can hardly follow the blow. And the terrible punishment which those two on the dais dealt out with only their bare hands and feet!* Darn sent a quick prayer winging to whichever god or goddess that might be appropriate under these circumstances, to please, *please* allow him to be found acceptable, whatever the cost may be. For to become one of these disciples, to never again fear another man's hand, was a prize worth his very soul.

Saura, too, was lost deep in thought as he looked out over the hall below him. A smile reached the old man's lips, for this was *his* Order and these were *his* warriors. *And by the blood of my mother, no fighting force in the world could stand against them in battle. Nearly every acolyte in this hall is already the equal of an armed guardsman. The senior adepts are each worth at least a hand of seasoned campaigners, and every master of the Order could hold their own against ten times that many. Elias, Tobani, and perhaps two or three others, I would match together against the King's entire cohort of Leopard Guards.* Saura barked out a short laugh then, and chided himself for his boastful pride. The elderly master reminded himself of his vow to uphold the Three Sacred Flames – Honor, Justice, and Battle; these iron bands of faith and duty were far stronger than any dream of conquest. *We shall be no kings then, no rulers. But by Lord Agni's Fiery Breath, for as long as I hold sway here we shall bring a measure of Honor to this land. And we will ensure that Justice – if it exists no where else – at least is known to follow in the footsteps of the Agni's Disciples..*

Grandmaster Saura shook himself loose from his musings, at last remembering the soaked, half-starved waif that stood entranced by his side. The elderly warrior had seen the same wistful look on the faces of a thousand young boys, all but a handful of whom had found the price for their wishes to be far too high. But for some unnamable reason, *this* boy, this scrawny, stick-limbed urchin, gave the master pause. This one possessed an intensity, a hunger that Saura had not seen the likes of since Elias had been abandoned at the gates as a six year-old, sharp-tongued whore's son. Saura relaxed his gaze, willing himself to a state of mind that would allow him to examine the boy at a deeper level, where internal energies each manifested their particular shading and form. Then he noticed that the boy shivered despite the heat of the room, and the master shamed himself for not attending to the lad's needs before all else. There would be time to satisfy his own curiosity later.

"Come, small one," said Master Saura, taking the boy gently

by the shoulder. "I will show you to your hold now." He turned and left the balcony through a small, arched doorway.

With a last worried glance backward, Darn hurried to follow. *Please!*

***

"You may rest here." Grandmaster Saura waved his hand to indicate the tiny room: barely four paces by three, with a single tiny window shuttered tightly against the storm that still raged outside. A straw-stuffed pallet lay in one corner, covered by a rough burdock-wool blanket. Beside the simple bed, a washbasin and oil lamp sat atop a battered wooden trunk: the room's only other furnishings. The old man walked slowly to where the lamp sat, and touched its wick with a forefinger; a tiny flame sprang to life, but Darn was simply too bone-weary and cold to be amazed.

Master Saura turned to face Darn, and the sharp edges of his face softened at the sight of the blue-lipped lad. "Leave those soaking rags you wear outside for now. Someone will be along shortly to take them away, and will leave you a dry robe and some warm soup in their stead. That, and the bird leg you availed yourself to in the guardroom, should hold you till breakfast. Sleep as you can. I will see that Elias comes for you in the morning." Saura brushed silently past Darn, slipping out into the hallway to leave. Then he glanced back in the doorway, and frowned at Darn's immobility.

"Be quick now, boy," he snapped in mock ferocity. "I'll not have you die of cold before we've a chance to test your mettle! Though I'll dare say the time may come when you'll wish that I had." Darn heard the old man chuckle quietly as the whisper of his steps faded into the darkness. A spasm of shivers shook the boy's thin frame then, breaking the strands of uncertainty that held him captive. He peeled off his rain-drenched clothes, setting his sling and stone pouch atop the trunk, along with the purse of coins that Elias had given him. After a moment's consideration, he reclaimed the purse and worried it deep into the straw of his pallet. Darn plucked the marshfowl leg from the pile of sodden clothes, then laid down and wrapped the wonderfully-warm blanket around him, its familiar scent a talisman against the bleak, unwelcome spirit of the room.

The rain outside hammered at the tightly-shuttered window, and the wind moaned a sorrowful plea for entrance. And inside the small chamber, a young boy fell prey to the quietly-creeping specter of loneliness, that haunting imp who leads tiny familiars of heartbreak and fear. By the light of a single, small flame, the boy hugged himself tightly and quietly sobbed until sleep stole away his tears.

Chapter Four
Striving

Darn cursed quietly as he picked another pot from the seemingly endless pile of crockery and dunked it into the wash tub. He cursed the water for being too hot; he cursed the strong lye soap that splashed and burned in his eye; he cursed whoever had left their porridge to dry on a plate till it was the consistency of granite. But most of all, he cursed his fate — and with it, he cursed Master Elias.

Elias had drawn him to this place – the *Pyre* he'd called it – with promises of power, of soulfire, and of martial skill. Granted, he had also promised warm food and a dry bed — and of those, he had kept his word. But *Lady Above!* it was nearly Midwinter's Day! He'd been here for nine moons, since the early days of Spring. And the only new skills that Darn could lay claim to so far were how to fold linens, how to rake the grounds properly, and – inarguably – how to wash pots. *Willing to eat with my bare hands the rest of my days, if I may only have to never again look at another pot!* he thought grimly, attacking some dried gravy with a vengeance.

The day after his admittance to the Pyre, Darn had been given a nondescript gray tunic – along with a list of chores. *These will build character,* he was told, *and will demonstrate to us your sincerity. Should you find them not to your liking, the door stands always open.* Still too much in shock to question or argue such directions, Darn quietly took his broom and got to work. As well he had, for it quickly became clear that complaints were answered with a swift slap to the head at the very least. Any who dared voice their anger to Grandmaster Saura were gifted with a bite of the master's fearsome staff, and would always bear the markings of their foolishness. No, Darn learned from the mistakes of those around him, and chose instead to bear his anger and his hurt in silence, as he always had.

Many initiates gave up in despair and chose to leave the Pyre for the world they had known before. Oft times, those who complained were shown to the gate and the dirt beyond it, and perhaps gifted with a swift kick to aid their departure. Others simply failed to return after a trip to the market, or left their tools in the gardens outside and fled for the city or the northern road. But a small few, of which Darn was numbered, endured their chores in grudged silence. For it was these younglings whose dreams were still plagued with visions of warrior's fire.

Perhaps it is all a lie, Darn thought, as despair nudged at his thoughts. *Perhaps they simply pick young fools such as myself, and use us until we are broken. Servants – nay, slaves! – for only the price of bread and a bed.* Thoughts of leaving had begun to weigh heavily on the young boy's mind, as did the bag of coins – Elias' bribe, as he thought of it – still hidden inside his sleeping pallet.

Just as a wonderful daydream was beginning to stretch across his mind, a sudden voice sounded at his elbow. Darn started at the interruption, and the bowl he held slipped through his fingers. He gave a hoarse gasp and fumbled with the vessel twice. Then a hand snatched in – impossibly fast – and claimed the crock just before it met its doom on the paving stones below

"I was saying," the tall adept continued, as he sat the rescued bowl on the drying rack, "you have been summoned to the Forge." He turned to look back at Darn once as he walked away, and the senior student's face held an odd mixture of humor and pity. Tek'ka, his name was: he was one of the only people at the Pyre who spoke to the initiates with anything other than contempt in their voice.

Darn knew better than to ask more questions. He wiped his hands dry and hung up his washing rag by the kitchen hearth. Fear and a sick feeling of anticipation yapped at his heels, hurrying him towards the doorway.

***

Darn glanced about the great hall, confused as the rest of the initiates who milled aimlessly about, seven or eight full hands of them at least.

"Prob'ly have us polish the floor with our tongues," one boy ventured out loud.

Others offered their own ideas or foolish suggestions, and laughed nervously. Darn felt it wise to keep his thoughts as his own.

A door set at the edge of the raised dais suddenly opened, and a score or more of Flame Masters filed into the hall. Several senior adepts followed behind, one of whom carried a long leather bag. All bore very serious expressions. Grandmaster Saura stepped forward to the front of the dais and fixed the assembled initiates with a glare that none could match. As he spoke, one of the senior students busied himself at the glowing hearth behind him.

"Each of you has entered here, entered Lord Agni's Pyre, in hopes that one day you would be accepted into His service. Many gifts beyond the ken of the rest of humanity await those who have walked the Land of Ashes, those who wear the Red Robes of His Disciples. The path is long and tortuous, aye, and filled with grave peril. Of those who stand here now, perhaps only a hand of you shall survive to gain your robe. And perhaps none." The initiates glanced at each other nervously.

"When you passed through our doors, the first step on a journey was begun. Many have already found the path too costly and have left our midst. Those of you who would remain must now make a choice. Will you stay this path, or will you step aside? For from this point forward, there is no turning back. For the Disciples of the Flames, there is no other goal, no other master, no other path. Lord Agni's Three Sacred Flames: Honor, Justice, and Battle — these will guide your lives for the rest of your days. There is no room for failure, and no room for regret. To a Disciple of the Flames, failure is oblivion. For one in His service, there is death before failure, death before dishonor."

Saura paused, giving his words time to settle. A few of the applicants muttered darkly between themselves, but the rest were too young to understand the subtly of his speech.

"There can be no mistake in your choosing. For once Lord Agni's mark is upon you, your body and soul both are but tools in pursuance of His will. Sworn by our Honor, to uphold true Justice, through the course of holy Battle."

"Hear the words I say to you, those who would become Agni's children. Your choice is now. For no one – not the lowest acolyte, not the Grandmaster himself – no one who bears the mark of His Flames may leave His service. To do so would be an admission of failure, and would bring dishonor on us all. Such an abomination would be hunted down, and his or her life forfeit."

"Lord Agni gave His teachings to Grandmaster Tyrin, the first of us all. And these gifts and skills have been passed down to each of us who would uphold His Flames. Such knowledge could do much harm, should it fall to any not bound by our strictures, not bound by Honor. And so it is that none may ever leave our Order, nor fail in its training."

"Be of no question: each of you who accept this path will one day wear the crimson robe of a Flame Master ... *or you will die in the attempt!* As I have said, there is no turning back." Grandmaster Saura motioned with one hand to the group behind him. "And now, you will accept Lord Agni's mark, as have all who claimed this path before you."

Master Tobani stepped to the huge hearth at the back of the dais, which was layered with a thick bed of burning crimson coals. A hand or more iron rods jutted from the coals, gleaming dull red like dragon's whiskers. Tobani reached forward, bare handed, and lifted one of the glowing metal rods from the fire. Despite the cries of dismay from the watching crowd, the air remained free of the foul smoke and stench of burning flesh. Tobani's hand was not consumed, though beads of sweat broke out on his brow. He turned back towards the young boys and girls who waited below, and a hush descended over them all.

The brand on the rod's end was a sculpted metal flame a finger-length tall, that seemed to leap and dance as if alive. It wavered in the heat of its own making, seeming to beckon to those who waited, calling to them in a voice that promised unimaginable amounts of both pain and glory.

Tobani stepped forward, and picked out an initiate at random.

"You. Come and embrace your future."

The gangly, pimple-faced youth swallowed strongly,

undecided. Even life as a soldier's son hadn't prepared the boy for this. Master Tobani took another step, to the edge of the dais. Then the master smiled, displaying the filed, pointed teeth which the Bandaran people found so charming — such a rare and awful sight that even the senior students in attendance quailed. The hopeful young initiate's courage melted like wax.

"Nah! Nah!" the boy cried, backing away. "They never told me it'd cost m' life!" He bolted for the open doorway. No one moved to stop him.

"And who next shall prove their courage," the master asked quietly, a whisper that echoed like a shout in the silent hall.

The next two initiates turned and ran also. But then a thin dark-haired child with arms like pointed sticks stepped forward, pushing past those who held back.

This time, Tobani smiled truly, with pride and honor.

"Ah, Sharphands," the master said, as he nodded acceptance. "I had hoped you would be the first."

The dusky-skinned urchin nodded fiercely, then swallowed once.

"I've 'ad t' pay in pain, b'fore, Master," the child said in a low, musical voice. "This time thoo, I give it gladly."

Tobani leaned in close, and whispered in the initiate's ear for a bit. When the master finished, he pulled back and stared hard into the child's face. The initiate answered his question with a fierce nod. Tobani straightened, lifted the hot iron before him, and reached out to steady the child with his free hand. One of the senior students pulled open the top of the initiate's robe. Then swift as pain, Master Tobani drove the ruby-red metal flame against the skin of the child's chest.

Darn watched in horrible fascination, unable to close his eyes. He saw the young initiate arch backward in sudden agony, but heard no scream — only a twisted harmony of breath forced through clenched teeth and the sound of flesh sizzling. A long oily wisp of black smoke danced over the dais for a moment or two, then darted into the open mouth of the great hearth.

The student staggered back half a step, blood pouring from a deeply-bitten lower lip, but recovered both balance and composure almost immediately. The child brushed aside a dirty crow's wing of hair, and fought to see up through a veil of tears.

Tobani looked down, a fire of admiration glowing in his strange, angled eyes. "I expected no less of you," he said. "I chose well." The young Adept nodded once more, then turned and left the dais, and was led towards the open courtyard door where the Order's Healer waited. What was moments before only another frightened and powerless child, was now an Acolyte to the Disciples of the Flames, a servant of Holy Lord Agni. And though pain marred the child's face, it was also filled with a pride born of something other than years.

Darn glanced at the new Acolyte's chest as they passed on the stairs. He immediately regretted his mistake, for the flesh was bubbled and blackened, with a pulsating rawness to it. A scream knifed through the air, slashing at Darn's already-raw nerves: apparently, the second new acolyte had failed to match the first's stoic courage. Even as Darn fought to quell the thunderous pounding of his heart, he heard Master Tobani intone the word, "Next," and realized with sudden terror that no one stood between himself and the swarthy-skinned master.

Darn climbed the last stair to stand on the dais before the master. The heat from the glowing hearth made his skin feel tight, flayed. He looked up and was trapped by the depths of Master Tobani's inscrutable eyes.

Tobani stared hard at the boy, weighing his worth. Then the master nodded as if he'd found the answers he sought. He reached out to grip Darn by one shoulder, and brought the glowing brand close enough for Darn to feel its heat. Then he leaned forward until his pointed teeth nearly scratched Darn's ear.

"By the mark of Lord Agni's sacred Flame, you are no longer part of the world," Tobani said in a quiet, surprisingly gentle voice. "You shall be one of His Disciples, to preserve His Honor, to carry out His Justice, and to fight His holy Battles. Only by death can you escape the bond which this mark lays upon you."

Darn closed his eyes and clenched his lip between his teeth, so as not to betray his cowardice with a scream. He felt Tobani's hand on his shoulder tighten, and braced himself.

Before there was pain, there was a sound: a sound like fat dripping onto hot coals. Then followed an unmistakable stench: the smell of burnt offerings and sacrifice. And then, almost as if it were an afterthought, the pain came.

At first, the pain seemed like ice on Darn's skin, sharp and biting. Then it flared crimson across his vision, blotting all sense and all thought from his mind. It was a feeling to dwarf any concept of pain that Darn had ever held. After the initial shock, the pain receded a measure, then surged back even stronger with the next beat of his heart. The fold of lip that Darn held between his lip parted, and blood flowed unnoticed into his mouth. The urge to scream , to open his mouth and give voice to his torment, was stronger than the urge to breath. So Darn didn't breath, and he didn't scream. He ground his teeth together in bitter agony, and willed himself to simply survive one heartbeat at a time.

Darn staggered as he opened his eyes, waves of pain radiating outward through him, centered on a tiny bit of the sun that lay embedded in the flesh of his chest. Dazed, his feet moved of their own volition, and Darn found himself standing in the courtyard outside the Forge, staring up at the night sky. He was dimly aware of other acolytes standing nearby, some weeping in pain, others bearing their agony in grave silence.

"Not a picnic 'long th' seashore," a quiet voice muttered by Darn's elbow. "But a far piece easier than a hand o' strokes from some slaver's lash, I be tellin' ya. Though I s'pose we're still slaves, all th' same."

Darn looked at the thin silhouette beside him. After a moment, he nodded in mute agreement, though in truth, Darn had difficulty imagining that anything in the world, death included, could hurt more than his chest now did. Still, the statement brought other thoughts to mind.

By the Lady, Darn wondered, *what price have I laid across my soul?*

* * *

The new students of the Order gradually grew lean and hard under the harsh tutelage of their masters. Many succumbed to the training and the heat, and no few failed to rise again. Those that survived, though, were pared down to the warrior's essentials:

blood and flesh, sinew and bone. From the moment Lord Agni's fiery chariot began its journey across the sky, till the ninth bell sounded from the city tower below, the acolytes performed an endless routine of stretches, body-hardening drills, balance exercises, and slow tension movements that chiseled their young muscles into iron whipcord. But over and above all else, were the thousands upon thousands of kicks and punches, stomps and strikes they executed. They struck at the air, at heavy sand bags, and at each other. They beat their fists and feet against hemp-covered poles till horny yellowed ridges of armored callus formed over their skin. They endured the crack of wooden batons against their unprotected shins until the nerves there deadened, leaving their lower legs to be used as shields or heavy bludgeons. And they thrust their hands into large drums of hot desert sand and jagged pebbles, again and again, till their fingers tired of bleeding and turned instead into stiffened rods of steel.

In one of the cavernous cellars beneath the estate, natural hot springs bubbled up to form the manse's bathing pools. Often times, the acolytes were forced to stand neck-deep in the scalding water for as long as it took them to punch a thousand times. Then they climbed exhausted from the pools, only to be ordered to perform a thousand kicks, wrapped in the stifling cloaks of steam which rose about them. Those that remained standing were marched out into the midmorning sun, perhaps to practice fighting atop a narrow wooden beam or on a slanted hillside covered with loose stones. Those that fell were carried to the cooler wine cellars to recover – or not.

Injuries were frequent, and death among the students was

not unknown. But the young boys and handful of girls that endured, once farmherds or ship's mates, beggars or ring-bearers, whores, maids, or kitchen-slaves, they gradually grew immune to the heat and pain, immune to the agony of muscles and tendons stretched far past their normal limits. Their limbs grew strong and hard, their strikes fast and sure. Once-impossible tasks – extinguishing a candle's flame with a kick or punch, dancing aside from the path of Master K'tarr's padded arrows, or simply holding a low horse-riding stance and punching until even Master Tobani tired of counting – all began to fall under the heel of progress, and the pain and drudgery of training faded away before a glimpse of the shining warriors they might one day become.

***

As he struck at the training post for perhaps the five-hundredth time, Darn's concentration faltered. His fist failed to hit the hemp-wrapped surface of the post squarely, and instead it skittered off low across one sharp corner, leaving the skin on the back of his hand hanging like a dead leaf from the trunk of the post.

Darn uttered one of the many Heshian curses he knew, spitting the word out harshly even as he kept his voice low; it wouldn't do to have Master Tobani hear him complaining about training. Tobani answered criticisms with a hearty thump on the head, followed by a spinning sweep that could drop an acolyte on his spine in the space of an eye blink – if one was lucky, that was. Tobani's punishments were legendary, and were far worse even than his training regiment, as many students could attest.

Darn cursed once again, granting his wounded hand only a brief moment's respite. Then the sound of Tobani's grating voice approached along the line, and Darn quickly regained his stance, striking the post once again as fast and hard as before. He bit down deep into his lip to keep the pain at bay and concentrated solely on his target.

"Change t' swordstrike, fool," a voice hissed quietly from beside him. Darn continued his punching, but glanced quickly over his shoulder at the student working the post to his right.

The novice practicing at the next post stood perhaps a hand's-breadth taller than Darn, but hardly carried any more weight. The student's punches snapped out fluidly, striking the target post with an definite *crack* each time. Granted, without much mass to back up the strikes, the acolyte's post didn't move half as far as did those struck by the larger boys. But the speed of the attacks was impressive – as fast as some of the seniors, Darn would wager. And as Darn had quickly learned during the endless sparring sessions they endured each afternoon, such quick focused strikes could prove to be devastating, inflicting much more serious wounds than the mere bruises handed out by the bigger, slower boys.

"Don' look at me, ya idjit!" the acolyte said, glancing at Darn quickly. "Master Tobani will av both our hides tacked up onna wall if ee cutches us talkin."

Darn turned his full attention back to his own post, but he couldn't help wondering at the other student's strange accent. Perhaps it held a bit of the Chak'ran tongue, though Darn couldn't say for sure. What was sure, though, was that the pain in his injured hand was growing to unbearable proportions. Each time he struck the post, fresh spatters of blood flew and painted the wall behind it.

"When I call out agin, switch t' swordstrikes with yer lef'

han' oonly," Darn's conspirator whispered once again. "Tobani 'll take no offence at th' change, long as we keep at it faster 'n b'fore."

Darn was unsure of the instructions. Some of the acolytes took great pleasure in getting each other into trouble with the masters and senior students. And Darn certainly had no wish to bring Tobani's wrath down on his head. He was still chewing at his indecision when the command came, and then it was too late. As he was learning, his body now often reacted without waiting for permission from his brain.

"Switch – *Now!*"

Without pause, Darn slid smoothly to a side horse-riding stance, drew his left hand up beside his right ear, and lashed out with a swordstrike. The solid chunk of his hand meeting the post fell the barest moment behind that of his new acquaintance. His irritation at being bested lent fuel to his soulfire, which laid coiled a few fingerspans below his navel as always, waiting to be fed like a hungry viper. Darn's next strike fell at the exact same moment as his companion's. He forced himself to move even faster, and this time was rewarded with the sound of his own strike hitting first - along with the spitting sound of a particularly foul Chak'ran curse. The other acolyte twisted sharply to add speed to the strike, and once again, the two struck their targets at the same moment. The contest continued, each of them striving to push their hands faster – never cheating on the full motion of their strikes, for to win in such a way would bring no honor to the victor.

Within the space of another full hand of blows, the two acolytes' strikes were moving so fast and in cadence that no observer – save for Master Tobani – could tell which one landed first. The striking posts vibrated wildly under the blows, but neither of the two faltered or missed a strike, their blows landing with focus, precision, and power, moving at speeds that would once have seemed inhumanly fast, but now were simply the current, tenuous limits of their abilities.

Tobani stood behind the competing pair, smiling inwardly as the two acolytes strove to outperform each other.

Both of them could use a reprimand for sacrificing too much control in their quest for speed, the dour-faced master thought. *Though I grant, both of these young ones have speed enough to match the seniors.*

Tobani held back his admonishment, though. For whereas Elias lusted for battle, and K'tarr strove for the elusive perfection of technique, Master Tobani lived to breath *spirit* into the youths who were put into his care, to help build and nurture the soulfire within them. The force and fire that the two acolytes before him demonstrated was like a finely-wrought elixir to Tobani. He savored their sweat, their bruises, their successes and their failures, as if they were his own. But he had no pity for their pain, for pain was a strong teacher and carried many lessons. In his way, Tobani cared a great deal for the students put in his charge. Cared enough to push them *hard*, to teach them to endure the pain now, so that they might be spared the pain of a dishonorable death or failure later.

This one, Tobani thought, nodding as the taller of the two students gained a slight advantage in the contest, *this one is one I would call my own.* Tobani had spotted the acolyte aboard a Crimian slave ship tied along the docks, fighting off a trio of men with only sharp teeth and a long sliver of wood as weapons, two bleeding men already dying on the deck. Tobani had dispatched one of the slavers, crippled another, then held the third so that the child could plunge the makeshift dagger deep into the slaver's eye. The scarred young child had never questioned Tobani afterwards, but had simply followed him home to the Pyre like an innocent puppy, happy to have a new master. And from that day forward, Tobani discovered he had a student more loyal, more diligent, and more driven than any he'd ever known.

The master grunted grudgingly, as the slighter student redoubled his efforts and gained a small advantage in speed. *One of Elias', yes,* Tobani thought. *The boy has fire. I cannot deny him that.*

"The rest of you slackards," Master Tobani shouted over the hall, "change to swordstrikes, NOW!" He clapped resoundingly, and the other acolytes in his charge changed positions and began their new task. "Match the pace set by these two!" he demanded. Raggedly, the tempo increased, amidst quietly muttered curses and black looks tossed about.

Palm-heel strike. Stamp of the Ox. Cutting Wing. Phoenix-Eye Fist. Dragon-whip kick. Over and over Tobani drilled his company, harder, faster, until some began to falter and faint and fall twitching to the floor. But no matter how the master harangued the rest, still the two acolytes nearest the doorway – Elias' mongrel and Tobani's own – outstripped the others, setting a cadence that none could match. Back and forth the contest shifted, with one having advantage during a particular strike or two, then the other taking the lead with the following kick or combination of techniques.

At last Tobani spoke the words which released the group from their tortuous training. Most of the acolytes shuffled towards the doorway which led to the baths. A few, sobbing with exhaustion and near to collapse, were helped towards the coolness of the wine cellar.

Darn sat back on his heels, trying to expel the soulfire from his mind, trying to rid himself of the flames' influence and to calm the shaking of his exhausted limbs. He stared down at the bloody ruin of his hands, fighting to banish the pain that pulsed within them.

The familiar sound of a fist landing on a training post echoed through the now-empty hall. One acolyte – Darn's competition from earlier – still stood before a post, whirling from one technique to the next, each striking the hemp-covered post with precision and fury, a deep-seated anger clearly etched on the student's dusky features. A final flurry of three kicks left the post rocking wildly in its anchor, and Darn wondered if his own kicks could land so well after such a grueling training session.

The acolyte walked back to where Darn sat and silently extended a hand. Darn wondered briefly at the thin, rather delicate fingers as he reached up; then his forearm was grasped in an almost painful grip and he found himself hauled to his feet.

"You're Darn," the acolyte said simply, in a low, smooth, somewhat husky voice. "Master Tobani 'll be mightily pleased, knowin thit I kin motch th' speed oof Elias' finest Spark." The student wore a huge, fading bruise that stretched from one ear to the bridge of the nose. Still, beneath the ugly shading the face was finely chiseled, with high sharp cheekbones and a slightly pointed chin. Coal black hair fell down over smooth dusky skin, and indigo eyes – startling in their brilliance – peered cautiously out from beneath the dark brows.

But grim lines cut the child's fine face into angry planes, outlining a harshness that should have been heartbreaking on one so young. In the Pyre, though, an unkind life was far from an unusual tale. Hard living had tempered most of the acolytes at an early age and had given fuel to their inner fires. And it was this quickening soulfire which could draw a master of the Order to a young street-urchin like some predatory moth to the flame. Granted, a few – a very few – were accepted as initiates from those that brought themselves to the Pyre's doors. But most of these – hopeful guardsmen's offspring, or third sons of some petty noble – were simply turned away without a second glance. None of them would ever endure the training, for they lacked the survival instinct of those who lived on the streets, those which the masters personally gathered. And so it remained that the Disciples of the Flames were groomed from the poorest and the most wretched, from those who had seen little but the back of Life's hand.

Darn's companion smiled suddenly, and the stern visage was utterly transformed by a brilliant smile that echoed in the indigo eyes.

"I answer to 'Sharphands', here in the Pyre," the acolyte offered simply, before turning towards the doorway that led outside. Just as Darn stepped to follow, the taller student stopped and looked back. "You may call me 'Eillena'. Twas not th' oonly name I wore b'fore comin' here, but twas th' oonly one I ever cared fer."

Darn stopped in his tracks, bewildered.

"But ... but Eillena is a girl's name!" he blurted out, wishing in the next instance to have considered his words more carefully.

The acolyte spun on him in an instant, anger building so quickly in the depths of her eyes that Darn took an involuntary step backwards. He could feel the heat of her rising soulfire.

"An' no mere *girl* can be a warrior, can b'come a Disciple o' th' Flames, is that what yer sayin?" Eillena spat out, her fists clenched tightly at her sides.

Darn raised his hands before him in a calming gesture. "N-no, truly I meant no offense, Eillena." Darn's mind whirled furiously, searching for the words that would placate his fiery-tempered companion. "Master Dorcell is a woman, and she is the finest archer among us!"

Eillena pounced on his words. "Oh, but she is no *fighter*, ya mean!" She took another step towards him, and Darn hurriedly backed another pace.

"No, no, those were not my thoughts!" Darn offered. "She is an fine fighter. Remember last moon, when she fought three seniors at once on the dais. Few of the other masters even could match her grace."

Again Eillena hurled Darn's words back at him, and again she advanced towards him, till they stood nearly nose to nose.

"Ya mean she's a fine fighter fer a woman, dontcha? She has grace a'plenty, but no real power, ya mean!"

Finally, Darn's own anger began to brew, and his voice rose to match Eillena's own.

"I meant nothing of the sort," he near shouted. "Should I have meant so, I would have spoken so. No, Dorcell has not the power of Tobani or M'tanno. And she cannot match Elias for speed or ferocity. These are not her shortcomings, but simply facts."

Eillena opened her mouth to argue further, but Darn walked over her words.

"But no one else has her grace, as I have said, and even Master K'tarr kneels before her skill with the bow. None can be so elusive in battle as Dorcell, and no other commands such subtle attack strategies. She plays on her strengths, and avoids her weaknesses, as we are all taught to do. And no one treats Master Dorcell with deference due to her sex." Darn's anger began to ebb. He smiled unwillingly, recalling the response of the diminutive female master when a senior student had offered her a half-hearted attack in recent training – the burly lad was left lying on the dais, calling for his mother. "At least, no one treats her so more than once," Darn added.

Eillena blinked slowly as the truth of Darn's words burrowed beneath her anger. She grinned slightly, and nodded in agreement.

"Indeed, Cheykar's nose shall always bear th' 'semblance o' Master Dorcell's foot," she said, the grin on her face turning into a full-born smile. She shook her head at her own foolishness, and laid a hand on Darn's shoulder. "Forgive me, Darn," she continued. "You didna deserve m' anger. Tis only .... all my life, I have fought 'gainst those who thought me weak. You can't be weak here. This is a hard place, you know that."

Darn just held up his hand in answer and grinned foolishly. His hand looked like something hungry had been chewing on it. "Hard, do you think?" he replied, and laughed.

Together, the pair turned once again towards the doorway and began walking towards the welcoming sunlight. After a few steps, Eillena turned and snapped a straight, sharp punch dead into Darn's shoulder.

" I canno b'lieve you didna know I was a girl!" she said ruefully, then turned and continued walking.

Darn rubbed at his sore arm as they walked, and wondered if he dared to chance more conversation. He gritted his teeth, and dove ahead despite his misgivings. "As to thy earlier words, I do not believe they carry the truth," Darn said. He continued on quickly, hurrying to clarify himself as Eillena's face began to cloud once again. "Indeed, thy strikes are fast. As fast as any of our fellows; certainly as fast as my own." Darn was relieved to see the anger draining away from his companion's face. "But Elias has many students, and I am far from his finest. Arak is the best fighter, by far. Though he ..."

"Arak is an ass, anna bully," Eillena interrupted. "A number o' th' Adepts command better skills than Arak, an' ee 'as not your speed. Ee 'as a great, unholy flame, aye. But ee 'as somethin' worse: a *heart-thorn* my people call it – a hunger t' do hurt t' oothers. Tis what makes him so feared, more th'n anythin' else."

"Thou do pay me undue respect, Eillena. The speed of my left-side kicks ..." Darn's words were struck from the air before he could finish.

"Oh, spare me yer humility," Eillena answered brusquely, though a smile touched her lips. "Ya got speed t' match any o' th' seniors. Yer kicks an' timin' are th' envy oof us ooll. Had ya size an' temperament t' match yer abilities, ya would prob'ly wear th' sash oof a senior, by now. Whether they like it er not, all oof th' acolytes strive t' match ya in ooll thot we do. Oonly a few o' them shall e'er claim yer abilities. Th' rest bemoan their fate, an' resent ya fer yer prowess." Eillena waved a hand in dismissal. "But as fer myself," Eillena slid forward smoothly and snapped off three reaping kicks in quick succession, each blow more than enough to crack a man's skull. "I choose t' foller in yer steps, an' adjust t' our lack o' size an' strength by being thot much better th'n any o' th' rest."

Darn bit back another argument, and instead simply nodded and accepted the compliment. He reached up cautiously, and squeezed Eillena's shoulder in thanks. She smiled at him in return, a pearly gleam that illuminated the lovely young girl who hid beneath a mask of sweat and scowls, pain and anger. Darn felt his own face flush hotly, and he dropped his head in confusion and embarrassment as they stepped out into the bright sunlight.

Master Tobani moved from the shadows where he had stood unseen, and watched the retreating backs of the two young acolytes. Concern, caution, perhaps even a bit of jealousy swirled over his normally inscrutable features.

She needed a companion, he accepted grudgingly, *someone to push her gently, to help her lick her wounds. These things I cannot give her.* Though he fought against it, anger intruded into his thoughts. *Still, did it have to be one of Elias' brood? The boy is good, I cannot deny it. But one of his curs can only bring her pain in the end.* Tobani worried at the end of his long mustache, lost in indecision. *True, the pain may help to temper her. But she has suffered so much already. And she is mine own, as truly as if sprung from my loins.*

Tobani cursed his own sentiments, even as he could not deny them. As he watched out through the open doorway, the dour master sent a warning winging towards the smaller of the two acolytes, who even now laughed and danced away as Eillena hit him sharply in the arm again.

Mark me, young Spark. Allow her pain more than her measure, and I will have your still-beating heart in my hands, Elias be damned!

101

***

Darn blinked furiously as another tortuous drop of stinging sweat fell from his brow into his eyes. The muscles of his thighs and lower back screamed long anthems of agony, as he continued to hold the deep squatting horse stance which Master Tobani had ordered the class to assume, seemingly days ago. And the heat! *Lord Agni!!* The shimmering waves of heat that surged out from the huge brass braziers set around the hall crashed against him like a physical blow, threatening to set his skin afire and blacken his very bones as he stood! But Darn had felt the crack of a training baton across his shoulders far too many times; he knew better than to move to ease his pain. So he focused his attention even tighter onto his breathing pattern and the sound of the master's voice, and made himself deaf to the chorus of pain within. And in the vacuum of that silence, Darn began to hear the growing roar of the flames that resided within him.

"With each breath you take, feed the heat to your soulfire." Master Tobani's low, commanding words drifted over the class of acolytes. "Let it flow down through you, and pool below your navel, in the place we call the *crucible*."

Tobani was a harsh disciplinarian, the only master ever to be accepted into the Order at the grand old age of sixteen summers. His indenture as a galley-slave was written in the hideous tattoos of barbed-whip scars that crossed his back. It was also mirrored in the way in which he pushed his students with no respite, no encouragement, no kind words: only the incessant drive to perform harder and faster. None of the students within the Pyre, and few of the masters even, would admit that they actually *liked* the swarthy, almond-eyed teacher. In fact, many outright despised the man, and he figured strongly in countless numbers of sweat-soaked nightmares. But neither master nor student could refute the fact that Tobani's teachings took those that were soft and quick to complain, and set them on the path of the warrior, a path who's walking left them either hard and impervious to pain, or wasted and dying by the wayside.

"Feel the flame pouring into your crucible," the master ordered. "Feel it burning brighter and hotter: as hot as Master Era's forge."

As he looked out over his students, Tobani relaxed his focus, searching for their auras. He began to perceive the edges of a different plane, where energies and fields of force flowed and collided and forged their material embodiments. Tobani could see lingering traces of psychic or emotional forces, which hung over the children like ghosts of colored clouds. The liquid golden glow of pure animalistic health surrounded most of the acolytes. Around a few of the students, Tobani could detect faint indigo traces where the craftings of magic had left their indelible stain upon all they touched. But here and there among his charges, Tobani saw several spectral clouds tinged with scarlet at their edges, evidence of newly-gained control over their inner fires. *Excellent!*

Master Tobani smiled in secret satisfaction and began to bring his focus back entirely to the material plane. Before he could complete the shift though, his attention was snared by a sudden flare of crimson light. Tobani's head snapped up in sudden surprise and his eyes narrowed in alarm.

Lord Flame! Tobani shouted to himself. *He cannot burn so bright! Few of the seniors even can fan the soulfire so high!*

But Tobani could not ignore or disbelieve what his altered senses told him. Darn stood immobile in the line, eyes locked closed, breath whistling through his teeth in long tortured gasps, thin frame trembling under the strain. But the boy's aura shone a deep and brilliant red, reflecting the inferno of the soulfire that raged inside him.

Tobani watched for a moment longer, concern tracing familiar roadways on his face. Such fire at this stage of development was almost unheard of. It *could* indicate a prodigy of vast potential. More likely than not, though, it marked a student with severe emotional instabilities. Tobani knew that some of the berserker clans of the far Northern tribes – despite having no training – shone crimson when their rage was upon them, somewhat tinted by the sick brown of insanity. The scarlet gleam of this student's aura, though, was pure and unflawed, like sunlight through the finest ruby. It could only be borne by one who had given himself over to the soulfire, who was master and slave both to the flames that resided deep in the crucible of his soul.

The Parthinian Flame Master was not a man easily ruffled. But Tobani stood quiet and unsettled for a long moment, then reluctantly shifted his sight back. But first, he made a strongly-worded mental note to speak to Elias about the matter.

Tobani returned to the lesson at hand. "Feed the soulfire until it grows within you," he continued, "burning through your veins, reaching every limb, every joint, every muscle in your body. Good . . . now, the Dance of Embers." Master Tobani finished the order with a resounding clap.

The students began to move together through the familiar

patterned form: circle block to the left, slide forward with a leopard punch, step through and sword strike to the throat, spin to the left with foot lashing out in a dragon whip kick. At this point in their training, the acolytes' strikes and counterstrikes had gained a serious measure of surety and power, already as quick as the cut and thrust of experienced swordsmen. Their kicks cut the air like a field of deadly scythes. Each student of the Order must master this Dance, an ancient pattern which contained all of the basic elements of the Disciples' fighting style. Some acolytes moved correctly, but stiff, like puppets or golems, while Darn and a few others danced lightly through the form, blows licking out to burn and sear their unseen opponents.

Until this day, Darn had always feared to surrender himself completely to the power of his soulfire. He had found it addicting, indeed, those tiny sips of power that he'd tasted so far. But Darn feared the obsession which gripped Elias and many of the other masters, the battle-rage which overcame them when they gave themselves over to the Flames. Yes, until this day, Darn had honored and feared his soulfire all the same. But somehow, somewhere after the ten thousandth strike of the day, after the tower bell tolled a second time while they still held a deep horse-riding stance, Darn's pain overcame his fear. It washed over him from head to toe, and poured into his *crucible* like paraffin on a flame. His fear and pain vanished, forgotten, burnt to ash as the cleansing soulfire blazed upwards, scouring every nerve, leaving only grit and desire in its wake. Darn surrendered himself to the primal force raging through his body, and reveled at the soulfire pouring through his limbs, drawing him through the motions. He struck, spun, leapt through the air to land and roll and strike from the floor. Faster, always faster.

The Flame, must be the Flame, his mind echoed. *My fingers are hot blades of steel, my heart a lump of molten iron, pumping the soulfire through my limbs.* He felt elated, drunk with power, invulnerable, untouchable. But still, a tiny gnat of fear bit at the back of his neck.

Darn began to move without conscious thought, his limbs flashing through the patterns carved deeply into his body's memory. He concentrated solely upon the soulfire burning fiercely within him, fanning it to greater and greater heights. His vision began to dim, as a hazy blood-red cloud rose to cover his eyes. Panic, too, began to rise, as Darn's body continued in the dance, while his awareness drifted outside of himself and he seemed to watch from a distance. He could hear Master Tobani's call to end the exercise. He could see, too, the fear-enshrouded faces of his classmates, who slowed and stopped their own practice and watched bewildered as Darn's body continued its frenzied storm of techniques, unmindful of Master Tobani's shouts or of the smoky tendrils twisting upwards from his tunic.

One of the attending senior students parted the circle of acolytes who gathered in fearful fascination around Darn. Swaggering with his usual disdain for those of the lower rank, Cheykar reached out to grab Darn by the scruff of the neck as the boy glided within reach. But a sudden fan-block swept the burly adept's arm aside, leading a flock of strikes as swift and vicious as wild Saira falcons, blows that drew bright floods of pain and blood wherever they landed upon Cheykar's face. The adept cried out once, sharp and piercing; then Darn's continued spin brought the heel of his foot slamming against the hands covering Cheykar's face, and the wounded boy dropped to the floor like a slaughtered bullock.

Silence slammed down over the hall.

Darn blinked furiously to clear both his head and his vision. His breath raced in tempo with the hammering of his heart as he slowly turned, honestly surprised at the scene that surrounded him. Darn wanted to voice his innocence, yet the blood on his hands shouted his guilt. It mattered little that he'd had no intention to harm the senior student. Darn looked up at the other acolytes and found varying looks of surprise, fear, even admiration and envy on their faces.

For the first time in his young life, Darn felt a vermilion rose of pride bloom to life within his chest. Darn breathed in the heady fragrance and found it much to his liking. He never noticed – or pointedly ignored – the wickedly-sharp thorns so carefully hidden within the blood-colored petals. Darn tried hard to hide the self-satisfied smile which played across his face, even as he turned to receive Master Tobani's admonishments.

On the balcony which circled above the training hall, a silent figure wrapped in the shadows of an alcove echoed Darn's smile with one of his own. Firelight briefly winked a pair of golden reflections as the figure shook in quiet self-satisfied laughter.

Chapter Five
Loon

Darn sauntered slowly along the dockside, relishing the stiff breeze and the salt tang of the sea, as they dispelled the stench of rotting garbage and fish guts for a while. He enjoyed watching the merchant vessels arrive from distant places, disgorging exotic people and wares into the melting pot of Shiningrock. And so Darn came to the wharves whenever the masters granted him the precious boon of time to himself.

Many of the local fishermen knew Darn by sight if not by name, and they always found time to toss him a few good-natured words or a wave of the hand. This small measure of companionship was an added attraction of the wharves, for Darn had yet to make any friends among the others acolytes – except perhaps for the Chak'ran girl, Eillena. Of course, another inarguable fact was that the working girls who trolled along the waterfront taverns often teased Darn and flirted with him. And at the vexing age of a full hand and four summers, he was beginning to gain an appreciation for such attentions.

Darn neared the end of Drunkard's Wharf, where Sott's Inn sat like a fat ugly toad, waiting for a drunken fly of a sailor to pass within reach. Sott's didn't maintain quite as bloody a reputation as did The Mortuary or some of the other establishments along the waterfront, but it was still a far cry from the crystal and light of the Rose Garden Inn uptown. Old Sott served several stews and slops of questionable origin, and stocked only the cheap local ale commonly known as "Boar's Piss." But his prices were the lowest along the wharves, and so the scrapboard tavern was filled to bursting both day and night.

Darn slowed as he passed the doorway, stepping carefully over the body of a sailor who lay face down in a steaming puddle either dead or dead drunk, neither condition being unusual along this section of the wharves. He walked a few steps further, to where empty kegs stamped with the porcine mark of Boar's Brewery framed an open window, and strained to peer in through the ever-present gloom and the drifting haze of sweetleaf smoke. Sott's serving girls were known far and abroad for their anything-but-modest attire. And as often as not, Sott's also served up incredibly foolish acts of ale-induced bravado, like the Cherramite sailor who bragged he could swallow a small sparking eel alive and whose eyes had turned black just before his lifeless body fell to the floor. Even on a slow night, it wasn't uncommon for some Perthan trader or Camdian sailor to lose a toe to Big Meg's knife in a game of mumbly-toss. And then there were the infamous and impromptu head-bashing tournaments, the last of which had been championed by a Kalthmus dwarf who left one of his opponents a blathering idiot and another one dead on the floor. With such quality of ambiance and entertainment, Sott's proved an irresistible lure for a young boy with time on his hands.

As Darn watched eagerly through the window, dodging an occasional thrown mug or leather jack, loud voices carried from around the side of the inn where a narrow walkway led out around the edge of the wharf. Darn ignored the commotion at first, as he strained for a better glimpse of Rhianna's naked breasts as she danced atop a knife-scarred table to the appreciation of patrons and staff alike. But the shouting from around the corner escalated several levels, then was punctuated by a loud splash as something landed in the harbor. An anguished howl of fear cut through the air, wresting Darn's attention away from Sott's taproom and putting the young boy's legs into motion before he had time to think better of it. As he turned the corner, a second braying howl, much louder than the first, sounded in answer.

"Aaahoooooo! Looooon! Oooooh-no-no-no!" The howling resolved itself into words. "Oh help me, help me poor lil' Peg! I'll save ya Peg! I'll . . . Oh swim Peg, swim! The fishes'll get ya! Oh Loooooooonnnnn! I'm a-comin' Peg!"

Darn skidded to a halt at the rear of the inn and leaned over the railing to spot the swimmer. He saw only choppy gray inlet water at first, a slick of fish oil covering the waves. Then a small, black-furred head bobbed briefly to the surface, and a vise clamped about Darn's heart. The little dog washed under several times, tiring quickly as it paddled in frantic circles. A human death he could stomach, for Darn saw one example or another of it nearly every day. But the thought of a helpless puppy drowning was more than he could stand. Darn looked about frantically for a dip net or long pole, some means of salvation for the hapless mutt. Then from behind him came the sudden drumming of pounding feet, and Darn stepped aside barely in time.

"Loooooooooooooooooonnnnnnnnnn!!!" A burly figure flew by Darn, gained the top railing in a single bound, and launched himself out over the choppy waves. The dog's savior landed behind the little dog, then quickly bobbed back to the surface and wrapped a big arm around struggling pup.

A wave of relief washed over Darn, followed quickly by

a surge of puzzlement, then a crashing breaker of alarm, as he watched the man in the water begin to splash and struggle to stay afloat. Darn slowly, almost unwillingly, realized that the fool who'd leapt in to save the dog couldn't swim himself, and was in equal danger of drowning.

"Help, Help, Help! Oh poor Peg! Oh poor Loon!" the gasping figure wailed to no one in particular. "Oh, we shall both be fish poop by morn, I fear ol' Peg. Oh woe, oh Looo-oooo-oonnn!"

Darn snatched up a coil of rope that hung by Sott's back door, ran back and tossed the coil out to the drowning pair. While the line landed within a few feet of him, the man seemed oblivious to it, and continued to splash about in circles, wailing and alternating gulps of air and seawater.

"Grab hold!" Darn shouted. The man in the water turned a wondering face towards the wharf, and was immediately washed over by another oily whitecap. Darn shook the rope up and down, slapping the water with it. "THE ROPE, MAN! GRAB THE ROPE!" The drowning man looked at the line floating beside him with astonishment, as if it had appeared by magic. Then he slowly reached over and secured a hold. Darn strained to reel the pair in, though his hands burned and bled as the waves jerked the rope through his grip time and time again. But at last, the wretched pair in the water drew up against the pilings below.

With sudden dismay, Darn realized that he hadn't a prayer of hauling his waterlogged catch back up onto the wharf. The pilings were two spans high at low tide, and covered with slime and barnacles besides. And the ramshackle sheds that clustered the wharf would prevent Darn from dragging the drowning fellow and his dog back to the seawall and shallow water. He knotted the rope around the top railing, then leaned over to regard the miserable couple dangling below.

"Hold on," Darn shouted. "I'll run to fetch a skiff from a'front of the docks. Just hold tight, my friend!"

The man below seemed not to hear Darn's words. Instead, he reached up with his free hand to grab high on the rope, then with a monumental heave pulled himself and his companion half out of the water. Darn stood dumbfounded, marveling at the fellow's strength, as the man secured himself with his feet and reached up quickly for a new grip, this time lifting himself free from the sucking grasp of the cold, gray water. Not knowing how to help, Darn simply watched and mumbled a few encouragements as the man and his dog continued their awkward journey to safety.

After an agonizing wait, Darn reached down and pulled the little black dog from the exhausted man's arm. The half-drowned fellow pulled himself up on the railings, then fell over onto the wharf in a sodden heap. He lay there breathing heavily for several moments. Then his red-rimmed eyes opened and a wide grin split his face as he looked up.

"Lady in White! That was no fun at all! Loon'll tell ya that fer sure, my friend! No fun fer ol' Peg either!"

At the mention of its name, the bedraggled dog squirmed from Darn's arms and ran to its master. The little terrier mutt danced about with the manic intensity of a natural-born ratter, though she ran with a curious hobbling gait. Darn looked closer and realized that the dog was missing half of one rear leg, and was fitted with a tiny wooden peg-leg held on by a leather harness, much like the one worn by the captain of the Sea Whore.

"Oh my goodness Peg – I've come close nuff t' drownin' already. Don't ya lick me t' death!" The sodden fellow sat up and hugged his pet to him, murmuring tiny endearments as the little dog squirmed to reach every spot on his face with her darting pink tongue. Then he looked up at Darn, and a gleaming smile lit his face with all the innocence of a pure soul burning behind it.

"You are a good man an' *my Friend*, t' save me an' Peg from th' fishes!" he said, as he stood up with a slosh.

Darn quickly stepped back to make room for the boy as he stood – for boy he was, as Darn could now see from the fine down that graced his face. But though the light beard marked him at no more than sixteen winters, the boy still stood as tall, or taller, than most of the men Darn knew, and he wore the thick muscles of a blacksmith on his stout frame.

"Ol' Loon sure is powerfully glad to have ya as a friend." The hulking boy smiled even wider, till his face looked ready to split, and stepped over to Darn. Darn smiled back – the fellow's charm was overwhelmingly infectious – and sketched a short bow.

"Darn is my name, and it was no trouble to . . . Oomph!!" Darn's eyes bulged with surprise and strain as he was suddenly caught up in the big boy's arms and lifted into the air, the breath crushed from him and his ribs threatening to crack. Darn shook his head in confusion and chagrin. He'd been caught flat-footed by a smiling attacker, and had never even noticed the danger. Master Elias would be disgusted.

With arms pinned at his sides, Darn instinctively reared back, preparing to smash downward with his forehead like a skrall ram.

But just as suddenly, his captor released him, and Darn dropped back to his feet. He slid back several paces, and his training brought his hands up into a fighting stance. But the boy named Loon never noticed, for he had already turned back to his hob-legged friend

There never was any danger, you fool, Darn chided himself. The monstrous fellow had simply hugged him in thanks. Darn dropped his hands, feeling quite foolish, and walked over to where the curious young man sat playing with his dog. He pondered several questions for a moment, then cleared his throat.

"Umm, Loon?"

The waterlogged boy looked up, and Darn continued.

"I . . I mean not to pry, but how came Peg to be in the water? And if ye cannot swim, why did ye leap into the harbor as well?"

A fierce scowl stole over Loon's face, and anger began to brew in the air with the feeling of unseen thunderclouds. "Oh, I'd fergot about that. Old Sott – twas him what threw Peg in wi' th' fishes, ya know. Said Peg was drinkin' some offis nasty stew right out o' th' pot. Why, ol' Peg's not so dumb as t' eat any o' Sott's slop! Is ya Peg?" The curly-haired mutt wagged her tail and yipped in agreement. "I tried t' tell Sott that, but 'e wouldna listen. An' when I turned m' back, 'e went an' tossed 'er right in! And see, Miss Peg here, she canna swim none too well, so I couldna let 'er drown all lonely an' such!" Now the dark clouds on Loon's brow broke open and dangerous lightning flashed deep within his eyes. "It was a bad thing t' do: a *very* bad thing! Why, Old Sott should have t' go in wi' th' fishes hisself fer treatin' my friend Peg such a way!" He rose slowly to his feet like a young mountain being born, and Darn quickly stepped back. Loon continued to mutter darkly to himself as he strode towards the back door of the inn. Peg danced about his feet and barked with glee as young man disappeared inside.

Uncertain of what to do, Darn waited impatiently through a brief silence. But just as his curiosity began to drag him towards the doorway, the clattering crash of pots and pans sounded from inside. Darn stepped back a pace as several voices began cursing loudly and the sound of shattered crockery joined the ruckus. Above all, he could hear Peg's high-pitched barking. Then a voice rose in sudden terror, and Loon came rushing back through the doorway – but he was not alone. Above his head, Loon held a large and greasy individual – who could only be Old Sott himself – who wriggled and hollered to no avail, while a cook and a pair of young serving girls hung ineffectively on both of the burly lad's arms. With a great cry of "Looooooonnnn!!!" he rushed to the railing and sent the old innkeeper sailing out over the waves like the afternoon bucket of garbage. His revenge fulfilled, Loon turned and simply walked away, his face once again fixed with a beaming smile. Behind him, the trio of kitchen staff tried desperately to fling the same rope that had rescued Loon and Peg out to their floundering employer.

"I s'pose it's time to go home now, Peg," Loon remarked evenly, all evidence of anger gone from his voice, as if he'd already forgotten the entire event. He stooped to pick up his small companion, then turned to Darn. "If ya like, ya can come with us, t' Peg an' Loon's house. Share some dinner even. None o' Sott's slop either, we promise. Friends should do such things, ain't that right, Peg?"

The happy little mutt barked her agreement.

Darn considered the invitation for a moment. This Loon fellow, though a bit addled, seemed like enjoyable company. Master

Shim *had* granted him the afternoon and evening free, up until the 7th bell – a very rare occurrence, especially from the dour-tempered spear master. But whispers in the hall said that Master Shim's ancestral spear had somehow been broken during a simple blood feud two day's previous, and the man had been contemplating ritual suicide ever since. That explained the master's unusual leniency.

With his decision quickly made, Darn tried in vain to smile as brightly as his companion.

"T'would be an honor to guest with you for the evening meal," Darn replied, to Loon's obvious pleasure. "But throw no one else into the harbor; it angers the fishermen to see such trash floating about."

Loon's smile dimmed just a small measure.

"Ya sure talks funny, frien' Darn," Loon said curiously. Then his face returned to its former radiance, and his voice tripled in volume. "Still, we care not! Tis good news! Loooooooon! Oh yes, good news Peg! We've company fer dinner, an' a new friend t' boot! Let's sing our friend a song, Peg." Loon commenced into a off-key ditty about two lonely sailors and a wall-eyed mermaid, and Peg howled a harmony as the three walked back to the main wharf. Darn fought to keep his hands from his ears, and tried to ignore the worst of the colorful applause they earned from those they passed.

Above all else, this evening shall not want for lack of attention or entertainment, Darn thought worriedly to himself.

***

"Ye live here all alone, Loon?" Darn asked, as he eyed the wooden clap-trap his friend called home. The shack perched perilously on the south edge of Sandali the Rug Merchant's wharf, a few feet away from the trader's main warehouse. While it wasn't much more than a large shed, it was at least fairly clean and dry, and its only window opened to a magnificent view of the harbor and – more importantly – a steady eastern breeze. The sides of the shack were cobbled together from odd lengths of salvaged boards, the sides of broken shipping crates, barrel staves, and a large faded sign from the now-defunct Belching Unicorn tavern. A rough stone fire pit squatted in the middle of the hut, and a draft-hole in the roof glared down into it from above. A heavy table and its attendant bench sat crookedly in one corner. A rope hammock and a pair of weathered chairs rounded out the room's furnishings.

"Oh, course not, friend Darn!" Loon chuckled amiably as he clomped around in the single room of his manse. He pulled a good loaf of coarse black bread and a questionable hunk of nania cheese down from a shelf, and uncovered a wonderful-smelling pot of cold honkfish chowder. Peg hobbled along behind him and yipped reminders now and again, worrying him like a little old lady. "Why, I live here wid ol' Peg, don't I Peg?"

Peg agreed happily.

Darn composed a silent prayer for patience, then pulled up the short bench to the table and began to eat.

"Merchant Sandali lets me live here for 10 coppers a moon," Loon continued, as he joined Darn at the table. "Long 's I keep an eye on his wares, an' holler fer th' Watch if I see anything amiss. Peg, she takes care of the four-legged rats, an' me an ol' Stick," he pointed a callused thumb to a large, iron-bound quarterstaff leaning in the corner, "we take care of them that run on two!" He guffawed at his wonderful jest, a half-chewed chunk of bread flying out with his laughter. Peg seemed to be expecting just such a gift, for she nabbed the doughy wad as soon as it hit the floor. "I calls it Loon's Roost! Ain't that jest as good a name as could be?" He bellowed once more and slapped his knee, again losing some of his meal. Loon seemed able to speak, cram food into his mouth, take a drought from his flask, and even manage to pick his teeth, all at the same time. But Darn had to admit, he was a much better dinner companion than the dour harsh-eyed boys back at the Pyre.

"Yes, Lord Loon – Lord of all I sees! An' his be-yoo-tee-ful queen, Queen Peg!" Loon laughed, spooned a large chunk of fish from his bowl and flipped it towards the waiting Peg. The little dog snatched it from the air and turned a little dance of delight before settling back down on her haunches to wait for more.

Darn tried in vain to wipe the grin from his face and speak seriously to his simple-minded friend. "But Loon, the employment ye held at Sott's, it has most surely drifted out to sea much the same as old Sott was wont to do." Darn hesitated for a moment, not wishing to insult his host, but unable to allow a friend to travel unsuspecting into trouble. The thought both surprised and warmed him, as Darn realized that he already considered the big, smiling boy a friend, the first true friend he could count in many years. "Ye do understand, do ye not, that without any money, Sandali will no longer allow ye to stay here."

Loon's heavy brows furrowed deeply, and his gaze flicked around the room uncertainly. He stood slowly, dropping his spoon back into the bowl with a splash, then turned and stepped heavily away from the table. Darn feared that he had hurt his friend's feelings, and he began to stutter an apology, only to be cut off by

Loon's conspiratory whisper.

"Haven't showed this t' anyone, 'cept o' course fer ol' Peg," he said in a low, quiet voice. The hulking, fair-haired boy walked to a corner of the room that was curtained off for the chamber pot, glanced around once more as if searching for prying eyes, then slipped behind the moth-eaten rug he had hung up for privacy. A moment passed, then Loon strolled back from behind the curtain with a smug look on his face, a definite swagger to his step, and offal smeared up past his elbow. Darn sat in horrored confusion, holding his nose while trying to imagine what else one would fetch from the chamberpot besides the obvious. Loon bent down to open a small trapdoor in the floor, then used a pitcher of grayish water to wash the filth off his arm and into the surging waters of the harbor below. Seemingly satisfied with the job, he walked back to the table, pausing long enough to shutter and bolt both the window and the door. Then, with a triumphant flourish, he dropped a long glistening gray lump onto the table.

"Gots t' have a treasure t' be a lord, ain't that so?" Loon whispered, and his moon-shaped face fairly gleamed with pride.

Darn swallowed hard to retain his recent dinner, then leaned forward to inspect Loon's unsavory treasure. About the size and shape of a man's pride and joy, the reeking lump defied identification. Then Darn noticed the knots tied at each end of the slimy package, and an old memory knocked at his mind's door.

"Tis burdock gut, is it not, Loon?" Darn asked, poking at the messy thing with his finger. It still stank horribly and squished a little as it moved, but Darn thought he heard a muted clink as the disgusting lump rolled over.

"That is th' truth, oh yes it is!" Loon crowed happily as he snatched the glistening tube up in one huge paw. "Old Jakko told me th' sailors all use 'em t' keep their treasures safe. Watertight as a fishes arse, 'e said!" At that, Loon raised his hand to face, and before Darn's stomach had time to lurch more than once, his host happily bit an end off of the gray lump and spat the piece to the eagerly-awaiting Peg. Loon glanced suspiciously around the tiny shack once more, then dumped the contents of his well-hidden "purse" onto the table.

An amazing assortment of booty dropped into a ringing pile on the scarred wood: a full hand of small silver tracham pieces; a white-gold chain and locket of exquisite craftsmanship; several larger silvers bearing the crests of the Jade Isles and a few of the sand-smoothed disks carried by the Scarab Folk; a lonely gold solari; two small, poor-quality emeralds; an adamantine ring with the falcon crest of the Jessari family; and incredibly, what appeared to be a blazing Parthinian fire opal as big as a man's thumbnail! Darn stared dumbfounded at Loon's small mound of treasure, his disbelief kicked swiftly aside as he fingered the opal and guessed roughly at its worth.

"Friend Loon, this gem alone is worth more coin than most men earn in a year .. or several years, for some! Such a hoard would quickly gain ye a cut throat, should anyone hear tell of it." Darn fell back onto his bench, lines of worry slashed across his brow. "Ye didn't st . . . how did . . . where did ye find such a treasure, Loon?"

The tall young man crossed thick arms on the table top, and his eyes shone with a strange glint of humor and cunning that well accompanied the corkscrewed grin on his face.

"Found most of 'em in th' moon-sheds b'hind Sott's an' some of th' other inns," Loon said, smiling like his namesake. "See, Sott an' them, they each pay me a copper dram ev'ry Moonday t' empty their pots fer 'em."

He paused. "I hear 'em sometimes: they laugh an' cal me names an' think poor dumb ol' Loon don' know no better." A scowl tugged in vain at the simple boy's carefree smile, finding no foothold. But that small glimpse brought Darn an understanding that Loon's life contained a great dollop of pain and hurt mixed in with all the song and foolishness.

"But dumb ol' Loon found that lots o' th' sailors got shallow pockets, an' wind up droppin' their coins along wi' their pants when they squat on th' pots. An' he found that drunk men's purses tend t' get hung up on all th' jaggely nails what's in there." Loon smiled broadly as he spoke. "So I tries t' keep lots o' rushes on th' floors fer those what got bad aim, an' so's they ain't bothered by th' sound o' their silver hittin' th' boards." Loon picked up a few of the silver coins and dropped them one by one into a small chiming pile. He giggled a bit at his own jest – a twitter, actually, that gave Darn a glimpse of the eternal child imprisoned within Loon's man-sized body. Then Loon continued: "I go by at dawn, b'fore Sott an' th' rest get up in th' mornin', empty th' pots fer 'em, an' pick through th' rushes fer all th' treasure!" Darn set the crimson-veined opal carefully back onto Loon's gleaming treasure pile. When he looked back up, Darn found that he held a new feeling of respect for his slightly skewed friend.

"An' do ya know, friend Darn," Loon's voice dropped back to a conspiratory whisper as he stroked the downy whiskers on his chin, "what we do ev'ry Moonday once th' sun goes down?" Darn shook his head in mute answer.

"Well, me an' ol' Peg, we sneak down t' th' end o' th' old Tanner's wharf, where no one can see. Then we takes out th' coppers what Sott an' them has paid me, an' one at a time we spit on 'em, an' then throw them little whore-sons as far out t' sea as we can! An' then we laughs – Looooo-ooooo-oooon! Yes, Frien' Darn, we laughs an' laughs, till we're 'bout ready t' sick up our dinner!"

Loon threw back his shaggy blond head and laughed deep and loud then, a roaring that sprang from his simple soul and mocked those forces that caused him to be born different from "normal" folks. His was a laugh of a child of the elder gods, one that held victory and defiance and the simple love of life in it. He flung his thickly-muscled arms out wide, as if to embrace the world as he bellowed out his joy. Little Peg sprung yipping from under the table to join Loon in his celebration. And Darn felt himself ripped from his chair by the power of Loon's laughter, as together the three danced about the little shack, fairly shaking the walls with their barks and shouts and howls of victory and pleasure.

Somewhere amidst the merriment a dull knock sounded at the door of the shack, but it was immediately and utterly trammeled beneath the dancing feet and shouting voices of those within. The door creaked a bit as the one who stood outside tried to force it open, but the bolt held fast. A low muttered string of curses began to fall, along with more solid blows upon the door. Still the bolt held, and still the three inside gave no notice.

The sound of the renewed assault upon the door finally penetrated the din of the raucous celebration, halting Darn in his steps. He cocked an ear towards the door, then tried to no avail to catch hold of Loon's attention.

"LOOOOOOOONNNN! AH, HA HAH!!! TAKE THAT OL' SOTT!" Loon continued his bellowing. "JUST PUT THEM OL' COPPERS RIGHT UP YER ARSE FOR ALL WE CARE, EH PEG?"

The first two times Darn struck at his arm, Loon just laughed all the louder and kicked up his heals in a fairly respectable jig. But a painful pinch just over the kidneys neatly captured his attention, and he finally noticed Darn, who waved frantically at the door and motioned for silence. By now the bolt on the door was beginning to bend as someone outside kicked at it repeatedly, and the curses had progressed to a steady stream of profanities.

Darn turned to the table beside him and carefully swept Loon's entire treasure into the earthen pitcher of ale which shared the table. In three long strides Loon reached the corner where his quarterstaff resided, then returned to stand in front of the door holding the iron-shod stave at the ready. Even Peg had sensed the change in attitudes, and she now stood quietly next to her master, her tiny white teeth bared in a silent snarl.

Darn stepped quickly to stand beside the doorway. The young acolyte felt the soulfire deep within him flare up from a quiet sleeping spark to a raging scarlet brand, searing its way through his veins and preparing him for battle. He raised onto the balls of his feet, his entire body tensed and poised to strike. At a nod from Loon, he waited for a pause between the blows at the door, then slid the bolt quietly back He counted silently, and on the next measure the door slammed back onto its hinges with a splintering crash and a burly figure stumbled awkwardly through the doorway.

A whirlwind of pandemonium swept through the room, heralded by Peg's frenzied barking. As the intruder fought to catch his balance, Darn's arm swung in a blindingly swift arc, the ridge of his hand connecting solidly with the man's forehead. Although the open-faced helm that the stranger wore bore the brunt of the blow, still his head nearly snapped from his neck. The man's feet flew from under him and he landed flat on the rough-sawn planks, the breath slammed from his lungs.

Darn leaned in to reach for a paralyzing nerve hold, a smug smile already worming its way across his face as he anticipated the tales of victory he'd proudly tell back at the Pyre. Then a whistling edge of steel flashed towards his legs, and only a prodigious leap – gained from the endless training sessions dodging Master Tobani's staff – saved Darn from being hamstrung. The shortsword in the intruder's hand slashed again in a return stroke, but Darn danced lightly out of range.

Peg darted in fearlessly to sink a mouthful of sharp teeth into the man's legging. Then Loon was there beside her, roaring like an enraged aurochs as he swung his quarterstaff in a tremendous blow that met the man's sword edge-on and shattered it like brittle glass. The stranger's arm was flung aside under the force of the blow, and Loon raised his staff high, preparing to end the fight.

The blow never fell, though. After an awkward pause, Darn glanced away from their attacker to see what held his friend in check. Loon stood frozen, a mask of frightened puzzlement hung over his face. The menacing quarterstaff fell in a clatter on the floor, and Loon loosed a cry akin to that of a wounded beast. He bent down to hook his hands under the intruder's arms, then snatched the man up off the floor and crushed him to his chest. Whereupon, to Darn's utter confusion, Loon began to cry in deep braying sobs.

"Jehred, Jehred! Oh, I is so sorry Jehred!! Please don' be mad! Ol' dumb ol' Loon didn't mean t' hurt ya, Lords of Fire, no! Looo-oo-oo-oonn is s-s-so s-sorry!"

The huge boy continued to weep and wail, tears and snot dripping steadily from his chin onto the helm of the man he held. His captive wheezed for a few moments more as he fought to regain his breath, then abruptly straightened up and struck at Loon's arms two, three times before finally freeing himself. As the man stepped back from Loon's blubbering hulk, Darn glimpsed a flash of mail beneath the stranger's hauberk and a purple cord knotted around his left arm. An old memory tugged faintly at the strands of Darn's mind; then the stranger erupted in outrage and most of Darn's confusion evaporated.

"Loon! Ya addle pated, anile, witless son of a cud-chewing bundhar! I could have killed ya, ya beetleheaded fool!! Left ya laying on the floor, trying t' hold yer guts in, while our good Mother cursed me a thousand times from her grave!" The soldier swore with a vengeance, spittle riding the winds of his rage. "By Volar's Three Hairy Balls, why dintcha answer me at the door? I thought ya were being set upon by some o' those porking wharf-rats, what for the bedlam I heard from in here!" He snapped his head about to glare at Darn. "And who in Chaka's frozen hell be thee? Like to 've cut yer porkin' legs off . . . and still might, mind ya!!" Fury stabbed from the soldier's eyes and Darn backed up a step, his earlier self-assurance draining away and turning his feet to blocks of ice. He stammered to find an answer to the man's demand, but

Loon leapt to his rescue.

"This," Loon paused to snort and wipe his dripping nose on his arm, "this is my new frien', Darn. He saw ol' Sott throw poor Peg in th' harbor – wasn't that a mean thing t' do? So I jumped in t' save Peg, then Darn saved me an' ol' Peg both from being food fer th' fishes." The tall boy ran a broad palm across his face and wiped the resulting mess on his trouser leg. Even as his sniffles slowed and the tear-tracks dried, Loon's sparkling-white smile – the doorway for the laugh that earned him his name – split the unsavory mess on his face, and the power of it was so strong that even Jehred's fury abated somewhat at the sight.

"Then we walked back t' here, an' we sang a song – ya know, Jehred, that one about Cappon th' Lucky an' Left-handed Loric an' th' harlot-daughter o' th' Sea Queen? An' we had some soup – oh, there's still some left, ya know – an' we talked an' I told a joke an' we laughed an' danced." Loon continued to prattle on, winding his way into a convoluted tale of his day that began with an interesting beetle he'd discovered in a rotting bundle of Sandali's cloth, and from there proceeded into a list of what he'd had to eat for the last three days that could have been the source of his current bout of flatulence.

The disheveled soldier tried in vain to slip the edge of a sharp word into Loon's unending narration. Failing that, he shook his head in despair and began to knock the dust from his clothes.

"Oh, an' Jehred," Loon continued. "I tossed fat Sott in th' harbor. I know ya told me not t' do that no more, an' I know it'll bring ya trouble, but he deserved it! Oh poor ol' Peg; he . . ."

Jehred threw both hands up as if to wrench the words from

the blond boy's lips. "Yes, yes, I know Loon! He threw her in with the fish; ye told me already!" Jehred spat crossly. He walked stiffly across the room and bent to retrieve the hilt of his broken sword. Staring at the jagged splinters of blade, Jehred sighed, then dropped heavily into a crooked storm-salvaged chair that creaked ominously as he settled into it. He glared silently for an unmercifully-long moment at Loon, who stood with his smile now clenched in his teeth and tears threatening again at the edge of his eyes. Then the corners of Jehred's mouth twitched awkwardly upward, as if unused to the motion, and the grizzled soldier shook his head as he smiled in spite of himself. On the heels of his brother's rare grin, Loon's grand smile escaped to shine out once again, brushing the red tint of anger from the air.

"Young fools, the pair of ya," the burly soldier swore without spite. "Shara's Teats, boy! Could've spitted ya both, if Mother Bes hadn't been smiling upon ya." Jehred untied the chinstraps of his helm, pulled it off and pushed back his mail cowl. He ran a thick-fingered hand through the grey-iron curls on his head, then closed his eyes and rubbed cautiously at the angry purple lump growing on his forehead. A silent gesture towards the table, and Loon quickly brought him a brimming tankard of ale.

"I ... umm", Darn cleared his throat and picked nervously at his sleeve. "I most truly apologize for any harm we may have caused ye, Captain. These wharves do deserve a measure of caution though, and we had no idea who ye might be."

"Did the thought never strike ya t' call out and ask?" Jehred replied quietly. The two boys glanced up at each other and a flush of foolishness stole across both their faces. Each began to sputter and choke as they struggled to find an answer, but Jehred waved them to silence.

"Ah, hell, tis no matter. I'd rather ya be a trifle too wary and impulsive, than t' end up floatin' face down in the harbor." The captain nodded a bit as he pondered his next thought. "An' I suppose no harm came of it. Told th' Lord Marshall that this new batch of cheap Yotian blades weren't worth their weight in used ass rags; now I can prove the point." He scowled at the shattered sword still in his hand and dropped it to the floor, then took a long pull from his tankard. "As far as harm to my person," he continued, "th' day that I can't hold my own 'gainst a pair of babes barely weaned from th' teat, is th' day that I trade in m' sword and cord fer a broom and apron, and find myself a fat wife in th' country." Jehred uttered a loud snort, an abortive attempt at laughter, and settled back to sip at his ale. His unoccupied hand rubbed at the rough-sawn arm of his chair, and as his eyes closed the deeply-carved lines of worry seemed to melt from his face, leaving only the white ghosts of battle scars behind.

The two boys shuffled their feet nervously, uncertain how to part the silence which draped about the room. Jehred hawked deeply and spat a wad of phlegm into the cold fire pit, then straightened up in his seat and stared intensely at Darn.

"My thanks t' ya fer saving this fool brother o' mine," Jehred said as he cocked a thumb and a crooked smile at Loon, who grinned and nodded his head as if proud of himself. "How many times I gotta remind ya, ya can't swim, fer Bess' sake?" Jehred asked Loon, not expecting an answer. The old soldier leaned over to scratch the waiting Peg behind the ears, then cocked his head back up to

128

look at Darn. "A 'Spark' from the hill, eh? One of Elias' boys, if I'm not mistaken."

Darn nodded in mute agreement, unsure of what to say. Loon dismissed himself and quietly went about fetching a bowl of chowder and another tankard of ale for his brother. Then he poured off the pitcher containing his treasure and discreetly stashed it away from view.

"I can always pick out those who are indentured to Elias, that bald-pated pain-in-the-arse," Jehred continued as he straightened back up. "Like the rest of yer order, yer all too cocky fer your own damned good – or anyone else's fer that matter." He took another sip from his tankard, then the guardsman winced as he explored the tender knot which Darn had gifted him with, and his lips twitched in the crude semblance of a grin. "But I will say this: that red-bearded whore-son does teach his pupils well. Thought I'd taken a bolt from a crossbow when I stepped through th' door."

Jehred watched intently over the brim of his tankard as Darn bowed his head in embarrassment.

"One thing ya obviously didn't learn from Elias, though," the Captain continued, "is yer humility. Ya got that, an' even a measure o' courtesy, besides."

The young boy's brow wrinkled in uncertainty, as Jehred proceeded.

"Elias, on th' other hand, was born without a humble bone in his body, I'm certain. Doesn't know the meaning of the word. Nay, nay, boy – put yer hackles back down," he said, as anger began to twist its way across Darn's face. "I understand Elias better an' have more respect fer his abilities than anyone else in this sewer of a city. Owe my life t' th' little bugger, in fact. But be certain o' one thing, boy: Elias holds no one in higher esteem than himself. Ever plan on Elias considering your welfare over his own, and you're planning on being terribly disappointed." Jehred sipped slowly at his ale, watching the dregs as he swirled his mug. It seemed to do little to calm his mood though, for he stabbed the air as he continued.

"It's that kinda damned attitude he infects all of 'em with, all those whom he deems worthy of his attention. It's *his* students cause me most of the trouble I get from yer Order: Flame Dancers or newly-robed Masters who wander down into the city like a pride of rogue lions. Come down t' drink an' wench an' maybe try out their moves on some unlucky loudmouthed sot, or occasionally even on one of my guardsmen! I've got no use fer such nonsense, an' Elias knows it. But will he reign 'em in? By the Lady of Scorn, hell no, he won't! He comes right along an' leads th' pack half th' time."

The grizzled soldier tipped his jack back for a long draught, then shook his head as if to fling any further gnats of anger from his mind. "Come, son," he motioned Darn towards the empty bench, "didn't mean t' offer ya nor yer master any ill words. Just been a unpleasant ending to an long bothersome day, fer a man who's been doin' a thankless job too long."

Darn warily sat down and Loon quietly joined the pair with a fresh round of ale for them all. The three sat in uncomfortable silence for several moments, then Loon's face lit up with a smile and he leaned forward to rest a hand on his older brother's arm.

"Tell us a tale, Jehred. Th' one 'bout th' Siege o' th' Dark Sun." Loon turned back to his new friend and his face gleamed with unclouded pride. "Jehred an' I was there, ya know! Held th' Western Wall fer a full-hand o' days against th' Klemish dogs. Could've held 'em forever, if'n they hadn't had them witches, them Black Sisters with 'em. Ain't that right Jehred? An' *I* even got t' throw a few rocks an' buckets of scaldin' water down on 'em. An' me only bein' eleven summers at th' time! It was ..."

Jehred cut his brother off abruptly with a snap of hand and tongue.

"It was a damned fool thing t' do, that's what it was! I had enough t' worry about that day, without you dancin' along th' top o' th' wall, waiting t' take a bolt in th' throat or get snatched up by one o' those Black Bitches' infernal beasts!" The captain shook his head sullenly. Then he noticed the wounded look on Loon's face and he dulled the sharp edge of his voice. "Even so, it was a man's job," he continued. "And ya did it well, when few were willing t' take th' chance, Loon." He closed his eyes and the weathered landscape of his face shuddered slightly, a faint tremor of old pain. He scrubbed at his face for a moment with a scarred hand that lacked half a ring finger, then looked back up at the boys, and his eyes blazed with fury at the remembrance.

"Aye, I'll tell it: th' Siege o' th' Black Sun. I'll tell what I know, and what I wish to recall. Listen well, young Darn, fer yer Master Elias played a large part as well." Jehred drained his mug with one long pull, then held it out to Loon for more. "A tale such as this requires some sustenance fer th' teller, little brother. You'll get yer story, long as this jack stays filled." He sat back in his chair and sucked off the foam that spilled from the lip of his tankard. Then he began.

Chapter Six
Siege of the Dark Sun

"Twas a sweltering night; night o' th' new Dog Moon, if I remember correctly. Anyway, twas one o' those nights when th' sheets on yer bed stick t' ya like horse-glue. Yer sweatin' so much, ya wake up wonderin' if ya caught a fever, or if mebbe ya pissed t' bed from too much ale. Ya can't sleep, ya ain't hungry, an' tempers are so short yer 'fraid t' talk t' yer old woman fer fear she'll snatch up a skillet an' start swingin'.

"I gave up tryin' t' sleep. Decided t' walk th' sea-side walls a while: jaw some with th' boys on duty there, an' mebbe catch a bit o' breeze comin' in. Twas too cursed hot t' wear that be-damned mailcoat, so I jest strapped on some steel over a short kilt, an' left Dhanna to soak th' bed by herself.

Jehred paused for an overly-long moment, staring out the window, and Darn began to wonder what smoky thoughts drifted behind those eyes of jet. Then the soldier took a long draw from his jack and continued.

"Found a little bit o' wind blowin' when I got up a'top th' wall. Even still, twas sorely temptin' t' jest take a runnin' leap, hoping t' miss th' rocks an' land in th' harbor. Found a couple o' th' night watch sharin' a bit o' icemint-liquor, so I joined 'em fer a dram er two. Blistered their ears good fer drinkin' on watch, first all, o' course." Jehred snorted as he lifted his jack, and the ghost of a smile tugged at one corner of his mouth.

"There wasn't much t' see over th' harbor that night, with th' moon swallered up an' all. Lot o' sea-mist come rollin' in too, an I remember thinkin' it was a bit odd t' have fog that time o' year. Couldn't see nothin' on th' water 'cept fer th' gleam o' some fisherman's lantern here an' there. So with a drop o' mint-juice t' cool m' throat an' warm m' belly, I curled up in th' corner of a balustrade an' tried t' catch what sleep I might find. Wouldna be much, though.

"I must've dropped off fer a bit, cause all th' sudden I found m'self sittin' bolt upright, wonderin' what th' hell I was doin'. Ya know how it is, when somethin' wakes ya, an' yer not sure what it was, or even if ya were asleep in th' first place.

"Anyhow, I sat there for a moment, rubbin' m' eyes an' scratchin' m' sack, when all th' sudden I hear it again: a *tink* an' then a scrapin' noise, like some careless idiot lettin' th' buttcap of 'is pike drag along the walkway. Well, bein' as I was inna bit of a pissy mood anyway, I got up t' find th' sluggard what couldn't remember th' first thing about keepin' quiet whilst 'e walked 'is watch. Figured I'd scare 'im outta 'is boots with a blade laid 'longside 'is throat.

"I got 'bout eight, nine strides along th' way, when out th' corner o' m' eye, I see somethin' leanin' up 'gainst one o' th' balustrades: figured it t' be that pike bein' dragged that I'd heard earlier. By Volar's One Eyebrow, now I was mad! A man on watch never sets 'is weapon down, not e'en t' take a piss er blow 'is nose! Nevermind that we was on th' Sea Wall, where nothin' but th' gulls an' th' broadwings ever come sailin' past. A man what was this careless on a secure wall is damn well gonna be careless when 'e walks the Harbor Wall or th' Valley Wall! An' wouldn't that be jest dandy if some soldier's standin' there aimin' a stream over th' edge, with 'is pike outta reach, when a hungry sand demon or some Tharian sell-sword comes pawin' up over th' side? Fer this mistake, I was bound

133

an' certain t' have a pound 'o flesh outta some watch-man's arse!

"I walked over an' made a grab fer th' pike, readyin' t' break it over some poor-excuse-fer-a-soldier's head. Only, when I lay a hand on it, it won't budge a finger joint. 'Now what the bloody hell is this?' I wonder. I turned back for th' torch I'd passed a few steps b'fore, an' brought it back for a better look. And whatta ya guess I found?"

Loon leapt to his feet and shouted: "A climbin' …!" He clapped both big-knuckled hands over his mouth, as if to stuff the rest of his words back down his throat as Jehred gave him a knife-edged glare. A few nervous giggles squirmed out around his fingers and Loon glanced nervously at Darn. Then with a well-practiced move, he snatched the pitcher off the table and filled Jehred's jack to the brim with the golden-red brew.

"Go ahead Jehred," Loon waved his free hand. "Tell us th' rest! I fergot what I was gonna say, anyway!" The towering youth tried his best to fold himself down into a small, unnoticeable knot on the bench beside Darn. Then he pulled on a foolish-looking, open-mouthed stare of rapt attention. Darn tried very hard to ignore his friend and quell his own laughter, not wishing to draw any measure of Jehred's ire.

"As I was sayin'," Jehred sent an unheeded scowl towards his brother, "I went back fer a torch. Got back t' th' strange pole, an' *Shara's Teats!* if I don't see that it's hinged in th' middle an' has got a length o' rope runnin' from it, down over th' edge!

"Couldn't be no climbin' rope, I figured. Jest ain't no way t' come up on th' Sea Wall. Can't land no boat on th' rocks down below; hell, e'en a good swimmer'd be broken t' pieces on them teeth! An' from th' top o' th' rocks, the cliff's carved smooth fer a hundred spans, then ya got nothin' but wall for another two hundred! Ain't no ladder that tall, and no hand-held bow that can shoot that far.

"The boys must be hangin' a cheese er skin o' wine over th' side t' age, I told myself. So I reached fer th' rope, an' started t' haul up its booty. Felt somethin' catch jest below the edge o' th' wall, so I gave it a good tug, then grabbed th' torch t' take a look.

"But by Volar's Bloody Head-Lice, an 'is Three Snaggled Teeth!" The iron-haired captain leaned forward in his seat, and his eyes blazed deep in their dark depths as he relived his tale. "Didna' get no wineskin er crock. What I got was m'self face-t'-face with one o' them bleedin' Klemish Toads instead!

"What, never seen a Toad, boy?" Jehred asked, seeing the bewilderment on Darn's face. He settled back into his chair, waiting while Loon topped off all their jacks with fresh ale. Then the captain took a long pull from his tankard, washing away some of his flush before continuing. "Well, th' warty little bastards've got faces like squashed, rotten stinkfruits: all greasy gray an' lumpy on th' outside, an' kinda pus-yellow leakin' out 'round th' eyes an' all. Stand only 'bout waist-high t' Loon, but with legs almost as stout as his are. Got sorta long fleshy hands, an' fingers that look like they couldna' break cheap yarn. But believe me, them long fingers can snap yer neck like a day-old chicken bone. Got a mouthful o' ragged teeth on 'em too, an' they ain't shy about usin' 'em. Why, I seen one bite off a man's hand at th' wrist once: one *Snap!* an' twas gone!"

Both of the boys grimaced at the thought. Peg snapped her own sharp little teeth together, and Jehred laughed as the pair jumped in their seats.

"The Klemish get th' Toads off some god-forsaken rock pile," the captain continued, "what sits somewhere out in th' middle o' their inland sea. Couple thousand of 'em live out there, breedin' like vermin. Can't sail er swim worth spit, so they're stuck there 'cept fer th' ones th' Klemish come an' take off.

"Some say that th' Toads are some half-breed cousins t' th' dwarves, what got shipwrecked there durin' the Great Troll Wars an' been inbreedin' fer a thousand years 'er such." Jehred paused for a long pull at his ale, then carried on, wagging a finger seriously. "Mind ya ne'er mention that idea near a dwarven axeman though. Cause ya open yer yap on *that* matter, an' sure as Chancellor Karlonos is a lard-assed buffoon, ye'll be walkin' home with yer head tucked unner yer arm!

"Th' Klemish often use a hand er two o' Toads as shock troops, 'specially if there's some climbin' t' be done, since them Toads can go up a wall er cliff-side like flies on a moon-shed door. Foul, unholy little whoresons cain't handle a blade half as good as m' blind Aunt Sophilia. But give 'em a mace er somethin' else heavy t' swing an' they're nasty little porkers t' cross! Ya 'bout gotta cut one in half t' make 'im lay down an' quit. An' hittin' 'em on th' head with anythin' less'n a war hammer generally only aggravates 'em." Jehred paused and spit into the hearth. "Nasty little porkers!"

"Anyways, as I was sayin', I'm standin' nose t' snot-drippin' nose with a Klemish Toad. It's got some kind o' heavy crossbow strapped 'cross its back an a short-hafted cudgel stuck in its belt. An' it looks more surprised than I am! Must've expected t' come up on a empty walk, or at least t' have only a couple o' half-sleepin' drunkards t' contend with.

"Course, I go fer m' broadsword. An' *Volar's Balls*! if halfway out it don't hit th' edge o' th' balustrade an' stop dead in th' scabbard! Well that ugly Toad peeled back them big gray lips an' smiled at me when it saw the state I was in. An' boys, I'm not ashamed t' tell ya I 'bout lost m' water then an' there. I was jest standin' there like a damn fool, with a hungry Toad stepping up top th' wall a-tuggin' at its cudgel an' lickin' its chops like I'm a lamb hung up neat an' trim fer slaughter.

"Now all this ain't taken but a couple o' heartbeats, an' I still hadn't passed th' shock t' holler out yet. But when that ugly little disgrace o' nature stepped up close, I could see strings o' old meat stuck 'tween its teeth. An' I figured that soon there'd be pieces o' *me* hangin' in there. Well that unfroze me inna hurry! So I leaned in close 'nuff t' get a good whiff o' th' dirty little monster's breath – *like a buzzard with screw-worms, twas! Whew!!* – an' I stuffed that pitchwood torch straight down its gullet! An I swear t' this day, I seen th' gleam o' that torch shinin' out through that Toad's eyes right afore it pitched out over th' edge an' sailed down t' th' cliff's teeth.

"Well, I kept m' wits about me long 'nuff t' get m' blade out an' set t' sawin' at th' climbin' rope b'fore th' next one showed up! Course, th' top couple arm-spans of it was wrapped in wire t' keep it from wearin' out on th' edge o' th' wall, so it took some time. Long 'nuff fer me t' take a glance down an' see what other vermin might be scalin' th' walls.

Jehred frowned and shook his head. "Bleedin' nasty sight, 'twas! 'Bout a hand o' Toads had lines o'er th' top o' th' wall. Sticky-fingered little bastards looked liked they'd crawled halfway up th' cliff face – somethin' no honest *man* would have a prayer o' doin'

– an' then they shot lines up past th' balustrades. Soon 's they got up th' wall, they wouldna waste no time in securing heavier lines an' tossin' 'em t' their masters below. An' though I could see naught below in th' shadows, I had no doubts that a full-scale raidin' party o' them Klemish vultures was waitin' there!

"I started hollerin' m' fool head off fer th' rest o' the watch, since them warty-hided little buggers were climbin' up faster 'n I could cut th' rope. An' every few moments that passed, I could hear th' rattle of another bolt comin' o'er th' wall.

Jehred broke off his story, setting his empty tankard back onto the table. Then he stood and stretched slowly, perhaps even carefully. He seemed a bit unsteady on his feet, testimony to the tankards of ale he'd drunk, and his words had taken on the ill-fashioned clip of the alleyways. But his mind and memory were still clear, and he could almost taste the salt spray of the night air as he shared his tale.

The captain sat back down and scowled darkly at the empty leather jack before him. The two ensorcelled boys sat quietly for a moment or two, then Loon jumped up from the bench with a start and grabbed for the near-empty pitcher which sat on the table behind them. Loon's big meaty hands seemed to have gained a life of their own in the excitement though, for they betrayed him and batted the pitcher off the table instead. Loon made a desperate lunge to save the crock, but it was over much too fast, and all they could do was watch as the pitcher sadly bled the last of its golden lifeblood onto the splintered floor boards.

"Oh, fish farts! Loon, ya ol' lunkhead!" Loon fumbled to pick up the shards of the pitcher, and the blond curls which hung past his face did little to hide the flush of his shame. "I'm sorry Jehred! I didn'a mean t' be a clumsy tater-head and spill it all! Ol' Loon is so stupid!! I'll getcha some more Jehred; I'll be quick! Oh, don't leave; don't be mad at me. I'll . . .

Darn glanced over at the captain, fearing harsh words for Loon's accident and the resulting babble. But instead, Darn found a sad soulful look of compassion on the grizzled soldier's face. Jehred must have sensed Darn's attention though, for an instant later the look fell away like a silk veil, leaving only the iron and worn-leather visage of a seasoned campaigner.

"Leave be, Loon," Jehred called out roughly, almost covering the crack in his voice. "'Tis less than enough t' be concerned about, though the crock's a mess. An' I told ya b'fore not t' let me hear that name-callin'. *I'll* decide who's th' tater-head 'round here, an' who's not!

Loon returned to his seat, his face still crimson with the stain of his embarrassment. He squirmed nervously for a moment, staring at the floor, then he silently handed Jehred his own mug, which was still mostly full. Jehred nodded a silent thanks, and leaned back to pull at the frothy brew. Darn, in turn, was thankful for the excuse to relinquish his own jack, as the brew was stronger than he was accustomed to. So he placed the ale into Loon's hands and closed the boy's sausage-thick fingers around it. The unquestioned ritual complete, Jehred resumed his story.

"Well, I finally managed t' wake up a few o' them worthless fools what were s'posed t' be standin' watch. Set most of 'em t' cuttin' th' ropes loose, an' tossin' a few javelins down through a couple o' Toad gullets. Lost one young whelp right off: a boy barely older than Loon, what didna know better than t' lean out o'er th' wall too far.

A grapplin' bolt whistled by an' ruffled 'is hair, an' 'e lost 'is balance an' took th' long leap." Though Jehred held his voice steady, he still felt the loss, the same as he did for every man who'd died under his command. Yet it was a soldier's burden to bear, so he shifted the thought to a more comfortable position and carried on. "Poor bastard; I'd like t' believe 'e took a couple o' Toads with 'im on th' way down.

"By then, a few o' them frog-eyed monsters 'ad made it t' th' top o' th' wall. But one er another of us spitted each of 'em an' sent 'em back o'er th' wall b'fore any could belay ropes t' th' rest o' th' hoard below. By then, th' general alarm was bein' sounded, an' th' Toads was scramblin' back down t' th' water as we bounced rocks off their flea-bitten heads! Ya should've seen 'em run boys: like beaten cur with their tails twixt their legs, 'bout killin' themselves on all them broken boulders down there. An' when they got ' th' water's edge, they found that their Klemish masters had already pulled anchor and left 'em, with nowhere t' go an' not a shield among 'em! Them Toads made fine nighttime target practice once th' archers got mustered! Ha!" Jehred took a long pull from his jack, and laughed with the boys when he spilled a great dollop of foam down his chin. He drew his sleeve across his mouth, and shook his head smiling. "Yes, m'lads, ya should've seen 'em run! *Volar's Fist!* It made us feel strong and heady with a quick victory." Jehred's smile faded slowly. "Should've known it's never that easy."

As he returned to the telling of his tale, the tiny hovel seemed somehow darker and closer, with hungry shadows lurking in the corners. "We was all laughin' an' slappin' each other on th' back fer chasin' th' heathen bastards off once again. Then outta th' fog drifts th' biggest raidin' fleet I e'er laid eyes upon! As they slid out o' th' night, each o' th' ships lit up ev'ry torch they had on-board, just so we could see 'em and start t' worryin'. At least six er eight full hands o' ships: big triremes, war galleys, an' a couple o' fat supply freighters, some with trebuchets an' towers already built an' lashed t' their decks. Each of 'em was flyin' th' Klemish rags: *Blood an' Black Iron*, they call it 'mongst themselves. An' lashed just below each o' them flags hung th' body of a Shiningrock guardsman, their gold an' purple clear enough in th' torchlight, dead with a black Klemish blade stuck twixt 'is ribs! Found out later that th' bastards had crept up on th' watch tower at Siren's Point an' butchered ev'ry one o' th' men stationed there. That's why we had no warning o' th' attack.

"But it wasn't th' site o' them ships that dried th' spit from m' mouth. Naw, an' it weren't all them Klemish soldiers standin' shoulder t' shoulder, what sent th' stones o' every man on that wall creepin' up fer sanctuary!

"On th' flag ship was a special group o' figures, standin' wide open there on th' bow with no caution fer arrows er missiles an' whatnot. Three of 'em – for I could jest make 'em out – three of 'em stood there surrounded by torches. But they seemed t' suck th' flames right inta themselves, cause e'en with all that light, they was jest as dark an' shadowed as a slaver's soul. We could hear a bit o' keenin' comin' from 'em, like carrion birds singing some ugly song. Then th' mist 'round 'em slowly started t' stain black, like ink from a cuttlefish spreadin' crost th' water. That foul-lookin' cloud started t' move through th' rest o' the fog that laid o'er th' harbor. An' ev'ry time that blackness swallered up th' light o' some poor harbor-waif's cookfire, ya heard a scream er two ring out like th' wail o' th' damned - which I guess is exactly what it was." The captain paused, and his two young listeners hardly dared to breath.

"That was th' first time any of us laid eyes on them Black Sisters. I stood there wi' th' sweat freezin' on m' back in spite o' th' heat, an' all 'round me I could smell th' rotten stench o' fear. I know none of us won't ne'er ferget it, long as we live.

Jehred straightened back in his chair, and shivered as if to throw off the tatters of a bad dream. He grunted and muttered to himself a bit, ignoring the boys for a bit as he dug a worn bag of leaf and a battered blackthorn pipe out of his pocket.

"By that time, someone had th' sense t' set th' alarm gong t' bangin'. Least it allowed most o' th' fisherfolk – them that lives on th' southern wharves, anyways – t' save themselves. Th' rest o' them poor souls out on th' harbor had nothin' but their prayers as they died. Most all o' th' rough trade drinkin' and whorin' 'long Drunkard's Wharf either didna hear th' alarm, er was too far gone t' care. Not much of a loss there fer th' most part. But a few good men o' mine stayed down there t' help get those out what wanted t' leave; all of 'em got caught by that be-damned demon-fog b'fore they could get cleared out.

Jehred sucked quietly at his pipe, the pungent clouds of blue-grey smoke dancing over his head for a while, then drifting slowly upward to search for cracks in the ceiling. Just as his audience began to stir, the captain spoke quietly around the stem clamped in his teeth: "Found all th' bodies afterwards, we did. Most had nary a mark on 'em, 'cept fer a few what looked like they tried t' scratch their own eyes out. But all of 'em had such looks o' unholy terror on their faces, it was all we could do t' bring ourselves t' carry 'em back t' their families, er over t' Fat Orley th' glue-maker if they had none. Hell, e'en th' cutpurses an' other such vermin was loathe t' pick them corpses over!

"Anyways." Jehred blew out a long plume of smoke that guided his young listeners past the morbid picture he'd painted. "That mist didna' come up no higher than th' deck o' th' least Klemish ship; just enough t' cover th' wharves an' creep a ways up th' Harbor Road. Scared th' hell outta all of us, till we realized that if we couldna' go down through it, then they couldna' come up through it either! Figured we'd give *them* somethin' t' worry 'bout fer a while, so I ordered th' big trebuchet loaded up wit' burnin' pitch an' sent 'em a couple o' awfully hot messages! Quick enough, that got 'em backin' over t' th' far side o' th' harbor, but not b'fore we sent one o' their galleys up in flames as a burnt offering t' Volar One-ear.

"Th' rest o' th' night weren't much, as I recall it. They sat out there on th' water, not makin' a move that we could see. An' we prepared fer th' siege we knew was comin': stackin' bolts an' arrows an' javelins; boilin' up tubs o' lard; tightenin' ropes an' stackin' shot fer th' onagers an' catapults; checkin' on th' city cistern an' th' grain houses; bringin' water an' supplies an' bandages up on th' Harbor wall. By dawn we was ready; e'en managed a bit o' sleep, most of us. Yer warmark, Elias, was up there by then, spreadin' out Flame Masters an' Dancers along th' wall, an' complainin' t' *me* 'bout some o' our preparations — as if that little grease-pated weasel could do any better 'imself!" The captain grumbled into his beer for a while, then blew the foam off his lip with an angry pout and continued.

"Long 'bout dawn, th' witches' black fog blew away, an' th' Klemish began t' ready themselves. They didna' bother sendin' no envoy with demands fer our surrender first – guess they knew we'd spit any flag-bearer inna heartbeat t' pay fer what they'd done t' our men. Th' Klemish front line troops hopped off down at th' south wharf, outta range o' our machines, an' started that long march up th' Harbor Road.

"Hell, I couldna' see any sense in it at all! They had t' know we'd be rainin' down rocks an' oil an' dung - anythin' that weren't nailed down, an' a few things tha' twere! Tossin' it all down on their heads th' entire length o' th' road! E'en them dirty blood-drinkers couldna' be *that* stupid!

"As we was all laughin' an' readyin' fer a slaughter, a guardsman called out an' pointed t' th' flagship crost th' harbor. I could see them Black Sisters out there again — couldna' hear nothin' at that distance, of course, but we could see 'em huddled 'round a small fire on th' bow. Ev'ry once inna while we'd hear a bit of a *pop*, an' a purplish cloud 'd go rollin' up from their fire. I sent a hand o' boys what were good wit' a crossbow t' see if they could creep in close through th' wharf shacks an' get a shot off at them unholy bitches. But they must not have made it past th' Klemish scouts.

"M' Second at th' time – Armsman Thrackar, it twas – was standin' next t' me, waitin' on further orders. All o' sudden, he lets out a curse an' slaps at 'is cheek. Pulls 'is hand away, an' he's got th' biggest damned needlewing I ever seen squashed on 'is palm, all full o' blood it'd just sucked from 'im. Seemed a might queer at th' moment, cause them little bastards usually only come out at night t' pester an' dog ya an' buzz in yer ear. Straightaway then, a couple more men start swattin' an' hollerin'. So I turned t' set 'em back a notch er two fer droppin' their guard on account o' some damned *bugs.* But b'fore I could say more 'n two words, a pair o' ghost-head hornets came soarin' up over th' wall's edge an' flew straight fer th' inside o' my helmet! One of 'em stung me right above th' eye b'fore I could squish it. An' th' other run up inside m' earpiece an' started gnawin' on th' side o' m' head!

"Well, I done jest what most o' m' men were doin' 'bout then: I ripped off m' helm – Klemish arrows be damned – then I tore that bloody little demon off m' head an' crushed 'it unnerfoot! Stood there fer a couple o' breaths, feelin' a mite foolish. I was 'bout blind with pain from them wasp stings. Then I quit worryin' 'bout such little things, as I heard a sound what liked t' froze my blood, never-mind th' throbbin' in m' skull.

"'Twas a far-off rumble at first, an' I thought it might be thunder. Then it got louder, an' I could tell 'twas comin' from th' south-west, out t'wards th' Endless Marshes. Th' Klemish pack began marchin' up th' Harbor Road, blowin' them damned shriekin' jontur-horns o' theirs an' beatin' on big man-skin drums. But that other noise kept gettin' louder an' louder, all th' while smoothin' out till it was just a steady *buzz* that began t' bore inta yer brain. An' then we saw th' cloud.

"Thought it twas a thunderhead at first, that th' witches had brewed up a storm an' sent t' dump on our heads. Then I realized it was movin' *towards* us, against th' wind. Tried t' ignore it – figured at worst we'd get wet an' have no fires t' work with; hell, the damned Klemish heathens comin' up th' road would have a harder time of it than us. Then th' whole city dropped inta shadow, an' I knew I'd made a mistake. Cause when that cloud fell on us, boys, I'll tell ya, th' Hell of the Seven Dark Gods would've seemed like a festival day!"

145

Jehred gritted his teeth as he spoke, and Darn thought he might have seen the captain actually shudder once.

"Bugs!" Jehred spat out the word, venomously. "Every filthy kind o' stingin', bitin' beastie ya e'er seen! There was blood-suckin' needlewings as big as a sparrow, black-water horse flies an' ghost-head wasps, bees an' locusts an' flyin' nose-wigs. Some nasty flat-bodied things 's long as yer finger, like a centipede with wings an' pincers what'd bite through a pair o' good leather gloves! An' ev'ry one o' them little bastards was intent on stingin' an' bitin' any patch o' bare skin whot it could find!

"Well, most o' th' men just dropped their weapons where they stood, an' tried t' clear their faces an' nose an' mouths. Some of 'em started rippin' off their clothes t' get at th' crawlies what had wriggled up their sleeves er down their necks, but them poor bastards just opened up more skin fer that witches' spawn t' lay siege to! A few of 'em dropped an' ran, an' all th' threats I could muster wouldn't do no good. I s'pose it was worse for some of us than others. Twas makin' me fearfully unpleasant is th' truth, an' I was ready t' rip out Klemish throats with m' teeth. But there was fightin' t' do, an' I hadn't time t' worry with bugs. Some o' th' men though – an' good men at that – well it just drove 'em crazy, it did. Seen three er four just fling themselves o'er th' wall inna fit o' madness. An' one poor soul 'bout burned 'isself t' death with a pitch torch b'fore someone could get it away from 'im!

"I guess 'bout half th' men on th' wall had either run er weren't in no shape t' fight. So th' Klemish dogs reached th' base o' Shiningrock's walls with nary a bolt er stone er pail o' oil dropped down on 'em, like they'd been invited fer a picnic er sumthin'! Next thing I know, they got siege towers rolled up 'gainst th' walls, an' a cohort o' archers set up behind shields sendin' a steady stream o' steel o'er th' wall. A testudo was rollin up t' batter at th' outer gate. An' th' biggest damned trebuchet I ever laid eyes on was settin' up on th' road, being loaded with stones th' size of a bullock!

"I'll admit t' ya here an' now son: if it weren't fer Elias and th' rest o' th' Flame Masters up on that wall, we'd o' fallen then an' there in that first rush. But them Red Robes didna seem t' e'en feel them damned bugs, though their faces an' arms liked t' been covered wid 'em. They knocked aside th' guardsmen that were assigned t' th' oil vats, an' three er four of 'em got th' biggest barrels tipped t' send all that boilin' pig lard out 'crost th' gutters an' down on them heathen bastards' heads! Seein' that got a few o' my own men t' doin' their jobs: firin' off th' small onagers loaded with burnin' pitch 'gainst th' towers, lobbin' rocks an' whatnot down th' walls, gettin' some pikes 'gainst th' ladders that were bein' thrown up. Somebody finally tripped th' gate on that pen o' boulders we keep set up above th' main gate, an' in th' space of a breath, they turned that damned testudo inta th' biggest coffin ya e'er seen!

"What about me, Jehred?" Loon asked in a rush. "I was up there too, fightin' like th' rest. Ya said so yerself – didntcha?" He scratched his dirty blond curls with a thick forefinger. "I 'member havin' a big ol' pail o' that burnin' soda water that I poured over th' wall. An' I sure did bounce a might many rocks off th' heads o' them that climbed on *my* side, I did!" He looked to Jehred for confirmation of his story. Finally gaining his brother's reluctant nod, Loon grinned as if his face would split.

"Ya did that for certain, ya bloody young fool," Jehred said gruffly. "I figured ya'd fall off th' bleedin' wall sooner er later. Jest hoped that ya'd take some o' them whore-sons with ya!" Even as he chided Loon for his foolhardiness, Jehred's eyes shone with pride. He coughed into his fist, then continued.

"Eventually, a couple o' th' Klemish made it t' th' top o' th' wall, what with so many o' my men run off, er useless with fightin' off th' bugs an' all. But them filthy heathens never managed t' hold a spot open at th' top fer long, b'fore me an' some o' my men diced 'em up real good an' fine. We lost a lot o' good soldiers though, let me mark that: damned Klemish shafts were as thick in th' air as was th' bugs! What with their bowmen dug in so well an' all, there was little we could do about it, short o' leadin' a charge out th' front gate – an' that bitin' swarm o' bugs made it purely impossible fer th' cavalry captains t' e'en mount their troops up. So we gave 'em all we had from th' top o' th' walls, till we'd burned an' squashed an' skewered enough of 'em t' give 'em reason t' pause.

"They finally run back outta bow an' ballista range, back t' th' harbor an' their ships t' sit an' lick their wounds. Fact was, they sat there fer th' next three days an' did nothin'. Nothin', that is, other than wait fer th' damned bugs t' drive th' last shred o' sanity from ev'ry person trapped inside th' city walls.

"A fair number o' people died from th' bugs in those three days, more'n what died from shaft er blade, I'll wager. Jest swelled up from th' stings an' bites till they couldna breathe any more. Some had fits, foamed at th' mouth an' ran mad; others jest fell t' sleep an' their souls slipped away in th' night, I suppose." Jehred sat quietly for an overlong moment, and Loon squirmed uncomfortably in his seat. Then the captain continued, though his voice seemed to have lost some of its bite, its hunger at the telling.

"Don't believe any of us ever been more miserable in our cursed lives. Chancellor Karlonos ordered th' city mages t' save us from th' plague. An' grant ya, th' storm they called up did help knock th' flyin' ones outta th' air fer a while. But still, it was almost more'n we could bear. Them creepin' horrors got inta most o' th' food stores, ruinin' ev'ry bit. They was *everywhere* I tell ya: in yer boots, unner yer armor, inside yer bloody helmet, among th' sheets on yer bed. I think some people jest went mad from havin' them little vermin crawlin' all over em all th' time!

"By th' third day, more 'n half o' th' regular troops were either dead er in no condition t' fight. O' those that remained, they was so ugly-tempered from th' bugs that they was takin' t' fightin' 'tween themselves. I was startin' t' feel that another two days – three at th' most – an' th' Klemish could jest stroll right in th' front gates, cause there wouldna be a sane soul left t' hold it against 'em. An' by Volar's Snotty Nose, ya could bet that them Klemish knew it jest as well!

"Then on th' mornin' o' th' fourth day, our greatest fear an' our most solemn prayer both came accord. Th' Klemish Dogs started back up th' Harbor Road. An' jest about th' same time, an elder Green Robe – one o' th' Lady's True Healers – showed up on th' walls with big tubs o' some foul smellin' grease. Told us t' cover ourselves with it, as it would keep th' bugs at bay. Hell, by that time, most of us woulda smeared fresh horsemud on ourselves whilst dancin' naked a'top th' East Tower, if it'd kept the bugs outta our pants!! By The Lady, boys, I never in my life smelled nothin' so bad. Liked t' burn th' hairs outta yer nose, t'would! But th' bugs seemed t' hate it worse'n we did. An' by the time them Klemish bastards were at th' foot o' th' walls again, we was ready fer 'em.

"Course, they figured we was all dead er insane behind th' walls, an' we didna let on either. Didn't drop a single stone er pot o' oil, an' only shot a few bolts down at 'em. So they was swarmin' up their ladders an' ropes, hangin' by their fingernails an' laughin' 'bout what fun it'd be t' bugger a bug-swollen Shinin'rock wench. And when they got nearly to th' top, we let loose with all that we had! I'd bet solaris t' coppers that a thousand o' them heathens died in th' space o' ten breaths. Why, twas plain butchery, pure an' simple. Not a one of 'em e'en had his shield o'er head; expect they thought we was most all dead er half insane by then. We took out so many o' them in that first rush that they couldna e'en get back t' th' base o' th' wall, much less climb th' damned thing! So many of 'em fell we began t' build a new wall with their filthy corpses! It was our turn t' laugh then, laugh an' spit down on them bastards' heads. Word began t' pass of chargin' out th' gates on foot: chase them dirty whoresons back t' their ships an' burn them an' their bleedin' Black Sisters like a big ol' pile o' straw an' pigshit.

"Well, I'd stepped down off th' walkway, an' was tryin' t' find any soldier willin' t' stand th' wall whilst th' rest of us went after th' limpin' mongrels. Then a scream sounded off behind me: a scream like no man ought t' e'er make.

"I remember thinkin': 'Volar's Balls! How much worse can it get?' Then I turned around, an' saw jest how bad ...

"A bug stood there on th' balustrades, but this weren't no kind o' bug ya e'er seen before — or e'er wish t' see. It stood half again as big as Loon here, stood upright like a man too. Had a couple o' pointed legs wrapped 'round a young guardsman, an' with another leg it was pullin' 'is head off, slow an' easy, like it wanted t' see how far his neck could stretch first. Three good men stood 'round that miscarriage from hell, layin' inta it with swords an' pikes. But that damned thing's shell was as tough as good plate, an' it didna seem t' take more'n a scratch. Hell, I seen a crossbow bolt bounce square off its chest, an' it hardly e'en flinched.

"I started hollerin' t' get one o' th' ballistas locked an' loaded with a spear. Knew that th' guardsman it held was meat already, but I hoped t' skewer th' demon what had 'im before it could grab another. Then I caught a flash o' flyin' steel, an' th' hilt of a dagger stood out from one o' th' beastie's ugly eyes. It reared back an' tossed th' boy out o'er th' wall. Then, as th' foul thing's tryin' t' pull th' blade outta its face, yer Master Elias appears right beside it an' starts shovin' another o' them delta-bladed daggers of 'is 'tween th' joints of that monster's shell. I imagine it didna like th' ticklin' o' Elias' blade in its guts much. That big ol' bug whipped 'round, almost knockin' two guardsmen off th' wall, an' started slashin' an' snappin' at ol' Baldy fer all it was worth!

"Ya seen Elias work when th' Fire is on 'im, aintcha boy?" Jehred asked.

Darn nodded deeply. Master Elias was nigh untouchable when he was filled with the soulfire, like a raging storm-cloud full of flickering, deadly lightning.

"Then ya know that can't nothin' hardly lay hand on 'im, should he wish it not." Jehred paused for a drink, then hurriedly wiped his lips, anxious to return to his tale. "Well, Elias started dancin' back down th' length o' th' wall – steppin' along th' top o' th' balustrades like he was skippin' through th' court gardens, he was

– wit that porkin' demon scrabblin' along on all six legs after him. An' ev'ry time that bloody insect would turn t' deal with someone what was pokin' it in th' arse with a pike er halberd, ol' Baldy would dart in an' slide a blade inta another knee joint.

"Finally, Elias had backed up till he reached th' wall o' th' eastern tower. He taunted an' stuck that walkin' horror till it was 'bout mad with rage. We hollered fer him t' jump down t' th' walkway, an' we'd deal with th' demon there. Course, bein' Elias, he jest ignored us an' kept gettin' th' damned bug t' swing harder an' harder at him. Then, as it lashed out one final time, Elias ducked 'neath two o' them claws an' kicked that horny-headed whoreson's legs out from unner it. Stupid bug bounced off a balustrade then fell right o'er th' side. Guess it never learned t' fly, cause it dropped like a stone an' spread a feast for th' harbor broadwings on th' rocks below.

Both boys let out long-held breaths as Jehred slowly pushed himself up out of his chair then took a slow measured step towards the privy. If the veteran soldier had hoped to redeem himself for his inglorious entrance, he failed miserably. His first step faltered only a bit, but the second and third tangled in upon themselves, and the captain nearly tore down the privy curtain trying to recapture his rapidly-retreating balance. He snapped a sharp eye about just in time to see the tail-tips of smiles whisk off the boys' faces.

"No!" he bellowed, as he jerked the curtain roughly aside. "Fer yer information, I have *not* yet had enough ale! Enough is when ye two smilin' idjits turn inta a pair o' flyin' toad-fish an' sail on outta here t' leave an old soldier in peace!" The curtain whisked closed, but the boys could still here him mumbling curses as he went about his business.

152

Loon turned to his friend, eyes gleaming wildly as he relived the battle, dying to add his own words to the tale. "Ya should've been there, Darn," Loon said. "'Twas powerfully scary, an' Lords o' Fire did them bugs sting an' bite! Didn't they Peg?"

Peg thumped her tail half-heartedly, then cocked a quizzical eye at her master and yipped sharply.

"Aawp!" Loon slapped a meaty hand to his forehead, and grinned down at the questioning mutt. "Course ya don't know. Ya weren't e'en born yet, were ya?" He scooped up the peg-legged little dog and shook her above his head, ignoring her growls and false threats. "Why, ya was just a little hob-legged drop o' yer daddy-dog's kindness, jest waitin' t' be spread around, weren'tcha?" Loon growled and snapped back at her, then dropped Peg to the floor, where she set about attacking his boot-tip in retribution.

"Boy," Jehred intoned, as he parted the curtain and walked back to his chair. "Ya keep messin' with that mongrel, an' one day yer gonna wake up t' find some important body parts missin', an' one fat, smilin', little sea-cap'n dog sittin' at th' foot o' yer bed!" He cuffed Loon lightly behind the ear as he passed, and settled heavily back into his chair.

"All right ya two," Jehred glared menacingly at the boys. "Ya wanna hear th' rest of it, dontcha?"

Loon and Darn both quickly nodded in mute agreement.

The captain reached into the top of one of his boots, and from underneath the fringes he pulled a tiny stoppered flask of blue clay. The bottle was covered with what could have been dwarvish runes, but the signels were too small for Darn to read. From his other boot, Jehred drew a slim dagger whose aged bone hilt seemed to Darn to glow with a faint inner light. Jehred used the blade to dig the stopper from the end of the little vessel, then motioned for his audience to approach.

"This is Spiderdew," he said solemnly. "Th' dwarves collect it from deep unner th' Kalthmus mountains, from th' webs o' some loathsome white beasts whot live down there. Say their bite don't kill, but it drives a man mad. Them spiders make this stuff like honey, I'm told. Say that it can conjure up th' past, ofttimes. E'en show ya what *will be* th' past once inna while." The iron-haired soldier stared at the encrypted bottle and swirled its contents slowly. "Don't know nothin' 'bout that," he said. "All I know is it helps ya remember, an' it lets me feel a hell offa lot better 'n I have inna long time."

Jehred motioned the two boys forward, and carefully loosed a single drop of the thick liquid onto each of their tongues. Then he took three or four drops for himself before restoppering the tiny flask and returning it to his boot. Darn felt his head spin for a moment, and when he reopened his eyes, a crystal clarity seemed to have descended on the room. He thought he could hear the mice burrowing in Loon's cabinets, could smell the moldering bolts of cloth in the warehouse outside, could taste the coming rain on his tongue.

Jehred sat back and closed his eyes. Smiles and frowns chased each other across his face, as long-lost remembrances danced their way through his mind. He ran a callused hand over the stubble on his cheeks and pinched tight at the bridge of his nose, face scrunched in pain as if he'd suddenly discovered a thorn in his heart. His face grew long then, and seemed to hang on his skull — and at that moment, he looked far older than the forty winters and three that sat upon his shoulders. He appeared as he was: an unhappy and tired campaigner, who missed the days of his youth on the trail and dreaded the endless squabbles and petty political backstabbing amidst this nest of vermin they called Shiningrock. But then he looked at the eager faces of the boys who shared the tiny shack with him, at the fire and sparkle in their eyes and the tension in their limbs as they hung on his every word, trembling like hounds to join in this world of men of which he was so tired. Jehred sighed, shrugged off the cloak of sweet sorrow and longing that threatened to choke him, and took a long draw from his jack that left nothing but foam on his lips. The tired coals in the depths of his own eyes began to burn with battle-fever once again.

"Didna have no time t' congratulate ourselves on turnin' that be-damned bug inta scavenger pickin's. Cause as I turned 'round, I saw a greasy black cloud that sort o' hung boilin' in th' air. Then somethin' that looked like a mantis with a man's head flew out o' th' cloud. That one didna' get too far, cause soon as it landed top th' wall, another Red Robe (*Tobani, I think twas*) scooped up a handful o' burnin' pitch what was loaded in one o' th' small onagers – picked it up with 'is bare hands, he did! – an' he flung it right square in that beastie's maw. By Volar's Headlice, did that one dance an' fly about, sizzlin' an' poppin' like some big ol' staghorn moth flittin' through a torch flame, till its wings caught fire an' it joined its brethren down on th' rocks.

"We coulda been stuck there all day, fightin' 'gainst whatever belched outta that cloud next. An' th' bedamned Klemish 'ad hit th' walls again, whilst we was busy wi' th' bugs. But th' White Lady blessed us with a small wind right then (*Course, th' bloody council magician claimed it was his doin', but that imbecile couldna spell a flea t' jump).* Anyway, that breeze moved th' cloud jest enough fer us t' see what was behind it: an ya know what we saw there?

"A Black ..." Loon shouted as he jumped to his feet, only to be cut off in mid-sentence by a withering look from his older brother. Loon's voice caught in his throat for a moment, then a toothy grin spread across his face as he walked towards the back wall of the shack.

"... bug," Loon finished. "A big, ol', arse-poundin', black bug jest a-climbin' up my wall like he was 'nother dinner guest!" Loon stared in a dark corner for a moment, then slapped his meaty paw against the wall. He examined the mess smeared across his palm, looked at it more closely and prodded at a few of the more easily identified remains. Then he shrugged and consigned the squashed insect to the seat of his trousers. He glanced back up at his other companions, and a flush of scarlet stained his face as he returned his attention to his guests.

"Big, ol' bug," he mumbled, even   as he liberated another pitcher of ale from the coldbox. The jacks were filled, and the story continued.

"A Black Sister, twas! A big pair o' scroungy wings stuck out th' back of her cloak, an' she hung there flappin' like some giant vulture eyein' a dead kine layin' in th' field. All we could see of her beyond that was her face; an' speakin' fer m'self, I'd have jest as soon not seen it! Ugly enough t' make a dog sick ... an' th' *smell*!! Lord Volar, the Great Molester Himself, would've turned away if she'd lifted her skirt an' laid a goldpiece tween her legs!

"One o' th' men let loose with a holler an' a bolt at th' sight o' th' black bitch. An' inna heartbeat, that devil's whore 'ad a hunnert pieces o' hot steel flyin' t' drink her soul. But that cursed witch held out her claws, an' coughed out some words, an' ev'ry one o' them bolts an' arrows jest stopped an' fell like dead pigeons. An' I 'member that laugh she sprayed in our foolish faces – th' blackest an' most vile sound I e'er heard – jest b'fore she swooped down an' pointed a finger at one o' my men an' a stream o' fire hit 'im like burnin' oil.

"So now, while we're fendin' off demon bugs, an' we got th' bedamned Klemish still climbin' th' bloody walls, now we got some arse-toastin' vulture-bitch flyin' 'round our bleedin' HEADS!! I hollered at m' men t' keep firin' on her, t' keep her busy whilst I dashed t' one o' th' ballista we had set-up fer javelins.

"I got th' damned stubborn machine cranked up, an' laid th' heaviest lance I could find in th' groove. Then I started prayin' that th' infernal bitch would fly my way! Didna have t' wait long, fer Elias saw what I was doin'. Straight away, he run t' where one o' th' onagers sat in front o' me, an' climbed up th' frame quick as a Reillan monkey-cat. Then he gifted that demon-porkin' witch with 'is last dagger.

"She seen it comin', o' course, an waved it off like she had th' rest o' our darts. Imagine her surprise when Elias' *silver* blade slashed right through her enchantments and slid twixt 'er ribs! That got 'er attention, what did!" Captain Jehred chuckled slow and drunkenly, an all-together unpleasant sound.

"That unholy harlot spun in th' air, searching fer th' one who'd drew 'er blood." Jehred smiled a bit crookedly. "Course, there weren't no doubt who'd tossed it. Cause when she got t' lookin' at th' top o' that onager, well there stood that flame-faced whore-son Elias, showin' 'is teeth an' grabbin' 'is manhood at 'er!!"

Darn fought down his laughter at the vision that sprung to mind. He could see Elias doing just that, acting the fool in the middle of a battle with some demon-summoning witch.

Loon, however, found the thought more than he could bare, so he laughed and choked and sprayed Darn, Jehred, and Peg with the mouthful of ale he held. His showered victims all leapt to their feet with various profanities, oaths, and indignant dog curses, which led Loon to laugh all the harder. Jehred snatched the jack from Loon's hand, and poured its remaining contents over his brother's head, cursing and laughing all the while. Not to be outdone, Peg hobbled up and gifted Loon's foot with a shower of her own making. The small shack literally shook with the sounds of laughter and company. And for each of those inside, it was one of the best and simplest of times they'd ever known. Or ever would again.

After a while, the four companions regained their seats and their composure. At the others' strong suggestion, Loon started a small blaze burning in the fire pit. Jehred sat quietly for a few moments to pack his blackthorn pipe with pungent sweetleaf again, then reached for a burning splinter as he began the end of his tale.

"Guess that Black Witch an' 'er sisters must o' been a bunch o' man-less ol' spinsters, cause she certainly didna find any humor in Elias' offerin'. She let loose a scream like th' wail of a marshhowler, an' dove down at Elias like some giant black crow. But when she got t' within a double arm-span o' where Ol' Baldy was standin', out came that steel whip of 'is — quick as a sanddarter's tongue. *Crack! Crack!* He hit 'er three, mebbe four times, b'fore she figured out whot th' hell was happenin' to 'er — ya know how fast 'e is wi' that thing! By then, 'er robe was in tatters, an' when she lifted 'er arm t' ward off th' next strike, Elias snagged th' hem an' ripped most of 'er cloak away.

"Aaaugh!! I'll tell ya true my belly knotted at th' foul smell that hit us. An' that weren't th' worse part!

"Oh, above th' neck she was ugly enough already. But what th' cloak had been hidin' looked more like a Crimian gut-buzzard than anythin' human! Black greasy feathers an' shriveled ol' dugs hangin' halfway down t' her scaly yellow feet. Nasty ol' hag flyin' 'round jest shittin' on men out o' sheer meanness, an' callin' us names whot made *me* blush! Hell, I seen one o' th' younger guardsmen faint o' sheer fright, an' I imagine more'n one needed a dry kilt. But she didna surprise any of us old guard, as we'd seen harpies before. Hell, after fightin' them unholy shamans in th' jungles o' Yot, I wouldna o' been surprised t' see th' Black Sister grow horns an' have a big, blue, baboon's arse!

"Well, that filthy bird-bitch must o' gone plain mad wi' rage once 'er full ugliness was revealed. She screamed an' swung down on ol' Elias — an' ya know, I'd swear I even seen *him* pale a little!

" She let loose with a blast o' flame that scorched th' ballista an' liked t' melt th' mail I wore. But through it all, I could see Elias standin' on top o' that onager, dancin' 'round th' black witch, holdin' 'er there with 'is insults an' whip. She'd burnt off most of his clothes an' all th' little bit o' hair he had left then. But he'd given me time t' get th' ballista lined up, an' when she dove down at 'im I sent that lance wingin' at 'er plague-ridden heart!

"Elias' steel whip snapped out one last time an' snagged th' harpy by one wing, pullin' 'er down inta th' path o' th' ballista bolt. An' he held 'er there till that half-burnt lance hit 'er full in th' chest.

"She ne'er made a sound, she didna. Skewered like some ugly marsh-grouse, she jest dropped outta th' air an' splattered all over th' Harbor Road. We heard a pair o' screams let loose from th' Klemish flagship all th' way crost th' harbor. Then we seen th' two other Black Sisters take flight an' head east out over th' sea, leavin' th' Klemish t' fight on their own.

Jehred stood up slowly and began to collect himself, and this time there was no disguising the wavering step of a thoroughly drunk soldier. He upended his jack, then tossed the empty vessel to his brother.

"That was th' end o' th' battle, right there. Th' cloud o' bugs let off a bit, an' th' next gust o' wind scattered 'em back t' th' marshes. The Klemish turned tail an' ran fer their ships: cowards an' scavengers – expected naught else from 'em. With th' bugs gone, th' horse-boys were able t' get mounted, an' they rolled down that Harbor Road like a threshin' machine. I bet they left a full company o' Klemish carcasses pounded into th' stones, an' knocked at least as many into th' harbor t' feed th' fish.

"We set a hand o' their ships aflame, b'fore they made it outta th' harbor an' 'round th' Point. An' we got a couple o' men back out t' th' Point tower jest as they passed, who dropped a load o' burnin' tar on th' deck o' their flagship as a partin' gift. Th' top o' their masts can still be seen juttin' up out there at low tide.

Eyes and memory now properly clouded with ale, the captain struggled to fix his cloak, finally catching it on his third try. His voice thickened, and found interest in his boots and shattered sword rather than the boys' eyes as he finished his tale.

"A lot died durin' that time; mostly from sickness 'er madness,

160

though more'n a few were claimed by th' steel. But fer an occasional sortie up- er down-coast, them filthy Klemish hyenas ain't come back yet fer more.

Captain Jehred straightened up, and his face grew hard, hard as flint and spark. "Me, I'd jest as soon they came once a moon. Then I'd ne'er sheath m' blade in nothin' but a black Klemish soul."

With that, Jehred pulled open the door, squinting into the evening harbor fog that had grown outside. He turned to nod quickly at the boys, and instructed them to bar the door behind him. Then he turned and strode off into the gloom, a hand on the pommel of his ruined shortsword and his stagger disguised as a military swagger.

Darn sat for a moment, still transfixed by Jehred's story. Then he stood to bolt the door and help Loon tidy up. The tiny shack was quiet for a few moments — even Peg seemed too overwhelmed to voice an opinion. Then Loon brought his own ending to the tale.

"Lords o' Fire, ol' Loon like t' 'bout itched hisself t' death, afore all them bugs finally flew away." Loon began to scratch at his head, and Darn fought the urge to join him. " But lots more people got real sick from th' bug bites, and swelled up like some o' th' dead kine ya find layin' out in th' northern meadows in th' Spring."

Loon's voice hitched suddenly, and a fat, salty tear scattered the dust at the boy's feet. "Jehred's wife was one o' them that died … died o' th' bugs. Dhanna, her name was. She was real nice t' ol' Loon, an' she always made Jehred an' me laugh. She could make this funny little voice, an' make it sound like it come outta th' cubberd er honeypot er jest about anywheres — twas pow'rful funny. An' she cooked us sweetbreads an' cookies, an' she always saved th' first ones fer me, cause thems th' ones she sprinkled th' faerie dust in, ya know!" Loon rambled on for a candlemark or two, while Darn sat silently and listened and smiled. Darn was honored that his friend would share such cherished treasures, for Darn had few such memories himself.

Loon rubbed a wide palm across his face and knuckled at his eyes. "Jehred didna know that Dhanna was dead, till after most o' th' fightin' was over," Loon said. "He knew she was sick an' all, an' he had me tendin' over her most o' th' time, as all th' Healers was busy tendin' th' rich folks. But one mornin', she jest turned blue all th' sudden, an' then she stopped breathin'. I tried t' do somethin' Darn, I truly did!"

"I'm sure that ye did all there was, Loon," Darn answered, as he handed his blubbering friend an old dishrag. Loon blew his nose mightily on the rag, then handed it back to Darn — who discreetly tossed it in the fire.

"I had t' be th' one t' tell 'im, e'en though I didna want to! There I was, bein' a big bawl-baby, an' my brother Jehred jest stood there still as stone, starin' out crost th' harbor. He wouldna bother t' keep 'is shield up er none such. I couldna get 'im t' crouch down 'er leave, an' I was powerful afraid, cause there was bolts an' stones an' arrers still buzzin' 'round our heads."

"Then up walked yer Master Elias, an' I told him what'd happened. He tried t' talk t' Jehred, but my brother didna pay 'im no more mind than 'e did me. I 'member ol' Elias standin' there, all 'is clothes an' beard burnt off, lookin' like a big ol' prairie hen been turnin' over th' fire fer a few bells. Elias, he slapped my brother right crost th' face — slapped 'im a couple o' times. An' jest when Jehred fin'lly turned t' look at him, Elias' hand moved so quick I couldna see it, an' it stopped with a black-fletched Klemish arrer held 'bout a fingerspan from Jehred's throat.

"Jehred, he ne'er flinched er nothin. He jest started t' cry. An' I'll always 'member how 'e looked at Elias an' asked: 'Why? Why didntcha let me join 'er? Why not jest push me off now an' be done withit?' "

Loon turned to look at Darn, and a torrent of tears streamed down big fellow's face. "I ... I ne'er seen m' brother cry b'fore," he choked out, adding his own sobs to the story. "But that day, Jehred, he bawled a bucket load o' tears. An' I had t' hold 'im like *he* was th' looneybird an' *I* was th' captain o' th' watch."

Chapter Seven
Eillena

It was a stifling afternoon late in the month of the Dog Moon. Along the low foothills nestled at the base of the surrounding Rendrac peaks, shimmering waves of heat rippled upwards from the rocks and the trees murmured their discontent. The saw-toothed soldier grass which covered the open hills no longer stood at stiff attention, but bent in supplication under the harsh command of the sun. A lone harrier hawk drifted lazily on the rising air currents, but found no prey senseless enough to venture out in such heat. *Only humans would be so foolish,* it thought.

An exhausted band of acolytes slowly trudged from a small door set in the Pyre's west wall, following a well-worn trail that led up into the hills. Their bruised young bodies ached abominably from the grueling "game" which they'd endured under the tireless direction of Master Elias. The drill consisted of sprinting between two lines of fellow students, each of whom was allowed one kick or strike. The challenger of this gauntlet was not allowed to block or parry any of the blows, only to twist and duck in a running effort to evade them. Eventually, Elias told them, they would be able to dance the length of what he liked to call the "Aisle of the Intrepid" without receiving a scratch. But for now, the exercise only showed them how poor their defenses were against multiple assailants, as well as how many bruises it took to cover one's body completely. The attending acolytes, each of whom nursed at least a blackening eye, a swollen lip, or a side full of battered ribs, dismissed both the master's humor and his assurances. Elias offered the students a chance to focus their frustration and anger, as he ventured a stroll down the Aisle himself. The master's successful and effortless evasion of every strike as he glided past the length of students did little to ease their misery.

The acolytes walked in solemn procession until the trail passed into a small dense grove of goldenoak trees, and they were finally hidden from the harsh eye of the sun – as well as from any Adepts that might be watching from the wall. Once there, weary smiles stole over their faces, and quiet laughter escaped from a few. In turn, the students skipped down the steps of an ancient oak's roots, and stopped beside a quiet tranquil pool of water. The Acolytes quickly shed their short tunics and underclothes, then rushed to soak their battered bodies in the bone-chilling stream that flowed down from the mountains – the cold helped to ease even the worst bone bruises and other pains.

The shadows slowly crept longer as the acolytes splashed in the stream or lay quietly, dreaming of solace from their pains and trials. By two's and three's, several of them slipped off upstream or down, some to play, some to tend wounds, and some to tend to other physical needs. By the time the sun had dropped a handspan in its course, only Darn and a few others still remained in the pool.

Darn cracked an eye open, and checked the activity and attention of those who still shared the blessedly-cold water. Peder and Ghetta were obviously engrossed in each other, and even as Darn watched, the hulking Ghetta pulled his companion up onto the bank and off into the sheltering trees. M'clutha woke with a start and a snort as his nodding head dipped into the water like a fishing swordbill's; grinning foolishly, he too retired from the greenwood sanctuary. Only Darn and Eillena were left, sharing the grove's shadowed, liquid embrace.

"Eillena!" Darn called quietly across the pool, feeling a bit like an intruder as he breached the silent magic of the glade.

The young girl who lay half-submerged by the roots of a cascading willow slowly opened a swollen eye in answer, and raised a badly-bruised arm to pull a lock of raven hair from her face. She scowled briefly at Darn for disturbing her quiet rest, then lazily pulled herself along the pool's edge, closing the distance between them. Just as she neared, Darn felt a hand clamp tight around his ankle, and with barely enough time to grab a quick breath, he slid under the icy waters.

Eillena laughed as Darn broke the surface, floundering for purchase and blowing water from his nose. Her indigo eyes and ivory smile sparkled and shone from the smooth expanse of her tawny-brown face, all together marking her as a native of the Chak'ran Isles. As well, the knife-scar which crossed her stomach and the lash marks which graced one shoulder with their macabre lacery named her as one who'd seen a life beyond her years. Still, the mischievous grin reflected in her eyes bespoke an unbroken and delightful wickedness. Darn felt the evidence a moment later, when a slimy ball of mud and pool-grass hit him square in the face.

"Hai, Darn! Water sprite get'cha? Or deed ya think ye'd becoom a feesh, now?" She laughed again, and splashed a handful of water in the boy's face as he waded near and reached out for her. She kicked and squealed like any other girl of threehands of summers, and wriggled to the far edge of the pool.

"Oh, no ya don't now. Hands t' yerself, m'dear. I can't be t' blame if ya can't keep yer feet unnerneath, an' yer haid above water." She pulled herself up on a large slab of water-smoothed stone at the edge of the shaded pool and patted the spot beside her. Then she drew her knees up and clasped them tightly to her barely-budding breasts. "Come now. Come sit beside me an' tell me wha' twas worth th' trouble oof int'ruptin' m' rest."

Darn sputtered and spat a few quiet curses – mostly learned under Elias' tutelage – bemoaning the treachery of females, then slid up onto the rock beside his slim companion. He determinedly ignored Eillena's nakedness, and willed himself not to blush. Failing this, he turned to search for pebbles to toss in the pool, and spoke back over his shoulder to her.

"Recall ye my friend, Loon? That large and, ah, happy fellow? We three met at Amran the Confectioner's stand in the bazaar, a few day-turns past."

Eillena nodded, and began to absently work at the tangled knots in her hair.

"Well, he has insisted that I speak to thee, a-about this. Umm ... I wondered if perchance ye might enjoy traveling into town-proper for the celebration of Hearthstone's Folly tomorrow eve. It ... it is tradition in our country to invite a young lady to the festival, and I ... Arrrgh!"

Darn writhed in pain as burning lances of white-hot agony radiated out from his shoulder. He could feel Eillena's fingers dug into a nerve plexus buried there, as painful and unrelenting as iron pincers. He twisted to break her hold, then whirled to his feet in outrage, only to find her standing already before him with her hands bunched into tight fists by her side and her eyes nearly glowing with fury.

"*Young Lady!*" she spat, as if the words burned her tongue. "*Young ladies* wear satin an' silks! They smell of ambergris an' cloves, with pale powdered faces! None o' *them* e'er consented t' bein' buggered by some filthy ship's mate, jest so she could get unshackled from an oar. None o' *them* e'er fought rats an' mongrels an' other street cur fer moldy crusts o' bread, er picked maggots from rott'n redfruit afore eatin' it, I'll bet!" Eillena snarled in anger and her entire body trembled as she fought unsuccessfully for control. "*Young ladies* 'av someone t' bathe their littl' bottums an' powder their littl' butt'n noses fer 'em! Know ye this, Darn: I been a slave an' a thief an' a whore; an' one day I shall be a true warrior. But ne'er 'av I been a *young lady*, an' ne'er will I be!!"

The young girl closed her eyes and fought to control her rage. Her voice began to lose some of its edge, but still Darn was wary. He had come to know Eillena well over the past few moons – well enough to know that her tongue was as quick as her hands, as sharp as Master Era's swords, and could cut to the bone in an instant.

"We're well enough friends, Darn. But ya call me that damned name agin, an' I swear by Lord Flame I'll drag yer arse out t' th' practice sands an' prove I'm just as much a fighter as any ooth'r acolyte bound in this bedamned place!"

Darn stared at her dumbfounded for several heartbeats. He had no response ready after such an unexpected outburst. But Eillena cast the rough moment aside by wrinkling her nose at him, then slapping him good-naturedly on the calf as she sat back down. Confused, wounded by his companion's anger, and mad at himself for provoking it, Darn lowered himself to the cool, wet stone. He slowly rolled his response over his tongue, tasting the flavor of his apology, checking for any tang of bitterness before offering it up to his friend.

"Eillena ... Eillena, my friend," he stammered. "Please accept my most heartfelt regrets for this unintentional affront." But Eillena gave him no quarter, only stared back at him with those dark, indigo eyes.

"I .. I truly meant no slight, but was only speaking in a manner which I thought was proper. Old Makheim, my teacher of the White Lady's tongue, had so instructed me." Darn swallowed hard, and his courage nearly failed him. But it was too late to quit. "I had never considered that such a term meant different things to different people. So please believe me when I say again that I meant no harm or dishonor by it. On the contrary, I meant only to show my respect."

A sad smile spread its way across the girl's face, and she swept an unruly lock of hair from her face again. She nodded in acceptance, then sat quietly for a moment. Stones of silence once again began to build a wall between them, when suddenly Eillena turned and flicked a playful backhand strike at the tip of Darn's nose. In his hurry to parry the blow, Darn lost his seating, which in turn sent him on a slow and inexorable slide down the slick stone surface towards the frigid pool.

"Course now, a *warrior* woman, would most likely be pleased t' join ya fer th' festival." Eillena continued sweetly, even as she watched Darn's fruitless struggle to retreat from the chilling water's edge. "Couldna ask fer a more merry pair o' companions than yerself an' that fool Loon. Boot you'll 'av t' lairn t' speak like normal folk, so's naught t' 'mbarass oos!"

The pearls of her smile sparkled and splashed brightly across her dusky features, as she watched the stunned expression on Darn's face disappear beneath a widening circle of ripples.

Chapter Eight
Hearthstone's Folly

As it was in many lands, few events in Shiningrock touched both the rich and poor alike. The rich fought among themselves for power and prestige. The poor fought simply to survive. Midwinter found the wealthy merchants enjoying roasted marshfowl and other delicacies before a roaring fire. The beggars more often spent the night of celebration trying vainly to stave off starvation and the deadly cold. Midsummer's Eve found the nobled gentry vacationing along the cool sea coast, while the peasants toiled in the fields, trying to save their dying crops from the unrelenting sun.

But Hearthstone's Folly was a celebration that knew no boundaries of affluence or social station. For no one could fail to welcome the early embrace of Spring, to smile as the first gleams of golden sunlight stabbed down through the grey curtain of winter clouds.

Indeed, Hearthstone's Folly was the remembrance of life, after the loosening of Winter's deadly embrace. These Rites of Spring were a time for the young to celebrate their strength and vitality, and a time for the old to congratulate themselves on lasting through another miserable Eldorn winter. In the old traditions, it was the night for the farmers to lay with their wives on the hearthstone of their hovels, that their vitality might help to fertilize the crops. The "Folly" of it was that for many who consummated the Rites, an extra mouth to feed was harvested later that year, along with the hopefully abundant bounty of the fields.

Three young people dressed in green holiday tunics strolled

arm-in-arm through the narrow cobblestone streets, following the crowd as it surged towards the south side of the Bazaar — the traditional center of festivities for the common people of the city. A towering blond-haired fellow anchored one end of the threesome. A slender dark-eyed youth who moved with an unconscious feral grace bound the group on the other side. And between them, a budding young woman of shaded beauty laughed unguardedly for the first time in more years than she cared to remember. Such raw joy radiated from the three that no one who noticed them could help but smile and feel a bit awed, much as one would at the sight of an incomparably beautiful opal rose, or when standing at the feet of a magnificent colossus-spruce. More than a few celebrants felt a sharp prick of envy when they noticed the group, then suffered a drawn-out scratch of regret. But all who encountered the three found their steps just a bit livelier, their smile a bit wider, after they passed the small group and exchanged their greetings.

Eillena stepped briskly down the worn stone steps of the street and hugged the arms of both her companions. She had particular reason to be excited this evening, for she had never attended such a celebration in the company of friends before. Indeed, before Master Tobani had freed her from the slaver who'd held her bonds, Eillena had known no such pleasures as festivals, or even simple companionship. For her, there had only been thoughts of filling her starving belly, and of escape from the life of pain and humiliation that she had inherited. But today, she had friends by her side, coins in her purse, a place to call home, and the growing martial skills which brought her closer to her dream of becoming a warrior. With these most precious possessions wrapped tightly in her hands, there was room for little else other than joy within her. So she tossed any doubts or fears over her shoulder, and allowed herself to experience the true pleasure of living a simple, uncomplicated life — if indeed, being a Disciple of the Flames could be called a simple existence.

The three youths scrambled out of the dim alleyway – spilled might have been a better term, given their earlier efforts at inebriation – and splashed into the sea of dancing, drinking, celebrating people who filled the wide courtyard with their laughter and song. A drunken Kalthmus dwarf carried some grossly fat and besotted woman past on his shoulders — or at least that's what the trio guessed, gauging from the stout little legs that they could see. A misaligned band of musicians leapt into "What the Maidens Keep Doth Make Me Weep" somewhere across the fray. A score of unsteady voices joined in, adding their own off-key harmonies to the cacophony which echoed from the surrounding sandstone walls.

"Come," bellowed Loon above the din, "let us find a wandering ale keeper, an' lighten 'im of 'is load, b'fore th' rest o' these bungheads does it first! Loooooonn!" Without waiting for an answer from his companions, the hulking young man pushed out into the swirling mass of bodies, driving through them like a great bull, pausing a few times to snatch up some prostrate individual snoring in the mud and deposit them safely beside a wall or under a table. At last, Loon caught sight of the tall floppy brown hat of an ale keeper, floating above the crowd. In spite of their protests, Loon caught both Darn and Eillena up by the arms, and drug them directly through a section of the Mermaid's Fountain in order to follow the sign of imminent refreshment.

"I'll say one thin' fer 'im , Darn," Eillena said, as she grinned and pushed her soaking hair out of her eyes. "It surely don' pay t' argue with 'im, once 'is mind is set!" She waved her jack of ale to where Loon stood: their large friend held a pudgy ale keeper aloft and hollering, while he drank straight from the tap of the barrel strapped to the man's back. Darn joined Eillena in her laughter, and together the pair moved to rescue the rotund distributor of happiness from his leviathan captor, and to reward him for both his brew and his good humor.

The third member of their group in hand once again, the friends wound their way towards the nearest source of he music. A band of misshapen, intoxicated, would-be minstrels sat on empty ale kegs, sending their raucous tunes into the night air to color it with the bright explosions of their celebration. A one-handed piper blew upon a simple herder's flute and beat in time on the top of a keg with his stump, while a gaunt swaying seaman from distant Parthus plunked jauntily on a three-stringed lute and wailed an off-key version of "Three Men and a Bag O' Bones" to the appreciation of the surrounding crowd. A pair of young girls – twin sisters from the look of them – danced before the merry musicians and clashed tinny cymbals in counterpoint, their red-gold hair twisted with early wildflowers, and their white smocks already stained from a tumble in the mud. Several other ragged musical mercenaries squatted together, blowing on makeshift whistle-horns and taking turns beating a small skin-faced drum. By far though, the oddest member of the little troupe was a massive stone-troll, down from his home in the distant northern peaks: uncommon enough to be seen in the city, yet rarer still to be found in the actual company of humans. But the flinty-hided mountain dweller never seemed to notice the difference, as he pushed a drooping scarf up above one eye and slurped mightily from a huge flask of fire-dew before passing it on to one of his fellow band mates. He held the tempo by clapping his great scaled hands together with the sound of boulders crashing, and hooted a wordless refrain to the tune. Occasionally, the troll would lift up a huge curved horn that sat by his side and blow a mighty blast or two — whether as accompaniment to the music or simply to hear the thunder of it, one could never tell, and neither did it seem to matter.

Even Loon seemed a bit taken aback by the troll's presence, having never seen a stone-troll up close before, and certainly never one in such a good mood! But Loon's odd silence lasted only until the hulking creature turned and snatched the tankard of ale from Loon's hand, to then drain it of its contents and throw the empty container out over the crowd, even as he passed a smoking pipe of *shisha* back in return. Loon bellowed out his laughter and took a long draw of the sweet mind-melting smoke, his chest swelled to bursting as he passed the pipe to Eillena. As he blew out the smoke and the gentle vapors played through his mind, Loon stripped off his shirt and tossed it in the air, then leapt into the midst of the musicians, to stomp mightily in the mud and add his own hoots to that of his new-found friend.

And so a night of merriment began. Tears of laughter were shed, and sorrows were drowned. Many a dinner found its way to the cobblestones, and many a head would split to bursting the next day. But for this one evening, all that existed was the celebration of life itself.

175

***

"I'll look fer 'im up 'long Cooper's Street, in case 'e started back on 'is own!"

Eillena shouted to be heard over the late-night revelers, who seemed determined to make up in volume for what they'd lost in numbers. Darn nodded in answer, hesitant to use the voice he'd sung to rags during the evening. He pantomimed that he would check the last few ale keepers who remained on their feet, to see if Loon, their lost and thoroughly inebriated companion, might be following along behind one of the keg-toting dispensers of joy.

Darn paused for a moment to shake his head, then laughed at his own folly. *As if that would force the ale from my limbs, and blow this cloud of fog from between my ears!* He wended a twisted way through those who still fought to claim the night as their own, and stepped over those for whom the battle had proven too costly. He and Eillena had lost sight of their staggering friend shortly after the last bellstroke – the second of the new morning. Neither of the pair was particularly worried for their companion, though, for every person in this quadrant of the city was either blinded by drink, asleep, or otherwise busy by now. And drunken or sober, few would be of mind to harass Loon even if he walked alone, much less as he wandered along arm-in-arm with his new-found drinking companion, the Carpathian stone-troll, Phredairittat Öonder-Grom.

Eillena and Darn were both ready to return to the Pyre, for there would be no holiday for them on the morrow. At the first rays of the dawn, they would be roused from their holds to begin the day's regiment, hangovers and holidays be-damned. But still, as they had agreed upon earlier in the evening, it would be wisest to see Loon home first. Certainly, it would be terribly embarrassing to hear the next morning that their towering friend had fallen off into the harbor, or had passed out too close to the still-blazing bonfire and slept through his own cremation.

Darn searched out the last of the wandering ale keepers, and though each of them remembered Loon – some fondly, and some not so – none of them claimed to have laid eyes on him recently. So when the third bell echoed dimly across the sleeping city, Darn gave up his search in disgust. *The besotted, walking ale keg shall just have to look for himself.* Darn felt guilty for his thoughts, but then again, Loon had managed quite well for himself for many years without Darn's guidance. Still at odds with his conscience, Darn trotted across the Common to try to locate Eillena. He dodged a weaving line of thoroughly inebriated mountain dwarves who still danced the Dragon Trot, leapt over a huge bellydancer who snored peacefully on the cobbles, then headed west through the city.

Eillena wasn't in evidence anywhere along Cooper's Lane, nor did Darn find her among the monuments in the Square of Triumph which laid at the end of the street. He didn't think she'd leave for the Pyre without him — though knowing her temperament, the thought was not outside the realm of possibilities. Darn's own good cheer of the early evening had been quite worn away, dulled by the edges of a headache which already scraped at the base of his skull. Without a doubt, Eillena's mood would be deteriorating at a much greater rate than his own by now, so perhaps reconsideration of her route was in order. Darn ventured that, had Eillena decided to return without him, she would most likely have traveled by the shortest possible route and taken the narrow, twisting alleys which skirted between the artisan's quarter and the deserted ruins of the temple of Get. Never mind that those pathways were generally unlit and considered by many to be an excellent place to be accosted or worse: Eillena openly disdained such cautions, and did not hesitate to quickly school any uneducated city dwellers as to her newfound abilities to protect herself. Darn quickly plotted a course which he hoped would intercept hers, and dashed off in pursuit.

***

The warped and twisted spires of the temple of Get reached high into the starry sky, in supplication for a return of its deity. Gaped-mouthed gargoyles snarled down blindly from the temple's eves, stone sentinels eager to be free, hungry for heavy-pursed parishioners to terrify again. Once, the ornate towering structure had sat next to a bustling thoroughfare, its pews and prayer rooms filled to bursting with merchants and artists who wished the god's favor in their transactions, and its coffers overflowing with their offerings. But the god Get had been abandoned a generation before by followers who turned to more fashionable divinities. His priests had likewise long since departed for more profitable religious pursuits, leaving the empty sanctuary to collect only dust in the darkness. Since then, Get's temple was gifted only with those offerings which the birds and rodents brought.

Darn shuddered unconsciously as he rounded the corner of Painters' Way and found himself confronted by the decaying temple, unlit except for the starlight which glinted off of its slender towers and for the eldritch gleam of grave moss which hung tenaciously low on the walls. He paused for a moment, unsure of his directions. He remembered that the temple wall had tumbled down in one spot, making passage slow at best. He scanned the ground there with little hope, but took a moment to relax his sight and search for more eldritch trails. He was rewarded with a barely visible path of footprints outlined in faint golden light leading to the left.

The doorway of the temple gaped open like an old man's toothless maw. One of its gilded doors, long-since stripped of its adornments, hung precariously by a lone rusted hinge. The other door was missing entirely, and currently served as a table top for a family of starving mimes in the ramshackle tenements across the avenue. Darn barely spared the doorway or its stone guardians a glance as he hurried past, scanning the ground for further signs of passage. He was several steps beyond the entrance, already deciding on his choice at the next intersection, when a muffled sound drifted from the shadowed interior of the temple to tug at Darn's attention. He paused without knowing why. Then a twin of the noise he'd heard echoed from the doorway. It was the familiarity of the sound which had brought him to a halt: the wet thud of fist on flesh, and the muffled groan of a struck combatant. The frantic scrabbling of rats Darn would never have noticed, nor would the quiet rustlings of some human scavenger have caught his attention. But the distinctive sounds of human combat surrounded Darn every morning, noon, and evening at the Pyre, and they were as familiar to him now as the labor of his own breathing or the beating of his heart. Darn's feet led him back to the foot of the stairs, below the dark temple doorway.

Darn slipped silently into the building's black interior, the hackles of his neck rising and the soulfire in his *crucible* pulsing into crimson life. He crouched against the wall, straining to detect a noise or movement, anything to help him orient in the darkness. A muffled curse sounded faintly from the far left corner of the hall. After a moment, Darn could discern a thin flicker of candle light squeezing out through a crack, battling with the silver beams of moonlight that pierced the decrepit roof and dimly splattered the floors and walls. Darn felt his way across the room as quickly and quietly as possible. As he neared the source of the light, his shin knocked painfully against the remains of a shattered pew, and it clattered to the floor, the noise echoing throughout the hall. He froze, waiting to see what notice the din would raise. After a hand of heartbeats with no response, Darn scuttled across the remaining open floor to the closed door – for now he could see the frame outlined in the darkness – and leaned forward to peer through a crack into the room beyond.

A flurry of motion passed through the small slice of room that Darn could see. He briefly glimpsed a tangle of legs, and the violent flailing of an arm or two. The movement passed from his view, but left behind spatters of scarlet wetness on the floor. Darn reached for the edge of the door and began to slowly ease it open. He had widened the opening by perhaps a fingerspan, and was leaning forward to gain a better view, when his world flashed a brilliant, piercing white, and for a time, he knew no more than that.

Darn awoke lying on his back, choking on blood as it drained down his throat. A long bewildering moment passed before he recognized his surroundings. Then the exquisite pain of his broken nose flared like a flash of winter lightning, and he returned abruptly to his full senses. Yellow torchlight from the open doorway filtered scarlet through the blood that ran from his forehead. He reached up, and his questing fingers traced the ragged edges of a gaping wound on his brow.

Through the intervening veil of pain and blood, Darn barely noticed the hand which descended from somewhere above him, reaching for the front of his tunic. But his body needed no notice, no conscious thought, trained as it had been to answer any attack with immediate action. Almost outside of himself, Darn watched his left leg cock and deliver a snapping kick somewhere into the haze above and behind him. His assailant answered with a satisfying *"Oomph!!"* as the blow struck home, and Darn allowed the recoil from the kick to help him roll forward to his feet. A quick glance behind him showed Darn the murky silhouette of a man bent in half, hands to his gut. Darn took a half-step forward and spun smoothly. As the retching figure looked up, the heel of Darn's foot took him flush in the temple, leaving him stretched out atop a moldering pew, a less than diligent parishioner for an absent god.

"Very impressive," a silky voice responded, sounding both sweet and venomous at the same time. Darn whirled with one hand at guard, while the other hand wiped frantically to clear the blood from his eyes.

A young man leaned arrogantly against the door frame, stripped to the waist and outlined by torchlight from the room beyond. The fanciful half-mask he wore hid most of his features, though the four bloody claw marks which raked down across one cheek and onto his neck stood out blackly against his pale flesh.

Darn had only a moment to register the sight, before his gaze was drawn to the limp figure that hung silently in the crook of the man's right arm. A thick cowl of blue-black hair hung forward

181

to hide the face, and the body's boneless languor made Darn fear that he was too late. But the small breasts which peaked through the ragged remains of the girl's tunic moved slowly as she took a shuddering unconscious breath, showing that at least the poor wraith still held on to life. Darn felt the flames of his soulfire leap and dance, raging up his spine, demanding to be set free. For of all the tortures beset upon humanity by its own kind, Darn considered rape to be the cruelest and most despicable. His hands drew themselves into claws, and his frame seemed to vibrate like a wire in the wind, ready to snap at any moment.

"Release the girl," Darn growled, in a voice so deep and feral he failed to recognize it as his own. "Face me coward, and pay for the hurt you and your companion have wrought."

"Does she mean so much to you, boy, that you would sacrifice yourself to defend her honor? If indeed she possesses any, that is," the masked figure replied mockingly. "Besides, in the end, I shall take it all the same." The corner of his mouth twisted in a cruel parody of a smile, as he shifted his grip to his prisoner's hair in order to raise her face to the torchlight. The man's smile widened as he heard Darn gasp.

Eillena's left eye was swollen shut, the skin there bright and shiny, already darkening from flushed red to an angry violet. Blood dripped steadily from the end of her once-delicate nose, and a slick thread of crimson saliva stretched from the corner of her mouth to a growing puddle on the floor. But her neck showed the worst of her attacker's abuse: the collaring bruises where he'd choked her unconscious conjured images of a hangman's noose. Darn's stomach knotted briefly in nausea, and tears of anguish and fury helped to wash the blood from his eyes.

"Oh, don't be crying on me now, like a little snot-nose." Eillena's captor laughed. "She's not dead; just needed a little quieting. Twasn't the least bit understanding about the entire situation. After all, it is the holiday tradition." He looked down at her face almost tenderly, and brushed a strand of hair aside with his free hand.

"She's a lively one, I'll give her that," the man remarked. "Shame she won't be awake for the rest of the festivities, as I'm sure she'd be quite a ride!" He chuckled, an evil liquid sound that echoed from the walls of the temple, waves of malevolent intent. Then he relinquished his hold, and Eillena slumped to the floor like an abandoned puppet.

Darn howled his rage, a sound of hatred and anger so profound, so elemental, that all who heard it – from the half-starved artists massed in their derelict shanties outside the walls, to the grizzled old rat who held sway over all the temple's vermin – all of them trembled in their homes and nests as visions of primal hunters rose unbidden from their ancient pasts. Even Eillena's assailant took an unconscious step backward. And as reflections of the scream still bounded between the crumbling walls and roof, Darn launched himself forward, the soulfire within him burning away all vestiges of human control, leaving only a blood-hungry beast behind.

Darn's flying kick somehow missed its mark in the center of the masked man's chest, and as he sailed past he received a sharp swordstrike to the ribs for his efforts. The spark of pain was swallowed up by his raging soulfire though, and Darn spun to renew his attack the instant his feet touched the floor. Never in his young life had Darn moved with such inhuman speed and power: the reaping kick he sent whipping up and across would have broken the man's neck, had it landed; the spearhand strike he thrust towards the villain's heart would surely have penetrated flesh and bone alike – again, if it had landed. But Darn's opponent seemed able to evade the deadly attacks with ease, and indeed even began to laugh as he led Darn on a chase through the temple proper. In some small part of his mind, Darn realized that the howling soulfire which drove him with maniacal fury also cast aside control over the accuracy and timing of his attacks. But only the sight of black heart's blood gushing from his foe's torn and mangled body could quench the inferno that blazed up from his *crucible* and engulfed him body and soul.

Darn snapped out a stabbing front kick that he hoped would crush every internal organ in its path. Again, Eillena's masked assailant slipped aside and escaped unscathed — but his step brought him within reach of Darn's follow-up attack: a short, chopping elbow strike that smashed into the man's floating ribs with the deadly power of a hard-swung mace. Darn's mind flared in a brief flash of triumph as he felt the ribs begin to crack and bow inwards. Then a white-hot explosion of pain burst inside his head as his foe spun with the force of the blow and delivered his own elbow strike a fingers-width above Darn's right ear. Darn fought to hold onto consciousness, and was only barely aware of the next six or seven crushing blows that drove into his face, his back, the side of one knee.

The gibbering demon of soulfire that danced within him commanded that Darn remain awake, on his feet and fighting. And for a brief moment, Darn thought that he might be able to hold on to the reins of his consciousness. But then a final blow landed on the point of his chin: Darn's teeth snapped together and a sizable chunk of his tongue dropped onto the dusty floor. Darn was unaware of it all, though, for an deep ebony blanket had wrapped itself tight about him. And despite his feeble efforts to drive it off, the encroaching darkness smothered the flames of his soulfire and pulled him down to a place of no thoughts and no feelings.

***

The tolling of the great city bell battered repeatedly at the darkness which held Darn in thrall. Several times it crashed ineffectively. On the sixth stroke, though, the low clear *Gong!* cast aside the velvet curtain that shaded Darn's mind, and he awoke with a start. His eyes were glued shut at first, until he scrubbed the dried blood away. A dozen screaming voices echoed their displeasure when he tried to move, and his mouth seemed inhabited by some swollen pain-lanced slug that barely responded to his commands. But he shut the pain away as a quiet whimper drew his attention off to one side. There, huddled in the gloom, he could just make out Eillena's thin form. He tried to rise to his feet, but a snarl of pain from his wrenched knee forbade him to do so. Another quiet sob from Eillena's direction overruled any such protests, and Darn used his good leg to push his aching body across the chilled tiles to her side.

Darn draped his arm gently around his friend's shoulder, meaning to comfort her. But Eillena flinched away from his touch, leaving Darn to pull back the offending limb in confusion. Denied the ability to give physical comfort, Darn fell back to words: a poor second choice, but the only one left to him. His tongue refused to cooperate at first, and his attempts to force it to work brought a fresh flow of blood to his lips. He shut the pain behind the iron wall of his will though, closed off the agony that echoed his every movement. For he knew, without even examining her, that his friend's wounds were far deeper than his own.

"Oh, Eillena!" he mumbled, just barely understandable. "Eillena, I am so sorry to have failed you. I . . ." Tears of frustration stained his ruined tunic, softening the blood which was caked there. "If only I had arrived sooner, the pair of us could have fought them off. Oh my dear friend, please forgive me. Gladly would I take this burden from you, had I the means." A sob fought its way past Darn's clenched teeth, and added itself to the air of misery.

When her friend's words finally reached in to where she hid and shuddered deep inside, Eillena straightened and shook herself, trying to cast off the cowl of despair which clung about her, if only for a few moments. She raised her head, and silently they stared at each other. Then Darn gently, cautiously, pushed back the hair from her face. That single touch, full of love and compassion, broke her silence. She reached out to wipe a tear in turn from Darn's cheek, then slowly replied.

"Twas not yer fault, sweet boy. Ye did more fer me than any else would've done." She ran her hands over her face, wiping some of the tears and blood away, barely wincing at the pain. "Donna cry fer me. I've survived much roofer handlin' than whot I seen t'nite. No, what happened t'nite was m'own fault, no one else's. M' fault fer bein' born a woman!"

"I ... What?" Darn shook his head, hoping that the pain

would clear it and allow him some meager understanding of Eillena's words. Darn had expected curses, tears, outrage, even stony silence. But this self-crimination was beyond his comprehension.

"Tis m' curse in life, Darn: t' wear this body," she slapped her own chest - hard - and Darn knew better than to try to restrain her. "T' try an' contain such rage as ya could ne'er imagine." Darn just stood quietly, as Eillena began to explain, and growing anger filled her words.

"I'm tired o' bein' powerless, at survivin' only through th' grace o' those around me, er by th' whim o' some faceless, lice-ridden buggerer I've yet t' meet." Eillena shook fists at the sky as she spoke, and her wrath ripped her face into angry tatters. "Oh, mebbe I got t' scratch out 'n eye, er give a good kick 'n th' stones now 'n then. But most o' th' time, I ended up bein' knocked flat t' th' ground, an' mebbe takin' it up th' back hole fer not bein' more accomodatin' an' appreciative." Though she fought hard against it, her rage pushed hot scalding tears from her eyes.

"I bin prey t' such men b'fore. But I had thought ... had hoped ... had prayed that wi' th' trainin' th' Masters gifted me, I'd ne'er need t' surrender myself agin. I believed a lie: believed I finally had th' weapons t' protect m'self from th' takers o' th' world." She shook her head in futility, and the rage which buoyed her up died suddenly away, smothered by hopelessness. "But now, such illusions have fled me: been blown t' rags by the winds o' th' truth."

She held up a small fist – clenched it until her knuckles cracked. "Th' skills I thought would protect me seem now like a flawed sword, one that broke when I needed it most. As I knew it once b'fore, th' truth is most clear: those wi' th' gold er strongest arms makes th' rules. Th' rest oof us can only lay back 'n smile er grimace, as is our wont."

Self-loathing stretched Eillena's mouth into an ugly sneer, and sarcasm dripped from its down-turned corners. "Perhaps t'would be better t' find m'self a fat merchant er trader who 'as a taste fer scars an' a sharp tongue." She laughed at herself. "Aye, long as he's got gold 'n guardsmen enough t' keep th' rabble at bay, I'd be willin' t' carry his blubbery arse through th' seven veils oof heaven each an' every night. Spend m' days drifting away on sweet clouds oof *shisha* smoke, I could! An' then, though I'll certainly pay m' way as I ooluays 'av, at least it'd be *my* decision, *my* choice as t' who I lie with, an' what coin I get paid in!"

The humorless smile she wore fell away, but the void of expression it left behind was somehow even worse. "That, er I'll slit m' throat with a jagged edge oof stone, er bite through m' own wrists, if I must. But ne'er, *ne'er* again shall I suffer such robbery as I did here t'nite! Ne'er again."

Darn sat speechless, unsure of whether a reply was expected, or even desired. But though his better judgment may have said otherwise, he could not sit idly by and allow her to drown in her pain.

"Speak not of such foolishness, Eillena," Darn replied gruffly. "For one day we shall both be true warriors, Masters of the Sacred Flames. And none shall harm us then, no matter who they may be. We shall take vengeance for such barbaric acts as what passed here tonight!" Darn regretted his bold words almost instantly, as he watched Eillena cringe at the memory.

Eillena shook her head slowly, and the ghostly hint of a sad smile graced her wounded face.

"Aye, Darn, ye'll be a warrior one day; haps th' finest e'er t' be forged at th' Pyre! An' I daresay that you'd protect me, should I ask it. But I shall always be a woman. I shall always live in fear, fer ev'ry man I meet may be th' next one t' break an' bruise me. I will always be th' weaker one, th' smaller one, th' one holdin' th' dark treasure most men desire more 'n life itself. I canna' change these truths, any more than I can sprout wings an' fly."

Darn possessed no answer to his friend's argument. He felt empty and worthless, and still he knew that his feelings were but a pale shadow to those that gnawed hungrily at Eillena's soul.

"Come, sweet Ei," he said quietly, as he gently lifted her to her feet. "Let us back to the hold, that we may clean and poultice thy wounds. Afterwards, we shall speak to the Masters, and see which of them shall accept the pleasure of hunting down the carrion-eaters which did this."

Eillena suffered his help to stand, then gently but firmly pushed Darn's hands away. She pulled up the tattered rags of her tunic, and tried futilely to knot the remnants into some sort of cover for her bruised and bleeding body. Darn paused for a moment, then whisked his gore-smeared, emerald holiday tunic over his head and handed it to her. He shook off her half-hearted refusals and willed himself to ignore the early-morning chill. A small but visible wave of relief washed over the girl as she covered herself. And the tiny grin which spread across her face, as she looked at Darn standing in his loincloth, may have eased both their burdens by the smallest measure.

"No, Darn," Eillena replied quietly. "No, an' no agin. I'll not be goin' back t' th' Pyre. I can see that m' time there has ended."

189

Darn began to stutter a protest, but she cut him off quickly and continued on.

"An' no-one will hunt down m' late-night playmates, fer they were our own. I saw a pair o' flames branded on th' one I marked, an' both of 'em moved like Flame Dancers." She hurried on, despite Darn's confused stare. "Dontcha think fer a heartbeat that I let sum street mongrels treat me so. No, such rabble as that would've given me no more than a bit o' enjoyable practice. I've sent more'n a hand o' their kind runnin' wi' their tails tucked, an' e'en left a pair er two t' feed th' fish."

Darn sat in stunned silence, more bewildered at his own lack of awareness, than at the thought that one of the Order would do such an atrocious thing. A sudden insight struck him.

"They must have been *slag*, those who break under forging and are discarded," he offered. "For surely none of our own would do such a thing."

The small measure of patience Eillena had possessed was exhausted, and anger brought a matching flush to her blood-spattered cheeks.

"Ye don' *still* believe all that they babbled o' honor an' justice?" she shouted. "Pah!! They're men, an' like most o' their kind, whate'er suits 'em best must be th' Gods' very own law." She paced as she spoke, running a bloodied hand unnoticed through her dark hair. She whirled suddenly and pinned Darn with a withering glare. "Do ya really think most o' th' masters care a copper if some wench is forced t' spread 'er legs fer one o' their own? Hah! Natural order o' things, they'd say! Fine an' good, they'd say." She spat on the floor in disgust.

Darn's mind whirled in confusion. For years he had greedily taken in all that he had been taught of the Order, and its obligation to protect the common people. He had been taught that, should he prove worthy enough, he would be forged into a hero, a righter of wrongs, someone to prevent abhorrent acts such as had been thrust upon his friend, a judge to ensure that evil was not left unpunished. To think that one of the Order would – with the knowledge or unspoken consent of the Masters – willingly bestow such pain and anguish on an innocent! It challenged the very fabric of Darn's belief.

"B-but who?" he asked half-heartedly.

"Ya fool!" Eillena screamed in frustration. " 'Av th' Masters stolen yer ears an' eyes, as well as yer mind!" she shouted. "Oo did yer *ears* tell ya it was, Darn? Oo brays when 'e laughs like a bundhar with tailrot? An' whot did yer *eyes* tell ya when ya saw that twisted ring-finger, an' th' lash-scars crost 'is shins an' arms? An' th' other one: oo else do ya know has got teeth as sorry-lookin as wharf boards, an' always smells like pickled lumpfish? Huh? Answer me that!"

Darn stood quietly, unable to deny the names to which her questioning had led him.

"Arak and Cheykar," he answered slowly.

"That's right!" Eillena pounced on his reply like a famished miercat on a rock-coney. "Arak an' Cheykar, Adepts in Agni's Holy Service. Cheykar's a fool, an' probably wouldn't have dared it on 'is own. But Arak," she spat the name out like poison, "our acclaimed senior-most student, oo most o' th' masters adore an' suggest that we should try t' follow." She shook her head once, quickly, as if to banish the name from her mind. When she spoke again, hatred twisted among her words like a viper.

"'That bastard an' 'is kind are a disease on th' face o' th' world. An' though I *might* not kill 'im fer wot 'e done t' me, I'd sure as hell geld 'im. Make sure 'e ne'er produced any more o' his kind. Take th' backbone outta that pathetic worm o' 'is!" Eillena snickered, and the unshakable fighter and former slave that Darn knew so well peeked out again for a moment. "'E's got a right little one, ya know — I tried t' take it off fer 'im at one point, but missed m' chance." She paused to gather her breath, and her hands, rigid as claws, ripped at unseen anatomies without her apparent notice. "Aye," she continued, "an' mebbe I'd cut out 'is tongue, so it couldna spread no more poison than it already 's done. An' while I was at it, I'd whack off 'is hands at th' wrist, since he ne'er seemed able t' keep 'em t'isself!"

Eillena looked over at Darn, and a fleeting smile graced her bleeding lips. "After all that, I'd let 'im live, so's 'e could appreciate th' error offis ways, an' hear th' screams o' them what looked at him. Ai," she smiled even wider, and a fresh trickle of blood threaded its way unnoticed down over the curve of her chin, "that jest moit begin t' ev'n things out tween us."

She dropped her eyes, and absently wiped the fresh blood from her mouth. Then she looked down at her scarlet-painted palm, and what little life had surged inside her seemed to drain out before Darn's eyes. "Course, ain't noon offit gonna come bout, cause I'm gonna be onna merchant ship outta this bedamned city b'fore th' noon bell. Old Samil will give me passage: he owes me since I saved 'is youngest boy's arse inna street brawl last Harper's Day. An' wi' whot littl' luck I got, an' th' Lady's grace, I'll ne'er lay eyes on this place agin." She seemed to collapse in upon herself then, and she turned to walk out of the tiny room into the empty corpse of the temple.

Darn limped as fast as his injured leg would allow. Eillena seemed to take no notice of his discomfort. She strode the length of the temple hall to the gaping doorway, where the milk of dawn light had begun to slip in thick streamers through the waning night sky.

At last Eillena heeded Darn's calls, and she stopped at the top of the steps that led down to the muddy cobbled street. The sight of Darn's face, screwed up from the pain that ate at his leg, brought Eillena back from the lashing storm that swirled within her. Her throat swelled as she took a good look at her friend, he who had risked his own life to protect her. Darn was almost unrecognizable behind the patina of dry crusty brown that covered his face and clotted in his once-blond hair.

Eillena noticed a sour, rancid flavor in her mouth — recognized it a moment later as the taste of shame. She reached out to steady her limping friend, then stepped close in order to wrap her arms about him.

"Do not leave, Ei," Darn pleaded quietly into her hair. "I will speak to the Masters myself. I will swear on the Flames of Honor and Justice as to Arak and Cheykar's guilt. Together, we will see them justly punished. I swear it; on my very soul I swear it." A sob hitched his chest, and he returned Eillena's hug desperately.

"No, m' dear friend," she said quietly, as she stroked the young boy's hair. "I must leave this place now, at my own choosin' an' unner m' own power. Fer whot little pride still remains t' me must last a lifetime. An' t' stand b'fore th' Masters' Council an' admit my defeat; t' be told that 'twas m' own fault, due t' m' own weaknesses ... I fear twould cause m' heart t' break wi' shame." Eillena loosened her hold and took a step back, dropped her eyes when she found herself unable to hold Darn's gaze. "Fer now, m' path must take me away from here. Haps the Gods deem we shall see each other agin one day. I sorely wish that 'twill be so, for ya've been a great friend t' me, Darn."

Darn's heart bled in pain and sorrow, staining his soul the same color as his face and hands. He read the truth in Eillena's words, knew that to stay in this place would surely break her courage — all she had left to hold her life around her. Without sparing time to think, Darn stumbled forward, crossing the cold space between them, to take Eillena's battered face in his hands and kiss her softly and slowly on the lips. She stiffened at first, and Darn began to pull away. But Eillena grabbed his arms firmly, and returned his kiss with a fierce passion. Then, as suddenly as it was born, the moment ended.

"Quite a good-bye, tha' twas," Eillena remarked, wearing a hint of the spry grin Darn remembered so well. "When I see ya agin, m' friend, ye shall be th' foinest warrior t' walk th' length 'n breadth o' th' world. An' I...I shall be somethin' more than I am." She bowed quickly, a final salute of equals. Then she turned and walked down the stairs, headed left, down towards the harbor. And with her, perched on her shoulder like some carrion bird, was the thought that despite her brave words, never again would she lay eyes on this boy who had captured her battered soul with a single kiss.

Darn stood still for several long moments after she passed from sight. A empty chasm opened in his heart, whistling with the raw biting winds of loss, and Darn feared to peer into its depths. Darn could feel hatred forming a fragile bridge over the rift in his soul: hatred for those who had hurt his friend so, and in part, hatred for himself and his inability to protect her. And though he knew the bridge was a perilous path, it was his only passage to the other side — where vengeance lay.

Chapter Nine
Test of Honor

The Masters' council chamber was surprisingly bleak and unadorned, its walls carved from the very bedrock beneath the Pyre. Unlike the vast Hall of Audience, the scarred walls of the Forge, or even the communal dining hall, here there were no tapestries or paintings of famous battles on the walls, no bas-relief carvings of ill-clad nymphs and rampant satyrs. The only embellishment to the room was a deep, stylized carving of the three Sacred Flames, cut into a lustrous plaque of dark bloodwood which hung behind the Grandmaster's chair. The chamber was a silent insistence of the paragon that when all else was stripped away, only these three ideals remained: Justice, Battle, and Honor.

A long curved table encircled half the room, and behind it sat every ranking Flame Master in residence at the Pyre. They stared, silent and grim, at the two students standing at the room's center: one clothed in the plain white tunic of an acolyte, the other wearing the scarlet sash of an adept. Behind the pair stood Masters Rekki and Chaka – two of the youngest ever to attain their robes, but already renown for their fighting prowess – who watched silent and alert, poised to prevent any unsanctioned violence within the room.

A great finger of stone, gnarled and twisted with age, grew from the floor in the center of the chamber. The Stone of Accusation, it was called. Here it was that the assembled leaders of Agni's Disciples met to discuss matters of great importance, as they had for centuries. And it was here, in the shadow of the great stone, that the Masters brought those who would bear their judgment.

Grandmaster Saura sat at the center of the table, his eyes closed in silent meditation. He released one more breath, long and slow, savoring the quiet before the impending storm. Then the wizened old man opened his eyes. He glanced left and right, as if to assure himself that none were missing. Then he nodded slightly to Master Tobani who sat at his left. The Headmaster of Training rose swiftly to his feet, and even the simple movement betrayed the fire and fury that simmered just below the surface of his scarred yellow skin. Clad in flaming crimson and turning in solemn silence, he seemed to Darn like one of the great scarlet spoonbills which fed at the edges of the southern marshes; Darn bit at his lip to keep a grin from his face, as his mind conjured a picture of Master Tobani, perched on one leg with a grasscrab in his mouth. Then the vision dissolved and was replaced by Eillena's battered and bleeding face. Darn cringed at the sudden sight, collecting Tobani's immediate and glowering attention, and all other thoughts fled before the master's fierce glare.

"An accusation has been made against one of our Order – a very serious accusation," Master Tobani intoned deeply. "His accuser is also of our ranks, and the charge involves yet a third Child of Agni, one who has taken her life by her own hand." Cold fire blazed behind the folds of the master's eyes, reminding Darn that Eillena had been Tobani's chosen pupil.

"Eillena 'Sharphands', a promising acolyte student of the Order, was attacked and taken against her will sometime on the eve of Hearthstone's Folly. On the following morning, by the account of Acolyte Darn here, she threw herself from the top of the Harbor Wall in despair." Tobani closed his eyes, and the muscles of his clenched jaw trembled as he fought to contain his pain and rage. His eyes snapped open, and he glared murderously at the senior student beside Darn. "The very fact that she was subdued at all says much of her attackers, given her well-known abilities," he said fiercely, making no effort to hide the accusation in his voice.

"Thou may not judge, honorable Master," Grandmaster Saura said quietly from his seat. "Bring forth only the charges; the Flame of Justice will bear the burden of judgment."

Tobani grew stone-faced once more, and lifted his eyes to stare straight ahead, too mistrustful of his own emotions to look at the two students before him.

"Acolyte Darn of Warden Woods, has lodged an accusation against this Adept, Arak mel'Ulbreth, charging him with Acolyte Eillena's attack and violation. The accusation includes a second adept, named Cheykar, who has since fled from our midst. Cheykar has been declared *slag*, and his life is forfeit regardless of the outcome of these proceedings."

Each of the assembled masters nodded or muttered an agreement: no excuse was accepted for violating the bond of the Order, and no punishment but death allowed for those who so transgressed.

Tobani continued: "As the Flame of Justice must ever shine through the ill mists of deceit, this matter has been brought before this Council, to discover which of the pair speaks falsely."

Master Tobani made a sound of disgust, and waved an errant hand in Arak's direction.

"You will speak first, being the senior most of the two," the master said grimly. "And watch your tongue closely, mel'Ulbreth, for this Council, and myself in particular, will suffer none of your pandering lies or disrespect!"

"Tobani!" Grandmaster Saura hissed in annoyance. "Look to thine own tongue, for naught has yet been proven. And till such time has arrived, we *will* abide by the strictures laid down by those before us!"

Master Tobani suffered to bite back the remaining words which hung upon his lips, and sat back heavily into his chair. Otherwise, the stoic Bandaran master ignored his lord's displeasure, and continued to glower at Arak with a palpable searing fury.

The hawk-faced senior student adjusted the knot of his sash, seeming in ignorance of the heated words tossed about him. The sly smile hidden in the corners of his mouth said otherwise. Arak looked up after several moments' silence and took a sudden deep breath.

"I demand satisfaction in the defense of my honor!" Arak shouted in defiance to the assembled masters. "This insolent 'Spark' charges me with foul deeds that shame myself and our Order. He has no proof ..." Arak's words faltered for a moment, and Master Tobani leaned forward eagerly.

"... no grounds for such an accusation," the Camdian student continued. "I say he lies!" Arak's face flushed scarlet, as if with rage. But to many, it appeared as a familiar mask, carefully fashioned and well-worn.

Grandmaster Saura uttered a soft low sigh, as if grief and dismay leaked slowly from him. The scene before him had been enacted several times, always with the same conclusion. Arak, the accused senior student, had been father to a hoard of bastard conflicts since his inception: vicious beatings, several brutal rapes, and possibly even a murder. But Arak was as cunning as he was wicked, and he ensured that there were no witnesses to his crimes — or at least none willing to speak against him. Unfortunately, Arak had also developed into an gifted and skilled warrior, and as such, many of the masters argued, he was far more valuable to the Order and to the city than was the welfare or questionable virtue of a few commoners.

Saura found such arguments a bile-covered mush of politics and class hatred. But, as were the many grandmasters before him, Saura was bound by the traditional rules and strictures of his Order. He offered no interference in these matters, though the twin daggers of his wisdom and insight easily pierced the screen of deceit which Arak hid behind.

"Acolyte Darn!" Master Saura commanded, bringing the attention of all to the slight white-robed figure who stood silently by the Stone of Accusation. "Before this council, do you swear by the Holy Flame of Justice that this senior disciple, Arak mel'Ulbreth, is the person who attacked your fellow acolyte, Eillena? And that she also identified Arak as her assailant before she leapt to her death?"

Darn gathered all the courage he possessed. He pictured Eillena's face as he'd seen her three nights before, beaten and bleeding, lying in the trash-strewn ruins of the temple of Get. And he remembered the face he'd glimpsed during the struggle with her attacker: the black half-mask, with four deep gashes leading down across one cheek and onto the neck, courtesy of Eillena's clawing strike. Darn glanced to where Arak stood, noting both the sure and arrogant smile on the senior's face, and the scabbed furrows that started abruptly in the middle of his cheek and wound their way downward. Darn's resolved hardened to bedrock as he turned back to the council.

"By my honor, and by my faith in the Three Sacred Flames, I charge that it was he," Darn answered in a small but firm voice. "Eillena claimed it also. But … but her shame was more than she could bear, so I will speak on her behalf."

Arak flicked a serpent's glance about the council room, face wavering in the glow from the torches that lit the barren hall. He glared balefully at Darn for a long moment. Then, almost laughing, Arak turned his face upward and crowed to the dark unseen rafters of stone above, a triumphant sneer already spreading across his face.

"By the Flaming Eye of Lord Agni, then, I invoke the Circle of Judgment!" he declared boastfully. In the flickering light he drew his lips up into a gargoyle's smile, a smile that hid row upon row of sharp hungry teeth.

Darn's heart seemed to falter in its steady beating, and he willed himself to hold steady and not betray his fear. Master Elias had warned him that his charge against Arak might very well lead him to this place, and so it had. The Flame of Justice charged that any who would accuse must also be willing to adjudicate and administer punishment. It ensured that those who would gain their robes not only possess the physical skills necessary to commence holy Battle, but also the conviction to use those skills in the service of Justice.

A dark pall of silence draped over the room, seeming to dim the light of the torches as they guttered and smoked in their sconces. Saura turned a weary eye towards the young initiate, who stood quiet and pale-faced.

"What answer do you make, Acolyte Darn? Will you meet Arak in the Circle of Judgment to administer the penalties you deem appropriate?" The brass of the master's voice softened, warmed by the heat of his sympathy for the young boy's plight. "Or will you admit to a lack of evidence, or name it a simple mistake, withdrawing your accusation? In matters such as these, where there is no other proof to substantiate your charges, we must rely upon you to shoulder the burden of both judge and jury." Saura paused, giving his words time to settle over the young student, who visibly trembled beneath the weight of his decision. "Rush not, Acolyte, but examine this decision well." Several of the other masters seated in the council chamber murmured their agreement, then silence closed its cavernous maw over the room once more.

Darn stood silently, lost in thought as his dignity and sense of justice wrestled with his fear, fighting to take control of his destiny. He gnawed his lip nervously and glanced to where Elias sat, stone-faced and resolute, stationed at Saura's right as befitted the Warmark of the Order. One corner of Elias' mouth danced upward briefly and his left eye seemed to twitch; for all else, the master seemed carved from the same dark wood as his chair.

The feeling of the worn stone floor beneath his feet offered Darn an anchor, a sanctuary in the maelstrom that surrounded him. Self-doubt buffeted him again and again, filled with a hail of fear, and strengthened by the oft heard whispers that no one intervened in a Judgment match. But in the eye of that storm, Darn glimpsed the unwavering gleam of a pure transcendental fire: the Flame of Justice. It called to him by name and demanded his loyalty.

The silence that covered the chamber was shattered, as Darn's indecision crumbled into rubble. He clasped his hands together behind his back to hide their trembling, but his voice rang clear and true, like the striking of a smooth silver bell.

"I will judge, Grandmaster Saura," Darn replied steadily, "and prove the lie of Arak's words. For Justice must be championed, as we were taught. And I would reclaim the Honor of my friend and sister, Eillena."

Grandmaster Saura's eyes widened in astonishment, while Elias' gleamed with a slick shiny pride, and Tobani's nearly shouted with righteous fury. But Arak's eyes narrowed, a volatile mixture of hatred, uncertainty, and dark putrid glee roiling inside them, refuting in part the cocky smile that snaked its way across his face.

The surprised muttering of the assembled masters washed over the room, a tide which left Darn unmoved, but soaked to his core.

"Foolish Spark, no sense about him . . ."

". . . understand the consequences?"

"He has the stones of Tyrin, he does!!"

". . . surely, Elias will forbid . . ."

"Enough!" Grandmaster Saura's voice was a sharp whipcrack, cutting through the din. He directed his smoldering gaze back to the young acolyte, and Darn fought to hold the old man's stare. "Tis a serious decision ye have made young one, one which may not be rescinded. However, I applaud your courage and conviction, if not your wisdom."

He raised his voice once again, unwavering, the strength of it as evident as that of the stone walls around them. "Hear me and hold witness, thou who serve the Sacred Flames. Three Weaversdays hence is the night of the Hidden Moon. At the first bell of the morn, these two before us shall meet in the Circle of Judgment, there to prove the guilt of one or the other, and exact payment for his crime. I, Saura, servant of Holy Lord Agni and bearer of His Laws, sanctify this trial. May the Flame of Justice burn to ash the bones of he who is found lacking!"

***

Darn lay on the thin cotton pallet that served as his bed, allowing the cold radiating from the stone floor beneath it to quiet the moans of pain his body uttered incessantly. Today, which Elias had claimed was his last day of physical training, had been spent in the Hall of Unseen Foes. There, Darn's feet had been locked in shackles, and he was left facing a wall that was pierced by countless small round holes. By some unseen mechanism, knuckle-size lead balls began to shoot from the holes, singly at first, then by two's and three's, and even more by late afternoon. The first few shots slammed into the young boy with sickening thuds, raising cruel painful knots all over his body. But gradually, Darn began to adjust to the unheard rhythm of the missiles, dancing in place, bobbing and weaving, twisting, turning, ducking his head to avoid the kiss of one shot, then dropping to the other side to elude the following pair. By mid afternoon Darn almost began to resent the rests he received at each bellstroke, preferring instead to again challenge the flying metal shot, to taunt the unseen operator of the wall and deny him the satisfaction of causing Darn further pain. The young boy flickered and wavered like a living flame, anchored to the floor but impossible to grasp or strike.

At the stroke of the fourth bell, Elias halted the training

and released the boy from his bonds. The guarded half-smile on the master's face bespoke the pride and satisfaction to which he would never admit. But Darn glimpsed enough to know that it was the same smile Elias wore when his favorite bundhar won at the races; the thought filled Darn with an uneasy mixture of pride and trepidation.

After Grandmaster Saura's declaration in the council chamber three dayturns before, Darn had been excused from his normal training and duties and given over to the constant tutelage of Master Elias. From the first light of dawn, till the stars glimmered and danced in the sky, Darn's mentor drove him through drill after drill: leaping over a hard-swung staff, practicing rolls and breakfalls among the rocks of the foothills, fighting atop a narrow wooden beam, bearing the unmerciful blows of the body hardening drills, running through knee-deep water for endurance. The young acolyte kicked at swinging targets and punched at butterflies to sharpen his timing; he drove full-power strikes into the wooden dummy and the hanging sandbags to increase his power. And always, Elias was there: pushing, driving, taunting Darn with curses and laughter until the boy's rage took control of his limbs and pushed him beyond the normal barriers of pain and self-doubt. At times, the rage grew so great that Darn wished to kill the bearded master who capered and danced just out of reach – indeed, would have gladly killed the man, had Darn been able to land more than a glancing blow. Instead, the young acolyte drove himself until he collapsed in an exhausted heap with tears of rage and frustration coursing down his face, while Elias calmly pointed out the boy's mistakes and criticized his techniques.

Alone at last in his own chamber, with the voices of his recent injuries fading to a monotonous drone, Darn was able to push aside the curtain of anger that had been his constant companion for the past dayturns. For the first time, he began to truly understand the sanity hidden within Elias' maddening routines and tests, and recognize the incredible improvements such lessons had brought to his speed and reflexes. Darn allowed his awareness to settle into his *crucible*, just below his navel: there, he could feel the pilot light of his soulfire burning slow and steady, waiting for Darn to feed it and send it bursting upward in a blazing fury. The raw power that the young boy felt simmering beneath his skin was intoxicating, addictive, begging the chance to gift him with its bounty. It also terrified him: a jeering, unpredictable, beserking demon that threatened to take control of Darn's body and soul and use them for its own destructive purpose.

It had been nearly five winters since he'd passed through the doors of the Pyre on a forbidding and storm-tossed night. But for the first time, Darn felt a sudden fear as he examined the changes that had been wrought within him. Then he shook has head, and tried to banish such foolish worries.

Enough to fear on the morrow, he thought. *Best I worry at that which may kill me on the sands, for I know well enough that may be the ending of it. I shall worry for my soul later, if I still possess one after this contest.*

Somehow comforted by the thought, Darn worried the straw of his pallet into a slightly less uncomfortable lump, and allowed an exhausted and dreamless slumber to bear him away.

***

Elias watched in grim satisfaction as the two combatants stretched and loosened their limbs, one boy lost deep within himself seeking Agni's guidance, the other preening and showing off for the crowd of students that filled the three balconies circling high above the floor of the hall. Even from where he sat on the masters' dais, Elias could see the nervous tremors that shook Darn's frame. He approved of the boy's fear: it would provide fuel for his soulfire to feed on, keep it burning high until the actual battle began. The boy had good reason to be anxious: the only other two students to face Arak in the Circle of Justice – both experienced Adepts – had been left hopeless cripples, and one had taken his own life afterwards in despair.

As mentor to them both, Elias knew that the two boys were decidedly mismatched. The older boy's skills were still far in advance of Darn's, despite the recent training. Arak had additional advantages of height, weight, reach, strength and experience.

But Darn had speed that few could match — Arak included. He also had a quick, calculating mind that spun out complicated strategies and subtle feints that fooled even Elias at times. In his mind's eye, Elias could see the courage and resolution that pulsed within Darn's heart. And in recent weeks, Elias had been witness to the consuming soulfire that raged within the boy, feeding on his anger and hatred and hunger for revenge. It was a glimmer of that same soulfire which had called to Elias years earlier, caused him to enter a dirty alley and rescue a scrawny dockherd's son from a band of street cur. Above all else, Elias lived to serve that Fire, that all-consuming elemental human fury. He was addicted to it, he freely admitted: addicted to the god-like power that filled his limbs when he abandoned himself to the will of his soulfire. It was the embodiment of his god, his credo, and it bound him to Darn more strongly than such effete feelings as loyalty or pity ever could. The boy's fire called to his own, and he could do naught else but answer to it.

If Darn fell in the Circle, it would be a tragic waste of talent. *Also a waste of my time and gold,* Elias thought as he frowned. But it was this battle which would temper the young boy's mettle; temper it, or reduce him to a worthless pile of slag, that is. *Gorrah's hell!* Elias cursed. He'd even miss the innocent little fool: he, Elias, who'd forsworn all but his own needs and desires. He'd never had a son of his own; the one wife he'd taken had tired of his lecherous pandering and sailed off with an Etruscan rug merchant before any issue had come of their rickety marriage. Elias had thought often of what his own son would have been like, of the things he could have taught him. And now, this boy Darn ...

Enough of this snot-nosed drivel! Elias berated himself, shaking loose the troublesome thoughts that made him so uncomfortable. *To the issue at hand!* Elias hadn't spent the last three dayturns doting on the boy, teaching and luring and driving him into a fire-spun fury, simply to sit here and watch the overmatched acolyte be beaten into a broken bleeding pile on the sand. Darn had much to teach the chattering hall of students and the bored assemblage of masters about the strength of the will, the true strength of the soulfire, Elias believed. Besides, the master had a full hand of gold solari wagered at 20 to 1 odds on the boy, and if nothing else, Elias *hated* to lose.

***

The muscles and tendons hummed within his arms and legs

like the bowstrings of a legion of archers, waiting word to let fly. Darn forced his breath deep into his diaphragm, then quickly emptied it to fill it again. He thought of each breath as fuel to the soulfire burning fiercely now within his crucible, and he willed the flames to course out through his limbs, riding the beat of his quickening pulse. He tried to ignore Arak's leering grin as they faced each other, and instead focused on Master K'tarr's instructions.

"Any opponent who will submit may not be slain, though punishment may be dealt out as the victor sees fit," K'tarr intoned solemnly. "Without a word of submission though, this battle will end in death for one of you." No other rules were given; nothing would be held back in this duel.

The two combatants each assumed a fighting stance, the back of their outstretched hands touching. At this distance, the first flurry of attack could easily end the match in the space of a single breath – and often did. As Elias had instructed him, Darn relaxed his focus and allowed his vision to expand; otherwise, he'd focus solely on his opponent's hands, or feet, or eyes, and miss an attack coming in from a different direction. So Darn ignored the barely audible threats which Arak whispered and spat, ignored the senior as he rapped his knuckles against Darn's hand, deafened himself to the mutterings and the occasional dark chuckle of those gathered to witness this honor-test.

The sharp crack of the signal blocks sliced through the din of the chamber, and severed the bonds which restrained the two combatants. Arak's lead foot lashed out towards Darn's knee, seeking to end the bout instantly with a crippling blow. But Darn leapt above the path of the attack, sensing the movement even as it began, and he slashed out with one hand towards Arak's eyes. The senior student never faltered even as he took the blow, and he whirled, ready for a second thrust. But Darn had already skipped back out of range and stood poised and ready. Arak wiped at the corner of his eye, then looked at his hand in hooded disbelief: a shallow gash wept blood where Darn's nails had parted his skin like so many blades.

Arak looked across the circle at his young opponent, and a viperous grin slowly twisted its way across his dusky face.

"First blood, eh Spark?" Arak mocked. He laughed as he licked the stain from his fingers. "Enjoy yourself now, stripling," he said, "for this is but a taste of the blood to be spilt, ere I leave this Circle." Arak laughed again now, a barking sound of contempt and ridicule, and he strode across the sand, hands held arrogantly at his sides. He walked calmly to within two strides of where Darn stood waiting. Then, with near inhuman agility, the Adept was in the air, spinning, twisting, cleaving downwards with an axe kick, his face holding the same lethal intent as an executioner's.

Darn danced to the side of the kick and felt only the sudden breath of its passing. He tried to counter with a kick of his own, but too quickly another strike whistled towards him, leaving him only time to flicker away once again. He dodged in one direction then another, wove and spun and ducked and danced, avoiding as best he could the hail of feet and fists that Arak rained down upon him, blocking what he could not avoid, and rolling with those blows that slipped by his blocks. Arak afforded Darn no time to rest, no time to counter; only time to flee and bear the scorn of his taunting laughter. Three times Darn circled the ring, running before Arak's fury. Echoes of laughter began to patter down from the balconies in the darkness above like harsh stinging rain, bringing a flush of shame to Darn's cheeks. Many of the masters muttered among themselves, and even Grandmaster Saura shook his grey head grimly. Only Elias watched the conflict and smiled, a knowing and calculating look on his face that confounded any who chanced to glance his way.

Eventually, as he knew he would, Darn missed a crucial block and his eyes screwed shut in anticipation of the impending impact. He tried to let his body roll and absorb some of the shock as the hard heel of Arak's right foot slammed into his temple. Still, he was stunned, and the spinning sweep that followed dropped him boy onto the sand.

Arak paused in his attack long enough to raise his arms and bare his teeth up towards the watching crowd of students. He shook the sweat from his body like an angry mongrel then leapt upwards, howling out his victory. He seemed to float for a moment, savoring his victim's helplessness. Then Arak dropped from the air with his knee aimed at the center of Darn's unprotected chest, bearing death as his only message.

Arak's cry of victory suddenly changed pitch, even as his deadly stoop downward came to an abrupt halt. He hung for an long agonizing moment impaled on Darn's foot, for the younger boy had somehow managed to roll and kick upwards from the floor. The senior student let out a surprised awkward squawk, and then he was flying to land on his back in a cloud of dust several strides across the sand. He regained his feet as quickly as possible, but one hand clutched involuntarily at his groin. The exploding web of pain there told Arak that the bone or something even more important had been broken or ruptured.

Arak squeezed his eyes shut just for a moment to blot the haze of pain from his vision. He reopened them a heartbeat later, just in time to closely inspect the callused ridges on Darn's palm before it smashed into his nose and loosed a scarlet flood of agony. Arak was staggering, half-blinded by the sudden wash of blood and pain when Darn's front kick took him cruelly just under the breastbone. Arak sagged and stumbled backwards, barely able to catch his balance and hold to his feet. To fall now would be fatal, he knew.

A single ragged cheer rang from the balcony above, emphasizing the stunned silence. Then several more voices joined in succession, till the hall quickly filled with the call of Darn's name. The young fighter felt a wicked unfamiliar smile stretch across his face. And even as Elias watched and nodded in satisfaction, Darn surrendered his will to the flames of rage that burned within his soul. He attacked suddenly: three snapping backhand strikes that stung Arak and brought the adept's hands up high, leaving the floating ribs to become kindling beneath Darn's palm heel strike. Darn began to drive the injured senior before him, unrelenting in his attack, as a hound harries a bleeding wounded boar. Darn felt his smile turn downward at the edges and drip with disdain. And the voice that spoke in his head was unfamiliar, stronger, darker.

This? This is the one who filled us all with fear? The one who cuffed us for the slightest reason, or for no reason at all. The one who belittled me before the other acolytes, and laughed that I'd be better off as a eunuch whipping boy! This one will have my fear no longer!

"Now will ye perish," Darn said lowly, just loud enough

for Arak to hear. Though his eyes never left his opponent, Darn's voice rose to the rafters. "For Eillena! For the Flame of Justice!" An unbidden scream of rage tour from Darn's throat, and he redoubled his attack, allowing no quarter, granting no mercy.

In an elaborate game of cat-and-mouse, Darn herded Arak before the masters' dais to allow them a clear view of his victory, even as he prepared for his final attack. Elias caught Darn's eye and gave a barely-perceptible nod, which the boy returned with a smug smile. Pride swelling within his chest, the elated young acolyte leapt forward to cut off an avenue of escape. Planning three steps ahead, Darn swept a sword-strike towards the cringing senior's exposed neck, already prepared for the follow-up knee-strike which would send mel'Ulbreth crashing down into the tarry pit of defeat. And once there, the Camdian bastard better prepare for his sudden and irrefutable passage from the world.

Darn's elation was abruptly dashed, as he felt his elbow caught in the battered senior's desperate grasp. He realized then, a moment too late, that his own soulfire had betrayed him. For as his hand reached the end of its arc with too much speed and fury, Darn heard an agonizing *krrrittcchhh* as something within his elbow tore loose from its moorings, and his arm bent backward in a manner which nature had never intended.

Darn stumbled away, trying to pull his injured arm back into place. His feet suddenly flew upwards, and he landed in the sand with a spine-jarring crash. Then a heavy weight slammed down onto his chest, crushing the remainder of his breath from him. Darn fought to see past the scarlet veil of pain, only to recognize the bleeding visage of Arak, who sat astride Darn's chest and gibbered with a dangerous maniacal glee.

"Ha, Spark! Had enough blood yet?" Arak crowed as he captured Darn's free hand and pinned it down. The half-mad senior coiled one hand back, then snapped two sharp strikes to the bridge of his captive's nose, mashing it into a twisted and bleeding twin of his own.

"Still not enough, eh?" he jeered. "Here, have some of mine!" Then he hawked a slimy wad of scarlet mucus straight into the wreck of Darn's face.

"Sing for me, Spark!" Arak laughed and twisted Darn's injured arm a bit, then leaned in close as if to savor the forthcoming cries of pain. Darn bit deep into his lower lip to hold back his cry and deny Arak his pleasure. But the blinding pain of his ruined elbow would not be contained so easily. Despite his efforts, Darn's scream of agony and rage reverberated among the high stony reaches of the hall.

The senior reached down to Darn's throat with one hand, and after a brief search, began to apply pressure to the blood vessels there. Black and crimson roses began to bloom across Darn's sight, and he felt both his strength and his life fading with every beat of his heart. Darn fought desperately to control his breathing, and purposefully jerked on his own injured arm, riding the brief wave of pain back to consciousness.

Arak leaned in close, and Darn could smell blood on his breath like the charnel panting of a corpse-eating dog. "Come now, little bird," Arak whispered, full of spite like a jilted lover. "Surely, ye can sing more prettily than that. Yer little friend, the Chak'ran bitch, sang *much* better when *she* laid beneath me!"

A searing white flame burst through Darn's mind like a fire storm, as all the hatred and rage and pain he carried flooded into the furnace of his crucible, then exploded upward with the fury of a new-born sun. The elemental power of his soulfire jerked Darn half upright, and he slammed his forehead into the pulpy mess of Arak's ruined nose. A feral smile danced across Darn's bloodied lips as he heard the soggy snap of cartilage and felt the bones in Arak's cheeks crumble under the impact. Arak reared back in a convulsive cry of pain, but Darn clung tight to him and bashed again at the older boy's face. The bloodied young acolyte hooked his fingers into the hollow at the base of Arak's throat – a grip that brings immense and sudden pain – and rolled the senior off to one side.

Arak fought to shake the crazy Spark loose and stand free. But even as he gained his feet, a tremendous blow took him in the meat of the thigh, and agony ripped through him as the large muscles there cramped. He dropped back heavily into the sand, still trying to free himself from the howling demon which clung to this throat, ripping at him with iron talons.

Darn held tightly to the senior as he fell, and rolled to end up astride him pinning the older boy's arms with his knees. Not waiting to gloat over their sudden change of positions, Darn arced a swift elbow strike down into Arak's face, driven by every measure of strength and fury he possessed. A second strike quickly followed, turning the adept's jawbone to paste. The third and final blow took Arak square in the temple, and upon its delivery the senior student's eyes rolled back and his hands fell away to reveal the bloodied carnage of his face. Quickly, with screaming sudden stillness, the contest was ended. Now, only the inevitable conclusion waited.

Silence flooded the sand-floored arena, leaving a pool of sullen stillness, rippling with the racing beat of Darn's heart. Then a single comment splashed down from the dark upper reaches of the hall: cold, simple, and inarguable.

"Kill him!" the voice demanded with quiet passion, and all the air turned to crystal, those two words frozen in its midst.

Without conscious command, Darn's left hand rose, an executioner's blade made of flesh and bone. Then it stopped, hanging above the exposed windpipe of the condemned. The fury and rage of the flames within him demanded to feed on the dark nectar of Arak's soul. Nothing else would redeem the loss of Eillena's honor or would revenge her pain. Nothing but the death of the young man beneath his hand now. Still, some unnamable sentiment, some doubt within him, held Darn back from the fatal blow.

Darn frantically looked to the assembly of masters, pleading, hoping for their intervention. Most stared back at him blankly. A few – Masters K'tarr and Tobani and Grandmaster Saura – held intense and uncypherable frowns tight to their faces. Only Elias conveyed any message at all: the smile on his face – more a feral baring of fangs – told of his pleasure at the fight's outcome. As he caught Darn's eye, Elian nodded his head quickly in agreement, and purposefully turned his hand over, palm down onto the polished stone of the table.

The young acolyte turned back to stare down at the form pinned beneath him. Suddenly he found his mouth dry, full of the sour dust of distaste. The flames which had roared throughout his soul earlier, driving him to savagery he'd never dreamed he was capable of, those flames were now gone. They seemed to have dwindled down to mere sparks, hardly enough to melt the lump of bitter ice which held his heart captive. Darn felt shame burn across his face as he realized what held him back. It was that emotion which Elias had told him once held no place within a Flame Master's heart: twas mercy. His confusion deepened as his Master's admonishments and teachings fought the unwelcome and unwanted truth within him. But Darn could no more deny its existence than he could deny the blood on his hands. This man deserved punishment, yes. But death – he could not be sure. And Darn must be sure as Death itself to be the vessel of its deliverance.

Darn struggled to call up pictures of Eillena's battered face and rekindle the hatred he had felt. But even the memory of his dear friend's hurt was not enough to enforce Arak's death, though it drove a ragged spike of pain through his heart to admit it. For did not Eillena still live? She was battered and broken and had the most precious of gifts stolen from her, something that should only ever be freely given. But still she lived on, somewhere. And despite the Master's teachings on Justice, still Darn held the White Lady's laws closest in his heart, and he would take no life except in defense or in payment of another. Arak had left Eillena with her life, and Darn could do no less. But Arak too, would lose much in his punishment, something that he valued above all else.

Arak moaned weakly and his eyes floated down from under their lids, struggling to focus on the slight figure that rode above him. The adept student fought to speak, but a vise of small sinewy fingers dug deep into this throat, cutting off all but the barest of breaths.

Darn shouted hoarsely, and the hall fell silent once again to hear his words.

"Know all here present, that his man," he gave his fallen foe a none-too-gentle shake, "Arak mel'Ulbreth of Camdia: this man's life is forfeit to me. I hold by the Holy Flame of Justice, and I denounce this man as he who attacked my bond-sister Eillena!" Darn's voice cracked on the last shouted word, and he paused to regain himself before continuing. A roaring din of cheers and shouts, curses and profane suggestions erupted from the uppermost levels of the hall, and even Grandmaster Saura's command for silence was not immediately answered. Darn bowed his head until the tumult passed.

"I spare his filthy soul," he continued, "for I shall not sully my hands by taking it!" With head bowed, Darn missed seeing Elias leap to his feet in enraged astonishment, only to be pulled quickly back down by Grandmaster Saura's whispered oath and command.

"The Justice that I decree," Darn shouted to be heard, "is that this man be branded with the mark of a coward. He held himself a brave and valiant fighter. But I name him Coward, for only cowards attack those weaker and smaller than themselves." Shouts of agreement rained down from the rows of acolytes perched along the high stone buttresses of the hall, for Darn had not been the only one who had suffered at Arak's hands.

"Ever did mel'Ulbreth secretly mock the Flame of Justice. So forever let him be mocked and despised by all he may meet, so that he shall hide his face in shame, away from the sight of all men! Let him forever by hunted, so that he shall know no rest and no joy."

A slim, bone-handled dagger stabbed into the sand beside the blood-slicked ball of Arak's topknot. Darn wondered briefly who'd had the courage to fling the blade, then shrugged and simply blessed them for their gift and their accuracy. He grasped the knife in his good hand, clenching his teeth against the sudden pain as his injured arm swung slightly. The narrow blade gleamed in the flickering torchlight as he held it close before Arak's face, and for a moment the desire to plunge it deep into his enemy's throat was almost overpowering.

"Now and forever more, the truth of thy cowardice shall be proclaimed for all to see!" Darn said lowly, forcefully, passing judgment for the first time. And even as Arak weakly struggled, Darn carved a shape deep into his fallen adversary's forehead: ø, the unseeing eye, the ancient signel of those who refuse to see the truth of their own lies and cowardice.

***

"This is a tincture of jobbery root: twill aid in thy sleep, and dull the sharpest edge of the pain." The grey-bearded healer held a small wooden cup full of vile brackish tea to Darn's lips. He then eased the sputtering boy back onto his pallet, and proceeded to rearrange the blocks of precious ice that were packed around the boy's splinted arm.

The old man muttered to himself as he worked, ignoring his patient as much as possible, snapping out an abrupt "Hold this!" or "Don't move!" when communication was deemed absolutely necessary. He snatched angrily at a wispy lock of colorless hair that escaped the viridian confines of his satin skullcap and stuffed the betraying tuft back behind his ear, then continued vexing at himself.

"Be damned, ye old goat! Have to see in on that one with the pox-fever next. And of course brought nary a leech with me, or even my bleeding implements! Bah! Someone is sure to have a sharp blade in this den of cutthroats!" The healer glanced out the corner of his eye, just to see if Darn paid any attention to the ramblings of an old man.

Darn bit at his lip, determined to look as healthy as possible. The healer smiled to himself as he finished the remainder of his preparations in silence.

With the pale unlined hands of one who knows money well, the healer smoothed the wrinkles from his robe out over the broad expanse of his belly, and daintily flicked a few imagined bits of dirt from the hem of his embroidered sleeve. Satisfied with both his work and his attire, the self-important little man turned away and began to gather up the tools and herbs of his trade.

Fading screams of pain still echoed from Darn's shattered elbow, but the mantra he muttered, coupled with the draught the healer had given him, helped to deafen the inner ear that listened to such things. He laid back and watched through half-closed eyes as the old man finished packing up his cases. Then the man lifted an emerald green cloak from the rack by the doorway and fastened it around his neck. Darn blinked in sudden surprise as the significance of the cloak struck him: this was a True Healer, not some mercenary's barber or leech. There had been a True Healer back in Warden Woods during Darn's boyhood: old Makheim, who had taught Darn to read the Lady's Holy Psalms and speak Her tongue. Such healers had the Lady's *touch*, and could heal even serious illnesses and mortal wounds if given enough time and the proper incentives. Some asked a king's ransom for their services, and some asked nothing at all. Makheim was of the latter variety, old and poor but gracious with his knowledge and healing. Someone must have been very concerned with Darn's health to have summoned – and paid for – one of the Green Robes to aid with his recovery.

The elderly healer turned just before reaching the doorway.

"Young ones such as thyself, think that they are both indestructible and immortal. I know, for once I thought myself so as well. But hearken to my words, boy: use that arm again before it has time to fully heal, and like as not ye'll end up a cripple." The man pointed his nose a bit towards the ceiling, and sniffed for effect. " I have done this all my life; heed my words."

"The ointment I've left," he pointed to a small wax-sealed pouch which lay atop the trunk in the corner, next to a bone-hilted dagger, "is made of Leopard's Bane and shark bones. It will aid the healing, and strengthen the joint. That – and a truly sufficient rest – are all that I may prescribe. The remaining pain ye must bear, as it will clearly call when rest is needed."

"My … my thanks, venerable Healer …" Darn managed, as he struggled to both to sit up and to pierce the fog which was steadily creeping across his thoughts.

"Save thanks for one who cares, for thanks will not buy my meat or bread, boy!" the emerald-cloaked greyhair answered gruffly. "But thy masters send me a monthly stipend to retain my services for certain cases. That, plus the generous gift promised by one of thy Order, will be fair payment for my own pain." At that point, Darn noticed that the healer's one arm hung at a bad angle, and his faced scrunched a bit as he moved. Still, the man didn't seem to mind all that much.

The healer lifted the curtain to leave, but his departure was interrupted by someone outside. The muted chime of gold coins drifted into the room, then the green of the man's cloak disappeared from the doorway.

The battered young lad began to slip in and out of a drugged slumber, alike to the cautious steps one used when entering the steaming hot springs that lay underneath the Pyre. But just before the warm and welcome waters of unconsciousness could close over his head, Darn sensed another presence in the room, and so he struggled slowly back to the surface.

A crimson-clad figure sat rigidly at the head of Darn's pallet; it took several moments to recognize the shadowed and chiseled features of Master Tobani. In the pause before the master realized that Darn was awake, the boy was shocked to see tears drifting down the man's face. The Bandaran people prided themselves on their stoic nature, and it was rare indeed to see anything other than the harsh tracks of anger or determination twist across their features. A quick swipe of a crimson sleeve left Darn doubting what he had seen, and he certainly wasn't fool enough to mention it.

"You are awake. Good." No pleasantries, no inquiries as to his health or condition. Indeed, Darn had expected no more from the austere master. The black stones of the man's eyes bore down at Darn with an avian intensity that the boy found terribly disconcerting, like the glaring inspection of a gyrhawk moments before it begins to dine.

"There is much talk of what you have accomplished this eve," Tobani said in a deep, somehow colorless voice. "Some of the masters claim the trial to be inconclusive – that only luck and mel'Ulbreth ill-fated pride allowed you to leave the Circle triumphant. However..." Tobani raised a hand to silence Darn's protests. " Grandmaster Saura has decreed that Justice burns bright tonight. Arak has been cast from our halls, and has been declared *slag*. Word is being sent by homing swift to all of our outposts, to tell them of his crimes and his punishment. Though he may draw breath until dawn's first light, his life is forfeit beyond that. He shall live in fear and hiding for the rest of his short days." The stoic headmaster of training sat silently for a long moment, some inner struggle straining his control. Finally, he spoke again.

"Elias should be very proud of his teaching. Proud as well, of his eye for judging the hidden potential of warriors such as yourself."

Tobani stared away towards the wall. "Few, very few, could have managed what you did in the Circle today." He again paused. "I felt that you fought well, given the evident difference in your abilities." The master's face darkened. "I also feel you showed horrendous lack of judgment for withholding the punishment that Arak so well deserved."

Tobani stood up and began to pace the length of the small cubicle. His long fingers moved without his knowledge, and Darn shivered as he watched them flex, the restless talons of some great bird of prey. The scarlet-clad master paused in his pacing, and his hands clutched at a invisible nemesis. "For his crimes, I'd have wished to seen Arak broken joint by joint, then laid outside the Gate of Bones, still alive, for the jackals and the kites to strip away his flesh. And had you," Tobani pointed accusingly at Darn, "had you failed in your trial, I would still have found a way to realize my wish, the Order's strictures be damned!"

The master dropped his hands, but his frame still quivered in anger. "Perhaps Eillena would not have claimed his foul life, and would also think your sentence a more fitting revenge." Tobani glanced at Darn briefly, and a hungry shadow moved within his eyes. "Still, she and I failed to agree on a large number of subjects," he finished simply.

The fierce hawk sighed then and seemed to deflate with the breath somehow, to look less like a fearsome warrior and more like a tired weathered old man. Tobani's words now seemed more self-admonishment than conversation.

"She was one of those few who are a true joy to teach. Who bring all their will and strength to whatever task I set before them, with no complaint. I plucked her from the docks myself," he continued, more softly now, "a daughter of my soul, if not my blood. And though she had yet to fully to embrace her soulfire, she was the finest Spark I have known, the one I've waited a score of years to find."

Tobani suddenly snapped up straight again, and rage stripped the years from him. "Then mel'Ulbreth simply stole her away from me, like some pretty bauble that had taken his fancy!" My only prayer now is that it be *my* hand that sends him to Gorrah's blackest hell!" He shook for a moment, and Darn half expected him to lash out somehow. But then the Bandaran master took a pair of deep breaths and regained his control. He stepped across the small room and picked up the dagger which lay atop Darn's trunk. He slid the blade into a sheath hidden inside his sleeve, the quiet hiss of a viper returning to its lair.

"The blade I shall reclaim, though I will say that you used it well. I may yet have need for it." Master Tobani smiled – a chilling sight at any time. "A hunting squad leaves at first light, in search of the outlaw slag mel'Ulbreth. And I will be their guide, for his blood calls to me."

Tobani's hand appeared again from his sleeve, this time holding a slim package wrapped in plain rice paper. He laid it beside the pouch of herbs on top the trunk, then stood for a moment, head bowed and hands folded secretly back within his sleeves.

"This should have been worn by Sharphands," he said quietly, almost too low to be heard. "You were the only one to stand in her defense. It is fitting."

At that, the master spun in a silent cloud of crimson silk and left without another word, disappearing into the dark like some blood-soaked phantom, which was exactly what he longed to be.

Darn lay quietly for some time, not really asleep, not quite awake, trying to gain some footing in the maelstrom of events, even as the jobbery root fought to carry him away. Then he remembered the package that Master Tobani had left. He worked his way up to his knees, fighting off a wave of dizziness, and managed to snag the bundle with his left hand. Untying the string around it was difficult with only one hand, but at last he had it unwrapped, and its contents fell into his lap.

The young acolyte could only stare dumbfounded at the worn crimson sash, which bore Tobani's name in elegant gold embroidery. *The Master's own sash!* Tears began to fill Darn's eyes, for this was a reward of priceless value, one which Eillena had often spoke wistfully of one day earning herself. And though later he would fairly shine with pride as he walked and lived with the worn sash riding on his hips, for now Darn could only think of his loss, and that of his friend. The gift would not restore Eillena to her proper place, nor would it release Darn from the prison of his own guilt.

***

Two dayturns had passed since Darn's trial in the Circle of Judgment, half a moon, and the healer's art had worked its particular magic. Though his arm still held a dim painful memory of the damage it had suffered, its internal structures had obviously repaired themselves, and each day Darn was able to move it a bit further than he had the day before. He felt anxious to return to his training, but Elias had bid him rest, eat, and nothing else until his body was whole once again.

Elias had been furious when he first laid eyes on Tobani's sash in the room. True, any master could award a senior's sash to any acolyte, and as headmaster of training, it was certainly within Tobani's right to do so. But Elias had planned to make the presentation himself, albeit not with the gift of *his* own belt, he had to admit. Even so, it was his right as mentor to the boy to present the senior's sash. Lord Agni knew the boy had earned it after his performance in the Circle. And besides, Elias had added ten hands of gold solaris to his purse, winnings from his bets on the contest. He owed the boy something, after all. There would be a reckoning upon Tobani's return! Still, the moment had passed, the boy had his sash, and the day was over for ill or gain; Elias had tomorrow's plans to lay.

Darn awoke to the sound of quiet footsteps from the end of the hall outside, then moments later, a dim approaching light. The steps and light paused outside the doorway to his room, and Darn felt a small gust of fear and caution begin to fan at his soulfire. A familiar cough punctuated several moments of low whispers. Then Elias strode into the simple chamber bearing a small clay lamp in one hand, and the arm of a darkly robed and hooded figure in the other.

Darn hastily began to rise to his feet, then thought better of it and grabbed the blanket off his pallet to hide his naked body. He crouched uncertainly, attempting to order his thoughts and prepare himself for whatever Elias was planning.

"Yes, yes, I did say that you would not return to training until your arm could be safely used. Though I doubt that it warrants such laying about as I have seen from you these past day-turns." Elias smiled to take the sting from his words. The bald-headed master placed his hands behind his back and began to pace, a sure sign that a lecture of some sort was to follow.

"You, Darn, have striven arduously to learn and perfect what I have taught you. You did so, even though at times the lessons I offered you were beyond your understanding at the moment. You have taken such knowledge, stretched it to its limits, even found new ways to apply it in combat. And now," Elias stopped suddenly, an odd smile on his face, "you have need of another master to learn from: one who will show you how to ease the pain of your training and your duties. One who will answer any question you may ask. Most importantly, this master will assist you in reining in those forces which race and tear throughout your young body and oft times seem to steal your thoughts and will, delegating responsibilities for your actions to that wily member which knows no loyalty or restraint." Elias smiled at Darn's confusion, and raised a hand to silence the questions which sat on the boy's lips.

Elias seemed lost in his own thoughts for a moment, then shook himself clear. "Ahh, yes, how impolite of me," he said, as he motioned for his silent companion to step forward.

"Master Katrïnn will counsel you for the next two days. I will return for you on Weaversday morn with a special task. Until then, obey every word as if it were my own." Elias set his lamp into a niche in the stone wall, then stepped to the doorway and departed.

The strange master turned to remove a dusty grey robe and hung it from a hook on the wall, then turned back to the lamplight. Darn waited in nervous silence, but the woman merely stood and smiled sweetly and serenely, clad only in a simple shift of undyed satin. She seemed an older woman, perhaps three hands and five. But the winds of time had blown gently past her, leaving naught of their passing save for a few strands of grey in her raven-black hair, and a delicate fan of laughter lines at the corners of her eyes.

Darn fought to control the wandering of his eyes; but as a boy who'd seen the seasons pass a hand and six times, that was as achievable as sprouting wings and dancing among the stars. He blushed high and brightly even as his eyes caressed the master's form, his gaze lingering here and there far longer than was polite to do so. But Lord Flame, such a form! The few female students at the Pyre were, without exception, whipcord thin and stringy as most of the young boys. The female masters seemed to be built the same, though it was hard to tell what they carried beneath their satin robes, and none dared take a peek. But this lady, this *master*, he reminded himself, had the high full breasts and curving hips of a waterfront tavern wench, albeit without the bitter hard-worn image that chiseled itself upon those poor girls' souls. Her skin was as smooth and lightly tanned as the finest buckskin, with a spray of freckles over the bridge of her nose and at the base of her throat, which seemed to highlight rather than mar her beauty. Deep gray-green eyes peered out at Darn from behind long kohl-darkened lashes, holding secrets and laughter in their depths.

With a strength of will which surprised himself, Darn clamped his eyes closed, as if shuttering the lids could shackle the unbidden visions which danced within his head. His nails dug cruelly into his palm, then he reopened his eyes, staring only at the floor.

"M-lady . . . Master Katrïnn," the words tumbled awkwardly over the boy's tongue. "Pardon my indiscretion. What is it ye would task me to do?"

She walked slowly and quietly to where Darn sat, then gracefully folded herself down till she sat on the pallet beside him.

"To begin with, you shall call me Katrïnn. Master I do profess to be, but Katrïnn is the only name that I bear." Her full sensual lips pulled back in a wide honest smile, but Darn felt the tension within him grow, rather than diminish. And now, much to his horror, that tension began to extend itself to other areas as well, evidenced by the rising covers that he'd hastily pulled across his lap at Elias and Katrïnn's arrival.

Katrïnn laughed at his apprehension, a bubbling trill like the unpretentious music of a woodlands stream. Somehow, Darn understood that she laughed *with* him, not *at* him, and he ventured a tentative smile in return. She reached out a slender hand, her nails glowing with the polished luster of pearls, he thought, and she swept back a lock of hair from Darn's face.

"I have much to teach you, young Darn," Katrïnn said, as she began to loosen the sash at her waist. "Though I daresay that you shall find my lessons much more enjoyable than those that Elias renders."

The colorless dress slipped from her shoulders then, and puddled around her drawn-up knees – an exquisite butterfly, shedding its drab cocoon to emerge in all its splendid glory. The smile on her face shifted slightly somehow, now more like that of a hungry vixen settling down with a quivering young coney trapped between her paws.

"Time for your schooling to begin," she breathed, as her hands gripped Darn's shoulders with a surprising strength, and she pulled him to her.

Chapter Ten
Greenheart Forest

Two lads trundled along the woodland path, stepping in and out of webs of sunlight that hung lazily down from the branches above them. One boy was slender and wiry, with a delicate grace of movement in his steps. The other towered over his companion, and walked with the solid surety of a mountain. They both carried light packs and sleeping rolls on their backs, and walked on unshod fee as would any other low-born traveler of the road.

The two friends had left the towers of Shiningrock a full hand of days behind them, traveling the rocky coastal trail. Halfway along, they had made a wide detour around a tiny town Darn named as Warden Woods. *Nothing good ever happens there,* was all Darn had said in answer to Loon's questions.

When they reached the fork that led off to Dagarr's Keep – the old tower that served as Shiningrock's northern watch point – the boys turned west instead, following a path that led through a wide scrub pine forest. Another day brought them to the edge of a long escarpment, where the land fell away: "split a'half by a sword stroke in a fight tween th' gods of war, Volar and Tattargi," or so Loon claimed. However it came to be, the bluff gave them an unsurpassed vantage point over a wide valley that trailed off into the distance. The land there was covered by a glowing emerald blanket of beech and alder and ash, with a few massive oaks lifting proud heads above the rest.

Greenheart the forest was named, for it was thick and rich with verdant life. Greenheart was an old, old forest – as old as the elves who wandered its columned halls. Still, these woods held none of the black menace that had woven itself throughout Haldcort and some of the other great forests. Here, the White Lady still held sway, and creatures both great and small lived and died by Her just laws, without the intervention of man or other agents of the Dark.

Even underneath the forest canopy it was a bright and wonderful woods, alive with the creatures of the day, distinctly absent of those of a darker nature which frequented the night. Easy enough, with a sling and snare and a bit of common woods-sense, for a pair of travelers to live quite comfortably and eat well. Though the forest held no dangers other than those that the forest always had, few humans were bold enough to settle their homes here. Elves were known to live beneath the great reaching arms of oak and ash, and only foolhardy boys or groups of well-armed men traveled the forest road without fear of reprisal.

Darn had received a special dispensation from Grandmaster Saura to be his personal courier, and to carry a message to the Order's outpost in the town of Hovill. The trip was a full-hand's worth of steady walking, and the return trip would make it nearly an entire moon. Saura's instructions, though, had been only that the newly-appointed Adept student return by the Sowing Moon, bestowing on Darn the unprecedented gift of freedom. Such reprieves from the Order's arduous training schedule were rarely granted. But Grandmaster Saura knew that Darn's spirit still needed mending, even if his young body was healed and ready to continue.

Darn had not questioned the Grandmaster's benevolence, but had accepted both the task and the gift with quiet calm. Saura's instructions also bade Darn to take along a traveling companion, and of course Darn had turned to his truest friend, Loon. Loon had eagerly accepted the invitation – perhaps eager would not be the proper term, although frenzied or raving might be a bit too harsh if closer to the truth. In the end, Darn was able to calm his dancing friend down long enough to inform Jehred of their plans, and deposit an extremely displeased Peg into the Captain's care. Then the two rushed to fill their packs and set off up the northern road.

***

"… an' Lucky an' Loric held tight t' their jewels, an' set sail t' follow th' sun!" Loon finished the last stanza of his traveling song with a grand flourish, singing at the top of his lungs, scattering birds and treerats through the limbs.

"Huzzah!" he cried. "That is my most very favorite one! That, an' th' one called 'One-eye Twilly, a Horny ol' Filly.' Do ya know that one, friend Darn? Here … I'll teach it to ya." Loon fumbled in his pack as he walked, finally extracting a battered tin whistle. As Loon's fingers began to scrabble over a pathetic and equally-battered scale, Darn tried hard not to grit his teeth, nor to regret inviting his over-exuberant friend.

Suddenly the wind shifted, and unexpected sounds drifted through the forest: shouts, voices raised in alarm, and animal bellows of rage or pain. Without a word spoken between them, Darn and Loon shrugged out of their traveling packs and dashed off towards the clamor.

After climbing a narrow ridgeline, the pair reached the top of a small knoll, beyond which the shouts and cries – now mostly fallen off – had been born. The two boys slithered through the underbrush until they had a view of the clearing nestled at the base

233

of the ridge. The scene they discovered set Darn's blood to boiling, stoked by the soulfire which was quickly growing within him. The young Flame Dancer started to tremble as his rage licked out in hot flickering lashes through his body, and he would have leapt to his feet at the moment, tossed aside their concealment, if not for the ham-sized hand which slapped on his back and pinned him to the ground.

"No, frien' Darn," Loon whispered as forcefully as he dared. "As Jehred says t' me time an' agin: 'Loon, ya tater-head, ya hav'ta use yer brain fer somethin' other than t' jest keep yer head round!' An' that's what we gotta do here an' now: use our heads. Now slide on back some." With a hand clamped like a vise around Darn's ankle, Loon snaked back through the underbrush, leaving his companion no choice but to follow or be drug along.

As soon as the pair was safely back over the edge of the hill, Darn leapt to his feet and spat out his anger.

"Loon, have ye no eyes? Did ye not see the harm they were playing at? Tis not the Lady's way, to cause such hurt, to bring such suffering. By the Flame of Justice, I will not allow it!" He turned to storm back over the hilltop, but again Loon's hand restrained him.

"Darn, these is not our folks. Ya don' even know why they're doing them thing down there. Could be they got reasons. Could be ..."

"Could be that they're ignorant fools, beset with the arrogance and madness that sharp steel and power curses so many with." Darn knocked his friend's hand from his shoulder and stalked a few paces away. He jerked several knots of grass from the ground, and began to rub the muddied roots and bruised stalks over his homespun tunic, quickly transforming it from pale yellow to a mottled green and brown. "I … I understand that ye seek to use thy head for a change, Loon, and that is commendable. But there are also times when one needs to act: when the heart must rule o'er the head. This is such a time."

Another sudden cry of pain shattered the forest stillness. At the sound, Darn dropped his arguments unfinished, and sprinted into the trees, leaving Loon to stand alone.

"Volar's Balls!" Loon swore fiercely. Red-faced, he hunkered down to his heels, and unfamiliar furrows stitched across his brow as he strained to plan a course of action.

Darn found that the climbing and stalking skills of his early youth had not forsaken him. Soon he lay unnoticed upon the limb of a large goldenoak, peering down through the leaves into a small dell. The boy still trembled with rage, and his mind reeled in an effort to find an answer to the scene below before his body delivered one of its own volition.

In the clearing stood a full-hand of finely dressed Sidhe nobles and guardsmen. The caste marking painted upon the forehead of the group's leader marked him as a *t'aacha*, a lordling prince and distant cousin to the Sidhe king in Courdeless. A second group of elves stood off to one side, though they were Sylvan-folk, dressed in leaf-and-bark patterned homespun.

The prince was a tall slender youth: tall for a Sidhe at least, which stood him only a hand-span above Darn. Eighty or ninety winters old by the gold of his hair and the gauntness of his frame; barely an adult, though his blood undoubtedly brought him far more respect than he'd have gained else wise. He wore a light burnie of moon-silver mail, worth a king's ransom by itself, and a cloak of finely-trimmed buckskin that hung down his back, though it was too warm for the latter and no call for the former. The Sidhe pirouetted delicately in his scarlet boots and a needle-slim rapier danced accompaniment in his hand. He laughed lightly as another squall of pain burst the quiet of the small glen, and tipped a slight nod to the applause it brought from most of his silk and fur-clad companions. Then short heavy claws struck near to his boot, and he hissed a Sidhe oath and slashed furiously with his sword.

The wounded bint'rong squealed again as the blade dug a long furrow through her foreleg, and she dropped back to all fours to scurry away from its stinging bite. The small kits hiding behind her snarled at the Sidhe and uttered their own little war cries. But the sow's long furry tail pushed her offspring back, still instinctively herding them towards the protective bulk of her mate, who lay in a bloody heap on the leaf-strewn floor of the glen. Her pointed snout swung back and forth and her long whiskers twitched as she scented hopelessly, searching for salvation from her hateful tormentor. But the moment that her attention wavered, the lordling reached in again to prick her shoulder or ribbon her ear with his sword, drawing forth the bawling cry which had called Darn and Loon from their trail.

At last the Sidhe prince tired of his sport and drew back from the growling bint'rong mother. He wiped his sword daintily on a swath of silk, then dropped the crimson-soaked cloth to the ground as he resheathed the blade.

"Enough of this," he said in the Sidhe's sing-song tongue. "Stupid creatures aren't worth the effort of a sweat, though I'll daresay the boar took more than I'd have guessed to lay him down."

He motioned to one of the elves. "Kill it, and take the kits. M'lady Dannella may fancy them for her gardens, as long as they're small. And they'll make some sport for the hounds once she tires of them."

The tall elven ranger scowled darkly at his lord's back, and the taste of his words were bitter in his mouth, as he nodded to his men.

"Be done with it," he said flatly.

Four of the Sylvan woodsmen pulled white-fletched arrows from their quivers and set them to their bowstrings. None seemed to relish the task, and one paused in his draw to spit to the side.

Hidden in the branches above, Darn tossed aside the arguments and doubts which echoed through his mind. He pulled his legs up under him and waited until he was perfectly balanced. Then with a leap and a scream that would have please a forest leopard – or even Master K'tarr himself – the Flame Dancer sailed from his perch and took the bowmen from behind. Darn's heel struck one of the archers behind the ear, who dropped as if poleaxed. Another crashed bonelessly into his companions spoiling their aim, after Darn's elbow spun into his jaw.

The elven ranger's blade appeared in his hand, and he lunged to place its point between the prince and the bewildering menace that had appeared in their midst. The Sidhe lordling stumbled over his own feet and fell back into the grass to lay and stare in slack-jawed fear. But the attack ended as suddenly as it had begun, for Darn's thoughts were more for the bleeding bint'rong which nosed at her lifeless companion, than for the group of armed elves facing him.

The *t'aacha's* Sidhe guardsmen had drawn their own blades and bows in the next moment, and only the Sylvan ranger's cry of "Hold!" kept them from searching for Darn's heart with their steel.

Darn turned to face the incredulous stares of the Sidhe. At his back, he heard the hiss and snort of the bint'rong female as she reared up, preparing to fight this new danger to herself and her kits. But Darn began to hum a quiet lilting melody, and at the sound the creature ceased her growls and perked her ears. Slowly, she settled back to the ground, ears twitching to catch the tune. Then the sow bint'rong stretched forward, trembling, to sniff at the seat of Darn's trousers. Satisfied for the moment, the bristling hair on the creature's shoulders smoothed down a bit, and she turned back to her brood.

Darn's sudden appearance had something less than a calming effect upon the Sidhe prince. A brush of embarrassment began to paint the *t'aacha's* finely chiseled features a delicate shade of crimson from his narrow chin to the tips of his ears. Anger glittered and danced within the lordling's emerald eyes as he leapt to his feet, savagely swatting the dirt and grass from his cloak. Then he hissed in outrage at his guards and the Sylvan woodsmen.

"A filthy human?" The Sidhe prince pointed at Darn, and the sneer of disdain he wore echoed in his voice. "Trained warriors, all. Taken surprised by one of the mongrel breed. And a whelp by the looks of him!" He glared at Darn for a moment, with eyes that bespoke the boy's worth, then whirled back and continued his tirade.

"And who shall pay for thy incompetence?" he asked, not waiting for an answer. "Myself, your prince, of course! Pray look at my cloak: it shall never be free of these stains, a candidate now for the scullery maid's rags!" He nodded towards the pair of woodsmen who still lay prone in the leaves. "Those two shall be flogged upon our return for failing to protect their prince. And as for this dirt-scabbed barbarian …," he waved a long-fingered and bejeweled hand in Darn's direction.

Darn interrupted the Sidhe's pronouncement, speaking in the same flowing language which the prince himself had used: the *Sidhest*, the ancient speech of the elder-folk, a grand tongue full of the sounds of waterfalls and birdsong and soft sweet chimes. And at Darn's words, the *t'aacha* froze, his jaw hung agape, to hear the music of his own people play from the lips of a human waif. Few outside the elven races were privileged enough even to have heard the musical tongue, and only the most learned of human healers were taught to speak the intricacies of the *Sidhest*.

"Nay, good Prince," Darn said fiercely. "Point no hand at me and call me barbarian. For even I understand twixt right and wrong, battle and butchery. As thou should know, in the *Book of Truths* the White Lady's words are clear: *Bring no war among those that know it not. For the children and the creatures of field and forest are the only true innocents.* She taught that there shall be no wanton taking of life, nor torture or gleeful infliction of pain!"

Darn's tone became harder, and sharp consonants full of anger began to stab into his speech. "The bint'rongs pose no threat to man, elf, or Sidhe *t'aacha*. They are simple eaters of fruits, the Lady's gardeners, planting new trees for the benefit of all. And by my word and oath, thee and thy men shall bring them no further harm! *Passaratt!*" Darn spat the last word to the forest floor between them. In the *Sidhest*, it meant a blood oath or promise, one that would be defended to the death. The air turned to crystal across the glen, as the deadly promise of the challenge froze the air.

Even the *t'aacha* seemed rebuffed by the blood oath. Such matters were taken quite seriously by a race that never died of old

239

age. But the dark mutterings of his men lent fuel to his arrogance, forcing the diminutive prince to answer the challenge.

"Hah!" the Sidhe barked. "Impetuous little fool! I, Thesspari let-Mernath, T'aacha of Jerrholm, hold domain over all these woods by decree of my father, Lord Mernath Trollbane. All the denizens of this forest hold their lives to me, to give or take as is my folly. These beasts raided our camp larder as we slept, and so I exact payment in kind."

"*Tsaa!*" the Sidhe cursed. "I have no need to explain myself to a barbarian." His voice rose again, cold and hard as midwinter ice. "No human wretch, particularly one who dares sully the music of the *Sidhest*, shall tell me 'Hold!' here in my domain. And now a blood challenge awaits fulfillment. Let it be so!"

The *t'aacha* snapped his fingers at his guardsmen. "Slay him," he ordered briskly. Then, after a moment's deliberation, he added: "And bring his tongue, after. Perhaps the Minister of Alchemy might divine what terrible defect would allow such an uncultured beast to speak beyond its normal growls and barking." He crossed his arms as his men lifted their bows, a carefully affected air of boredom masking his face.

"Caution, I would offer, my prince," a raven-haired Sylvan ranger said, as he stepped before the Sidhe. The woodsman's leathers and roughcloth seemed as homely as uncured furs compared to the lordling's silks and shining mail. Yet the ranger shone in a way that would ever be lost to the pampered Sidhe youth, and the guardsmen paused in drawing their bows to hear his words. The ranger motioned to where Darn stood, and laid a gentle hand on the *t'aacha's* shoulder.

240

"He is but a poor human youngling, without so much as a blade. Murder 'twould be to kill him, plain and simple. He has brought us no real harm, and the blood oath means naught coming from one such as he." The ranger drew the *t'aacha* around to meet his eyes. "Truly," he continued, "twould be foolish to bring about the boys' death, and gift us with even more ill-will from the human townships."

The woodsman's words were answered with a sharp *crack*, and an imprint of the *t'aacha's* delicate hand began to flush red across his cheek. The ranger never moved to block the blow.

"Dare to call me a fool!" the Sidhe prince screeched, as he shoved roughly at the gilded half-helm he wore, which threatened to slip down over one eye. "Untitled bastard of a Sylvan whore! I shall have thee imprisoned for thy insolence upon our return to Jerrholm; thee and any others of thy mongrel band which refuses to obey me!" He sneered as he turned away, knowing that his blood and station protected him from the Sylvan hunter's wrath. "And perhaps my father will have thy hand removed as well to remind thee of thy station!"

The golden-tressed Sidhe stomped passionately, in the way of little children, to stand before his entourage of Sidhe guardsmen and Sylvan woodsmen. Rage and renewed arrogance had charred all hint of the subtle beauty of his people from his face, leaving only cold sharp angles in their wake.

"I ordered the whelp shot!" he screamed into the face of the nearest guardsman, the eloquent sounds of the *Sidhest* giving way to the gutter patois of his childhood. "Are your ears filled with dung?" he continued. "He assaulted members of my retainer, and insulted the son of your lord! Do as I command!"

The small group of Sylvan woodsmen held their ground, ignoring the prince, looking only to their own leader for instructions. But the Sidhe guardsmen hesitated no longer, and eight bowstrings sang a deadly song, each a separate note of the dirge.

The soulfire licked though Darn's limbs, forcing his body into motion before the boy was truly aware of it. The first arrow whispered through a lock of his hair as he twisted from its path, and the second pair slipped by within a kiss of his heart. The next three, Darn slapped aside like so many flying pests, and the following one he broke in midair with a flashing sword-hand strike. The last shaft Darn simply captured in mid-flight, snatched from the air like a lazy bumblebee, its steel stinger held a hands breath from his chest. The young Flame Dancer sent a prayer of thanks winging to Master K'tarr for training him in just such tactics. Darn held the feathered dart out towards the dumbfounded Sidhe guards, then in unspoken contempt, he snapped the arrow in two and tossed the splintered halved to the ground.

The *t'aacha* was the first to recover from his surprise. With a deadly whisper his slender rapier slid out from its jeweled scabbard. His curses shocked the guards into action, even as he himself backed away from Darn towards the protecting bulk of an ancient goldenoak tree at the edge of the glade. "A sorcerer! A … a forest demon!" the prince screamed, terrified as a lost child. "A dark agent sent by my enemies for my soul! Slay it! Slay it! Protect your lord!"

The Sidhe warriors dropped their bows to pull their blades, and hesitantly began to step forward to where Darn stood waiting. The Sylvan ranger, however, motioned his own men back, even as he watched another unnatural occurrence unfold. A stout limb seemed to stretch slowly down from the goldenoak, down towards where the *t'aacha* huddled and cried hysterically. Then, with a hollow clang, the oak limb rapped the Sidhe sharply on the crown of his fanciful helm, cutting him off in mid-screech and settling him in a quiet heap at the great tree's base.

The ranger flashed a quick hand signal to a group of his woodsmen, and three of them pulled circles of woven grass from their pouches. With the green bands to their lips, the elven rangers each blew a high-pitched keening whistle, one towards the group of Sidhe guardsmen, one towards the cowering band of courtiers, and one towards the unconscious prince and his conquering tree. Instantly, the sword-wielding Sidhe warriors froze in their steps, and Darn was left standing guard against a group of statues. The nobles paused forever in their panic. And the *t'aacha* continued his slumber. But from the branches above him, a large figure crashed to the ground ungracefully, there to share the sleeping prince's dreams.

Darn pulled his attention away from the frozen Sidhe guardsmen as the Sylvan leader stepped towards him, stopping just outside sword's reach. A crooked grin twisted its way across the ranger's face as he crossed his arms, hands far away from his swordbelt. He motioned with his head back towards the goldenoak.

"A companion of thine, perhaps?" he asked, the smile on his face echoing the lilt in his voice.

"A-ay, my lord," Darn stuttered an answer, marring the beauty of the *Sidhest* only a small measure. "Though I knew not he lay in the tree. He …"

The tall graying elf cut off Darn's protest with a wave of his hand. "A disservice ye do me, by calling me 'lord' and placing me with his kind," he answered. "I am a simple Sylvan ranger, as my father before me. Not a noble, not a courtier."

The ranger swept the feathered cap from his head, then bowed elegantly, waiting patiently for Darn to belatedly join him in the gesture before rising again.

"Belerand Longshin of Greenholm, I am. Leader of my band by way of wisdom and age, but in no way 'lord' And how shall I address thee, young warrior?"

"Uh … D-darn. That is, I am Darn of .. of the Pyre," the bewildered boy answered, still unsure if he was rescued, or playing an unknown part in some odd elvish conspiracy or practical joke. The elves – high and low-born both – were ever a convoluted people. Still, here in the White Lady's domain, Darn held out that Her will prevailed, so he answered the ranger's honesty with more of his own.

"My friend, he is named Loon. I know not his given name, but he is brother to Captain Jehred of Shiningrock." Darn stepped as he spoke to slowly put himself between the ranger and Loon. "Please sir, do him no harm. For in his mind, he is still but a child."

"Then most blessed is he of all the Lady's children," Belerand answered with a small nod of his head. "For the precious brilliance of the little ones' minds bring sunshine and starlight into an otherwise dreary existence. No, we shall bring him no harm." He gave a hand signal, and two of his group – then two more – struggled to lift Loon's snoring bulk off the ground and away from the drowsing *t'aacha*.

The Sylvan hunter rubbed the back of one scarred hand along the edge of his jaw, and cocked his head to the side as he stared at Darn. "Now as for thee, young Flame Dancer – or is it Flame

Master? No, one of the Red Robes would either have allowed the prince his fun, or slain him where he stood, depending upon their judgment. Flame Dancer it is then, though well-versed by what I have seen here today." Belerand's smile widened, and he glanced sideways at one of his companions. "Of course, had it been *Sylvan* archers ye faced today, rather than mere Sidhe bowmen, the grass would already be stained with life's blood." The gathering Sylvan woodsmen smiled among themselves, and laughed as one of them kicked the broken arrow shards towards their frozen cousins.

"I suppose that I should have ye trussed and staked out, to await the *T'aacha's* displeasure," Belerand continued. The elf pondered for a moment, tapping a finger to his chin and purposefully ignoring Darn's sudden tensing. "But of course," he then added, with a mischievous grin, "such a mighty wizard as the one that beset the prince and his court – invulnerable to the arrows of mighty Sidhe warriors, and able to command the very trees of the forest," he gestured grandly, "a malevolent force such as that could most likely vanish into the very forest floor, or shape-shift into a tiny sweat-gnat and fly away. Yes, I believe that would be the most fortuitous conclusion to this day's events: preserving the lives of two brave young travelers, and dashing the pride of an arrogant Sidhe *t'aacha*."

One the elves across the glade trilled a quiet note into Loon's ear, and the burly young man slowly opened his eyes, a dreamy smile of contentment draped across his face. He gazed up at the group gathered around him for a moment, then the smile fled from his face.

"Looooon," he began, speaking quietly to himself. "What ya be doin' down here on th' ground? Ain't s'posed t' be here. S'posed t' be helpin' Darn!" And with that, Loon broke the last bonds of sorcerous slumber and lurched to his feet, swatting his massive fists at the elves who simply danced aside and laughed with the voices of swallows.

"DARN! DARN!!" Loon's bellows crashed through the glade, scattering the quiet and setting the sow bint'rong to hissing and puffing again. "Oh Loon, ya stump-humpin' fool! Ya hadda fall, dintcha?" He continued to curse himself and swing ineffectively at the elves, never hearing his friend's shouts from across the glade. Then Loon's eyes lit on a nearby sapling elm, and with a great roar he grabbed hold and ripped the young tree from the ground. He snapped the end off across his knee, and turned to brandish the makeshift staff with a great wad of dirt and rocks caught in the roots at the end. Loon began to swing the formidable maul around his head in large circles, and the surrounding elves were beginning to lose their patronizing grins.

"DARN!" Loon continued his shouting. "Whaddidya do wi' my frien', ya point-eared…."

"Loon! Loon, I am here! I am unharmed!" Darn dashed between the encircling elves, frantic to calm his lumbering friend before he either gave or received harm. It took Darn several moments to convince Loon that they were indeed in no danger, and several more to get him to relinquish his makeshift club. At last Darn took his companion by the arm, and by tugging and pleading and finally a swift kick in the rear, he managed to wrench Loon's attention away from the Sylvan woodsmen. Then he walked the big fellow back to where Belerand patiently waited. One of the elves picked up Loon's fallen club, straining under the weight of it, and the others gathered around murmuring in their liquid tongue.

Darn introduced his traveling partner to the elven ranger, translating for them both. Loon began to ramble off into a fanciful version of the boys' journey, when a mournful cry from the edge of the glade silenced his tale. The sow bint'rong was nudging her dead companion, trying to force life back into its stiffening limbs. All the while, the wounds that she had taken herself were slowly proving to be mortal, for the crimson seed of her life trickled from a dozen bloody mouths, staining the grass around her. The bint kits cried for their mother's attention, but the female could only spare them enough mind to herd them close with the long sweep of her tail. The rest of her energy she spent mourning over her mate.

Darn turned to Belerand with tears standing in his eyes.

"The bint'rongs hold their mates for life. I have seen one nearly dead from starvation, sitting on the forest floor next to the moldering corpse of its mate. She will mourn him until she dies, then the kits shall perish also." The young boy shook his head in a helpless gesture. "Perhaps I could bind her wounds, as I know a bit of the healing arts. But she would never leave the bandages be."

The tall elf nodded and murmured his agreement. The he walked cautiously to where the bint'rong huddled. The shaggy beast turned at his approach and hissed once, long and thin, a sound more of lost hope than of warning. Though the bint'rongs were indeed fruit eaters by choice, they were known to take an occasional frog or lizard or even a slow-thinking forest hen on rare events. And the Creator had equipped the waist-tall brutes with a bristling mouthful of needle-pointed teeth, more than adequate for halving a squashfruit or mangling a man's arm. But Belerand ignored the sow bint's threats. Instead, he began to hum a quiet melody as he sat down beside her, a tune similar in measure to the one that Darn had sang for the bint earlier. But this song was somehow richer – a golden message of ease and solace.

The mother bint'rong quieted immediately and settled back on her haunches. Then she sank slowly to her belly and laid sprawled over a small mound of grass, heavy lids drooping over the glittering stones of her eyes. Her breathing deepened and grew quiet, and she failed to respond even when her kits howled in protest, captured by their long coarse-furred tails by the Sylvan woodsmen.

Belerand knelt beside the entranced creature while continuing to spin his spell of comfort around her. He motioned for Loon and Darn to join him as he gingerly prodded at the animal's many wounds, and a furrow of anger etched itself across his forehead. The wordless turn he sang wound softly to an end, and the bint'rong continued her blissful slumber.

"Indeed," Belerand said in a sad, quiet voice, "her wounds are not deep, but she'll not walk easily. And soon, the green-rot will begin eating at her." Belerand hung his head for a moment, and when he raised it again a flush of shame colored his pale cheeks. "Twas I who caused this poor creature's pain, as surely as if I wielded the fool's blade myself." He spat in disgust, then sat quietly.

Loon looked to Darn for a translation of the elf's words, but Darn only shook his head in answer. With a heart-felt sigh Loon stood, then glanced uncertainly at the elf band which now stood quietly around them. A crystal-eyed elven huntress, who barely reached to Loon's elbow, stepped forward and silently handed the teary-eyed boy one of the crying bint'rong kits. Elf and human stared at each other for a moment, speaking clearly without words. Then

Loon turned his attention to the armful of black wiry fur he held, and walked off cooing a spell of his own concoction.

Belerand seemed to finish some internal debate, and he pulled a long hunting knife from his belt, its staghorn handle carved in the likeness of a diving Saira flacon. Darn closed his eyes as the blade plunged downward, and he began a short prayer commending the poor creature into the White Lady's care. Belerand's dagger, though, did not find the bint'rong's heart; rather, it stabbed deep into the forest loam by the sow's side. The Sylvan ranger dug through the moist earth till he reached a layer of heavy red-brown clay. Then he used the blade to cut a fist-sized chunk free.

"This is a different healing then ye may have seen before, young master," Belerand answered to the questions poised on Darn's lips. "Tis the Lady's work, have no fear – but of a taste perhaps not to thy liking." He sank the knife back into the ground nearby, then reached down to pull the lump of clay free. "This poor bint was born of the forest, of the Greenheart. And as a part of the White Lady's domain, the soil here holds a bit of Her power – at least of a type to aid Her children."

As he spoke, Belerand kneaded the clay between his hands. He leaned forward, and with a gentle fingertip he wiped a crimson drop of blood from a long gash in the sow bint's shoulder, then added it to the clay. After a moment's thought, he reached out again and drew his thumb against the sharp edge of his own knife, adding a bit of his own blood to the mass. He sang a line of Sylvan verse then, and began pulling and twisting the clay until the misshapen form of a bint'rong began to grow in his hands. He plucked a few coarse hairs from the back of the sleeping sow and worked them into the back of the clay figure. He eyed his creation critically, then set it on the ground and turned back to face Darn. Certain wonder and uncertain fear warred within the boy's eyes.

The ranger pulled his knife free from the loam, flipped it over to catch it point first, then handed the blade to Darn.

"Mark this figure with the same wounds as the sow has received," he instructed. "Make them deep and long, as are the ones she wears. Check her for point-wounds also. And hurry, young one, for even in sleep she fades from the world, and my paltry skills have no way to bridge that gap." The elf laid back into the grass then, and seemed to withdraw into himself. "Call me when ye have finished," he said quietly.

Cautiously, as if the clay doll might turn and suddenly bite, Darn picked up the figurine and began to score it with the knife in imitation of the bint'rongs wounds. Though he barely understood what he did, Darn followed Belerand's instructions in detail, even rolling the she-bint gently over onto her back that he might copy the bleeding gash that crossed her teats and stomach.

Finally, the figure was complete, except for a tiny cut across the pointed nose which Darn hurriedly added. He looked up from his work and seemed to suddenly reawaken, as the trill of the birds and the twittering speech of the Sylva hunters sounded again in his ears. Darn began to call Belerand's name, but hesitated, fearful to disturb the ranger and possibly interrupt some casting or preparation of sorts. But even as Darn worried to himself, the laughing-eyed ranger suddenly sat upright, brushing twigs and grass from his hair.

Belerand took the bint'rong doll from Darn's nervous fingers and examined it closely, checking every nick and scratch against the sleeping sow. He paused once, removing a clay toe to match one with the bint had lost to the *t'aacha's* sword. Then he nodded his approval, and adjusted himself to a cross-legged position.

"Listen well if ye understand the high-tongue, young Darn, for this is a powerful calling," Belerand said solemnly as he stroked the sleeping bint'rong's head. "By such words may the attention of the White Lady be gained, if the cause is worthy of Her notice." His face darkened as he continued. "But be warned: such a venture should not be taken lightly, or for one who deserves the gift not. For the Lady's Light is death to those that hold the Shadow in their hearts."

With that, Belerand closed his eyes and breathed deeply for several spaces. Then his lips parted and a sweet wordless melody began. It sounded like the wind playing games with its tail up among the tree tops, or the bubbling laughter of a brook dancing over rocks and rippled beds of sand. But slowly – so slowly that Darn could never be sure quite when it began – a song began to wind itself into the elf's tune. Words in the ancient high-tongue of the elder-folk began to take wing, a beseeching psalm to the patron of the woodland people, drifting out across the quiet glade, out among the trees and hills where She held sway.

We praise thee, White Lady, who brings us the gifts
of life and of joy, of sunshine and mist.
Look down, oh Fair Lady, look down and give heed.
For one of Thy innocent children has need.
Elandril, our Lady, the White One Who Smiles,
Please grant me Thy gift to heal pain, for this child.
For one who lies broken, for one whose wounds cry;

my own blood I shed, that this one shall not die.
Oh bind her and mend her, and knit her flesh whole.
These things I would beg Thee: bring end to her woe.
As this clay from whence her own form Thy once gave,
Let her limbs be unblemished, let her wound be unmade.
Reach down with Thy fingers, our Lady we pray.
Reach down and caress this child's harm all away.
Our dances and songs shall praise Thee through the night.
Elandril, Caretaker, our Lady in White.

And as he sang his song of healing, Belerand gently stroked the clay figure, smoothing closed the tiny cuts and gouges which scored its surface. Darn could feel a whirlwind of power spinning around the glade, centering around the ranger's hands. He relaxed and shifted his gaze just so, and could discern a shimmering aura of emerald green draped about both the doll and the sleeping bint'rong, a web of verdant power connecting the two. And as the blemishes on the figure disappeared under Belerand's questing fingertips, so the gaping wounds in the sow bint's hide knitted and closed completely, leaving only thin snaky lines of pink scar tissue to trace their leaving. And even though the toe which the bint had lost did not reappear, a smooth rosy stump was left in its place. The bint'rong's breathing deepened and lost the frightful liquid burbling it had held. And though he could never swear to it afterwards, Darn believed he saw a furry smile on the creature's, face, as it sighed and licked its chops and climbed after overripe squashfruit in its dreams.

Belerand blew out a sigh of relief, and Darn glimpsed deep lines of exhaustion on the elf's face. The ranger swayed a bit as he rose, staring out from hollowed eyes, and Darn hurried to clasp his elbow and steady him.

"Your concern is much appreciated, young Darn," Belerand said in a quiet weary voice. "But feel no alarm for me, my friend. The Song of Healing drains the body, tis true. But ..." he paused as he lowered himself onto a large moss-covered stone, "... in turn, the Song feeds the soul with a bouquet of such Light! Ahh, in a lifetime I could never fully describe it. The Lady willing, one day perhaps ye shall feel Her gift as well." The Sylvan hunter smiled blissfully, his eyes straying to a clump of nodding dwarves' cap which grew by his feet. He picked a single blossom, and held the delicate crimson funnel to his nose for a long draught of its perfume. Then he absently tucked the flower behind his ear, and returned to his thoughts.

"The sow will live. She will awaken in a 'mark or two, then we'll send her and her kits on their way." The ranger waved towards the corpse of the male bint'rong several paces off, carrion insects already buzzing about it. "For her mate, I can do nothing. The Lady forbids us reopen that door. Not that a simple forest-walker as myself holds such knowledge," he added. "We shall ensure that she is far from this glen when she awakes. Hopefully, she'll just gather her kits and run."

Darn smiled sadly, nodding in agreement. A whisper of off-key song drifted to his ears, and he turned to search out his traveling companion. Loon sat beneath a spreading parchment elm quietly crooning an inane sailors' chantey, one which he'd subjected Darn to time and again. One bint'rong kit slept cradled in Loon's arm, while another crouched on his broad shoulder, its tail secured around his neck, fishing in his ear for any interesting objects or morsels that might be hidden therein.

Darn's smiled fell away though, as he glanced from his happily-occupied friend to the unconscious Sidhe prince and his frozen entourage. Darn turned back to Belerand, and the hurried rush of his words tripped over his lips in anxious confusion.

"B-but the *T'aacha*! And his guards and retainers! What of them? For surely they will not sleep forever. And when they too awake, what then of the bint'rongs and ourselves? He shall …."

"The lordling shall do nothing." Belerand interrupted the boy's frenzied questions with his out-turned palm. "For after subduing his royal personage and the remainder of his company, the barbarian sorcerer – thyself, that would be – disappeared in a cloud of black mist, even as our shafts pierced his scabrous heart. The bint'rongs – which were obviously the foul warlock's familiars, designed to lure the *T'aacha* into just such a trap – disappeared along with their ebon-hearted master." The elf finished with prevarication with a flurry of slender arms, and added a mock bow to his obviously self-satisfying performance. He smiled a wicked grin and patted Darn on the shoulder. "What could be more fortuitous, I ask, young friend? The bint'rongs and you both make good your escapes, while I and my men receive the *t'aacha*'s grudging respect and his father's generous thanks. And the *T'aacha* himself? He receives a well-deserved dose of humility and a hearty thump on the head besides!" Belerand laughed heartily, and several of his hunters joined in. "A more fitting end to such an unfortunate display of Sidhe arrogance I cannot imagine!"

Darn thought on the elf's proposal for a few moments, scratching the back of his head as he searched for a proper reply.

He had no wish to doubt the ranger's words, but Darn's fears were still not vanquished.

"But thy lord – will he not suspect ..." the boy began.

"*He* is not *our Lord*, young sirrah! Words as such could bring much grief upon thee!" Belerand barked suddenly. Elven moods were known to shift quicker than the wind. "*He* is a *Sidhe t'aacha*, to whom we hold no ancestral rights or homage!" The infuriated elf broke off abruptly, as the slim hand of the female ranger laid lightly on his arm in a gesture of restraint. Belerand stared hard into the younger elf's eyes, and for several heartbeats a wordless conflict strove between them. Then, just as suddenly, Belerand turned back to Darn, and the anger which had cut his face melted and drained away like cold dew in the morning's light.

"Forgive me my rudeness, my friend. Gell'rin reminds me that my anger belongs to myself. Such bitter fruits should not be offered to an innocent. The folly of my people is no fault of thine." He paused for a long moment, eyes downcast in embarrassment. He motioned for Darn to join him as he folded his legs and sat down humbly in the grass. Then he continued.

"Once, the *Sidhe* and my own *Sylvan* folk were of one people – merely cousins which lived on opposite sides of the Rendrac range. But when the first Troll Wars began, our chieftains united under a single warlord – Corin let-Doran, the Silver Wolf – who was of the Sidhe people. A great leader and warrior he was. And once the scaled-ones were driven back to their holes, all of us, Sidhe and Sylvan alike, pronounced Corin king over all the Elder Folk, from Greenheart to Skypoint to the Great Fangs of the Rendracs. And when Corin finally fell under the black mace of Fangdrool the

Troll King, his son Gellad Skyseer took his place, and led us again to triumph." Belerand closed his eyes and sighed deeply, and his proud elven shoulders slumped a measure or two as he continued.

"Once the Lay of Peace was laid down between the trolls and ourselves, we no longer needed a warrior-king. But so strong was our people's allegiance to Gellad and his father, that we begged him to remain as our king, and lead all of us as one. The blood and get of the Silver Wolf each then took their stand as our king or queen: Vana of the Black Bow, Rolanda Mistwalker, T'aasla the Cold, and many others. And for a span of uncounted turns of the seasons, our people grew and prospered. The Sidhe stayed in their great walled cities west of the Rendrac peaks. They befriended the doughty stone-folk of the Kalthmus mountains, who taught them the working of metals and jewels and helped them to fashion arms and adornments of great beauty and power."

The sunlight shifted then and fell full on Belerand's face, driving away the clouds which had gathered there. He opened his eyes and smiled, full and bright. "But my people, the Sylvan folk, we preferred the green light and mists of the endless forest to call our home. For many generations we were content to dwell here, and leave our cousins to their politics and courtly intrigue. And it was also here that we came to know and love those we call the *Let-mon-Marnath*, the children-of-the-world – your own human-kind. And it was from your people that we learned to sail the great seas. "

"We still answered the call of the great-king or queen in time of need, and many of our people traveled among our cousins to the west. But slowly, the Sidhe came to regard themselves as our superiors, and claimed the right to rule over us all. As our honor bound us to the rule of Corin's clan, we endured the burden of their arrogance." Belerand's face darkened once again.

"Eventually, we began to believe their claim to our homage, and many gained employ and took service with our Sidhe cousins within their palaces and courts."

"As they have lost the knowledge of the forests, the *t'aacha* and his court sent message to the elders of our village. They had need of woodsmen to guide them through the Greeheart as they travel to meet with the human king in Lorring. Thus, were my friends and I burdened with the responsibility for these fools and their ignorance." Belerand looked at the frozen *t'aacha* in disgust, then spat to the ground. Gritting his teeth, he said, "Tis our duty to the king, but tis a chore of great reluctance."

He sighed and shook his head. "I am deeply tired, my young friend, and I sorely miss my home and family. Still ..." the ranger slapped at his knee and the ghost of a smile lit across his face, "tis no reason to gift you with my pain." He accepted an ornate drinking skin from the elf he had named Gell'rin, and took a sip of the golden liquid it contained. Instantly, his almond eyes sprang open wide and shone with a crystal brightness. Belerand rose smoothly to his feet, as a blade of grass straightens after the wind has passed, and all traces of spell-induced weariness fell away from him. His smile grew broad as he looked to where Loon and several of the Sylvan hunters sat playing with the bint'rong kits and sharing in the common language of laughter. Darn stood to join the ranger, and shared his smile at the sight. There, where Sidhe guardsmen and courtiers stood frozen as statues, several small greenleaf-thrushes gathered on the shoulder of one aristocrat to sing and preen and stain his silk gowns.

"It pains me to lose such fine company," Belerand said, as he guided Darn towards the rest of his group. "But the wind-snares which were woven about the *t'aacha* and his company will not hold much longer. The pair of you must prepare to leave, and take the furred ones along. I am certain that thy stalwart companion can mange the bulk of the sleeping sow, and the small ones will follow wherever their mother leads."

They stopped beside the small group, and at their approach Loon handed his furred playmate to one of the elf rangers and hurried to Darn's side.

"Darn!" Loon nearly shouted with excitement. "Gell'rin Springleaf – that's 'er wi' th' scarlet cap; powerfully pretty, ain't she? – well she speaks a bit o' th' man-tongue. She says that they're bound fer a camp only a day's walk from Hovill, once they get rid o' their satin-panted friends here." Loon patted one of the Sidhe noblemen absently on the head as he spoke. As an afterthought, he reached out a thick finger and transferred a healthy dollop of bird droppings from the elf's shoulder to the end of his bladed aristocratic nose, an act which brought pealing bells of laughter from the surrounding rangers.

Darn grimaced an embarrassed smile, and jerked his companion away from the begrimed figure. But the biting words which Darn had prepared melted under the pure glow of Loon's foolish grin. Loon couldn't possibly know that such an act was a deadly affront to one of the elvish folk. But then again, Darn mused, Loon wouldn't possibly have cared, either. Darn dropped his anger, and quickly explained Belerand's plan to his friend. Loon nodded his understanding and went to gather the sleeping mother bint'rong. A child-like sylvan huntress rose from the seated group of rangers and carried the bint kits along behind him.

Darn paused for a moment, as if chewing on his words. He wished for their parting to be done properly. Elvish customs were notoriously complex at times, and slights were easily taken. He turned to the tall elf, then bowed low, hands pressed together in front of him.

"My thanks, Belerand, for thy kindness and understanding. For aiding two foolish young ones who'd struck a hornets' nest – with all good intentions. And for finding a way to spare the lives of the innocent bear-cats."

"Nay, young friend," the Sylvan ranger answered, returning a bow as elegant and simple as a clear running stream. "It is I who must offer thanks. Ye saved me from allowing my habitual sufferance of these foolish Sidhe children to displace the vision which the Lady bestowed upon my people. But for thy intervention, these innocent creatures would lie dead, or worse yet confined to a life in the garden zoo of some Sidhe dumpling. Nay, it is I who am truly in thy debt, young sirrah," Belerand finished, laughing, as he waved towards the *t'aacha*. He clapped a hand to Darn's shoulder and began to walk towards the tree line, leaving the Sidhe *t'aacha* and his retainers as resting stoops for the silverbelts and nutfinches.

Belerand spoke with the boys for a short while, warning them of a pack of bandits that had been raiding along the main road, and of the griffin they'd spotted a day's travel to the north. The elf maid Gell'rin handed Darn a pair of baby bint'rongs. Then she slipped up to Loon, pulled the towering young man down to her level and whispered quietly in his ear for a moment. Her words had a power that Darn had never before seen, for Loon blushed from the roots of his disheveled blond mop to the line of his jaw. Later that evening, Darn would try unsuccessfully to pry the words' secrets from his friend.

The huntress smiled and laughed, high and sweetly, like the song of a morning rose-warbler. Then she winked at Darn and skipped back to her companions.

"May the Lady's Will be that our paths cross again, young masters," Belerand said to the boys with a bright smile, as he moved to rejoin his band. "May She rain sunlight and good fortune on your journey!"

Darn and Loon drew up their bundles of coarse black fur, and set out to retrieve their packs left hidden beyond the small ridgeline. Both, in their own way, was loath to leave the company of their new-found acquaintances. But perhaps the journey to Hovill now held a bit more promise than it had at the start.

***

All day long the two boys walked, talking and laughing as carefree boys are wont to do. They took turns carrying the mother bint'rong as she slept her healing sleep, though they stopped often to let the bint kits nurse and have their play.

Just after lunch, Loon announced that from that moment onward, he would make his way in the world as a wandering minstrel – though he wouldn't give up his job emptying honey pots, as it paid so well. Said he was made for the work, and he found the status of a minstrel to be quite to his liking. He then offered a sample of an off-tune ditty he'd spent the morning crafting, concerning Sidhe courtiers and their penchant for bird droppings. Loon thought the song quite good, and the woods rang with the sound of it as they marched along. Darn found the tune horrendously distasteful and incredibly funny; it could also quite possibly get both their throats slit, should the wrong pointed ears ever catch wind of it.

Near evening, the mother bint'rong began to stir restlessly. So Loon laid her gently in a soft mound of moldering leaves, piling her babies around her. The boys hid themselves downwind and sat guard over the dreaming sow and her brood until stars began to prick the growing shroud of night. The hunting call of a horned owl woke the sow bint suddenly, and she gained her feet with a menacing growl, if still a bit wobbly. After assuring herself that nothing threatened her kits, the mother bint'rong nuzzled each of her young in turn, puzzling over their decidedly man-like smell. Then the sow turned to futilely search for her mate. The father of her kits, though, laid cold and stiff in an empty glade a day's walk to the south; a creature who once ate from and planted the trees, now slowly providing sustenance for them in turn. The sow bint seemed to sense the completeness of her loss, for she raised her head and crooned a high lonesome cry of heartbreak to the moon. At the sound of her cry, the smiles dropped from the faces of the two hidden watchers like late autumn leaves, and fat tears dripped silently to the ground.

Her lament complete, the mother bint'rong gathered her kits to her with a sharp bark, then slowly waddled off into the underbrush. Ahead of her, an uncertain future awaited. Behind her, she left two boys to wonder and curse at the cruelty of those who walk only on two legs.

Chapter Eleven
R'hagnarost

The sun broke free of the sea's cold desperate grasp and stepped up above the waves, sending gleams of gold and rose towards the sleeping mainland. The first light of the new day traveled countless leagues, passing over the rounded hills of the coastland then settling across the emerald carpet of the Valley of the Dawn.

Hidden within the great green forest, a boy slept fitfully atop a wooded rise with his back to a large boulder. A single beam touched his thin, worried face, and the shadow of a dream drifted across his brow. The boy woke with a start and gained his feet inhumanly quick, quick enough to startle the forest leopard that had been watching him curiously from the trees. He looked about wildly for a moment, still in thrall to the dark dreams he'd suffered throughout the night. Then the warm welcome of the sun drew him fully to his senses, and he grinned in self-conscious folly.

Even as he relaxed his guard something moved by his feet, and Darn leapt back a full stride, hands at the ready. But it was only a shadow – a small funny three-legged shadow – that danced and jigged, surely made by the dawnlight shining through the branches. The figure flattened and melted even as he watched.

A terrible grinding sound began to crash across the quiet glen and Darn studied the undergrowth around him, searching for the source of the noxious droning. He found a clump of feather ferns off to his left that moved in tandem with the awful sound, so Darn strode up boldly and applied his foot in a less than gentle fashion.

"Wake! Wake and be thankful that we both still have our

heads this morn!"

Loon snorted and snuffled, and tried unsuccessfully to pull a long green frond back over his face. But the insistent prodding at his posterior was past the point of ignoring. He grudgingly opened an eye, yawned hugely, then levered his bearlike frame to a sitting position, unaware or uncaring of the twigs, leaves, and small scrambling creatures inhabiting the tangled curls of his hair.

"Quite the watchman, ye be!" Darn quipped. He tried hard to glower at his large companion. But as always, he found frowning to be an impossible task in the light of Loon's beaming smile.

"Th' Lady's Mornin' to ya, frien' Darn!" Loon answered in kind, oblivious to his friend's admonishment. "I had the most funniest dreams last night," he continued. "I dreamed I was a big ol' bint'rong, scarfin' sweet pears an' honeycombs, just climbin' around an' eatin' an' poopin' on things. It was a real nice life." Loon stretched and rubbed his face, and looked about hopefully. "Anyways, all them dreams made me mighty hungry. Got t' break our fast an' fill our bellies?"

"Breakfast!" Darn answered, as angrily as he could. "Loon, we could very well have been eaten for breakfast ourselves while we slept! Ye were supposed to keep the watch, once I turned in."

Loon scratched his head, brows knitted seriously, as he rose from his feathered nest to stand, towering over his slight friend.

"Well, Darn, I was watching. Watched fer a long while. I e'en watched the night whispies fer a while, an' listened t' all of 'em sing. But then they went away, an' there weren't nothing left t' watch at! So I set ol' Peg t' watchin', an' I took m'self a nap."

"Peg?" Darn exclaimed. "But Loon, Peg is not even here! We

left her with Captain Jehred and the Lady Beatrice, at the Lamplight Inn. Remember?"

Loon snorted. "Well just cause she had t' stay wi' Jehred don't mean she can't still take her turn at watch," Loon explained slowly, mocking Darn's petulant tones. "She jest left her fur an' toenails behind. Travelin' light: that's what Peg calls it."

Darn threw up his hands, conceding that his argument would never be won. He turned and squatted to pack his bedroll, and laughed just a bit at his friend's foolishness, even as he refused to dwell on the decidedly dog-shaped shadow that had guarded their sleep.

***

Darn and Loon followed an easy trail across a small meadow, tossing laughter and tales between them. The stately trunks of Greenheart Forest bounded the small glen on three sides, while a high rocky outcropping rose up on the far side. It was a beautiful day with a clear sky above them and nothing but an easy walk before them.

Then a scream knifed through the air, sharp-edged and ugly, slicing each of the boys to the bone. Both of them froze in mid-step, fighting the crawl of their flesh. The rest of the forest went silent: no chattering of treemunks, no bird calls, as if all the world were hiding.

"That ... that weren't no person," Loon whispered. His eyes were as big as saucers, and Darn would've laughed at the sight had he not felt his own face bugged out in fear as well.

Again, the throat-wrenching scream tore though the forest silence. The source seemed noticeably closer, and it had something else to it this time: a hungry, purposeful quality – the sound of hunting. Nothing else stirred in the forest; even the breeze had died away. The two boys turned about uncertainly, trying to determine the direction of the awful sound.

Darn wet his dry lips, and tried desperately to calm the trembling of his limbs. He felt the soulfire quicken within him, feeding on the fear that pooled in the pit of his stomach. "P-probably just an injured hare screeching its head off, or maybe a brown-faced eagle hunting up its supper." Darn felt little consolation at his own explanation. But he could feel Loon trembling behind him, and so he was determined to quench his own fears. "In either case, we certainly have no cause for worry."

A stiff breeze kicked up suddenly. Darn's hair blew forward into his eyes, as tufts of grass and last year's leaves tumbled past them to catch up against the legs of the trees.

"Darn," Loon said quietly, "we might have us a cause t' worry after all." The strain in Loon's voice was warning enough, but the lack of even a hint of laughter in his friend's words brought a chill to Darn's bones.

As Darn turned and stepped from behind Loon's bulk, the scream they'd heard earlier buffeted them again but now many times stronger, and Darn cringed involuntarily. High-pitched and rusty-edged, the noise drove a spike of pain straight through his ears and into his brain. Mercifully, the sound finally ended, and Darn forced his eyes open. For a moment, his legs felt like water. Then the soulfire lapped greedily at his fear, and sent fire racing through his veins instead.

"I think I'd jest as soon be home 'bout now," Loon whispered, almost to himself. Darn couldn't help but agree.

Large golden eyes stared unblinking back at them from across the clearing. Below the eyes, a wicked notched beak the length of Darn's arm opened and the ear-shattering scream came forth once more. Iridescent feathered wings stopped their fanning, and settled closely along the sleek tawny body. Thick scaly forelegs clenched restlessly, digging furrows in the soil with their dagger-length claws. A huge avian head cocked at an angle as if to study the boys better, and a long tufted tail twitched nervously behind it all.

Above and beyond his fear, Darn had to admit that the griffon was the most magnificent creature he had ever seen. Half again the size of a sturdy horse, the beast possessed a regal air about it, a fearlessness that marked it truly as a king of the forest. Darn felt honored for the sight. Then the creature loosed another scream and took a long step forward. Darn's admiration was dashed aside by the sudden sense of being *prey*.

"Loon – to the woods," Darn whispered. "It is our only chance." He nudged his friend lightly back towards the closest trees. Loon gave no response, only staring dumbfounded at the griffon. Then he finally managed a slow step backward.

Immediately, the griffon leapt into the air, its powerful hind legs propelling it up and forward. The great wings barely unfurled before it settled back down, standing between the two boys and the trees that held their safety. The creature glared fiercely at the pair, its great feathered head cocked at a quizzical angle. Then it took a sudden step forward, closer. Darn could see a dried brownish stain along one side of its beak.

"Do ya think it's gonna eat us?" Loon whispered loudly, as he and Darn stepped backwards again.

Darn stopped in his tracks, all fear and other thoughts fled from his mind. He turned towards his tall friend.

"Eat us? Of course it means to eat us, Loon!" Darn replied incredulously. "Did ye think it meant to ask us to dance?"

"Well, I dunno 'bout that, frien' Darn," Loon answered, wonderment banishing his fear like water to a flame. "Do griffons like t' dance? I seen a parrykeet one time in th' Bazaar that'd dance an' sing an' wear this little sailor's suit. Twas pow'rfully funny, it twas!"

"I should say it may dance about our entrails," Darn responded lowly. His patience in the face of imminent and life-threatening danger was beginning to wear a bit thin. "But I do not think that we will be able to enjoy it much!" he finished.

The griffon stood silently, cocking its head while the two boys talked. It looked from one to the other, then stepped forward and once again released its ear-splitting shriek. Darn and Loon backed up until their heels scraped on the rocky rise behind them. The griffon was less than a full body length away.

Loon took his hands away from his ears, and shook his head to clear it. "Lords a' Fire, but that birdy-beast is a loud one!" he said, as he dug a finger in one ear experimentally.

The griffon swung its great feathered head around, centering directly on Loon as he finished speaking.

"Loon," Darn warned quietly, "I do not believe that our guest appreciated thy comment."

Loon wiped his sweaty hands on his pants leg and tried unsuccessfully to look the griffon in the eye.

"I didna mean it weren't a nice voice or anything," Loon stammered. "Just as it was a great loud one, is all. I mean, loud voices is good if yer hollerin' fer someone er singin' er whatnot." Loon began to visibly wither under the griffon's relentless gaze. The creature stretched its neck forward, bringing the scythe of its beak nearly within Loon's reach. The boy swallowed with considerable effort, then continued. "It's a really nice voice – ah, fer a bird, that is."

At his words the griffon once again opened its beak, and the screech it released this time made its previous cries seem like the cooing of a dove. Loon and Darn were driven back against the rocky cliff by the shear force of the sound, and both pressed their hands tightly to their ears in a futile effort to lessen the pain. Just as abruptly, the griffon closed its beak and the echoes of its cry faded out through the surrounding woods. The beast settled back onto its haunches and looked from one of the boys to the other, finally settling on Darn.

"*A bird* he calls me," the griffon said, its words clear and distinct with an imperious matriarchal ring about them. "Tell me, young human: do I look like a bird to you?" The griffon tilted its head in question. "Answer well."

"Well," Loon began, "ya do have feathers an' all. An' I … Oww, Darn!"

Loon bent to nurse his bruised shin, while Darn struggled to find an appropriate and lifesaving response to their fearsome interrogator's question.

"Well, I would say … that is .."

"Quit quibbling," the griffon ordered sternly. "If there's one thing I've learned in my many years, it is that when a male starts stammering, it's only because a lie is stuck in his throat."

Darn paled, caught red-handed as it were.

The griffon rustled and settled a long wing feather. "I am no more a bird, than either of you are monkeys," the griffon stated. "Oh, most certainly there are avians in the far reaches of our ancestry. But griffons, as a species, have lived here since the earliest memories of the elves. And that, my young lad, is quite a long time indeed."

"Forgive my friend and I our ignorance," Darn said, as he nudged Loon discretely. "We certainly meant no disrespect. Quite the opposite, in fact. For we were both struck by the magnificence of a regal griffon." Darn tried to wipe his sweating palms on his tunic, and hoped the creature didn't notice.

The griffon nodded her great head towards Darn. "I did not expect to ever encounter a human with such fine manners. They normally just scream, running one way or the other until I nip their heads off. Thank you, young man." She eyed them imperiously for a long moment, then decided to gift them with her name. "In your tongue, I am called R'hagnarost, Countess of the Carpath Peaks." She made the announcement with great aplomb, then stood waiting.

Darn reached out and rapped Loon with the back of his hand to gain his friend's attention. He bowed low, as gracefully as possible, and was relieved to see that Loon performed a surprisingly good bow of his own – though Darn wished he hadn't seen the redbird feathers that waved from the side of Loon's cap. Darn swallowed as he straightened, and cleared his throat.

"My name is Darn, of the Pyre, if it please thee, my Lady. And my companion is Loon, umm…" he looked at his puzzled friend for just a moment. "Loon the Merry, a minstrel of much fame and renown."

Loon stood up, loosing interest in his sore shin, and he eyed

269

the great beast warily, unfamiliar lines creasing his brow. Darn winced at the sight, knowing it meant that Loon was thinking hard before speaking. He dreaded the results, given their present circumstances.

"Darn said yer gonna eat us," Loon stated matter-of-factly. "I guess I'd jest like t' know if that's true."

The griffon swung her great feathered head about suddenly, eyes wide in surprise.

"Eat you?" she asked. "A human?" The disgust was evident in her voice. "Why, I'd rather eat a dead marshhowler." She seemed to consider the prospect a moment longer, then ruffled her feathers in disgust.

"Why, what's wrong with eatin' a human?" Loon asked, oblivious to the look of horror on Darn's face. "I bin tol' that human meat was mighty tasty."

"And just *how* many cannibals do you know," the griffon asked, haughtily.

"Well, um, none. Least ways, none that I know of," Loon answered back undaunted, honest as bedrock.

"Then who told you such nonsense?" she shot back immediately, the menacing beak moving decidedly closer.

"A ... um ... well, a troll, fer one."

"A troll? A troll would eat anything. A troll eats rocks, for goodness sake!" She shook her head once again, a rather dainty shudder of distaste for such a large creature. "I wouldn't touch human flesh."

Loon paused just a moment for thought. "Ya did say ya snipped off a few men's heads now an' then."

"True," R'hagnarost answered, nodding in agreement. "Yet that was only to stop their screaming. Horrible voices your people have when running in terror. So yes, a head now and then, but never for purposes of dining."

"But I bin told that th' Klemish eat their dead." Loon seemed determined to hold onto the subject, despite the fact that Darn has pulling at his arm. "An' they eat some other dead folks as well, so I hear, if they was fierce warriors, er such."

The griffon cocked one eye. "The Klemish? Do you mean those filthy black-flagged barbarians that live across the Great Water?"

Loon nodded his head in answer.

"Uggh! Well of course they would eat dead flesh. Horrid, pestilential creatures! They never bathe, so the collective reek over one of their cities: oh, you cannot imagine!"

Before Loon could delve deeper into the eating habits of griffons, Darn wrenched the conversation back away from him. One important question remained unanswered.

"Forgive my directness, Countess," Darn began. "But if ye had no intention of eating us, then why work so hard to scare us so?"

If it was possible for a creature as fearsome as a griffon to looked chagrined, this one did. When she answered, her tone carried a bit less surety.

"Well, all else aside, I was truly hoping that you'd drop your packs and run. Much easier that way, you know. None of that fighting and bloodshed, and all that other ghastly mess." The griffon stretched out one magnificent wing, and began to preen it delicately with a talon the size of a short sword. "As I'm sure you can imagine, few men are willing to hold a sword against a griffon.

Pah! They usually just drop their things, stain their pants, and run willy-nilly off into the bushes. Makes my life so much simpler, when all is said and done."

Darn and Loon looked curiously at each other. Darn's pack was of fairly decent construction, made of cured leather and sporting a pair of brass buckles. Loon's pack though, was little more than a roughcloth bag with a pair of shoulder straps stitched on. The only item of value that either of the pair held was Grandmaster Saura's letter, which Darn was tasked to deliver to the Order's outpost in Hovill. Darn cleared his throat politely and searched anxiously for words that held no disrespect.

"Again, forgive me, Lady R'hagnarost. But our packs are simple and rough affairs. We carry no gold or other treasures. Of what interest could they possibly be to you?"

R'hagnarost leaned in till her beak nudged at Loon's shoulder bag. Then she closed her eyes and drew a great breath. "I do believe," she said, "that the contents of this pack includes at least three potatoes. And," she paused to inhale a second time, "an onion: one half gone bad, if I'm not mistaken." She clacked her beak together hard and fast, twice – obviously a sign of relish, but one that both the boys would rather have not been so close to observe.

For Loon, the fearful aspect of the beast before him vanished under a sudden thought. "Taters an' unyuns?" he asked, loud and slack-jawed. "A great griffon like you likes taters an' unyuns?"

"Oh, more so that you could ever know, young man," R'hagnarost replied, once again snapping her formidable beak in an alarming fashion. "It gets to be so tiresome, eating rock goats and dragonettes and the occasional dwarf day after day after day.

Few green things grow in the mountains we call home, and those that do are scant and bitter." She sighed glumly. "I've tried raiding a village or three, and digging up my culinary desires once the people had all run off." She held up a fearsome talon. "But alas, these are no groundpig claws, and they are little help for digging. Besides, the idea of rooting around in the dirt holds little appeal for me. Oh, I suppose I could tear the top off a storehouse in one of the cities and raid to my heart's content. But with so many arrows flying about, it's simply not safe."

The griffon looked sad – if a creature capable of biting one in twain could be said to look sad. Indeed, Loon even thought he heard the great beast sniffle a time or two. He glanced over at Darn, who shrugged and raised his empty hands, then nodded finally. Loon turned back with his smile on full shine.

"Lady R'hagnarost," Loon announced brightly. "My frien' Darn an' myself would be honored if ya was t' join us fer our supper: unyun an' tater stewpie."

The griffoness blinked oddly, and looked back and forth between the two young men. "Why, you would share your dinner with me?" she asked. "Even after I threatened you both, and tried to take your packs by guile and force?"

"Well," Loon replied, his grin still plastered across his face, "after all, ya was only lookin' t' scare us. Not really kill us an' all that."

R'hagnarost lowered her great feathered head and shook it slowly. "Oh, oh no," she said, low and solemn. "I am afraid that I have misled you once again. For you see, once we share our sup, I must still end both of your lives."

"What?" Loon and Darn cried together. "But … but … but,"

273

Loon stammered.

"Here now!" Darn stepped in front of his blubbering friend, feeling the boiling rush as the soulfire burned up through his veins. "Though we would share our meal with thee, still our lives are to be held forfeit?" His hand cut the air between them. "I would not expect such ungrateful treatment from royal personage, my Lady!"

The griffon lowered her head even further and began to waver it back and forth, unmindfully ripping at some nearby bushes even as she replied. "Oh, indeed, young sirs. Ye have both been the very model of graciousness and manners. Tis truly rude, what I must do. I pray ye will forgive me. But you see, long has our legend survived, and the legend itself protects us."

"What legend exactly do ye speak of, my Grace?" Darn asked casually, even as he surreptitiously plucked his sling from the back of his belt.

R'hagnarost shook her head as if in disbelief, then settled back and began to lecture the boys.

"Why, of course, the legend that says no one, ever, survives an encounter with a griffon. I mean, if the human folk began to hear that two defenseless younglings walked away from a hungry griffoness, well, they might start to lose some of their fear of us. And then should they discover that we have the gift of tongues, the next thing I know, there'll be a legion of net-wielding fools showing up at the edge of my nest, trying to capture a griffon nestling for the whim of some idiot human noble." She tore violently at the bushes now, shearing a small tree in half. She stopped speaking and seemed to catch control of herself, slowly dropping the torn foliage to the ground. Her actions did little to calm the boys, but perhaps the time for calm was past.

"My Lady," Darn replied forcefully, now trembling with the heat of the soulfire, "with all measure of courtesy, I must make clear that my friend Loon and I will defend ourselves, should ye so force us to act." Darn turned to glance at Loon for support and found his stalwart friend already beside him, grin vanished, gripping his stout iron-shod staff with serious intent.

"I see that neither of you has encountered a griffon before." R'hagnarost turned to look at Loon for a moment, eyeing the staff he held at the ready. Then with a movement blindingly fast for a creature so large, the griffoness' head shot forward. Before either boy had a chance to even cry out her huge beak snapped shut, nipping Loon's staff off by more than half, as easily as a gardener would trim an errant branch.

The great beast settled back onto her haunches again, and leveled a stare that was cold, smug, and utterly terrifying. "I am R'hagnarost, Countessa of the Cold Peaks. I have scattered legions of elven hunters with my cry. I have seen the dwarven armies of King Balinog cringe in fear, huddled like cornered conies, from the mere sight of my shadow. You have heard of the troll-king Ooderdunglazz the Left?" She paused only to take a breath, not really expecting a reply. "Ask him for the tale of how he lost his hand, and watch him pale under his scales at the remembrance." She looked at each of them long and hard, her point well-made.

She focused on Darn, her huge eyes widening even further. "I see the color of your anger, young one. And I grant you my respect. I had not known your kind could shine so brightly. Fiery like the setting sun. Like the great scaled wyrms of the West." She shook her great head, then continued. "Enough. It is not my place to speak of such."

The griffon stood to her full height, easily as tall as the giant draft horses Darn had tended as a child. She looked down at them both. "My sorry young lads, here is the truth. Should I decide to dispatch you both, there is nothing short of divine intervention that should save you. What would you do – hit me with a *stone*?" R'hagnarost uttered a series of short high-pitched hiccups. Darn reddened as he realized he was being laughed at, and dropped the sling he thought he had hidden in his cupped hands.

"I suppose that you may smite me with your bare hands, or perhaps kick me in the leg as you did with your jolly large friend here earlier," R'hagnarost continued. "In all the millennium, I have never seen such foolish bravado. I … *BWAWK*!!" In a sudden flurry of movement, R'hagnarost cried out in pain and disbelief.

The griffon's scorn had been more than Darn could bear. As the great beast articulated her pride and scornful humor, she paused a bare moment to blink. And in that moment the soulfire had raged up through Darn, forcing his limbs into motion long before his mind decided to move. Darn had skipped a long step forward and launched himself into the air, the heel of his foot whipping around and up impossibly far to strike against the griffon's beak with an awful *Crack!*

As Darn landed back on his feet, he realized that his life would most likely end in the following few heartbeats. But the soulfire inside of him had demanded no less. He was a Flame Dancer of the Pyre, and Lord Agni's Honor must be upheld. He had earned his sash with pain and fortitude, had been baptized in his own blood, and the blood of his opponent. Darn would endure much. But he would not endure the taunts of a bully. And while the griffon was a magnificent monstrous beast, she was still playing the bully. And Darn could not allow it to stand. If he died, so be it; he would die defending Honor both great and small.

R'hagnarost sat back on her haunches and blinked slowly, repeatedly.

"That, young sirrah, was completely uncalled for," R'hagnarost said, shaking her head slightly. "I retract my earlier comments on your good manners."

"Manners! Manners?" Darn dropped all pretense of caution, and marched to stand in front of the griffon. "Uncalled for, ye say? Yet thee have vowed to slay us, simply to keep the false shell of some ancient legend intact. And after we have offered to share our meal with thee, food from our hand. Perhaps no one has dared to speak thus before to thee, Countess. But the White Lady lays rule to all of this land, and by Her laws, such unwarranted deaths are not only ill-mannered, but are truly an act of the Shadow. Already on this trip we have stood against such deeds. I promise that we will answer no less in our own defense."

R'hagnarost looked admonished, or at least as much as much as an avian beast could seem. She hung her head, looked up, looked away. She began to protest twice, but both times her argument caught in her throat and died before she could give it voice. Finally, the great griffon lifted her head and looked at the two boys for a long quiet moment, truth shining her eyes. And when she spoke again, it was in a quiet mournful tone that none would have expected from such a fearsome creature.

"Thy words ring true, young Darn. And indeed, I am shamed." R'hagnarost sat quietly, scratching at the ground. "But you have little understanding of the suffering that would rain down upon myself and my kind, should I allow you both to leave this forest alive and with such knowledge as you hold."

"For if even one survives a meeting with a griffon, then others will be emboldened. And eventually, the manlings would come seeking our eggs. The elves thought to do so, eons ago, before we taught them to fear the skies. But the manlings, you humans, you are so many. I could slay them until my talons grow weary and still they would come. And should they succeed, should they steal an egg or hatchling, then I would be made an outcast, shunned and hunted by my own kind."

"You see, we have so few, so very few of our own young any more. Even the loss of a single fledgling would be a barb in the heart of each of my kind. Aye, a loss that would bring down the vengeance of all griffons upon any who played a role in such a tragedy."

Loon dropped the broken stub of his staff and sniffed loudly in a vain attempt to hold back his own tears. He stepped forward, unmindful of the danger, and laid a hand full of comfort on R'hagnarost's winged shoulder.

"Don' cry, m'Lady. We won' let no un get yer babies. An' we wouldna tell no un nothin' bout meetin' ya here."

R'hagnarost lifted her head, questioning Loon with her glance.

"Nope, we'd swear by th' White Lady's grace that we'd never ever tell a soul. Wouldn't we, Darn? Why, I wouldna even tell Jehred, an' I tell him most ev'rythin' in th' world."

R'hagnarost eyed them both with shaded disbelief.

"Beware of what you offer, youngling. For to swear by the name of She Who Brings the Rains is a bond for life," she said fiercely. "It is not an oath taken lightly, nor without full intention of the heart. For he who swears falsely by the Lady's name may forever bear the scorn of Her forest children. No creature will ever come to your snare; no green thing will grow under your hand. And the beasts of the woods, from the most fierce to the smallest, will forever worry you unto death. No, it is not a pledge to be forsworn."

" Lady R'hagnarost," Darn began, as he stepped up beside his friend, within beak's length of the fearsome creature. "We would indeed make such a vow, and hold it to our graves. Neither thee nor thy brood would ever come to danger from our words or deeds. Assuming, that is, that we are allowed to continue our journey – by your Grace's leave, of course."

R'hagnarost considered the pair of young men, staring intently at each of them in turn. Then she stretched out one glorious wing, and with precise and delicate care, she tugged loose a pair of gold and crimson pinions. She turned back and stretched her head forward, offering a feather to each one.

"There," she said, with proud satisfaction, "these will be my token to you each. No harm will come to you from my claws or voice. And should any other of my kind chance upon you, only show them the feather and they will know it for one of my own. Tell them I said to show you the courtesy of the Wind Kings."

"But how will they know that we did not find these, or steal them, or take them after ye had been slain?" Darn asked, apprehensive at the thought of a griffon not even hungry, but bent on vengeance.

"Well, most certainly by the smell," R'hagnarost answered, seeming a bit surprised. "Can ye not tell: there is no essence of violence, no taint of blood upon these feathers. Ahh," she nodded slowly. "Forgive me, I had forgotten that the sense of smell was lost to thy kind when thy ancestors climbed down from the trees. Still, it is no matter. Accept my word, that any griffon will know that these tokens were freely given. Speak my name, if any doubts remain, for no others who wander on two legs hold the knowledge of my true name. None that still draw breath, that is." The griffoness bristled just for a moment, seeming to grow half again her already formidable size, and the boys were reminded of the elemental force that they faced.

Darn looked to Loon before voicing his acceptance of the griffon's offer. Loon was already nodding so vigorously that Darn was amazed his friend's head managed to stay attached. He turned back to the Countess with a smile on his face and in his heart.

"My Lady R'hagnarost, I most fully offer my pledge. I swear by the name of the White Lady, that I shall carry to my very grave the knowledge that ye have shared with us. I will tell no others. None. That is my promise to you, on my own honor, and by the Flame of Honor that I am bound to follow."

"And myself, also," Loon nearly shouted in his haste. "I will ne'er tell a soul. By th' White Lady, I so swear."

R'hagnarost nodded at their words, then looked at Loon. "And what of your shadowy friend?"

Loon tipped his head to one side for a moment, then straightened and smiled. "She says she swears by Mother-of-the-

Wild."

At the name, the great griffon dropped her head and sketched a bow. Then she stood up, shook herself to resettle her feathers, and visibly relaxed. Darn looked around in confusion, but only for a moment. He knew he had missed some part of the conversation, but he was accustomed to Loon's rambling and imaginative retorts.

"Wonderful, wonderful then," R'hagnarost continued. "In truth, the griffon Speakers tell no tales of humans bearing such dignity and honor. Be sure that when I return to my aerie, I will sing of my welcome discovery, and of the two humans I call Wing Brothers – without the wings, of course, you know." She turned her head from side to side, and the once-menacing beak snapped open and shut several times with a bone-chilling *Clack!* "Now," she said, as she eyed the pair with a humorous glint in her eye, "there was some mention of an 'unyun an' tater stew pie', I do believe."

Loon dropped his pack, and began to rummage through it for the makings of their meal. "My Lady," he called out over his shoulder. "Have ya a taste fer some song, t' drown out th' grumblin' of our bellies, while frien' Darn here starts a fire. I am a minstrel, after all."

"Why, of course, young Loon," R'hagnarost answered happily enough, puzzling over the frantic waving of Darn's hands. "I do not believe that I have ever heard the songs of men before."

"Oh, you'll surely like it, as not," said Loon as he straightened from his pack, holding a sizeable mound of vegetables in his hands and a smile of unbridled proportions on his lips. "This un's called 'Loric an' Lucky', an' its one o' Darn's very fav'rits. It goes like this …"

Chapter Twelve
Belerand

Loon panted heavily as he struggled up the steep, rocky trail. Beads of sweat clung to his forehead, and gasped and wheezed with each arduous step. A rock suddenly rolled from beneath his foot and Loon fell square on his face, his arms too sluggish to break his fall. Worse than the pain in his head though, was the wretched churning of his guts.

Oh, Dear Lady, oh please help me. I bin poisoned, sure as can be. Oh Lady, please no more. If I have t' heave one more time, I'd jest 's soon die right here.

Loon's prayer either had no effect, or the Lady looked upon his punishment as just — for a moment later he clenched up into a tight sorrowful ball, fighting a hopeless battle to bring up something from his long-emptied stomach. All the while, he slid steadily back down the mud-slick trail, till at last he fetched up against an unyielding young oak that gave him a stout poke in the kidneys as penance. Loon laid against the tree a long time, fighting back tears of misery and pain.

A rock from up above, dislodged by Loon's failed passage, came bouncing down the steep trail, gaining speed with each hop. It was a small stone really: as big as a bundhar's eye perhaps. But in any case, it had been freed from its ancestral shelf by a recent traveler, and now it was enjoying one of the few journeys of its existence. The stone laughed as it careened from boulder to tree stump, and rejoiced when it rolled from the clutches of a sand puddle that sought to capture it. The rock wondered, in the slow, ponderous way that rocks do, what would be its final destination.

As if in answer, the stone fetched hard up against a small roundish boulder covered with some kind of fine, curly yellow moss. The stone bounced a considerable distance into the air, then came straight back down to plunk hard against the mossy rock again. This time it wedged itself in between the boulder and the sand underneath.

The drilling pain that shot through Loon's skull jerked his thoughts away from his quieting stomach. He had just begun to reach a hand up when the pain hit a second time, right on the crown of his head, like one of those little *extra* whacks old Nanna used to give him after a spanking. Loon uttered a little squeak of pain and felt the top of his head. He jerked out a fair-sized rounded stone and held it up to a critical eye. Loon growled at the chunk of stone for a moment, then with as much force as his watery limbs could muster, he flung the stone down the trail behind him. For a moment, Loon thought he heard a tiny voice wailing. Then a quaking aftershock rocked his bowels, and Loon recalled with despair that his ordeal would not end until he reached the summit of the trail. He pushed himself slowly to his feet, leaning heavily on his staff. His chest swelled as he took a long, slow, deep breath, hoping that it would help to rid his body of its poisons. As he exhaled, he grimaced and wiped the tears from his face, then started to climb once again.

∗∗∗

Darn smiled out into the sky. From this ridge top he could see the entire Lodren Valley, the ripening fields of wheat and barley stretching from one side to the other like golden blankets across the land. And there were the white walls of Hovill, gleaming in the sun some three leagues distant. They had left the town at daybreak, choosing to break their fast along the trail — normally an unreasonable request in Loon's mind. But Loon's affliction that morning had prevented any complaints, only a weary, glazed-eyed nod of agreement.

It had cost them only a copper apiece the night before to convince the stable boy at the Barleycorn Inn to let them sleep in the hay. The boy had warned them to be clear of the stables by dawn, for the groomsman would be in shortly after that and it would bode none of them well should he find them there. But neither of the pair minded the thought of an early start; and besides, Loon had added as they headed into the inn, the coin they saved on a room meant more ale and roast for their bellies. But Loon was paying double now for their decisions. The innkeeper had warned them that the local brew he served was potent, and he wasn't known to be a liar.

"Not like th' wodderd down stuff, wot we send down th' coast," the proprietor had claimed merrily, as he slammed down a foam-topped crock before each of the boys. He had wiped his hands on the towel tucked in his belt, and, as an afterthought, pulled the rag free and ran it over his rosy cheeks and forehead. "An dontcha e'en compare arr draughts t' th' swill they cook up down at th' Rock: Boar's Piss, i' tis! No lads – this be th' finest stout y' aiver drunk. And when yer dun them, I'll bring ya two more — an then I'll have ya drug ootside." He had turned then and trundled back towards the kitchen, squeezing his considerable buck through the crowd with surprising ease. The barrel-waisted innkeeper had taken a shine to the boys, and true to his word, he'd kept both their mugs and ears filled throughout the evening. But today, he generosity had a cost.

The sound of heavy, pained breathing brought Darn's thoughts back to the moment. He turned in his seat, and looked down at his weary friend from atop the sun-drenched boulder where he perched.

"Ahh! The late arrival of Loon the Merry. I was beginning to worry," Darn said with a grin. Loon stumbled over the last rise of the trail, then collapsed into the cool shade beneath the stone's overhang with the bone-weary sigh of a galley slave.

"And how are we feeling, brother Loon, after our early morning excursion?"

Loon took a long shuddering breath in, and let it out slowly. Then he answered as quietly as he could: "I've died. Died, an yer a demon whose job it is t' see t' my punishment."

"Did I not warn you?" Darn asked self-righteously. In truth, only vast quantities of water and some measure of moderation had saved Darn from sharing in Loon's affliction. But Loon was loud and jolly when their roles were reversed, so Darn felt no need for pity. " 'The brews of Hovill are not to be taken lightly', I believe I said, just before you impressed the serving maid by downing an entire pitcher." Darn shook his head lightly, and smiled into the morning breeze. "No, blame me not for the pounding twixt your ears. Curse only yourself, my heavy-headed friend."

The slender boy twisted in his seat to grab at his pack, and began to root through the contents. After a moment, he found what he was looking for, and stretched out across the rock till he hung just above Loon's shady shelter.

"Fear not," Darn called, as he tossed his treasure down to his companion. "I did, after all, promise to break fast along the trail."

Loon stared at the object in his hand several moments before recognition swirled up through the pain-laced fog in his mind. At that, he drew a quick, involuntary breath — and the greasy scent of the salted jerky coated his nose and throat before he could stop himself. He only crawled a pace or two before nausea gripped him and twisted his guts into knots.

Darn laughed at the sound of his friend's gastronomic distress. But as the sounds of retching continued, Darn found his own stomach heaving in sympathy, and the joke lost most of its humor. He plucked the water skin from where he'd laid it, then dropped lightly over the side of the overhang to land next to Loon. Darn pulled a rag from his pack and drenched it in water from the skin. Then he knelt and handed the cloth to his quaking friend, who mopped at his soiled face while Darn sat in shamed silence.

***

The pair of tired young travelers crested another sharp ridge, pulling themselves along only by handfuls of stout, prickly shrubs that charged a high price for the help. They reached the top and Loon fell upon the ground, while Darned leaned panting against a gnarled, wind-beaten oak tree. The trail they had followed since early morning had apparently been laid by a drunken goat, for the path ran straight up and down every ridgeline, plunged through thorn-choked thickets, and curved back on itself time and again. Worse, the trail was covered with fist-sized stones that rolled beneath one's feet and threatened to break an ankle at every other step.

"Darn!" Loon fought for the breath to speak. "We've been following this bedamned path all day, an' still we ain't seen no sign o' th' elf camp. The stable boy said this trail led straight there!"

"I know Loon, I know," Darn answered. Surely, they should have arrived before now. This had to be the right path, but Darn couldn't imagine the elves using such a poorly-laid trail themselves. Several times Darn had left Loon in a shady spot while he searched for an easier way. But it was as if the bushes and trees themselves conspired to block his passage, for more than once Darn found himself herded back to his starting point by angry hedges of firethorn, scrabbling arms of thick pine groves, and even once by a swarm of enraged honey bees. Exhausted and confounded, Darn began to consider turning back. Then someone coughed – discreetly – from nearby.

Darn and Loon struggled to their feet in alarm, standing back to back: Loon with a newly-cut staff at the ready, and Darn coiled and poised to strike. But no intruder appeared. Darn tried to relax, to search for the telltale colors of the hidden watcher's aura. Then just before the spectral clouds began to appear in Darn's sight, a voice spoke out.

"A rather drab emissary, the Keepers of Agni's Flames send us," a musical voice sang in a lilting tongue. "Two footsore and dusty young layabouts hardly seem appropriate ambassadors, particularly as representatives of the Scarlet." Laughter echoed out from the air itself, as sweet and unbridled as a rushing stream. The trunk of a huge, hoary oak seemed to shift, and a man-shaped form stepped away from the bole. The brown-and-green patchwork jerkin he wore had concealed him perfectly against the oak's bark.

"All the same, dirty or not, you will find only welcome in these lands," Belerand said, as he ducked into a deep bow and opened his arms wide. When he straightened, a wide smile split the ranger's well-worn features.

Loon smiled and waved wearily before slumping back into an exhausted heap, ignorant of the elf's speech. Darn laughed in surprise, and bounded forward to meet their Sylvan friend. He stopped short to perform a bow of his own, but was swept up in a brotherly hug by the elder elf.

"Glad we are to finally find you, friend Belerand," Darn said in the *Sidhest*, the silver language of the elves. "We had all but given up hope of reaching your camp. Another half-day of this unforgiving travel, and I believe Loon would have cut me to pieces and marked his way back home with my fingers and toes." Darn shook his head and motioned south, towards Hovill. "They told us back at town that this trail led to the Sylvan camp. 'An easy day's hike', they said. Was anything but easy, I can assure thee."

Now it was Belerand's turn to laugh, and he looked closely at the scratches and brambles that covered his young friend from head to toe. "Indeed, the men of Hovill spoke the truth: this path does lead to our home. But I would wager my cap that they made no mention of the need for a Sylvan guide to walk it, did they?"

Darn shook his head, puzzled.

"Aah! Tis true, my young friend. The woodlands and trees here have known my people for untold generations. They would never allow someone to come upon us without an invitation. So with no Sylvan guide to show the way, never will the path lay true. Instead, ye will only ever find a twisting, bramble-filled goat path leading through every thicket and over every rock-face in the forest. And in the end, should ye persist in following it, the trail would carry thee round the entire valley, and back to Hovill again." Belerand shook his head at his visitors' battered appearances. "Yes, I am afraid that the good innkeepers of Hovill have enjoyed a laugh at thy own misfortunes. Others have attempted the same unwelcome journey. Though I will admit, I know of none others that persisted so far."

Darn laughed at his own foolishness, and together he and the ranger walked to where Loon lay. Belerand greeted Loon in passing Eldorn speech, then gave up his attempts at conversation and let his actions speak instead. He pulled a small horn flask from inside his pack and passed it to Loon, motioning for him to drink.

Loon shook his head, and tried to push the flask away. "Tell Sir Belerand thanks much fer 'is offer, but I made a solemn vow ne'er t' drink agin — least not till m' head stops a-poundin'." Loon smiled weakly, and tried to pantomime the ache in his skull. But the motion set his head to spinning again, and his stomach lurched in nauseous agreement.

Darn began to translate, but Belerand waved him to silence.

"Indeed, our friend Loon has no need of any further abuse," Belerand said. "I myself have fallen prey to the powerful brews of Hovill on occasion. But tell him that this is *Sinta-del-Luín*, the Dew of the Moon. Not only will it dismiss the misery he carries, but it will return to him the smile that he has lost." The tall elf laughed and tossed the horn to Loon despite the boy's protests. "It is painstaking to harvest, and few of the man-folk have tasted it — but I fear that we shall be forced to carry him if he does not find some relief."

Loon eyed the flask warily, despite Darn's translation and encouragement. He finally drank a few sips, as much to bring an end to Darn's insistence as to hopefully end the demon band that played between his ears. The elven liquor had almost no discernable taste, a silvery coolness that flowed down his throat and seemed to run out to the end of his fingers. The barest hint of sweet flower nectar calmed the storm that raged in his stomach, and Loon felt a blissful silence descend over the screeching imps running rampant inside his skull. Even as the elven liquor worked its magic, his namesake smile stretched across Loon's face, once again reminding him that he was the happiest person he knew. He handed back the flask and stretched deliciously in the fading afternoon sunlight, marveling at how good he felt.

Darn shared a small sip of the liquor himself, and felt the aches and pains of the tortuous hike melt away. Even Belerand allowed himself a swallow – purely for social purposes, or so he insisted. As the elven ranger stashed his flask, the boys slung their packs on their backs and declared that they were ready to move onward.

Belerand turned smoothly and began walking towards an impassable thicket of gorse and dwarf pines, motioning for his companions to follow. "Stay close behind me," he warned, "for the forest can be impatient with unknown travelers." Darn wondered out loud how they would pass through the barrier, but Belerand just smiled. Loon simply trudged along trustingly, whistling an odd tune as they walked. As they reached the veritable wall of brush and trees, Belerand turned sideways and slipped into the thicket, following a trail that was invisible from more than a few paces away. Darn and Loon crowded in close behind and found to their amazement that the path opened before them as they traveled, leaving a close – but passable – corridor for them to follow. Once, Loon strayed too far behind, his attention captured by an insect that looked more like a walking stick than a bug. When he looked up, though, he found himself enclosed in an impenetrable cell of brambles and branches. His cry for help brought Belerand's laughing return, and upon his arrival Loon found the pathway once again clear.

Within the space of a candlemark, the group reached the top of the ridge. And as the sun fell into the sharp-toothed maw of the western Rendrac peaks, the three travelers looked down into a long river valley, just beginning to fill with the smoky dusk. Belerand waved towards the darkening valley below, and by his hand, it seemed, a thousand tiny lights began to glow across the vale.

"Welcome, my friends, to the Dawnwoods." The elven ranger smiled broadly as he spoke. "Leave your troubles outside its halls, and carry away all the peace and contentment that your heart may hold. For here is the home of my people, and here is a peace and happiness such as you may never know again. Be welcome now, but be prepared for sorrow when you leave. For once you have known the Dawnwoods, no other place on this world will ever seem as lovely and full of peace."

As the three began to make their way down into the valley, the trilling song of a night warbler rang out, beautiful and eloquent. But the notes held a certain odd lilt at the end that tugged at Darn's attention. He knew the bird's song well from the endless days he'd spent in the woods as a young boy: this one simply didn't sound quite right. He mentioned the point to Belerand, and received the elf's respectful nod in return.

"Aye, friend Darn. I had not thought that round ears could tell such a difference. But you are correct all the same; that song was never made by one of the feathered kind. It was a signal that we have been cleared by the warders to pass into the Dawnwoods."

Darn stopped and turned slowly about, searching the growing darkness for some telltale sign that would pinpoint the sentries. "I had meant to inquire about watchers, since I have seen no one who would block our way."

Belerand laughed and shook his head. "You will not see them no matter how you squint or stare. But be assured, should you have somehow managed to gain this spot without my guidance, you would now find yourself sprouting more feathers than any of our winged friends." He raised an arched eyebrow knowingly. "And *Sylvan* archers miss nothing."

Darn frowned as they continued walking. "I had not thought that there was danger here for your people to fear. As I was taught it, the peace between the elves and the troll folks has stood for four hundred years. There is war no longer; is that not so?"

"Aye," answered Belerand. "Indeed, we have set aside our differences with the scaled ones. But there is still no love lost between our peoples. Remember, our races both have long lives and longer memories." The elven ranger seemed lost inside himself as he led the boys down the path. Slowly, finally, he continued. "I myself fought in the last great troll war. And may the Lady forgive me, but I doubt I will ever look to those desolate peaks without feeling the bite of loss, and a gnawing for vengeance still in my heart. These days, trolls rarely travel down from the mountains. Yet still," he added solemnly, "there are evils that stalk the land, even here in the Lady's domain." The graying elf shook his head sadly, and walked quietly for a moment. Then the smile returned to his face and he clapped Darn lightly on the shoulder.

"But enough of this dark talk. No darkness walks within the Dawnwoods, for the starshine of our laughter would be a spear in the heart of any who serve the Dark Master. Here is the one spot in all of Eldor where man or elf may lay aside his sword, and have no fear for its need."

Despite his friend's reassurance, Darn felt his back itch under the gaze of the hidden watchers. Set thy sword aside if ye wish, my friend, he thought. But my hands shall stay wary.

The odd trio followed an well-cared path that seemed to open through the gorse and brambles before them, and close just as neatly behind. They wandered lazily down the flank of the high ridge line, and when they reached the valley floor, it seemed the forest reached out to swallow them up.

***

An growing pain in his neck made Darn realize he'd been staring upwards for far too long. When he looked over to Loon, he found that his large friend seemed decidedly smaller, dwarfed by the tremendous bole of the ancient goldenoak they stood before. Loon, too, stood gazing upwards, enraptured by the emerald sky above them and the tremendous rough-barked columns that supported it.

The great tree extended up, up into the sky, seeming to brush the clouds aside. A full-hand of men could not have linked arms around the base of the forest leviathan. Its roots cradled a mass of great boulders as easily as a child's hand holds a collection of pebbles. It was an awe-inspiring sight, a humbling experience to stand before it. Darn could only feel that an entity such as this, who had lived as long as the elves themselves, who watched the years pass like leaves blowing by, such a force must certainly have collected a vast treasure of wisdom and power.

Belerand smiled at his awestruck companions. "I see that neither of you have beheld the majesty of a grandfather tree before." He stepped up to rest a hand against the heavy, silver bark, closing his eyes as he stood quietly. A wash of serenity poured over his face. Belerand's breathing slowed as he settled deeply, deep like tree roots, oblivious to all else save his touch upon the tree. With slow cautious steps, Loon moved up beside the elven ranger and laid his own huge hands on the tree's skin. Almost at once, his eyes took on a dreamy slouch, and Loon motioned for Darn to join them beside the great tree.

Darn stepped forward, curious and cautious. He laid tentative fingers on the thick scales of wood, the texture rough but somehow still curiously slick. He closed his eyes and felt a deep, throbbing pulse from the great tree. Darn was sure he could feel the tree slowly drawing life and vitality from the soil and stones beneath his feet, pushing the green lifeblood up to the farthest unseen reaches of the branches above, then at last breathing that life into the cobalt sky. Darn could feel the emerald life-force of the tree gently – but inexorably – tugging at him, as if he stood on the banks of a wide, deep river. A streamlet of the tree's power began to flow down Darn's arms, and a small eddy of verdant power began to swirl within him, growing, enveloping him. His heartbeat slowed, matching the steady pulse of the tree. The urge began to simply relinquish his own will and surrender to the patient, peaceful life enjoyed by the ancient tree. But something tugged insistently at his shoulder, pulling him back to the world of those-that-walk.

Darn blinked his eyes open and found Loon beside him,

looking as stunned as Darn felt. They slowly turned in unison, and found their elven friend standing behind them with tears in his almond-shaped eyes. Darn realized that he felt a dampness on his own cheeks as well.

"That, my friends," said Belerand, "is but a taste, a glimmer of a true earth-power. *Löthari*, we name this one: Watchful Grandfather. He draws deep from Lord Gröme's power, tapping the strength of the earth and the stones. And he melds it with the growing, green strength of the White Lady's grace." The elven ranger laid a reverent hand against the trunk, and looked quietly into the hidden secrets of the canopy for a moment. "This tree has guarded the entrance to our valley since my people first came here. He listens to the voices of the wind, and holds all the wisdom of the land. He has rejoiced the birth of every bird, heard every cry of pain and felt every sorrow. Aye," he nodded, "this tree is a power."

Darn tried to translate Belerand's words for Loon's understanding; but in truth, Darn wasn't sure he understood them himself. The tree was lovely, and certainly very old. But Belerand went on about it as if it were a person, an entity with a will and a mind. Darn's confusion begged for an answer, but to question a belief that Belerand obviously held so strongly seemed hardly polite.

Loon, unfortunately, failed to reach the same conclusion, and blurted out his thoughts.

"I believe that ol' tree's got some pow'ful juice flowin' through its veins," Loon remarked. Then he sighed and shrugged his shoulders. "Shame, though, that somebody witha sharp axe an' a mean spirit could bring ol' Grandfather down t' kindlin' wood." Loon spoke frankly, no slight intentioned or mirrored on his brow.

Belerand's eyes opened wide in sudden alarm as a great cracking sound split the air. The tall elf grabbed both boys by the arm and drug them quickly from beneath the oak's spreading canopy. Moments later, a branch as thick as Loon's thigh crashed to the ground where they had just stood moments before. The ground trembled, and one of the great boulders held beneath the tree's roots split down the middle with a crumbling wail.

"Friend Loon, friend Loon," Belerand said reproachfully, in his poorly-accented Eldorn. "I know your heart harbors no dark wishes. Still, such words should not be spoken within Löthari's hearing or reach. Even to think such thoughts is not safe. Grandfather is .." Belerand looked to Darn for the word. " ...ah.., perceptive. That is it: he hears much more than what is merely said."

At Belerand's odd warning, Loon and Darn turned back to stare at the great goldenoak. An overpowering feeling of being watched, of being known, fell over the pair. Grandfather Tree now seemed to loom over them, menacingly. A harsh wind began to whip through the leaves, and all over the great tree, branches clattered together with a threatening sound like spears and swords rattling in their scabbards.

Belerand stepped forward, his palms upraised. "*Deena àthorn*, Löthari. *Deena àthorn!*" he said quietly, but powerfully.

Slowly, the wind faded till it was once again a playful breeze. The leaves reflected softly like jade, and the scampering, twittering sounds of life stirred again among the branches. Belerand backed slowly away, lowering his hands. When he turned back to his two companions, his face radiated a calm, deep power. Even so, beads of sweat circled his brow. The elf ranger smiled as he turned his young friends and led them deeper into the forest. "As I was saying," he added, "Grandfather is not to be trifled with."

A visibly-shaken Loon said nothing, only nodded his head violently.

Belerand led them along a wide path, the columns of massive trees flanking either side and holding up an emerald sky. After a while, Loon wondered aloud how long it might be to Belerand's village, as lunchtime had long since passed.

Belerand laughed and raised his hands upwards. "But we are already here, Friend Loon. This is where we choose to make our home."

It took a few moments of staring, then the shape of structures began to appear, resting among the branches of many of the great trees: something part nest, part house. Some of the buildings seemed to be woven of tightly-knit branches. Others looked as if after generations of growing, the limbs had simply melded together, sheathing the dwellings with walls of living wood.

Some of the trees were wound about with long graceful stairways, constructed entirely of living branches which sprouted from the great trunks. From the lowest branches, great nets of interwoven vines and branches hung downwards, adorned by purple and white blossoms that grew upon them. The boughs of many of the great trees were wide enough for three to walk abreast. And upon them all swung a joyous community of elven people, young and old alike, singing and laughing and talking among themselves. Cabled walkways hung between a few of the larger trees, but they seemed to receive little traffic. For as demonstrated by the children who played and scampered and leapt among the branches, the people of the Dawnwoods were as home among the trees as were the squirrels and the martens who also made their lives there.

The two boys followed behind their elven guide, speechless in their wonder, for the trees formed a living city, more grand than anything hewn of stone. Even Darn had never been honored with the sight of a true Sylvan hold before. The elves of his childhood near Warden Woods had all belonged to the wilder, nomadic clans who lived near the edge of the forest, close to the human pasturelands and easy hunting. Those elves wove simple lean-to's on the ground or in the crotch of a tree for a single night, then moved on in the morning.

As Darn and Loon began a babble of questions, Belerand pointed to some of the younger trees nearby, and the workers who moved slowly among the growing branches.

"See how the Warders sing to their trees the songs of strength, of growing, of being. It is dangerous work, for always they must venture out where the branches are still young and easily convinced to follow the warder's commands. The old branches have their own minds about things, and are not easily swayed from their chosen paths. Still," he continued, as he directed his friends towards a particularly grand goldenoak, "in times of need, they too may be sung to awakening. And as our earlier taste of Lothari's anger has shown you, the Forest Kings are not to be trifled with."

Belerand motioned to where a wizened elf sat on a broad limb. As the elf crooned a quiet tune of power, he bent several thin branches upwards. At his insistence, the branches sprouted new growth, quickly intertwining as they grew and stretched. The tree warder moved back and forth, minding the new branches and singing to them quietly. Finally, his song ended, he pulled his hands away and moved back. A woven wall of green and brown stood, moving only a little in the lazy breeze. The warder moved to a cross-limb, and began to form a second wall. And once again, Darn marveled at the simplicity and beauty of the elves' lives.

***

Loon turned his head slowly, staring with wonder at the "room" he'd been granted. The entire place was woven of living tree branches: the walls, floor, ceiling, even the furniture. The room rocked ever so gently as the giant tree it perched in swayed slowly in the evening breeze. Loon had never imagined such a place, never even dreamed of such a place even after a double helping of kidney pie and too much beer before bed. By the light of the glowstone that Belerand had left in a niche by the door, Loon could see two broad limbs, as stout as flour kegs, that supported the little cabin. As well, the many smaller branches the limbs sprouted wove back and forth, providing a solid, if disconcerting, flooring. The walls were made of woven branches also, growing and twisting together, leaving room for a window on either side and a doorway facing back towards the trunk of the goldenoak. Slender leaf-filled branches crossed the doorway, providing some measure of privacy, but still allowing the whispering breeze to play through. The bench that Loon sat upon grew from the floor along one wall; the branches that formed it were quite supple and strong, though they gave alarmingly when Loon first lowered his considerable bulk down on it. But Belerand had assured him that it would hold his weight, and true to the ranger's word, the bench settled only enough to shape itself to Loon's backside. Loon had to admit he found it all-in-all to be quite comfortable — even if his legs did hang over from the knees down. Of course, nice as it was, Loon would just have soon made camp on the ground, not up in a tree like some drunken squirrel. But Loon knew that he seldom won any arguments once Darn's mind was set, and Darn was determined to stay in a living cottage the same as their hosts.

Loon looked to where Darn slept in a hammock of verdant ivy vines. Thinking about the big hurts what Darn carried, after losing Eillena and having that big fight and all, caused tears to leak Loon's eyes like some big foolish taterhead. Darn had told Loon only the roughest tale of what had happened during his fight with Arak: a Test of Honor, he'd called it. The battle had left his friend scarred, inside as well at out, Loon knew. And even though Darn had survived, and had given Arak his justice, it hadn't lifted the cloak of pain his friend had worn ever since Eillena's death. Loon knew that Darn felt terribly bad about Eillena, not being able to rescue her from her attackers. Loon felt bad too, since he'd been of no help at all, sprawled in a drunken heap with two round young ladies and his trollish friend. But Eillena was gone, and neither of them could do anything about it now. In Loon's mind, that was the end of it, for he had enough trouble concentrating on today's troubles and needs. Wishing for things he couldn't have just wasn't Loon's way of living.

Wishing fer things b'fore me is another matter all t'gether, Loon thought, as a child-sized figure slipped quietly through the doorway of their room.

Gell'rin smiled when she saw that Loon was awake, and her eyes sparkled mischievously. At first glance, the elven huntress might have been mistaken for a waifish, human child. But upon closer inspection, it was clear that she bore no relation to the clumsy race of men. Slight even for an elf maid, Gell'rin seemed almost kin to the fairy folks, with her sharp bright beauty and tiny delicate features. With brilliant violet eyes and the tips of upswept ears peeking through the ringlets of her hair, Gell'rin Springleaf was beauty enough to turn the head of any male, Sidhe, Sylvan, human, or other.

Yet the blood of elvish warriors flowed through her veins. Gell'rin's mother was born of Belerand's Sylvan people, while her father was a distant cousin to the Sidhe king himself. Some said the spirit of Vana of the Black Bow, the great warrior-queen, lived again in young elven maid. Campfire tales told how Gell'rin had once shot out the eye of a charging warg, and had never readied a second arrow, so sure was she of her aim. She could run the deer of the forest to exhaustion, then sing them a song of rest and healing as they laid their heads in her lap. And while she was too small to wield a proper sword, Gell'rin had more than once proved her mettle with the long boot knives she normally carried.

Though she was most comfortable wearing the leaf-patterned jerkin of her mother's people, for tonight Gell'rin was dressed as befitting a cousin to the king. Her knee-length shift of glimmering silk changed colors as she moved, from silver-grey, to blue, to the purple-green of her eyes, and back. A belt of hammered moon-silver clasped about her waist, holding an embroidered purse on one side, and a finely-etched dagger on the other. She was barefoot, which somehow seemed more perfect and elegant than any satin slipper would have been. Her hair fell in rippling golden streams, splashing over her shoulders and cascading the length of her back.

Loon looked at the elf maid silently, without comment, drinking her in. And at that moment, Loon knew, in the roots of his simple soul, that his heart was no longer his own, but now belonged to another.

Gell'rin pretended not to notice Loon's stare, as she swept into the room almost dancing. The towering child-man intrigued her a great deal. Much more than any of her sylvan suitors, or especially the foppish Sidhe lordlings who pursued her. The elven huntress understood that the one named Loon bore a special gift — for despite his size and strength, in thought and action he still held the unencumbered joy and spirit of a child,. He was handsome too, even with his round ears and broad features. Of course, she couldn't seem too interested, for that would water down the thrill of the chase. But the human filled her with a delicious shivering, and she was forced to turn away before her blush became evident even in the room's dim emerald light. Gell'rin stepped to where Loon's companion snored in his hammock, and tickled his foot until he work with a start.

"I believe that you humans would sleep your entire short lives away, given the opportunity," she trilled, the music of her native speech infecting the Eldorn tongue with a liquid joy and rhythm. She laughed at Darn's tousled hair and bewildered look.

"My uncle Belerand has requested that I fetch you, for the dawn is soon approaching and preparations for the feast are nearing completion."

Loon squinted out through one of the windows, and frowned at the darkness outside. "Dawn? Well dawn ain't no where near t' comin' about, Gell'rin. Why, it's the middle o' th' night, just as sure as ol' Peg's got fleas!"

It was Darn's turn to laugh, as he tumbled from his hammock and began to brush his hair into submission and knock the worst of the creases from his tunic. "No Loon. Gell'rin is speaking of the Silver Dawn — the rise of the full moon. Tonight is a special night for our Sylvan hosts."

"Your friend knows much of our customs, Loon," Gell'rin said, as she smiled at Darn. "For this is the *Donée-d'Londra*, the Night of Passage, when the spirits of our ancestors may once again join us in communion and song. And for the Mistress-of-the-Night to smile fully on such a night brings an even greater presence and joy." She cocked her head and looked a bit perplexed for a moment, before continuing. "You are both very honored tonight. In my memory at least, no child of man has ever been allowed to attend this celebration. And while you may not participate in the Summoning, still you will join us for as much song and food and wine as you can hold." She looked at each of the boys in turn, then nodded. "My uncle must think very highly of you both, for there was much opposition to his decision."

Gell'rin shook her head in sudden exasperation, planted her fists on her hips and frowned mightily at the pair. "Come, laze-abouts! There will be time for talking later. For now, we will speak of naught else until you are changed into something more appropriate than those travel-weary rags you wear." She divided the pile of cloth that she held, tossing each of the young men a shimmering grey tunic of exceptional weave and hand, delicate shifts that felt as light as spider silk and just as strong. Darn suspected that the short robes may have been just that.

Gell'rin smiled wickedly as both of the boys shuffled their feet and stammered, waiting for her to turn her back before they doffed their clothes. At last she relented and turned about, not stealing more than a peak or two. But before long, she lost her patience and turned back around suddenly, laughing as the two boys tugged the hem of their tunics hastily into place. "Ye'll have the chance to bathe when we cross the river Tuínal; her waters are still cold this early in the year, but at least it will wash away the taint and dust of the man-cities." Gell'rin wrinkled her nose and chuckled sweetly, and neither Darn nor Loon could take offense in the face of her bright smile. "Though we have become accustomed to it by now, our ancestors might find the smell a bit repugnant."

"I don' think we smell," Loon began to argue. "Why, I had a bath jest th' last moon, didn't I Darn?" The towering boy cast a fearful glance at the doorway. "Besides, ol' Loon don' much care fer walkin' these tree branches in th' dark. Didna much care fer it e'en in the light, come t' think offit."

"I'll have no arguments now," Gell'rin said forcefully, her sweet child's voice turning as gruff as it was able, nearly as gruff as a thrush's song. "We must make haste. The Elders will have harsh words for me if I allow our guests to arrive late and smelly." Gell'rin stepped forward and took hold of Loon's littlest finger, which filled her grasp. She tugged insistently towards the doorway and the huge hulking fellow followed along, suddenly docile as a lamb, but with a pronounced pout riding his lips.

Darn smiled to himself at the sight: burly Loon, in an elf-sized tunic that barely covered his arse, being bullied by a elf maid a third his size. Gell'rin's spunk reminded Darn much of Eillena's fiery spirit, and he smiled at the reflection. But then the rest of that memory wiped the smile from his face. Darn shook his head, and wondered how long it would take to dispel the shadows that threatened him each time he thought of his lost friend. He followed the odd pair through the leafy doorway, then laughed in spite of himself at Loon's wailing protests as Gell'rin led the towering young man out onto a precarious walkway of branches and darkness.

Chapter Thirteen
Night of the Silver Dawn

"Aah! Welcome my young friends!"

Belerand turned from the group of elves he'd been speaking with, as Gell'rin brought Darn and Loon out of the shadows between the great trees. "I see that my niece has been thoughtful enough to provide you with fresh clothes and a bath. It is a much-needed improvement, I might add, over the pair of bedraggled travelers I found limping through the woods this afternoon," he said with a merry smile. The tall Sylvan elf was dressed in a tunic of the same fashion as those that Darn and Loon both wore. But there, the similarities ended. Belerand's short robe was patterned with the finest silver stitching, outlining delicate patterns that shifted and swam in the low light. A wide belt of scarlet-dyed leather cinched at his waist, studded with smooth stones that shimmered and blazed and appeared – to Darn's untrained eyes, at least – to be Parthinian fire opals. Grey hose of the same material as his tunic covered his legs, and a pair of magnificently-polished black hunting boots rode up to just below his knees. A circlet of silver carved in the likeness of twisted vines of ivy held back his raven hair. And from a heavy necklace of broad silver links hung a faceted oval of blackest onyx as large as a fishhawk's egg.

Had it not been for the elf's crooked smile, Darn doubted he would have recognized his Sylvan friend. *A long cry from his leathers and mottled jerkin*, Darn thought. He'd had no inkling that Belerand was anything more than a band leader of sylvan rangers. But from what elven lore he possessed, Darn knew that the ivy circlet his friend wore named him as Cuthain, the shepherd or chieftain of this valley and its people.

A discreet cough from Belerand's elvish companions brought Darn's musings to an end. The Sidhe couple wore a garish array of unmatched jewelry and clothes of rather startling hues. Both of the elves had the white-gold hair and delicate brittle features of the high-bred (or, as some rumored, in-bred) Sidhe nobles. Standing beside Belerand, they seemed like rainbow-hued tropical birds far from their accustomed element. In addition to their obvious overdress, the Sidhe couple both wore carefully-held masks of aristocratic disdain. Darn immediately disliked the pair, or perhaps he felt sorry for them: he wasn't sure which. Loon wondered if perhaps they were performers, a carnival-clad pair of fools costumed for the upcoming festival.

"Ah, please forgive my lack of manners," Belerand said in the *Sidhest*, one corner of his mouth turned up in a mischievous smile. "My friends, may it please me to present the esteemed Lord Othel and Lady Mesmerand of the House of Iet-Türin, far from their home in the city of Türin-väal. My Lord and Lady, please honor me in welcoming Lord Agni's disciple, Darn of the Pyre, and his stalwart compatriot, the renown bard, Loon the Leviathan." At this last, Belerand winked conspiratorially at Darn, who bit his tongue to keep from laughing. Loon, who understood nothing but the mention of his name, simply bowed deeply, leaving Darn to stand awkwardly for a moment before following his friend's lead. The Sidhe couple barely nodded in return, dismissing the human barbarians from any further consideration. Then they turned their attention back to their earlier conversation with Belerand, in which they had been complaining about the apparent crudeness of their accommodations.

Belerand, however, was ready to surrender neither his dignity nor his courtesy for the sake of the Sidhe's prattle. Instead, he waved a hand and cut off Lord Othel in the middle of his first sentence.

"I am sure, my Lord and Lady, that you will excuse me while I attend to my young guests here. They are strangers to our land and customs, and we would surely not wish for them to leave the Dawnwoods with any tale of elvish boorishness." Belerand smiled sincerely and sketched a deep bow. Before the Sidhe could compose a response, he continued: "My niece Gell'rin – whom I believe you have had the pleasure of meeting earlier – will be glad to attend you. Indeed, I am sure that she will provide better company for you than I could manage: she is a second cousin to the King himself, and was schooled for many years in the treasured halls of Corinväal. I am sure that she will find your tales of the court a welcome respite from our base and uncultured existence here in the woods."

Without waiting for a reply, Belerand turned his back to the Sidhe and gathered Loon and Darn to accompany him. Gell'rin moved to push back a strand of golden hair from her face, and from behind her hand stuck her tongue out at her uncle. Then she turned back to her Sidhe guests with a dazzling smile on her face and words of court flattery on her lips.

Belerand led his young charges through the trees, asking forgiveness for the rudeness of his Sidhe cousins. "They are as they are. I should not fault them for that, for others of their ilk can be far, far worse, as you saw in the forest when we met, " Belerand said. "But courtesy – and the Elder Council, I might add – dictate that I suffer their ungracious presence during this time of rejoicing. After all, I would be as bad as they, should I refuse their hosting." The elf smiled at his human companions, and shrugged off the ill-grace of the Sidhe.

"My friends, I would trade a legion of their kind, with all their finery and gold, for a simple camp and the companionship of two fellows such as yourselves. Ah, but enough of my ramblings, for here we are," Belerand said, as the trio emerged from the thick column of trees to find themselves at the edge of a wide open meadow. The verdant gleam of glowstone lanterns dotted the glade, and Darn could just make out a long trestle table at the center of the glade. A drifting breeze delivered a host of wonderful smells: fresh pepper bread and roasted crab apples, boiled fire kibbig, seared venison, the foamy tang of hardened cider, and the dusky breath of early musk melons.

Just then, someone blew a long, lonesome note on a elven horn, like the plaintive cry of a night swan. And as one, the green glow of the lantern stones winked out. Belerand, too, closed the door on his lantern, and the three companions joined in the darkness that spread across the meadow. Darn began to frame a question, when Loon's exclamation stole the words from his lips.

"Oh, Darn! By the Lady's Breath!" Loon said, almost a whisper, as he pointed towards the far edge of the clearing. As they watched, the full moon began to rise, larger, closer, more brilliant than either of them had ever seen before. A silver titaness, she leapt from the mountain tops into the night sky, beaming down on her children. And as the moon rose, she painted the meadow with her soft silver dawnlight.

"Come, my friends," Belerand said with a laugh. "Be Welcome to the Silver Dawn! Now is the time to leave the woes of human-kind behind. Come discover why there is such joy in the hearts of the Sylvan elves." And indeed, never again did either of the boys chance upon another place of such gentle grace and beauty.

***

The Mistress of the Sky had danced from one edge of the meadow to the other as the night passed by. To Darn it seemed as if the night had drained away far too quickly, like the final cup of a fine wine. He belched contentedly, then flushed at his own rudeness, remembering too late how the elves disdained such common displays. But Belerand laughed merrily and slapped Darn on his knee.

"Ah, my friend, it has been far too long since I enjoyed the raw company of the *Let-mon-Marnath*. The joy with which your people live life brightens my day. Though it also fills me with sadness for my cousins, the Sidhe. For many of them have forgotten how wonderful it is to be alive!" Outlined in sharp moonlit shadows, Belerand savored another drink of wine, then laughed loudly and passed the skin along to his young companion.

Darn took a long draught and laughed himself, for the bright elven wine seemed to loosen all the joy in his heart, while gifting him with none of the spinning sickness that accompanied his other attempts at drunkenness. The wine shared the same eldritch brilliance as the moonlight, and Darn thought he could feel the silvery glow of it sinking into his skin, drenching him with a crystal purity. But Belerand's words caught at Darn's attention just before they drifted off into the night. In turn, they brought questions of his own to the boy's lips.

"Belerand?" Darn began, then he broke off into laughter again when the elf waggled his eyebrows like flying seabirds in response. Once he collected himself, Darn continued.

"Are Loon and I truly the first humans to join in the *Donée-d'Londra*? For surely the Sylvan folk and humans have known each other for many years? I know that some of the old tales speak of High King Ælfred as 'the Elf Friend', but that may be only a tale. Gell'rin, though, she speaks Eldorn as well as most humans I know, and better than many. Yet I had thought there was little discourse between our peoples. For in the village of my youth, only myself and old Makheim the healer had any contact with the Sylvan folk, and we were both considered quite odd for it."

"Any more questions, before I begin answer?" Belerand asked teasingly. When Darn shook his head, somewhat abashed, the elf continued.

"I was not a young elf when the boats of thy people first touched this shore, and I saw them build and destroy and build again, like warring colonies of ants. Our cousins the Sidhe chose to simply watch, unmoved and uncaring in their stone towers, while your people wasted their lives in petty disputes over land and gold. But my Sylvan brethren and I greatly cherished the quick, flaring beauty of the *Let-mon-Marnath* – like swiftly fading blossoms of the cherry tree. On several occasions, I led my people on a journey of aid, bringing food and clothing to the tiny fishing village that called itself Shiningrock. And once, when that town had grown to a great city, I knew a certain Lord Marshall there who walked as a man into the desert, seeking death. He emerged as something quite different, something both less and more than a man."

Darn sat bolt upright as the significance of Belerand's last words struck him. He grabbed wildly at his dancing thoughts, and it took several moments before he was able to bring the words to his lips.

"A Lord Marshall? Ye speak of Tyrin, do ye not?" Darn asked, his mind whirling from the implications.

"Indeed I do, young Flame Dancer. We knew him as *Köndi-let-Tonal*, the Warrior Who Wanders, when he ventured and lived among us for a time after the wars. But among his own people, he was known by his battle-name, Tyrin." Belerand sighed softly, and an old pain marched quietly across his eyes. "Later, he became another: *Atärr-ni-Agni*, Agni's Sword. And I knew him no more."

Darn frowned, at odds with himself. The memory was clearly not a pleasant one for Belerand, but Darn could no more contain his questions than he could forgo breathing.

"Belerand — please forgive my questions, for I see it brings ye no joy. But I must know more of Tyrin. It is his example that I and my fellows follow, his teachings that have determined who we are – and who we may become."

Belerand looked at him sadly. "Be wary of who ye may become, my young friend. Be careful of what ye wish. The Tyrin I knew was a good man, a fierce – but fair – warrior. We spent many days hunting together, he and I. And though we often disagreed on the nature of things, of certain justice and the right of dominion, still I felt his compassion, his sense of the gray areas that border between black and white, right and wrong." The elven ranger rubbed at a spot between his brows, trying to ease the pain of his remembrance.

"We had no word of Tyrin's fate until after his sentencing was already carried out. By then, there was nothing we could do to save him, for the Land of Ashes is denied us and to step upon its sands is the death of any elf." Belerand lowered his head, and darkness seemed to gather in the hollows beneath his brows. "But later," he continued, "we heard the tales of Tyrin's return, and our scouts saw the flames as the council building was scorched to the earth."

Darn smiled grimly, but proudly. "Indeed, our teachings tell that Tyrin destroyed those who had corrupted the city. He brought Lord Agni's justice among those that knew it not, and instilled peace and order once again."

Belerand's eyes clouded over. "And do thy teachings tell," he asked quietly, "of the innocents who died, of the women and babes who perished in the flames of Tyrin's 'justice' when he burned the houses of the councilmen?"

Darn's stunned silence was answer enough.

The wineskin seemed to bring Belerand no solace, though he gulped its cold ruby blood eagerly, almost desperately. He flicked a drop from the corner of his mouth with a fastidious finger, and handed the skin to Darn as he continued.

"I tried to speak to Tyrin only once after that," Belerand said sadly. "But the man I knew was no more. This man, if man he still was, had room in his soul only for Agni's Flames, for Justice and Battle and the *Honor* he spoke of so highly."

"Ye speak as if justice were a thing to be shunned," Darn said, aggravation clipping his words, marring the birdsong of the elven tongue which they spoke. "But Tyrin and his Flame Masters brought justice to all the people, wresting Shiningrock from the choking grasp of a corrupt council."

"Aye, he brought justice," Belerand answered, "and it was sorely needed. But the justice he meted out was brutal and fine-edged, with no room for compassion, no consideration for human frailties. I saw such justice call for a stick-ribbed street urchin to be flailed for stealing a heel of bread. And Tyrin's justice was often bent to serve the 'Honor' that he and his pupils swore to uphold."

Belerand drew a deep breath, held it, then let it out slowly. "I had traveled to Shiningrock one last time to speak to the *Atärr-ni-Agni*, this man who had once been named Tyrin, in hopes of discovering the whereabouts of my true old friend."

"On the last day I ever set foot in the city, a simple cooper too deep in his cups spoke drunken words besmirching the reputation of the Disciples. Within the space of two bells, he found himself hopelessly crippled in an 'honor match' against one of Tyrin's followers, a contest he had no chance of winning. No longer able to work, the man and his entire family were unhomed and turned out into the street within a hand of days, forced into the ranks of the street beggars. Such was the *Honor* that Tyrin expounded."

Darn searched his memory for the teachings he'd been given. But within them, he found no answer, no excuse for Belerand's tale. "But there must be some honor in the world," Darn argued weakly. "Else we are all simple savages."

"I have known many men, many elves and dwarves and troll-kind too, who died for their honor," Belerand said slowly, thoughtfully. "Whether their honor was of any benefit beyond the grave, I know not. But of this I am quite sure." Belerand took a long drink, closed his eyes, and sighed. "They are all still very, very dead." Belerand was silent for a moment, following the flight of a golden-winged nightmoth as it fluttered clumsily in front of them. "As for me," he finally continued, "I believe that I shall remain a simple savage."

Silence laid down with the two companions, a silence that only the nighthawk dared to break with its call. Darn felt angry, for Belerand had cast doubt and blemish on the only thing in Darn's life that made him feel worthwhile: the honor of being called a Disciple of the Flames. He doubted that his elven friend had wished him pain, but still, an insult to Darn's Order was an insult to himself. Perhaps worst of all though, Belerand's words had touched on subjects that had troubled Darn since the first day of his training. Darn had listened to many long-winded lectures by the Masters, expounding on the duties and obligations which their skills and robes inherently brought: to defend the weak and unprotected, and to bring justice to the land. And most often, it seemed as if Grandmaster Saura enforced the strictures fairly, but firmly. Generally, those that could not abide the discipline left before their first branding.

But as age and experience opened Darn's eyes, he began to see things somewhat differently. Many of the Flame Masters, it seemed, were more concerned about their own honor, and that of the Order, than they were about the welfare of ordinary people, those supposedly in their care for whom justice supposedly must be served. Darn noticed the petty way that Elias would take offense at the merest slight given in public, and how he enjoyed intimidating an entire tavern with his glare. Or the way that Master K'tarr was so compulsively concerned with the cleanliness of his archery students and their equipment, while his servants were not allowed to even bathe in the manse's pools. Beggars were turned away hungry from the doors of the Pyre, and were lucky if they didn't receive a beating for their troubles. Red-sashed senior students were known to roam the city's bars and brothels, searching for drunken sailors to test their skills upon. And yet they received little or no admonishment when confronted with such dishonorable actions.

The arguments found no certain place to rest in Darn's mind, for the loyalty and dedication that he had first pledged to the Order had not waned with time. He acknowledged his induction as one of Agni's Disciples as the most powerful event he had yet experienced. It was undoubtedly the defining feature to his otherwise empty existence. Yet still, he could not ignore the hypocrisies he witnessed.

Such quandaries brought a grey cloud of anguish to the young man's mind. At an age when life should feel clear and bright, instead he felt haunted. It seemed the warring questions would hardly have been bearable, had it not been for the elegant sylvan wine.

Darn and Belerand laid silently in the grass, both fearful that their discussion had somehow blemished their friendship. But the moon's silver dawnlight, the clarity of the sylvan wine, and the joyous nightsong of the elves as they danced in the meadow below, would allow no discomfiture in their presence. The night breeze carried away any sting of their words, and soon the pair found themselves sharing the names of the stars. Belerand named one pattern the Frozen T'aacha, which sent them both to laughing over their meeting in Greenheart forest.

"Darn, my young friend," Belerand said, as he sat up and lithely stretched his spine. "My fondest wish would be for Loon and thyself to abide here with us. For there are so many wondrous things to behold in the Great Greenheart: the Rainbow Webs of the ancient spider-masters in the hidden towers of Turinth; the endless Falls of Forever, that leap from the shoulders of great Skypoint to fall silently into the depths of the earth. And the springtime gathering of the faeire-wights, as they dance and sing to celebrate their rebirth, is a beauty to make the hardest heart weep. Ah," he clapped Darn lightly on the shoulder, "and to rediscover such wonders in the company of young inquisitive souls, full of the bright spirit-spark of the *Let-mon-Marnath*, would bring back the joy of my own first adventures.

"I wish that we could stay as well, Belerand. Though I do not understand why ye would crave the company of humans," Darn said quietly, his words carrying only the slightest of slurs. "Except for my friend Loon, and my brother Mardon, and Master Elias on occasion – oh, and dear sweet Eillena, of course, though she is gone from us – I care not for the company of humans. Most have ever gifted me with nothing but spite and anger. In Shiningrock, even as it was in Warden Woods, greed and suspicion rule the day. And a smile seems to mark you for abuse or disciplining." Darn shook his head angrily, and tipped his head back for a long pull of the wineskin before continuing.

"When I was small, my fondest wish was to wake up one morning and discover that I had become an elf, like the Sylvan children who lived in the forest nearby. For their parents never raised a hand to them, nor spoke to them in anger. Their lives seemed only for living, and the their playground in the trees held no seeds of dissention." Darn sighed and ran a hand unconsciously over the rounded tips of his ears. "Back then I could think of no finer a life than to be born an elf, to live with the beasts of the forest and dance among the trees day and night."

"Ye know so much for one so young," Belerand said quietly, as he shook his head and smiled sadly to himself. " And yet ye know so little. Indeed, thy people are oft times a harsh lot, treating women and children less kindly than beasts. Rarely have I traveled in one of the human towns and cities, that I have not witness some random act of cruelty, some slight or blow handed down with no thought given to how deep it truly cuts. I cannot fathom how some lout could gift a sweet young child with an offhanded blow, merely for enjoying the gifts of their childhood. Aye, many times I have fought to keep my blade in its scabbard." Belerand leaned back as he spoke, resting his elbows in the feathery embrace of the sweet timothy grass.

"Indeed, many of the human kind take to harshness like a drunkard to his bottle, unable to let it go though he knows it poisons him body and soul." He took another drink from his wineskin, and reflected a sad moment. Then he shook off the malaise and sat upright, the smile returning to his face.

"But indeed, the beauty of a race cannot be judged based on its ugliest members." Belerand said in an excited rush. "Thy kind holds a gift that my people can never know. Human lives are sweet and precious, simply because they are so short. Every day is irretrievable, every decision can hold the weight of a lifetime in the balance." Belerand waved a hand towards the meadow, where his people still danced in the waning moonlight and sang their eldritch songs. "After so many years, an elf comes to realize that nothing ever has to be done right now...today. Well, almost as good as nothing. Planning for a simple picnic here may last a full turn of the seasons. The decision to form a new nest may take ten times that long. With no sense of urgency, every decision, every act can be debated, delayed, studied and measured till the last drop of joy and wonder has been drained from it. The years meld together and lose their color, till they take on the same grey tone."

He turned towards Darn, the shadows and moonlight each claiming half of his face. "Have ye any guess, how many years I have seen?" he asked.

Darn thought hard, studied the fine tracery of time that marched from the elf's almond eye. The elven folk lived long lives, he knew, and Belerand looked to be in the prime of his middle years. Darn made his best guess, then added a few decades to be sure.

"Four hundred?" he answered softly, praying that Belerand would take no offense.

The Sylvan ranger laughed long and loudly, falling back into the grass, and Darn had to rescue the wineskin before it bled the rest of its life onto the ground. Darn felt his cheeks flush with embarrassment at first, then he shrugged and joined in his friend's laughter until it slowly died away.

"My friend, my friend," Belerand chuckled, as he wiped a tear from his eye. He plucked the wineskin from Darn's grasp, arced a long drink into his mouth, then wiped his lips with the back of one hand. He tipped up his chin to speak to the dimly-lit stars, and his tone became as serious as the wine would allow.

"I, Belerand Longshin, was born during the reign of Gellad Skyseer. I fought beside my father, Tomron-lin the Treewise, during the Great Troll War, and took his place when he fell in the Battle of

Jhandar's Plain. I stood at the coronation of the Black Bow, and I wept when King Tregolas leapt from his high tower in madness. The High King Ælfred named me his friend, and I mourned for three winters when he died beneath a trollish mace." Belerand raised the wineskin once again, and frowned when it sputtered a mournful empty gasp, the last drops falling on his tongue.

Darn sat quietly, his mind whirling as he tried to make sense of all Belerand had said.

"B-but High King Ælfred died five hundred years ago," Darn muttered, almost to himself. "And a poem that old Makheim once read me, of the Sidhe King Tregolas, spoke of eight hundred winters past." The boy looked at his friend in sudden wonder. "So that would mean ..." He was struck dumb as he pondered the impossible number of years.

Belerand nodded, then said solemnly, "I have watched the leaves fall nearly twelve hundred times. And though it still fills my heart with gladness to witness the birth of the first green shoots of Spring, its joy quickly fades into the ever-hungry maw of time."

"But thee!" Belerand nearly shouted, his eyes sparkling in the dim silvery light. "Thy people cannot afford to waste a day, or even the space of a single breath! And that makes the sacrifices, the goals, and the victories, all so much more important, so much more precious and sweet."

"So here is advice that I would give to thee, Darn of the Pyre," Belerand continued. "Wish not for the wearisome life of centuries. Instead, decide which things make life worth living, then leap out after them like a hound to the hunt. Come live with us, if that is thy wish. Or chase down this young lass who holds thy heart captive, and claim her as a life-mate. And do not forgo the chance to sing some lighthearted chantey with thy friend Loon."

Belerand sat up, his tone more serious now. "In truth, ye should learn well the lessons that friend Loon has to share. For life holds naught but surprises for such as he: some joyous, some less so. Still, he wakes every day with a hunger for adventure in his soul. And every night he goes to sleep with a satisfied smile on his lips, for he knows that he has lived his life that day, not simply existed through it." Belerand was silent for several moments, as if unsure whether or not to carry on.

"Our friend Loon," he finally added, "burns fiercely in the gloom of the world. His *las'ona*, his soul-cloud – ye have seen this, yes? He is marked by the Lady to be a beacon of Light to all who seek it. Cherish him well, young Darn, for such bright fire seldom burns long."

Belerand peered into the waning darkness, searching the meadow below them. "And as we speak of thy mountainous friend, I do not see him among the dancers or musicians. In fact, I do not recall seeing much of him this entire night."

Darn turned to look down the sloping hillside, noticing with some surprise that the eastern sky was tinged with rose, heralding the night's departure. Indeed, the last time he'd seen Loon, Gell'rin Springleaf had been dragging the towering young man from among the sylvan musicians to join her in dancing the *Telspäat*, the elvish Dance of the Stars. And since then...

Oh no! Loon alone with Gell'rin! Oh buzzard brains and bundhar droppings! Why did I not watch more carefully? Darn knew that Loon had been more than a little smitten with the child-like sylvan huntress. And though Loon's mind worked slowly in many areas, amorous endeavors caused him no difficulties at all. In fact, the tall handsome fellow was well-known and well-favored by Shiningrock's professional ladies and merchants' daughters alike. But now, Loon and Gell'rin were off alone — and here Darn sat with the girl's very uncle! Swallowing thickly, Darn began to stutter an answer, aiming for as vague a truth as he felt Belerand might believe.

"I believe that I may have seen Loon last in the … uh … company of … umm … the huntress Gell'rin." Darn was forced to look away quickly when Belerand raised a crooked eyebrow, and he stumbled to find some innocent-sounding answer. "I believe she was about to show him the, uh, the …"

"The entrance to her sleeping quarters, if I know my voracious little niece," Belerand finished for his beleaguered young friend. He smiled and chuckled quietly to himself as he shook his head. Then he looked away over the tops of the trees, seeing easily through the dim light of dawn. "Ah, yes," he remarked, evidently finding what he expected. "I see the glimmer of a glowstone from her nest, atop that towering elm across the glen there. I should have known that Gell'rin would not allow such a remarkable young traveler – one with locks of gold at that – to pass through her fingers untried." Belerand shook his head again at the folly of youth, and picked up the wineskin with a smile. Halfway to his lips, he remembered that they'd finished all their wine, and he flung the skin back to the grass with a childish pout.

Darn blew out a sigh of relief, for he had feared Belerand's anger. Darn still remembered an unpleasant encounter at Loon's shack one evening with an irate silk merchant and his softly-swelling daughter: it was an episode he'd as soon not repeat. Still, his curiosity gnawed at him until it was a physical pain at the base of his skull. He had to ask the question, though he knew that he might quickly regret it.

"Belerand?"

The ranger looked over lazily from where he lay in the grass, nibbling a tender shoot he'd selected.

"I mean no disrespect, and please forgive my rudeness in the asking ..." Darn paused, unsure of how to properly frame his question. The elf smiled slyly, enjoying Darn's discomfort. At last, Belerand relieved Darn of the weight of his discomfort.

"But ye wonder how it is that I do not mind a mixing of the races? Not even when it involves my own blood. Is this the question ye seek to ask?"

Darn rushed on, eager for answers, and he let the wine in his veins deal with his embarrassment. "Indeed, it tis. Surely, I harbor no ill feelings over such a union. As I have told, I would have traded anything as a child to be born even part elf. But many of the adults in Shiningrock – in fact, most of the people I have known – they frown on such pairings between the races. Many call such offspring ill and blasphemous names, though I fail to understand why."

"Unfortunately," Belerand answered, as he shook his head in disgust, "such hatred is not an illness known only to humans. Most of the Sidhe, and even some of my own Sylvan folk, feel that to mingle our blood with others makes us less than what we were. Among the trolls, the dwarves, their cousins the gnomes, and particularly thy own human peoples, half-blooded children are often received with spite. It is the curse of small nasty minds, bringing misery to those that deserve it not." The pain of the thought laid silence over him for a while.

"Foolish hate-mongers!" Belerand finally continued. "They will never know the joy that such a child can bring among his or her people, the new strengths and talents, new wisdoms and challenges." The elven ranger stood suddenly and began to pace, smiling as he talked, his fine-boned hands helping to shape the liquid vowels of his elvish speech. "Many of the fosterlings hold the best traits of both their lines: the stalwart doughtiness of the dwarven stone-folk and their kind; the strength and tenacity of the scaled ones; the courage and fecundity of your own people; aye, and the wisdom and joy and long years of the elves. It is true that these children often live hard lives, and may bear the fear and distrust of both their kinds. Tis a heavy burden they must bear. But in truth, they are a gift to our world, a bridge between the different races, a salve to heal the many hurts we have bestowed upon ourselves. And in return, I feel that all of us are obliged to give them all the love and nurturing that we are able. For these are the healers of our world: without such children to guide and teach us, we are as so many quarrelling beasts."

Belerand stopped his pacing as his words ended, and he smiled sheepishly as he turned to Darn.

"Forgive me my tiresome preaching, young friend. But tis a subject that stirs my soul. And the reluctance of many of my own people to hear such words only makes them burn more strongly inside me." Belerand laughed at himself, and gestured to his companion. "Come. Let us break our fast with the others." He wagged the shriveled wineskin in his hand. "And perhaps we may find more life'sblood for our poor friend here."

Darn laughed in return, and stood to join his host. "Then, by thy own words, ye bear Loon no ill will for pillowing with Gell'rin?" he asked, as he brushed off the seat of his tunic.

"Indeed not," answered Belerand. "Our people have few children these days, and those that are born seem smaller and weaker with each generation. Should Gell'rin quicken from union with our friend Loon, she would surely beget a lineage of warriors and minstrels not known since the time of Gellad Skyseer."

"As Loon's children," Darn added, as they started down the long grassy slope, "they may even teach the Sylvan folk a few new things about love of life."

"Tis true!" Belerand agreed. "But let us pray that they do not inherit their father's gift of song!"

The pair began to laugh again. And as they walked, the sound of their joy mingled with the birds' morning welcome. Several elves in the meadow below turned from their breakfast feast to smile at the odd pair approaching: the tall, graceful elf lord, and the small slender human boy. But only the growing dawnlight picked out their differences, for the common voice of their laughter bound them as brothers.

***

Though they were pained to leave the companions they had found in the Dawnwoods, after a turn of days both Darn and Loon had need to begin their journey home. Darn was expected back at the Pyre before the crescent moon. And Loon feared leaving Peg without his company for too long.

"On account o' she starts t' peein' on yer bed when she gets lonely er mad atcha, an' Elias will be all kinds o' pissed 'imself if that happens!" he had said with a worried grimace.

Belerand provided the pair with enough provisions to carry them home. That, and a small flask of *Sinta-del-Luin* for emergencies of all types. He exhorted the young men to visit again, then bid them farewell, before grudgingly returning to his ungracious Sidhe guests.

Gell'rin brought Darn a parting gift of an ornate wooden flute, carved from a goldenoak branch gifted to them by Löthari Grandfather. For Loon, the gift was even more personal, as the wiry Sylvan huntress literally climbed him like a tree, planted an exuberant wet kiss on his lips, then whispered in his ear till the towering young man once again blushed crimson. Gell'rin and her rangers laughed among themselves as she hopped down and moved to join them, though she turned once to smile widely at Loon and blow him a kiss. Then she led her group away, preparing for a sortie through the mountains to the dark edges of Haldcort Forest.

The trip back to Shiningrock was long and wearisome, as they had to follow the quicker Coast Road, with no such adventures to recount besides sore feet. But the boys relived their tales every night by the campfire. And they laid extravagant plans, as young men are wont to do, to climb to the top of Skypoint, and to sail to distant Parthus, and explore the jungles of Yot. To return to the Dawnwoods, and live among their new Sylvan friends, and discover all the wonders that lay hidden in the deep, deep forest.

But plans have a way of turning, whether we will or not.

Chapter Fourteen
Darn's Rage

Darn flew across the cobblestones, squeezing through the evening crush of vendors and tradesmen that filled the narrow streets of Shiningrock. The message he'd received, delivered by one of the serving girls from the Rosey Nose Pub, had been in no uncertain terms: Loon needed his help NOW, a matter of great urgency. Darn was well aware that "a matter of great urgency" to Loon could mean anything from a Klemish invasion to the loss of his lucky feather. Still, the message had caused the hair on the back of Darn's neck to stiffen, and his stomach felt suddenly sick. So he'd begged and pleaded his way through Master K'tarr's reluctance, promised to sweep the archery range every day for a month, and finally left the Pyre in a dead run for the wharves.

As he rounded the corner from Crock Street onto the boards of Shrimper's Wharf, Darn ran bodily into a swagger of Perthan sailors. One of them made a grab for Darn as he untangled himself, and was rewarded with a stunning strike that left him with one arm dangling like a dead coney. The rest of the group was sober enough to recognize Darn's crimson sash, and they hastily grabbed their compatriot and moved away towards the nearest tavern. Darn gathered speed again and headed south, where Loon's tiny shack perched on the edge of Sandali the Merchant's wharf. Halfway there, the ebon thunderclouds that had hung overhead all day ceased their threats and posturing; with a thundering crash, a cold harsh rain began to lash at the city, as if trying to flay away the layers of filth.

Loon's weather-beaten hut sat quiet and forlorn as Darn

skidded to a halt before it. He tried the rope latch, and found the door unbarred. Caution and concern slashed deep lines across Darn's brow. Loon rarely left the door unlocked, preferring instead to exit through a small false panel that led into one of Sandali's warehouses, where Loon occasionally worked. For the door to be open, with no one at home, was a certain sign of trouble.

Obeying his instinct, Darn slammed the door wide and dove through the opening, tucking into a roll that brought him instantly back to his feet, poised to do battle. Almost as quickly, the room's other occupant snapped to his feet, and a deadly hiss heralded the arm-length of sharp steel that sprouted from his fist and pointed towards Darn's heart. The two held their stances for a heartbeat, then recognition swept the taint of death from the air.

"Damned good way t' get yerself skewered, boy," Jehred spat gruffly, his words slightly slurred, as he slid his sword back into its sheath. He righted the chair he'd' been sitting in, then flopped back down with a "Humpfh!" and reached for the flagon of wine he'd' been nursing before the interruption.

Darn looked around him with growing shock. The tiny crude hut that Loon called home was roughly furnished with a simple sleeping pallet and a collection of storm-salvaged furniture. Still, Loon normally kept his modest abode remarkably clean and tidy. Now, though, Loon's Roost looked as if he'd' hosted a pack of rabid wolves for a three-day celebration. The chairs had been smashed and torn apart, along with Loon's only table. The rough cupboards and shelves which lined one wall had been ripped down, and every bag of flour or crock of beans strewn across the floor. One of Loon's table benches protruded through the only window, and a gust of salt-laden wind blew in, as if to bemoan the little hut's fate.

"What has happened here? Where is Loon?" Darn whirled on the captain. "Angelique brought me urgent word that he needed me here. Is he hurt?" His mind tumbled in a confusion of fear and rage and worry. In the two years since Eillena's departure, Darn had counted Loon as his only true friend. They were closer than a brothers. Loon simply *had* to be all right.

"Loon was fine when he left here," Jehred said, unhurriedly. He looked around at the wreckage, and sipped at his wine. "Calm down now, Darn. Seems like a few of the local street rats broke in t' spread a little misery. Loon came home t' find the place like this, an' his mutt run off inta the rain. Ya know how Loon feels 'bout that useless bundle o' fur." Jehred shook his head and smiled crookedly. "Loon didn't take a second look at this place, once he noticed Peg was gone. Just grabbed 'is staff and rushed out into this god-forsaken storm. I tried to tell 'im he'd never find her till the rain stopped. That she'd be home on her own by the morn. But o' course, there weren't no reasoning with him – not that there ever is!" Jehred's weather-beaten face softened a bit as he talked about his brother – the only time Darn had ever seen the old soldier look to be made of anything other than leather and steel. Although he often spoke as if otherwise, it was plain to anyone who cared to look that Jehred held his younger brother at the center of his heart.

The captain stood and finished off the rest of his wine, then frowned a bit. "Still, it worries me as t' why someone would come t' Loon's looking fer anything o' value. Surely, there's nothin' t' find here that ya couldna steal better of somewhere else." He shrugged, then pulled down his oiled cape from where it hung behind the door, and began to fasten it over his mail. Standing in the shack's crooked doorway, the soldier muttered to himself.

"Curse this damned rain! Every man in the Guard will be wearing a shirt o' rust if I don't make sure they get their gear dried and oiled proper." The guard captain made to step out into the rain. "*God's Tears!*" he laughed without humor. "Hah! More likely the' gods are jest pissin' down on this forsaken place."

Jehred glanced back at Darn as he grabbed the latch rope and mad to swing the door closed. But the worried look on the boy's face snagged at the captain's instinct for trouble, and it yanked him back inside as if by the curls of his beard.

"What is it, boy?" Jehred stepped back into the room, and grabbed Darn roughly by the shoulders "What is it that I don't know?"

"The treasure in the honey pot! Ah, by the Sweet Lady, Loon! Who have you told?" Darn slapped Jehred's hands away and was gone, out the open door in a flash, disappearing into the sweeping curtains of rain.

Jehred stood dumbfounded, his shouts unanswered. He turned in confusion towards the garish Etruscan rug that Loon had nailed up across the privy for his privacy – a violet and viridian piece of eye-wrenching madness that Loon had proudly claimed from the beach out of some storm wreckage. With a bitter oath, the captain ripped the curtain aside, then knelt to probe with his dagger after the unsavory secrets of Loon's latrine.

***

Darn ran blindly through the rain to the end of Merchant's Wharf, fear pulling frantically at his heart. He tripped over street trash twice in the darkness, and the second time he caught himself tottering at the unseen edge of the wharf. Recognizing his madness, Darn settled into a slow familiar breathing pattern, one which gradually lent a cloak of warm calm to sooth his racing mind. It also allowed his senses to make a gentle shift, granting him the ability to perceive certain energies that regular people weren't attuned to. Now looking around him, Darn could detect slight foggy streamers scattered in the darkness that seemed to glow with their own inner light. *Aural clouds*, Master Tobani called them. Darn glanced over at the *Narwhal*, docked nearby, and could discern the pale blue veil which lay over the carven sea-beast on the prow of the ship, evidence of a simple enchantment meant to find safe harbors. A few fading snakes of pallid yellow mist wove their way through the downpour, each attached at one end to some unfortunate drenched soul. Looking behind him, Darn could see the traces of his own aura: a bright orange-gold stream shot through with darker threads of vermillion that stretched from the pale cloud surrounding his body, running down the length of the dock and around the corner towards Loon's humble abode. There, his own path tangled with another wispy trail of deep gold, one that Darn recognized as Jehred's by the streak of indigo at ankle height, left by the rune-carved dagger which the captain kept hidden in his boot.

Panic began to tug and tease at his attention once again, as Darn observed with despair that no trace of Loon's peculiar spectral path still endured. Such trails only lasted for a candlemark, even under the best conditions. As the calm began to flee his mind, Darn felt his vision slip back to the material plane once again.

NO! I must be calm. Darn ground his teeth, trying to control his frantic monkey mind and twitching limbs. *Focus on my crucible.*

Slow down and regain the pattern. Ah, there it is. As he relaxed his breathing the lines of force returned to Darn's vision, showing him the rainbow-hued remembrances of recent passersby once again.

Darn turned and strode down a crooked lane between two warehouses. He hopped a low fence and crossed the garbage-strewn yard behind some squalid tavern, ignoring the muttered growls of the sodden watchdog who watched and shivered beneath the eaves. At the next choice of avenues, Darn turned inward towards the city proper in hopes of crossing Loon's path. A hundred paces revealed nothing; neither did two hundred. But just as Darn was beginning to consider turning back south towards the wharves, he somehow tasted or perhaps even heard a slight change in the air. He stopped and willed himself to relax even further, calming his mind, then slowly scanned the ground around him.

At last! The barest hint of color hugged the damp earth, its shade hardly distinguishable. But Darn could feel Loon's presence about it. Ever since their trip through Greenheart Forest the year before, Darn knew Loon's aura as well as the young giant's booming laugh. Darn leapt forward with renewed hope, following the ever-strengthening trail.

The seventh bell of the evening rang out, muffled to a dull, flat chime by the rain that continued to flail at the city. By now, Darn was sure that he followed the right trail. The gauzy, spectral rope held a distinct violet strand twisted around the blazing gold of its core, as if Loon was wrapped in an enchantment that was woven into his being. Even Master Tobani, who prided himself on his knowledge of such matters, was unable to explain Loon's unusual aura, saying only that the god-touched were often in tune to other planes in ways that regular people could not comprehend. But tonight, Loon's distinctive aura was a gift, marking his path through the confusion of smoky trails that criss-crossed the city streets, allowing Darn to now him swiftly and certainly.

The path he followed led Darn into a section of the city deemed seedier than most. From the corner of his eyes, Darn noticed several shadowy figures who peered silently from crumbling doorways, and one who even dared to follow him for a few dozen steps. But either the sight of Darn's sash or the unceasing onslaught of the storm convinced the padfoot to quickly give up his game.

Now Loon's trail merged with several others, these new ones all a pale piss-yellow, touched with licks of black and scarlet: hollow men, full of anger and sickness – dangerous men. Darn's heart began to race faster and his legs matched its beat as he turned sharply left through a half-hidden archway. A sweet-sour tang assaulted his nose when he stepped into the small shelter from the rain: the rank sickness of slaughter. Instantly, Darn's focus narrowed to a sword's point, and the soulfire smoldering in his crucible began to pulse hot and quick. He danced through the shadows, silent as a shade, and peered out into the weed-infested courtyard at the end of the walk.

Darn cursed silently. The pouring rain seemed to soak up the darkness as it fell through the night sky, only to release it again in torrents upon the tiny courtyard. An impenetrable blanket of night lay across the square, with no moon or torchlight able to pierce it. Unlike the learned masters of his order, as long as the flames burned hot within him Darn could not discern any type of astral markers. But without the aid of his altered senses, Darn was unable to see who or what might be waiting hidden in the darkness ahead.

Again, he cursed the rain to no avail. Nothing stirred for two full hands of heartbeats, but the steady droning of the rain drowned out any sounds there might be. Darn fought the urge to leap ahead, slowed his breathing once again, calming himself to the point where his sight might slip through the veil.

At once, the courtyard seemed to fill with a tangled knot of smoky tendrils. Loon's trail twisted over and around several of the straw-colored ones, and in two places along the courtyard wall there hung a gauzy cloud of carmine to mark some violence who's memory still lingered. Darn slid through the shadows across the courtyard. As he'd expected, two large, ill-defined lumps lay huddled against the wall: the flare of a lightning stroke revealed them as corpses, neither one large enough to be Loon's. Then Darn made out his friend's trail, snaking out of the courtyard and into a divided breezeway. Darn followed quicker than thought.

The covered breezeway shielded him from the storm's onslaught. At one end a pitch-root torch lent a feeble, flickering light, revealing a stout ironwood door barring the way into an otherwise featureless building. Towards the other end, splintered crates and empty kegs piled under the eaves in confusion. An enormous gray rat, sleek-coated and fat as a mild-fed pup, darted out from under one of the piles with a scrap of cloth between its teeth. It paused and raised its head to sniff and glare in Darn's direction, then scurried away back to its bolthole.

Darn crept up to the door and listened: the muted sounds of raw laughter and occasional shouts seeped through the worn wood. He searched the surface of the door and the surrounding stonework for a hidden trip-latch, but found only a spy hole, cunningly disguised as a knot in the wood. Even as he continued to probe at the door, several faints sounds drifted from the far dark end of the breezeway, behind the refuse: what sounded like a man's curse, and the thud of something heavy being dropped or thrown. In the space between breaths, Darn was hidden in the midst of the rubbish, crouched besides a rotting barrel that reeked of sour wine. He slipped silently along a crooked path that wound its way through, over, and even under the moldering heaps of wood and garbage. Another hand of creeping paces, and he caught a glimpse of more torchlight ahead, outlining the open doorway of a low cellar or storage room. Continuing on his belly, Darn crawled to the edge of the opening and lifted an eye above the sill.

The stump of a torch guttered fitfully along one wall. Under it, a large figure lay slumped to one side, its face hidden in the shadows. Darn struggled to lay still, unsure of his next action. Then a long, thin shadow next to the seated figure resolved itself, and Darn realized he was looking at Loon's iron-bound quarterstaff.

Darn hurled himself down the stairs, abandoning all pretense of caution as he came to his friend's aid. But as he jumped through the doorway, a hand reached out from the gloom and tangled in the shoulder of Darn's tunic, swinging him through the air until a mailed fist slammed into his stomach. The shame of being taken unaware burned a thousand times worse than the pain in his body. So Darn took all of the pain, all the fear and shame, and channeled them straight into his crucible where they fed the flames of his rage. Darn barely felt the next punch, just bent and absorbed it, then rode the hand back to its owner even as he unleashed the tethers on the fire inside himself. Darn felt more beast than boy, as he slipped in close, biting, slashing, clawing, gouging. He grabbed his opponent up close then snapped his head forward with the speed and concussive power of a Skraal mountain ram, feeling the man's face crumble under the blow. The assailant toppled sideways into the shadows, and Darn heard a satisfying crack as head met hard stone floor. Then a quiet moan brought Darn spinning about, and he quickly stepped to his friend's side.

Loon lifted his head a bit, and a hiss of pain fought past his clenched teeth. Darn gently eased Loon upright, and tried to push the hair back from his face. But Darn had to bite his own lip to keep from crying out at the sight, for he could barely recognize his affable companion through the veneer of blood that covered Loon's broad, guileless features. Darn looked away from the sight of Loon's battered face and moved to untangle his friend's legs, one of which seemed to be bent back beneath him. With fingers still trembling from battle rage, Darn reached to grab the knee of Loon's trousers, meaning to free the leg pinned underneath. But instead of coarse broadcloth, Darn's hand found a leather belt wound tightly around Loon's thigh, below it only a ragged mess of shattered bone and torn flesh. Darn jerked back his hand in horror and surprise.

Loon's eyes flew open wide and a hoarse scream of agony floated from his swollen lips. The injured boy's eyes rolled wildly for a moment, and his good leg kicked and jerked as if to run away from the pain. Then slowly, he quieted again, and his eyes finally focused upon the white-robed figure squatting beside him. Loon's lips pulled back in a grimace or smile, revealing a mouthful of broken and blood-stained teeth.

"M' good fren' Darn," he gasped. "I knew if I waited long 'nuff, ye'd come fer us." A bubble of blood, black in the dim light, formed at the corner of Loon's mouth. Still, his lips stretched back into his namesake smile, and he reached out to lay a heavy hand on Darn's arm. His eyes drooped nearly closed and his shaggy head nodded forward, then a sudden stab of pain reached through his private fog to stir the injured fellow back to consciousness.

"Loon! Oh Loon, thy leg!" Darn stammered foolishly. "What can I do?" Even as he stared at his friend's terrible wound, Darn knew they were the words of a fool.

"Whore-sons chopped it right off, they did! Loooon!" The young man howled softly, almost gently. "I chased 'em here, an' me an' ol' Stick set three more of 'em down fer good along th' way. But they was hidin' when I came in here, an' they all jumped me an' held me down. Kept askin' 'bout my treasure. Then I kicks one of 'em in his choppers, an' *Whack! Whack!* next I know, here I sit lookin' like ol' Peg!"

Once more Loon's head nodded forward, and Darn reached out to hold him from falling. But at his touch, Loon looked up and his pale blue eyes blazed with a brilliant, cold fury. He clawed feebly at Darn's arm for purchase to stand, and a fresh flood of black liquid spilled thickly from his wounded leg onto the floor.

"Peg!! Oh, by th' Sweet Lady, Darn – them filthy bastards've got me poor Peg! They hurt her bad leg an' made her cry! LOOOOONNNNN!!! I WILL KILL THEM DEAD, EV'RY BLEEDIN ONE O' THEM!!" Loon's huge frame shook with the force of both his rage and his sobs. He made one last bold effort to push himself up on to his remaining leg, but gave up and fell back even as Darn caught hold of his arms to restrain him.

"Please, Darn – my good fren' Darn," Loon whispered, even as he fought to keep his head up. "Save ol' Peg from them rotten, porkin', sons-o-whores. I'm – I'm bein' afraid I can't help her no more. But I know that ya can save her. Yer our very best fren' in th' world. An' yer one o' Agni's Sons, th' best there's ever been. An' I know ya could beat a legion o' them bastards if ya need ta." His eyes closed fully now, and Darn gently leaned Loon's head back against a makeshift pad of torn clothing.

"I'll jest rest here a while, till th' pair o' ya get back," Loon muttered so softly that Darn had to lean in close to hear him. "Damn, Jehred's gonna be awf'lly mad at me fer lettin' 'em chop off m' leg." Loon chuckled lightly, and hummed a few bars of his favorite sea chantey. "Oh well, mebbe now he'll let me ship on th' *Sea Whore*, since I look jest like ol' Cap'n Malachi." The simple-minded, sweet-souled young man laid quietly for a moment more, then he sighed softly. The lines of pain and worry drifted away from his gentle, smiling face, and his broad, muscled chest fell one last time.

Darn sat quietly holding his friend's hand, as the shards of his broken heart danced and spun inside of him, cutting him over and over again, laying his soul to ribbons. He felt tears fill his throat, but the heat of his rage burned them away long before they reached his eyes. With the utmost care, Darn laid Loon's weathered hands together. Then he slowly stood, and with eyes like flat, black stones, he stared about the room.

Two more bodies lay nearby in the gloom, their heads decidedly flattened, testament to the fury of Loon's staff. Several rats chewed steadily at one of the corpses. The sight of the vermin brought back a fleeting moment of sanity, sending Darn searching

338

for another torch to light and mount above Loon's body. That accomplished, Darn stood and looked down at his departed friend, took in the sight of the battered and mutilated body, and fed the anger and rage straight into his *crucible*. The flames surged through him, and he would have screamed in ecstasy and horror, had he cared about either thing any longer. When his eyes cleared, they settled on the only other person left alive in the room. Darn bared his teeth and moved forward, soon the remedy that.

The man who had attacked Darn from the shadows still lay on the floor, moaning unconsciously and clutching at the pain of his broken ribs. The cutthroat's hair was bound in a warrior's braid, and the sword and loose ringmail he wore showed the hard use of a professional's tools. Fresh blood flowed freely from the man's face and scalp, and one of his arms was bent back at an unnatural angle. Even dazed and badly wounded, the sellsword still grasped at the hilt of his weapon, struggling to pull the sword free.

The sight of the bravado mewling in pain brought sour bile to Darn's mouth. Lips pulled back in a feral snarl, the young Flame Dancer darted forward and slammed his foot into the man's lower back. The injured fellow moaned and moved, and Darn kicked him twice more, even harder than before.

Excruciating pain jerked the rogue back from his safe cocoon of darkness, and he woke to ill-remembered waves of agony. His first vision was of Darn's soulless eyes boring into his own, digging down into the depths of his skull. With a start, the man began to cry and beg for mercy, all the while slipping a knife from a hidden sleeve-sheath into his palm.

With careless disregard, Darn ignored the knife whipping

towards his face. Instead, he drove his stiffened fingers straight down, a spear of flesh and bone, burying it deep just below the sellsword's breastbone. The knife flew from the man's hands as the pain froze his limbs, and he lay helpless, gasping for breath. Darn stripped off the thug's swordbelt, then strapped it back around the man, pinning his arms tightly to his sides. After checking the bindings, Darn reached for the braid of hair that hung down the mercenary's back, looped it once about it's owner's neck, then dragged the man to the far side of the chamber. A large hole gaped in the wood where the wall met the floor, rat droppings and tufts of hair marking the entrance. With no hesitation and even less remorse, Darn walked to the man's feet, took a firm grip, and drove his prisoner's head into the hole with a violent shove.

It only took a moment before a high-pitched shriek sounded from behind the wall, and Darn tightened his grip as the man's legs bucked and thrashed about. For a score of heartbeats Darn held his captive's tight, and muffled screams resounded dully from behind the wall. Finally, Darn jerked back on the man's legs, then walked up to stare down at the remains of his face.

The hired thug had been born no natural beauty, but at least he'd previously had the proper compliment of features. Now he was missing an ear and an eye, and his nose had been chewed down until the pale cartilage shown through in several spots. His face was pocked with bite marks and scratches, and his scalp laid bare in a hand of places. The man continued to scream hysterically till Darn grabbed his throat in an iron grip and pinched it closed. With his breath shut off, the mercenary was forced to focus on Darn's face; the grim visage he found there left him little doubt that his last day was ending.

"For the death of my friend," Darn said, in a dull, flat tone, "ye too shall perish. Whether quickly or more slowly, is the only choice." The boy straightened up slightly and looked towards the doorway. "Tell me quick who it is that ye follow, and where they hold the little dog."

"Kirt! Black Kirt Smith-son!" the bloody apparition fairly screamed. " 'E pays Klem an' Johan an' me an' th' rest t' swing our blades for 'im, keep th' rabble in line. Twas 'is idea t' take th' simpleton's mutt when we couldna find 'is hoard. I never touched th' big saphead; twas Kirt that cut 'im. I was jest supposed t' make sure th' idjit didna . . . AAAIIIEEE!!!"

Darn let go of the broken finger he held, then grabbed a fresh one. He bent it back nearly to the man's wrist, then savagely jerked it sideways. The mercenary's renewed screams almost covered the sounds of bones snapping.

The Flame Dancer's face flushed with rage, and he jerked up on his captive's braid, then slammed the man's head back down against the floor once again.

"NEVER!! ... NEVER again shall ye speak of my friend!" Darn screamed into the mercenary's face. "Too pure was his spirit to be sullied by mention from lips such as thine! He was more a man in his way than ever those of thy kind could dream to be! He ne'er brought harm to any that deserved it not, and for that he was maimed and broken!" Darn fought to keep his hands from the man's throat. He took several deep breaths to calm himself, just a measure. Then he reached out to grab his prisoner by the hair, aid laid his thumb atop the man's remaining eye.

"This Black Kirt: where shall I find him?" Darn questioned, and his tone was once again as flat and hard as cold pig iron. "Answer quickly, 'fore I take the other one."

"In th' tavern, th' Devil's Womb! Long th' walk, then knock twice, three times," the bound and bleeding man spat out as quickly as he was able. "Kurt'll be in thar gamin' an' whorin'. Black topknot, lots o' cheap finery, short an' broad, th' loudest o' th' bunch. You'll know 'im."

Darn released his hold, and looked impassively down at his captive. "Tis far better than ye deserve," the boy intoned flatly. "My wish would be to kill ye over and again." Then the calloused edge of his hand slammed down into the man's throat, crushing cartilage and trachea with a soggy snap, like sticks broken in the rain.

***

Darn eased the heavy oak door open and stepped quietly over the fresh corpse of the watchman who lay across the threshold, empty eye sockets gazing into infinity. Steep stone stairs led upwards into the darkness, and a single oil lamp nestled in a wall niche halfway up cast a fitful glow that only seemed to accent the gloom. The sounds of raucous laughter drifted down from above, and Darn counted at least a double-hand of separate voices. Then a series of shrill yelps punctuated the ding, and Darn flashed up the stairs, an argent-clad specter cast burning with hate and revenge. The young disciple paused when he reached the top, hanging back in the shadows. Darn struggled to control his rage, which urged – no, demanded – that he leap among the revelers inside intent on their wenching and gaming, then rend and tear and crush them all till none still held breath.

Several double-hands of human decrement gathered in the smoky interior of the filthy tavern: slavers, worn-out street whores, cutpurses, chancrous beggar-masters, and the like. Most sat at knife-scarred tables, or stood at the counter where an obese, dough-faced eunuch traded leather jacks of cheap ale and wine for copper marks. A few of the inn's besotted patrons gazed unimpressed at a couple who rutted atop one of the tables, while the rest of them watched the ongoing action in the gaming pit, laughing and cheering each time another squeal of pain rose from the pit's depths.

Darn scanned the crowd quickly. At once, his focus was drawn to a squat swarthy fellow, hair pulled back in a greasy topknot, who stood at one end of the counter and laughed harshly with several large, wolfish men. Every finger on the dark man's hands were encrusted with gaudy circlets and rings. Likewise, the lice-ridden curls of his hair were held back with a tarnished silver band. Blood dripped slowly from the corner of his mouth, and the cheap silk handkerchief wadded in his jeweled fist was soaked with it.

In his heart, Darn knew that this foul-faced villain was surely the source of Loon's pain and death. And at the sight of the man, a fury blew through the young boy like a searing desert wind, fanning the flames already raging within his *crucible* into a roaring hellfire. Every muscle and fiber of his body screamed for release, straining to bring death upon the black-haired man. But his promise to Loon – to first find and rescue Peg from these heathens – held Darn fast, if only for the moment.

A sudden howl of terror and pain rent the air, answered in turn by curses and laughter from the motley crowd gathered around the gaming pit, and Darn realized with a foolish start where poor

343

Peg was being held captive. In a flash of muddied samite he dashed from the shadows of the doorway, leapt atop a table near the edge of the crowd, and launched himself over the heads of the bewildered spectators to land in the middle of the shallow enclosure. There, the shattered remains of Darn's heart crumbled into dust as the nightmare of the pit pressed in around him.

At least two full-hands of large rats lay dead in a rough circle on the boards of the gaming pit, necks snapped or throats torn out. And in the center of the circle lay a battered and bleeding Peg. The pitiful little dog had suffered many bite wounds: both of her ears were no more than tattered rags, and one of her front paws was missing most of its toes. A huge black rat, half again the little mongrel's size, lay dead beside her, a twist of wiry black fur stuck between its gore-smeared teeth.

At the sound of Darn's approach, Peg tried to turn and face him with tiny teeth bared. But in the heat of her last battle, the wooden peg upon which she normally hobbled had been wrenched loose from its straps, leaving her to stand awkwardly on three injured legs. Darn squatted in front of the wretched dog, quietly spoke her name then reached out his hand. A crockery mug half-full of ale glanced off Darn's head, but the boy hardly blinked, and never took notice as a stream of blood crept through hair to run from his cheek, a crimson replacement for the tears he was unable to shed.

At her name, Peg's ears tried to perk up, and she sniffed tentatively at his hand twice. Then her inky little eyes slowly focused on Darn, and her scruffy tail thumped twice weakly against the floor. Secure at last, she pushed herself forward to lean against Darn's leg, hushed whimpers of pain escaping with every movement. Once beside him, a faint sigh eased from the poor mutt as she settled down at Darn's feet.

Darn gently examined the dog's mutilated foot, and realized with despair that the flow of blood there was visibly weakening with every pulse. He stroked her head, ignoring the curses and crusts of bread that peppered against his back. Peg stared straight up into Darn's face, her eyes full of trust.

You always watched over the Boy and I. You are a true friend. a tiny voice seemed to sound in Darn's mind.

Peg licked his hand just once, a tiny thank-you, then she laid her head back down. As a bitter blade of anguish plunged into his soul, Darn tenderly took the little dog by the head and shoulders, and with a sudden snap he dislocated her spine from her skull, ending both her life and her suffering. Darn continued to stroke Peg's head for several more moments, then he set the tiny corpse aside, and slowly straightened to his feet. And when his eyes lifted, the hate and rage and fury of all the Seven Hells glared through them like devils' lanterns.

The crowd which had cursed and belittled the boy only moments before quieted suddenly, and several of the spectators turned to force their way out through the press behind them. Darn strode towards the pit's knee-high wall, his pace quickening with each step. He spun suddenly at one point, and his hand shot out to snatch a dagger from the air in mid-flight. He continued his spin, and as he reached full circle the dagger flew from his hand and buried itself in the chest of its owner, a burly bald-headed man who stood just outside the pit with another blade ready in hand.

A white-robed, crimson-painted demon who had once been

a boy stalked wordlessly through the crowded room. One painted trollop stuck out her foot to trip the blood-veiled figure – without breaking stride, Darn stomped outward, snapping the harlot's leg like a rotten tree branch. He continued on past the outcry, and when a cadaverous scoundrel with the pock-marked face of a kritt viper addict reached out to grab Darn's arm in passing, that man too was left writhing on the floor in agony. The rest of the audience cringed back in silence, and more than a few slipped quietly out the back door.

Darn halted several steps from the rough-hewn bar. A crude rendering of a female daemon, sprawled back with legs agape, hung crookedly from above. The sign creaked as it swung slowly back and forth, echoing across the tavern like the quiet personal laughter of an insane old woman. Three cloaked men – Tharian mercenaries by the swirled hilts of their swords and the moon-and-stars tattoos on their faces – barred the way between Darn and the man he sought. Sweat began to weep from the men's faces, and waves of heat began to inexplicably crash and break upon their brows, as the thin, blood-smeared youth stepped boldly into their semicircle.

The boy's eyes strove to burn a hole past the three, to the one they'd been hired to protect. Without so much as a wary glance towards the three men, the unarmed stripling spoke in a voice that trembled and threatened to crack but still held an uneasy sense of doom about it, like an impending storm full of death and fire.

"Back away now, and ye may see the sun in the morn. Draw steel instead, and the kites shall pick at thy flesh outside the western walls."

The first Tharian mercenary flickered a glance towards his

companions, and saw their eyes fixed on the boy. He grasped his sword hilt, but an old memory stayed his hand – a remembrance of his cousins' bodies returned to their homeland from this same damned city, nearly flayed of their skins and wrapped in unacceptable explanations. The hired soldier felt an egg of fear hatch within his bowels, and a capering imp rose to claw and dig at the base of his spine. He looked once more to his fellows as his free hand clutched his purse: finding both to be worth less than the value of his own life, the brigand whirled suddenly and dashed from the room.

"Johan, ya snivelin' gutless pig!" one of the remaining swordsmen swore, his face flushed with embarrassment. "We'll cut yer sword hand off, once we finish wi' this milk-pup here." The Tharian slid an elegantly etched, slightly curved longsword from its scabbard, the trademark tool of his guild-tribe, one which bore scars of frequent honings and frequent use. With a bored look of disdain on his face, the man stepped forward and swept an arc of steel death towards the insolent boy before him.

The blade uttered a thin hungry cry, cheated of its anticipated feast as the mercenary staggered off-balance, swinging through empty space where the boy had once stood. The man's eyes widened in shock, and the muscles of his arm strained to bring his sword back for a quick return cut as a samite and crimson specter sprang from its crouch on the floor. But time about the Tharian seemed to slow, and he stood as a spectator inside himself.

One heartbeat: his right knee buckled backwards, and he began to float down towards the floor.

Another heartbeat: a burning ribbon of agony began its lazy journey up his leg, joined by slow-blooming explosions as four, no, five of his ribs shattered and pierced the Tharian's lungs like ancient spears.

A third heartbeat: a bloodied face suffused with pain and rage loomed in the mercenary's vision for a long moment. And after staring into the hell which burned within those eyes, the Tharian was almost thankful when a thunderbolt crashed into his jaw, his head spun about to look briefly down at the back of his own cloak, and a cold grasping darkness reached out for his soul.

Darned stepped over the lifeless hulk at his feet, stepped over into a land where caution and mercy had no meaning, where only vengeance and hatred held sway. At the boy's solemn approach, the remaining Tharian swordsman dropped his drawn sword to the floor, an offering to a vengeful spirit. Arms raised in supplication, the mercenary slowly stepped back two paces, then turned and fled, cradling his life in his empty hands.

The once-white robe the young Flame Dancer wore was now stained crimson, colored by the blood of his friends, his enemies, and himself. A baptism from which he had emerged in the garb of a master. And truly now, Agni's Flames consumed him, burning all vestiges of human weakness and mercy from him. Tiny tendrils of smoke began to slowly reach upwards from the edges of his tunic, and the smell of burnt offerings, of smoldering blood and cloth, rose and spread about him. Through the blackened, scarlet streaks of blood and dirt on his face, the boy's eyes smoldered like the heart of a smithy's forge.

Darn fought to speak, to curse the man before him with unimaginable death and torment, to accuse him of Loon's foul murder, then tear the tongue from the killer's mouth if he dared to refute it. But the whirling wildfire that raged through Darn's soul robbed him of all words, and he could only stand silently, working his jaw while his frame jerked and twitched as if in palsy.

Black Kirt's lips pulled back in the semblance of a smile, like that of a death adder, the crumbling shards of his teeth awash in blood like crimson poison. He uttered a sudden snort of derisive laughter.

"All ri' now, boyo – Agni's *Pup*. Ya wanna piece o' Black Kirt Smith-son, ya come t' th' right place. Wha' did I do? Lay hand onna bit o' girl-flesh that belonged t' ya?" Smith-son paused to poke at the stump of a tooth with his tongue, then winced as pain answered his probing, and he spit a broken shard into his hand. Without looking up, he continued: "Mayhaps it was a bit o' boy-flesh? Mebbe e'en a bit o' simpleton flesh?" A sneer of ebon mockery stretched across the man's face, and bloodlust whirled together with madness within his muddy pig-eyes. He lifted a jeweled hand holding a jagged-edged war axe, gummy clots of crimson still clinging along a notch in the blade.

" 'E didna want t' share, th' half-wit dint. I seen th' greenstone 'e gave t' that slut Angelique," Smith-son offered, as if any sin might be forgiven for the right price. "Weren't none too nice about it, he weren't. Still, since I got th' stone in th' end, I figured me an' ol' Chopper here would leave 'im sumthin fer 'is trouble." He laughed, loud and braying like a mad mule. "Lef 'im lookin like dat lil' cur dog of 'is! Ha! Dey can both gimp 'round in Gorah's Hell t'gether!"

The dark man's laughter ended suddenly, and he motioned for Darn to approach. "Cum'mon den, lil' man. Ya want sumthin from Black Kirt Smith-son?" He stepped forward away from the bar and took a double-handed grip on his bloodied axe. "Well here it is. Ah got sumthin fer ya!"

In response, Darn raised his right arm, his hand empty, fingers curved and rigid like talons. The air about his hand began to shimmer, and the sleeve of his tunic began to smolder and blacken. Then Darn smiled, ivory teeth gleaming through the blood on his face like a predator baring its fangs before taking its prey.

"Oh, yes," Darn answered, a lilting touch of maniacal glee in his voice. "I have something for ye as well: a gift from my friend." He raised his hand higher, and in the dim smoky gloom of the tavern an eldritch gleam began to course along Darn's fingers, growing brighter and steadier until ghostly flames blossomed, running up and down his arm, feeding upon nothing, it seemed, but the rage in his soul.

Smith-son cringed back and held his war axe before him as a shield against the phantom flames and the insane bearer of their torch. But Darn slid forward, moving between one moment and the next, and plucked the axe from Black Kirt's hands in a motion so swift the weapon simply disappeared.

"Tis the last gift ye shall ever receive," Darn continued. "One for which ye shall beg, before it is granted." He smiled even wider, as Smith-son fumbled for a dagger at his belt.

"Tis Death."

Then Darn laughed quietly and danced forward, all three of Agni's Flames resplendent upon him. And soon, the screams began.

***

Some time later, Darn stood above Loon's mangled body, holding Peg's tiny limp form. Crimson gore stained the young

Flame Dancer from head to heel, like some capering madman from a lunatic's nightmare. His eyes were flat and lifeless; the raging of his soulfire had left him a burnt-out husk. Only the barest spark of will drove him to keep moving. He laid the little black dog gently in the crook of Loon's folded arms, then sat down beside his lost companions. Knowing naught else to do, Darn cradled Loon's head in his own arms, and with his tears he tried in vain to wash the blood from his friend's quiet face.

***

A trio of garrison soldiers were dispatched to a particularly shady corner of the harbor district early in the morning hours on a call of multiple slayings. Upon leaving the scene of the crime, the three chanced upon another room full of corpses, this one guarded by a blood-soaked apparition that would only snarl at them and utter a single name. Upon his arrival, it took Captain Jehred the greater part of a bellstroke to convince Darn to relinquish his hold on the bodies of his friends.

Chapter Fifteen
Out of Darkness

Slowly, so very slowly, a conscious thought wormed its way past the veils of despair that draped Darn's mind. It was a smell, actually: the smell of rotting straw, reminiscent of his father's burdock pens, where he'd spent many hours of his youth. And something else – a pain. Not the throbbing ache that echoed dimly through the muscles of his arms and legs, nor the tormenting itch of the shallow gashes that crossed his chest. This pain was fresh and bright, a spark down by his ankle that only flickered at first, but then grew bit by bit, till it was a searing flame that pulsed up his leg like a living thing. It was almost a welcome sensation after the featureless void into which his mind had retreated. Darn followed the thoughts, followed the pain, and for the first time in several days, he truly awoke.

After some time, his body tired of waiting for directions, and Darn's hand flashed downward under its own volition, down to the source of his torment. His fingers closed around a sleek, furry form, which squirmed in his grasp and lit new sparks of pain in his hand. Again without thought, his arm whipped outward and a wet, crackling thud sounded from off to his left. Now, Darn could discern other sounds: a myriad of tiny rustlings, the scrape of dirt upon stone, the clink of chains as he shifted up onto one elbow, and the labored drag of his own breath echoing from nearby walls.

He sat up and fearfully touched his face to see if his eyes were open, for nothing but darkness met his sight. He felt his lids blink as he touched them – felt also the unconscious tears upon his cheeks – and rejoiced that they had not taken his eyes, at least. For all the good that did for him in this foul hole.

A quiet, drawn-out, mewling cry echoed from somewhere in the distance, a human sob empty of all hope. Darn stood, and cautiously stepped forward, but something caught at his leg, forbidding him to move any distance into the darkness. Cold links of rough iron met his questing fingers. Darn followed them back to where they joined a large ring embedded in cold stone. He traced the range of the chain over the cold, cobbled floor. With his boundary established, Darn crawled to the base of the wall, and huddled against it. *Back to a wall, if nothing else, Elias always told us*, he thought

That he resided in a cell of some kind was obvious. In all likelihood, he thought, he was in the city dungeons. But then again, it could be some private hell-hole, fashioned for the security and amusement of any one of several well-known and despised city stalwarts.

Darn tried to concentrate, to dredge up some memory of being brought to this place. He fought to remember, but then his mind suddenly reeled, torn and bleeding as if still in the clutches of a terrible nightmare. His last full memory was of practicing strikes against the wooden dummies in Master K'tarr's class, sometime in the past. Everything after that yawned like a dark, fathomless chasm in his mind that he dared not approach. It was as if some formless spirit had taken a bite out of his memories, leaving nothing but the raw, ragged edges that showed where something precious had once been.

The boy took his head in his hands, wincing as the crusty

scab of an old wound crumbled beneath his palm, shedding crimson tears to join those already on his face. But Darn took the pain gladly, gathered it up together with the bright lances that still darted up from his gnawed ankle, rolled it together with the aches that echoes from every limb and joint of his body, and fed the whole bleeding mass into his *crucible*, the furnace of his power and passion.

His soulfire was flickering feebly, nearly extinguished beneath the weight of an unnamable sorrow. But the fire licked hungrily at the pain which Darn offered up to it, and a reflected glimmer shone faintly in the boy's eyes. As the flames began to slowly grow, they sent tendrils reaching out through his body, searching for more fuel for their dance. After the pain, Darn fed his anguish and grief into the soulfire, then a hidden pocket of blackest rage, forging his emotions together into a single will, a single purpose – survival. Darn sat up straight, lifted his chin and squared his shoulders, breathed deep and slow, and felt a trembling of strength return to his limbs.

With his soulfire to give him strength and courage, Darn took a purposeful step towards the dark, hollow space that hung in his mind. At his first step forward, an ebon wave of sorrow rose from the depths of the emptiness and crashed down upon him. Terrible pictures played themselves against the back of his eyelids. But Darn shook off the dark waters, straightened himself again, and licked the drops of pain from his lips. He was one of Agni's Disciples: he would not shy from any pain or task. Accepting his loss, breathing in his pain, Darn began, piece by piece, to mend the holes in his soul with memories of his dear friend Loon. As he did, Darn hummed a silly little sea chantey to keep himself company. And it seemed once, if only for a moment, that another voice sang along.

***

In the unseen distance Darn heard the sound of voices –
sane voices, the first he'd heard since arriving here. The guards
which brought him moldy crusts of bread and withered vegetable
peelings on occasion neither gave orders nor answered questions,
but simply tossed his meager meal through the open doorway and
left him to fight the rats in the darkness.

Darn crouched quietly against the wall of his cell, carefully
coiling his tether of chain behind him in order to hide its true length.
He knew that at full stretch, he could just barely reach the frame of
the iron-bound door which sealed his cell. *With the Lady's Grace,*
he thought, *I might have the barest chance of snagging the guard's
arm when the daily measure of garbage is tossed in.* And any chance,
any hope, no matter how small, was better than slowly rotting away
in this dank pit.

As the first glimmer of light shone through the tiny, barred
window set in the door, Darn began a rhythmic breathing pattern,
one used to draw the soulfire out into the limbs and imbue an extra
measure of speed and strength. But the lack of adequate food and
water had begun to tell on the boy, and his weakened limbs trembled
as they tried to contain the forces which his soulfire commanded.
Finally, the light of a torch flared outside his window, and Darn
strained to catch the words which drifted in from its bearer. At
their understanding, an unexpected smile slowly stretched across
his face, even though his cracked and bleeding lips protested.

"I'm tellin' ya, sirrah! 'E's an idjit! Ain't spoke a word since
we drug 'is arse in 'ere. You'll be wastin' yer time … *Errrack!!*" the
voice choked off in mid-sentence.

"And *you*, my good fellow," a second voice answered, pitched so quietly at first that Darn could barely make it out, "shall be wasting the very last breath you shall ever take, unless you cease your incessant babbling and open this door this INSTANT!"

A hurried rattling of keys followed, accompanied by the sounds someone might make whose throat was being crushed. Then the heavy door swung back on its hinges. Darn squeezed his eyes shut against the unaccustomed brightness, and waited tensely for whatever was to follow. Two figures stood silhouetted in the doorway: the one holding the torch was doubled half over and gasping for breath, while the second, shorter figure stepped unhesitantly into the cell.

"Stand up, boy!" Elias' voice lashed across the small cell. "A Disciple of the Sacred Flames does not cower in the corner like some whipped cur. They've not stripped you of your Honor, have they?"

Darn stopped rubbing his eyes and snapped to attention before his teacher. "No, Master. They have not. Nor shall they ever," he answered quickly. Elias was *very* touchy about matters of Honor.

Elias looked the boy up and down slowly. His nose wrinkled as the foul smell of the room fell fully upon him. Without turning, he spoke back over his shoulder to the guard.

"You there! I believe that this prisoner has yet to be fed this day. Scurry off to the kitchens then, and bring back something fit for the pair of us, for I too am feelings the pains of hunger."

"Th' cooks 'av gone fer the night, sirrah. There's naught left till morn," the turnkey quickly answered. Even in the dim light, his words reflected the unseen smirk on his face.

"Then perhaps you would be gracious enough to gift us with

that roasted haunch I noticed lying on the table in your post-room," Elias replied just as quickly, winking at Darn. "Oh yes, and best to bring along that bottle of good Elibran wine that was perched there as well. It would not do to have a man of your austere position found with drink on his breath."

The guard mumbled a few quiet curses, then a fit of coughing further tortured his bruised throat. Elias moved as if to turn his ice-blue gaze in the guard's direction, and the man bent and hurried to light a second torch and comply with the master's request. The crimson-robed master turned back to face his student, his anger and anxiousness betrayed by the twitching of his callous-edged hands and the beads of sweat that clung to his brow.

"Master," Darn began, "I … am truly sorry …"

"Sorry! Yes, sorry is an accurate description of the state which you now occupy!" Elias interrupted in a lashing voice, a Master's voice, under which Darn could only bow his head and endure the flaying. "Filthy! Beaten! Cowering in a cell eating refuse! What state is this for one of Agni's Chosen?" he thundered. "Ten hands of corpses should have lain with your own, before you let yourself be captured and chained like a rabid dog!"

Elias' face and tone softened a measure, a bare measure only. "In the defense or revenge of your friend, I support your actions wholeheartedly. A true warrior stands for his comrades. And besides," he motioned to a corner of the cell, where the straw rustled, "vermin such as those you exterminated need frequent thinning of their ranks." But then the Flame Master's face clouded darkly, and he shook his fists at the ceiling as he brayed out his frustration.

"But you cut them down in the midst of a room full of

witnesses! Then admitted to the bedamned city guardsmen that you put them to death! Agni's Blood, boy - have ye a wish to dance the Gallows' Trot?" Elias shook his head angrily, then pulled a finely-woven silk handkerchief from a hidden picket and used it to wipe the sweat from is bald pate.

"Could you not have hunted them in the alleyways, with no one to see? Or scattered the rest so that no witnesses remained? Or at the very least, simply have denied the act?" Elias stalked back and forth, his harsh words rebounding off the stone walls.

"At the very least, Chancellor Karlonos will demand a public lashing. Possibly even the loss of your hands," Elias added. "That fat, greasy pig would die himself before relinquishing the opportunity to put a member of our Order under his thumb. For he – and many of the other human dregs which walk our fine city – would as soon be rid of us, allowing them to peddle their darkness in the bright of day." Elias ground his teeth in frustration. "We shall be damned hard pressed to fight off his claim, being that you do not yet wear the crimson robe of a master."

At that moment the jailer returned, balancing a roasted haunch of fenlock, a tray of ripe bloodfruits and nania cheese, a torch that threatened to light the ends of his greasy hair afire, and an unopened bottle of dark, musky Elibran wine. He resented the forfeiture of his dinner – particularly the wine, which he'd taken great pains and greater risk to lift from the Chancellor's private stock in the wine cellar on the level above. But his fear of the short Red Bastard, as well as the difficulty which still impaired his swallowing, kept the man's tongue in check. He set the food and drink in the doorway of Darn's cell, and shot a hateful look at Elias' back.

Fer two droma I'd slide a blade 'tween yer ribs right now, Baldy, the guardsman thought blackly. *Ya better bet too that I'll be trottin' back down 'ere soon 's yer gone. Take back ev'ry bit o' ma supper, an' make yer pup bleed a little fer ma trouble!*

A smug smile twisted the ends of the jailer's lips, and he turned to go. But before he'd taken his second step, Elias' words drifted out of the tiny cell like smoke to slip and swirl around the man's soul.

"Guardsman! Should I discover that this wonderful repast – which you have so graciously supplied us with, I might add – should it be taken from this cell before my young friend here has had his fill, then I shall be forced to return to this cesspool: a task I shall find highly unappealing. And in trade, I shall then see how many of the snake-tailed vermin that infest this boardinghouse I can stuff down your gullet – alive!"

The sound of pounding feet brought smiles to the faces of both prisoner and his guest. Elias speared a chunk of the roast fenlock on a slim dagger, kept it and a sweet-pear for himself, then sat the tray with the remainder of the food within Darn's reach. The pair ate in silence till Darn had wolfed down several large portions. Then, with food in his stomach to bolster his strength and courage, Darn quietly asked his teacher the question which had plagued him since he'd regained consciousness in this dark place.

"Master ... had ye stood in my place, what course would ye have followed? Although I am unsure of things now, on that evening the soulfire possessed me so that I had no thought for my actions, but only acted."

Elias smiled behind the curve of his hand. *At last!* the master thought, before answering. *He has fully surrendered himself to the Flames. I had feared he would never lay his control aside.*

"On that night," Elias pronounced proudly, "you acted as one of Agni's Children, with no thought, no reserve, no mercy, and no quarter. You allowed Agni's Flames to guide your hand and dispense the Justice which was required." Elias grinned broadly as he tore a bite of meat from the knifepoint. "In response to your question though, the answer is simple: I would have killed them all, rather than just the pitiful few which you laid cold." He almost choked then, trying not to laugh at the shocked expression on Darn's face. Elias waved a hand for patience, then swallowed, and continued.

"After spending eight winters under my tutelage, after all I have taught you, how can you be so surprised at my answer? Yes, I would have killed them all. I would have bathed in the blood of those responsible for my friend's death. Then I would have cut down the rest still in the room simply out of principle, for there are no innocents in an establishment such as the Devil's Womb. And that would have saved us the problem presented by any surviving witnesses."

"Smith-son, though," Elias continued, "he, I would have spared. And I would have him tucked away in some quiet cellar, yet, to extend the pleasure which his demise was to bring to me."

Darn looked up at Elias, but could only bear it a moment before turning away. The smile on Elias's face, so simple, so chilling, was something Darn prayed he would never see in a mirror.

Darn shook his head in violent denial. "It brought me no pleasure then, but only fed the bloodlust in my heart. It brings me no pleasure now to think of it, for all of their deaths do not equal the value of Loon's life."

"You avenged your friend's death, and brought Honor to you both," Elias interrupted. "You used your skills to dispense a just sentence. It is our Way, and you did it well."

The young man gnawed his lip in indecision as he digested his master's words, unsure whether to reveal his next thought to his teacher. But his anguish was such that he could not hold it inside. "Master," Darn began quietly. "I know I did honor to my friend Loon by rescuing his dog and avenging his murder. I understand, and believe, that those which I slayed were deserving of their fates. But still, their shades, they haunt my sleep, and I am unable to dispel them."

Elias stood and stretched, then began to fastidiously knock the straw and dirt from the hem of his robe. "I have many such shades, my young friend," he answered lightly, almost proudly. "You will come to appreciate them in time, for they may keep you company on a lonely night – aye, and provide a moment of sweet remembrance at times."

"I have never killed before, and my soul rebels at the thought of it!" Darn answered flatly, angrily. "I shall not do it again!" He pushed the tray of food back with his foot and huddled back against the base of the wall, head cradled in his arms.

Elias stepped forward and squatted down in front of the boy. And when Darn failed to raise his head, Elias snatched up a handful of lank, straw-colored hair and forced the boy to meet his feral grin and blazing eyes. "Oh yes, you shall young Spark!" the master replied angrily. "Your hand will fall, and a man will drop dead at your feet. Over and over again, until you are unable to remember the number or the reasons." Elias's trip tightened, and he jerked Darn back to face him when the boy tried to turn away. "For that is what Lord Agni's Justice often demands in this world. It is ugly, yes. And sometimes not easily accomplished, or stomached. But it is *what we are* – the destiny we were born to fulfill, you and I. Anger and violence are what the soulfire feeds most heartily upon – so in a world filled with both, it is no wonder that the fire within you grows with time." He released his hold on the boy and stood. "There is naught you can do but answer its demands."

Elias stepped to the cell's doorway and turned to look back on the young man, his prize student, whose thin frame shook with barely-suppressed tears. An unfamiliar sorrow softened the master's harsh features, and he was pained to utter his next words. But he cast off his doubts, for he knew that regret and shame held no place in a Flame Master's world. Darn must be consigned to his fate.

"Before I go, I must say that I inspected the bodies myself. The Tharian mercenaries were disposed of quickly, thoroughly, and with grace. The wounds on Smith-son, however, were well-chosen for great pain and a slow death. I was remiss in not commending you for such fine work. Justice was served." Elias stepped outside then, and without another word he shut the cell door and walked quietly away.

Horror, pain, and remorse wrestled together within Darn's chest, each struggling to emerge the victor. Worse yet was the odd, slime-coated feeling of pride that tainted his thoughts. Unable to bear the strain any longer, Darn leaned to the side and spewed his dinner into the corner. Once his body stopped convulsing, the young man wiped his mouth and dried his eyes on the edge of his filthy tunic. He laid his head back against the cold stone wall and breathed deeply for a while. Then he began to search for some way to reconcile Elias' words – and the fearful dawning of their truth – to the sick pain he felt gnawing at his soul.

***

"The lad is a Disciple of the Flames," Elias fairly shouted, and his words carried a dangerous edge to them. "He performed as he has been trained to do, in service to the sacred Flame of Justice! He discovered an evil matter, and took actions to resolve it. The facts are above question!" Elias' wiry, red beard fairly sparked with rage, and the Leopard Guards who stood between the crimson-cloaked master and the seats of the Council members glanced nervously at each other and tightened their grips on their weapons.

An immense, pale-fleshed man sprawled in the center chair on the Council podium: he appeared quite bored with the proceedings, as he worried at a large boil that grew from one of his chins. Chancellor Karlonos had schemed, bribed, and – some said – paid for a few fortuitous accidents, in his steady climb to the top of Shiningrock's Council. To those who knew him not, he appeared to be a stupid glutton of a man, a market-fattened pig dressed in silks. But the subtle play of his words belied his appearance, and he fenced with the scarlet-robed master as none other in the audience room would have ever dared.

"In first, I agree with you, venerable Master: the lad is a *disciple*, not a robed Master." Chancellor Karlonos paused for a moment to sip from a goblet which his attendant held ready, allowing the weight of his words time to settle. "He has not yet proven himself to hold the impeccable judgment for which those of your Order

363

are so famed and revered. And as such, he cannot be entrusted to always discern between just and unjust."

"The boy has better judgment and reserve in these matters than any others of his station!" Elias interrupted. "Better, in fact, than some of the masters of our Order. Be assured, Karlonos, that had I been in his stead, many more would have died. And none of you would have dared question *my* judgment!"

"Then I suppose we should all be thankful that you were not involved in the affair personally, my dear Master Elias," Chancellor Karlonos replied, stifling a yawn with the back of his hand, and ignoring the terrified stares of his sub-chancellors and advisors. "Nevertheless," he continued, "I do not question the fact that the boy's companion was killed, for we have the body as evidence. But what is also unquestionable is that this disciple of yours – this, *Darn*, is it? – this Darn murdered at least three citizens, possibly as many as seven. He also seriously injured half a room full of others, none of whom are proven to have had any connection with the demise of his friend."

Elias took a single step forward, ignoring the guards as they shifted in their stances, disregarding even those who lowered their swords from at-arms to ready position. Several members of the Leopard Guard shared sheltered glances, for Master Elias' fighting skills were a whispered legend even among such decorated warriors as themselves. Elias, though, had no thoughts or words for the armed soldiers facing him.

"They found Loon with one of Smith-son's bully boys dead at his feet, ye great bloody fool!" Elias bellowed up at the Chancellor. "The boy had signs of Tharian knife-work all over him, and a Tharian sell-sword was found dead beside Smith-son's corpse – he who was known to travel with the greasy bastards!" Elias' face was flushed with anger, matching the robe he wore. His hands flexed open and closed unconsciously, like a great cat baring its claws. "Darn deduced, as would I, who the obvious culprit was behind this heinous deed. He then exacted the punishment which he saw fit. What more proof is needed?"

Chancellor Karlonos' voice dripped with choking sweetness, and he smiled as if his reply brought a taste of it to his fleshy lips. "Why, I need proof, Master Elias, that the cutpurse and the mercenary were in any way connected to either this young man's death, or to Krolluck's son. What proof I do have … ," the chancellor raised a ring-encrusted, doughy hand, and motioned to a servant at one of the small side entrances to the council room as he continued, "… is a full hand of citizens who testified that this student of yours did illegally enter a private business establishment, assault a number of its patrons, then attack and kill several men in cold blood with no provocation."

A ragged voice cried out from a dimly-lit alcove to one side, where a small knot of administrators and the like waited.

" 'E kilt ma boy!"

A barrel-chested, grey-haired man pushed his way through the crowd of trustees, who drew back in open disgust at his touch. His clothes were of decent make, but his skin and clothing alike were grimed with soot. The ill-kept figure gripped the railing in front of him with large, powerful hands, and his bloodshot eyes rolled like those of a maddened horse.

"Lil' whoreson broke both ma boy's arms, an' both 'is legs.

Ripped out 'is tongue too, an' took 'is eyes afore 'e kilt 'im!" The smith swore, and wiped angrily at the tears leaking from one eye. "Weren't no part of 'im that weren't broken, an' 'is face looked like dogs 'd been at 'im!" he continued. "I had ta check th' rings on 'is hands ta be sure it was ma boy." Krolluck strained against the low railing and stabbed a blackened hand towards Elias. "Crazy! That's what 'e is! Like a weasel wi' th' foam-mouth, jest like th' rest o' ya bleedin' Red Robes! Burn 'em all, I say! Afore they turn on th' rest offus honest folks!"

Elias turned slowly and silently until he faced the speaker. The master's ice-blue eyes glared with such frozen malice that Krolluck began to fidget and visibly sweat, adding to the smith's already heady aroma.

"Krolluck, the black-hearted Smith," the Flame Master spat, as if the name burned his lips. "Quite an impassioned speech, for an 'honest citizen' such as your self – *slaver*! Oh yes, I know of your little bands that prowl the darkened alleyways, hunting for prey to sell off as toys of pleasure or pain. And I know of your arrangements with the pirate lord Q'intaz, to supply fresh arms for his galley holds." As Elias spoke, Krolluck fell back, his earlier bravado falling quickly aside.

"Were I you, Smith," Elias concluded, "I would look to your bolt-hole even now. For the time that you live on is not even borrowed, but indebted to 'foam-mouthed weasels' such as myself. Consider the execution of that vicious cur you called a son to be but a mild portent of your own morrow." To anyone listening, the threat of violence rode proudly on the winds of the master's words.

Even beneath the layer of grime and soot that coated his

face, Krolluck waxed pale at the master's words. He stumbled backwards, and moved to hide himself in the cloaking shadows of the alcove once again.

A thin, bitter smile crossed Elias' face, and he turned back to face the Council. But before he could return to his protest, an armor-clad figure walked slowly into the room, and the newcomer's presence silenced even Elias' tongue.

Captain Jehred's eyes held only the barest, smoldering spark of life, and his face seemed carved from stone. Jehred gave Elias no acknowledgement as he shuffled towards the Council's dais, but only stared dully at the polished marble floor before him.

Chancellor Karlonos, purposefully ignoring the smith's interruption, continued on with the proceedings. "Our distinguished Captain here found your disciple near the scene of this heinous deed, apparently unconcerned for the wanton damage which he had caused." Karlonos waved a hand at the soldier. "Perhaps Captain Jehred would be better suited to explain what he found – Captain?"

Jehred's jaw worked silently for several moments before he found his voice. That voice held none of the crisp authority, the sense of command due a captain of the Imperial Guards. It was not the voice of a man who had stood solid under siege, fire, and witchcraft. No, it was a voice drained of all spirit, of all life, the dull croak of a man who had lost the last strand of his soul.

"I – I found the accused boy sitting with th' c-corpse of another boy in his arms. He …" Jehred's voice failed him, and he stared at the floor until it returned. "He was crazed at that point, cryin' an' blubberin'. I couldna get a word out of him, 'cept that when I pointed to another body that lay nearby, an' asked him if he done it, he nodded *yes*. That one had been beat t' death. Th' first one – th' one he was holdin' – that one had died o' blade wounds."

"And the rest?" Chancellor Karlonos demanded impatiently.

"Found one more 'long th' walk, an' two more inside. They all bore th' mark o' hard hand-work on 'em, like a Flame Master would leave."

"There, you see," Karlonos remarked to Elias, as he dismissed the captain with an absent wave of his hand. "From the lips of one of our most experienced guardsmen. And then, as I said, there is the matter of the witnesses."

Jehred turned to leave the audience chamber, never looking up, and his feet drug morosely as he shuffled towards the door. But his apparent mourning drew no sympathy from Elias. As he passed nearby, the Flame Master sank his fingers into the soldier's arm and whipped him about to stand face-to-face.

"I thought you were a *man*, Jehred!" Elias spat low and venomously. "They will hang the boy for revenging Loon's death, and yet you …" Words failed the fiery master as Captain Jehred lifted his face from the floor and looked back. Misery dripped instead of tears from the man's eyes, and the agony in their depths spoke of his sorrow as no words or cry of pain ever could. Elias' fingers lost their grip, and the wash of Jehred's pain forced even the brash Flame Master to retreat a step.

Jehred dropped his gaze, and as he slowly turned for the door again, Elias strained to catch the words he left behind:

"'Tis my job, Elias. S'all I have left, now."

As Elias stared at the broken soldier's retreating back, the rage inside him burst forth again, fresh and bitter.

Jehred is a warrior, dammit! A man of uncommon heart, deserving to die with a blade in his hand! Not one to be left to this shambling, lingering decay! Another debt that Karlonos owes me!

Elias whirled back to face the Council seats, and none of the Leopard Guards stationed before him could fail to feel the waves of heat and loathing which poured from the small crimson-robed man. Elias trembled as he pointed an accusing finger up at the Chancellor.

"You quivering mound of bundhar dung! Jehred's testimony offers no proof. Yet you would condemn this disciple on the words of some street vermin, while parasites such as *he...*" Elias pointed to the half-hidden figure of Krolluck the Smith, who tried to disappear in the shadow of a column, "...continue to enslave and slaughter as is their wont! I warn you now, you pox-ridden ass: dare to bring this disciple, *my* disciple, to dance on the gallows, and my brethren and I shall bring this hall down upon your lice-ridden head!"

A tall graying man in gilded breastplate and helm, who sat to the Chancellor's left as befitting the city's Lord Marshal, spoke in a deep imperious voice.

"Thy words ring of treason, for thee and thy Order, revered Master. Guard them well, or perhaps more than one shall perform upon the gallows' stage in the morn."

Elias grinned dangerously, and took another step forward. The Leopard Guard before him whipped his blade up, resting the point against the cloth over Elias' heart. The soldier's eyes held more than a measure of fear and caution, but his training and pride as one of the Eldorn kingdom's elite troopers held fast, and he prepared himself for battle – and death, if need be. At the least, the Flame Master halted his advance, even though his eyes took on an unearthly, ruddy glow.

"Lord Marshal Vin'Dall. It galls me to no measure to see such a poor excuse for a warrior seated in the chair of our Firstmaster, Tyrin." Elias shook his head at the folly, then continued, almost laughing. "Be assured that even with chains of cold iron bound 'round my neck, I would still find the strength to walk from the gallows and search your entrails for the soldier's heart which you claim to possess." He did laugh then, as he saw the Lord Marshal pale beneath his helm. Elias, after all, was not known to make idle threats. Satisfied with his rebuke, Elias turned his attention back to the Chancellor.

"As for you – foul despoiler of innocent young boys and confused farm animals! Ignore my words at your most sincere peril! I ..."

"Master Elias!" the Chancellor interrupted the master sharply, surprising even Elias. "I would have expected one of your station to be more eloquent, if not more convincing, in his arguments." Karlonos stifled a yawn with the back of one fleshy hand. "Unfortunately, your speech beings to offend, and – even worse – bore us. I will not descend into the gutter with you. Therefore, this audience is at a close."

The head of Shiningrock's council moved to stand, and two of his personal servants quickly stepped in to assist him. But the gold-threaded robe that the chancellor wore snagged on a corner of his heavy rosewood chair, and he flopped unceremoniously back down into his seat like a large, stranded goosefish. He slapped away the fluttering hands of his servants, and fought to regain his composure. But the crimson flush of embarrassment crept up the wattles of his neck to stain the expanse of his face. For the first time, a hint of anger and irritation sounded in the Chancellor's voice as he finished addressing Elias.

"You may commend my apologies to your Grandmaster Saura, but the decision of the Council stands as given: the boy, Darn, shall hang for his transgressions as would any common criminal. Sentence shall be carried out at sunrise tomorrow." Chancellor Karlonos paused dramatically, as if hoping for an outburst in return. Receiving none, he waved his hand impatiently. "Begone now, Elias. Scurry back to your manse on the hill. We grow weary of your presence."

"You'll grow much more weary of it, Chancellor, should my student come to any harm," Elias replied lowly and evenly, a blood-sure promise. The sword point at his chest increased its pressure a measure, and for the first time the Flame Master seemed to acknowledge the arm-length of sharp steel and the soldier who wielded it.

"You, at the least, have some stones, my friend," Elias quipped lightly to the guard. "Courage is the highest card in a man's hand." He stood for a moment longer to tighten the blood-red sash that wound about his hips, then turned to go. But in the midst of his movement a whirlwind seemed to catch the diminutive master up, for he spun like a top in a tight circle, robes streaming out behind him in a crimson cloud.

A loud *Clang!* rang out through the chamber. And though nothing was seen to touch him, the sword-wielding guard sailed backwards several paces to land flat on his back. His companions hurried to raise their own weapons, but Elias was already striding arrogantly towards the main doors, unconcerned with his unprotected back. For who would be foolish enough to strike?

The Leopard Guardsman fought for breath and clenched his teeth against the pain radiating from his broken ribs. He opened his eyes to meet the gaze of his fellow soldiers, who stared slack-jawed at his chest. The guardsman strained to look down at himself, and for a moment his pain was forgotten. The perfect imprint of a fist was fixed in the tough, layered bronze of his breastplate.

"However, a flush of speed, power, and timing, trumps courage every time," Elias muttered to himself as he walked through the open doorway. The soldiers stationed there allowed him a wide berth as he passed.

"Well," Chancellor Karlonos remarked to no one in particular, as he attempted once again to rise from his seat. "That certainly was – engaging. Perhaps we should spend the afternoon in the company of Master Elias more often!" None of the other council member knew if the Chancellor was joking or not. Karlonos preferred it that way.

***

Although he could not be sure, Darn believed that he was awake. He eyes stared upon darkness, but that proved them neither open nor closed. He felt the rustle of a furry form in the straw by his hip, and his hand slapped the chisel-toothed scavenger away. But still he was unsure if he slept, for he knew that he performed such actions in his slumber now. The dreams which spoke to him as he slept seemed more real to him than anything else that occurred in this dark latrine of a cell. And the brief moments of light, when the guards came to taunt him and throw scraps at his feet, seemed insubstantial, barely remembered. But when he heard his name whispered once softly, then again with a sharp bite behind it, Darn knew that he was truly awake.

He padded over close to the iron-bound door, and tried to peer out through the tiny barred window set in it. At first, it seemed that a glowing wraith stood in the hall outside, for its form shone with a wavering, greenish light. Then the figure pulled a small crystal pot full of glowing grave-worms from under its cloak. The writhing, eldritch gleam from the worms pushed back the gloom just a measure, but enough to reveal the gleam of gold earrings and the bright smile of the man who wore them.

Darn felt his knees threaten to buckle as the implication of his diminutive master's presence fell full upon him. He remembered the sadistic laugh from the guards who brought him his daily rations. They'd told him to enjoy the scraps, as they'd be his last – but then, the black-hearted bastards always had something ugly and hope-breaking to say. Still, Darn had spent the remaining unknown candlemarks (or days – who could tell in such blackness?) since then steeling himself for the moment when they came for him. He was at peace with himself for the execution of Loon's tormenters, and was not afraid to die if that was the price for his revenge. But Darn also was not fool enough to eagerly await his own demise, and so he had decided to attempt an escape even as he was led to the gallows. But Elias' appearance in the middle of the night pushed those half-hearted plans aside, and brought a gleam of salvation into the gloom of the dungeons.

"Pick up your chin, boy," Elias chided. "Dare not to tell me you doubted I would secure your release. After the veritable mountain of coins which you have won for me time and again, twould be like allowing a prize bundhar to starve to death after winning the

King's Dash. Besides," Elias grinned as he fished through his pocket and extracted several slender iron rods, "the pleasure that I shall receive watching, Karlonos' piggy face when he is left with an empty gallows in the morn, is a confection that I would not easily forgo." Elias pushed the jar of grave-worms closer to the door, then knelt to begin prying at the lock with the pick's he'd brought.

"Swilling bastard must have a hiding hole for his keys, for I found them not," he said quietly, as he set to work. "These will have to do, though it is not a skill to which I lay great claim." Time passed, and still the red-robed master failed to unlock the secrets of the cell's door. The quiet oaths he'd been uttering grew slowly more passionate, then rose suddenly to a low-pitched but steady poisonous stream, as one of the picks snapped off deep within the lock's mechanism. Darn could see the fury rising in his mentor's face, but Elias seemed to be controlling his anger. Then the second pick broke off within the lock as well.

"By Agni's Burning Beard, I will *not* be *denied*!" Elias swore, as he leapt to his feet. He danced back a pair of steps, then launched himself at the door. The thundering sidekick which the Flame Master landed just above the jammed lock seemed to have no effect upon the stout wooden timbers, though ancient dust flew from the edges. Undaunted, Elias sent another powerful kick into the door, followed by a third and a fourth. A dark circle of scorched wood began to form on the door's surface where Elias' heel landed again and again, and the iron hinges began to squeal in protest. The hollow booming of Elias' attack echoed up through the dungeon tunnel like the sounding of a giant's war drum, bringing wordless howling in answer from some other prisoner. Darn held his tongue, though, for he knew that when Elias burned at such a fevered pitch any comments or cautions would go unheeded.

A crack appeared at the edge of the door's lock plate, and with each assault the small split grew upwards bit by bit. A rivet which held the middle hinge to the door shot from its mount like a slung stone, clipping Darn just above the ear. Elias' attack seemed to redouble in fury, and at the next blow the lock bolt screeched a short high-pitched wail and snapped, half of it falling to the floor in surrender.

Elias stepped into the tiny dank room, his eyes fairly gleaming from the flames in his soul. He limped slightly on one leg, but no pain could survive the soulfire which burned so brightly within him. Darn rushed to stand before his savior, but the chain which bound him to the wall brought him up cruelly. The rattle of the cold iron links seemed to snap Elias' trance, and he stepped quickly to retrieve the shining jar of grave-worms from the hallway. Elias cursed again as he set the jar next to the shackle on Darn's leg, for it too was locked: a simple lock, albeit, but formidable still for one without a key or lock pick to effect its opening.

"So *now*, what? Ya gonna chew off his leg?" a deep, grating voice questioned suddenly from the dark hallway.

Elias stood and whirled and leapt in one movement, so smooth and quick that even to Darn's eye he seemed like a molten jet of flame piercing the black hole of the open doorway. But a short command bark in *Dolat*, the warrior's cant, halted Elias in mid-flight, though he landed in a fighting stance and stood poised to explode again in an instant.

A solitary figure stepped into the feeble light of the grave-worms. Though he still wore the pallor of a corpse, there was no mistaking the stern bearing and chiseled features of Captain Jehred.

"My thanks to you, Elias, fer leaving my simple guard th' gift off his meager life. Not that he deserves it; but it is so hard to round up any idiot willin' t' stand watch down here in th' sewers. I wasn't lookin' forward to th' chore." Jehred spoke casually and quietly, but his eyes were bright with life-spark and there was iron in his voice again.

Elias continued to hold his stance, and his eyes darted to the shadows that boiled in from either side of the tiny light. Perceiving no other threats, the master relaxed somewhat and straightened, but his voice still held fire within it.

"A tap behind the ear, and a bit of rope and a rag for his mouth, and he fit quite nicely there in the pantry. He never laid eyes upon me, so Justice demands that I spare him – no matter his other shortcomings," Elias answered. Then he shook his head, and a touch of sadness rode upon his words.

"You should not have come alone, Jehred," Elias said, unexpectedly somber. "Indeed, you should not have come at all. For the boy leaves this offal pit with me tonight. And if needs be I must carry him out on my back, crost your corpse and a legion of dead guardsmen, then so be it." The master sighed deeply, and seemed to shrink in on himself for a moment. But with the inrush of his next breath, iron seemed to infuse his spine, and the diminutive Flame Master snapped back to himself, an arrogant smile on his lips.

"I will not stand to see Darn dance for Karlonos' amusement, even though Grandmaster Saura has declared that the Order must abide by the Council's decision. Therefore, I have come as another *criminal* to this place, to free one of my own and to piss in the Chancellor's fat face. So leave now, my friend, and let me be about my business. Forget what you have seen here, return to your bed, and face the sun in the morn."

The ghost of a smile drifted across Captain Jehred's face at Elias' insolent words. He'd expected some such outburst – in truth, had hoped for nothing less. The captain flicked a hand suddenly up and forward from where it had rested at his belt, and a gleaming flash of steel darted towards the Flame Master. A scowl darkened Elias' face as he contemptuously snatched the tiny missile from the air.

"Apparently, I have your answer," Elias spat, as the soulfire licked through his limbs and he took a resolute step forward. But then he paused, confused at the smile which had solidified on Jehred's face. Elias looked down, then opened his hand and tilted it to the fitful gleam of the grave-worms. A slim burnished key lay there winking in the gloom.

Jehred laughed as Elias looked up dumbfounded, and he stepped forward to relieve the Flame Master of his slight burden. "I, too, have some pissing to do," Jehred said, "though I have vowed to gift the Chancellor with my water only as a dying request." He walked into the dank cell and fitted the key to the manacle about Darn's ankle. Then he looked up into the young Flame Dancer's eyes, and pain washed over the scarred warrior's face.

"Darn," he began quietly, "ya must understand: I believed ya, but I couldna ..." His voice broke, and Jehred hung his head silently for a moment, then sucked in another breath and continued. "I had t' act as if I'd been unmanned. E'en whilst I was collectin' th' names I needed, an' other important details. I had t' play at bein' th' grief-

377

stricken but loyal soldier. Anythin' else, an' Karlonos would guess I was plannin' revenge. They been watchin' me fer days now, so I couldna e'en see that ya got some decent food. It was awful poor thanks, after all thatcha did fer Loon." Then the grizzled soldier, proud survivor of a hand of major campaigns, victor in a hundred or more battles, hung his head in shame at Darn's feet, and tears of sorrow and shame splashed onto the cold stone floor.

Darn laid his hand on the man's bowed head, and felt some of his own pain melt away in sympathy. Elias, meanwhile, had stepped to the doorway and found reason to examine the darkness of the corridor beyond. Darn felt Jehred's loss, as fresh and mortal a wound as his own, but understood that Jehred's loss was even greater than his own. And knowing the captain as he did, Darn recognized what torture the graying soldier had born to maintain the façade of a broken man.

"Come, good Captain," Darn urged quietly, as he lifted the man to his feet. "Ye saw more clearly than any else would have. I know that ye did that which was necessary. But now, so that those deeds were not in vain, we must leave this place."

Jehred stood and quickly recovered himself. Once again, the seasoned campaigner was all iron and hard leather.

"Son, one day ya got t' lairn t' speak right." He half-smiled and shook his head, then it was back to the business at hand. "Now then, time t' decide fer where yer bound. I can get ya on a hand o' diff'rent ships in th' harbor, off t' most anywhere ya'd choose. Or ya could head back inta th' north country, up t'wards Hovill er beyond. Otherwise, it's either hole up in th' Pyre, er hide out in th' city somewhere."

"He cannot leave!" Elias interjected hotly, before Darn had a chance to answer. "He has not yet been tested. To leave now, regardless of the cause, would violate his vow and his Honor. He would be named *slag*, and would be hunted down as would any other deserter."

"Then he must hide in th' city, er else th' Pyre," Jehred answered. "At least till certain events take their course, an' Chancellor Karlonos has more pressing issues to attend to."

"No!" The single, irrevocable word silenced both men, and they turned to look at their young companion.

"I will neither run, nor hide," Darn answered. "The path I must take has been laid down by countless before me – and it leads to none of those places." At the young man's words, Jehred frowned in confusion, while Elias' eyes gleamed in fearful anticipation.

"Lead me to the Gate of Bones," Darn stated flatly, finally. "For there lies the only escape I will accept."

Jehred looked to Elias, comprehension slowly growing within him. Only the burning maw of the Escarp Desert lay beyond the Gate of Bones. And no one ventured through that wasteland alone, not even the Scarab Folk. No one, of course, *except* for the lunatic Disciples of Lord Agni's Blessed Bloody Flames! Jehred took a deep breath to begin his argument, but one look at Darn's face made him realize he'd have more success reasoning with a stone. He turned to Elias, but the Flame Master only shook his head and motioned gruffly for Jehred to lead the way. The captain looked from Elias to Darn and back again, mouth open as to question their sanity. Then he gave up, shrugged, and started off down the dark corridor, mumbling as he went.

"Long bloody way t' walk in th' dark, jest so's th' fool boy can kill himself, ya ask me! Volar's Hell! A good draught o' belladonna here an' now would serve the same purpose, an' I could be back in m' bunk b'fore th' next mark. Instead, my old bones gotta walk half th' night, jest so his bones can get gnawed by jackals in th' morn. Jest don' make no sense."

With Jehred to lead the way, the trio passed unseen from the dungeon then traveled silently up through the Council building. The Captain possessed keys that opened long-unused passageways and storerooms, and he knew the touchstones which opened secret stairwells. He had long memorized the sentries' schedules and routes, and knew as well which ones were apt to be asleep or away from their post for the comfort of some warm ale or warmer flesh. Once outside the building, Jehred led his band of conspirators a crooked path down dark streets and alleyways and once even through the sewers of the city, three fleeting shadows that were seen by none.

It took the three men most of the night to slip out through the city unnoticed. They traveled up the steep hills west of the city proper to the high summer meadows that lay at the feet of the surrounding girdle of mountains. There, like the gaping maw of some vast subterranean serpent, lay the opening of a tunnel at least three wagons wide, a tunnel which led straight through the heart of the great pinnacles that towered overhead. And at the end of the tunnel, on the other side of the curtain of stone, lay only one thing: the ravenous Escarp Desert.

***

Three carrion birds drifted lazily in the thermal currents that spiraled up from the warming desert sands. Their eyes searched hungrily for any remains from the nightly struggles of life and death, hoping to find an early breakfast before the sun's burning rays drove them to their caves high in the cliff walls. All else was still and calm, save for the whirl and play of several small dust devils dancing on the wavering horizon.

Three warriors stood upon the weathered edge of the sandstone battlements, looking out over the bleak, barren wasteland. Darn wondered at the forbidding expanse of rolling dunes, marching endlessly onward. And he felt a stirring at his elbow that could only be Death, preparing to join him on his journey.

"Though he must travel this way at last, as all of our Order have done, this is not his time," Elias said quietly aside to Jehred, an unaccustomed softness easing the edge of his tongue. "We have room to hide him within the Pyre. Grandmaster Saura will never allow Karlonos' guards to enter our halls, and they haven't a prayer of forcing their way."

"Politics is an evil, cursed thing, Elias," Captain Jehred grated, the words obviously causing him pain. "The Council members – an' those who line their pockets – will demand Darn's return. For Krolluck's gold an' fear mongering will inflame many t' speak agin yer whole Order. In the end, it will be civil war if the boy is not given up. And though yer Grandmaster may not fear th' Council, neither will he allow chaos to take th' city. Th' boy is a pawn t' be sacrificed – nothin' more, as they see it."

Darn stepped between the two older men then whirled to face them, his figure silhouetted against the brightness of the desert sand. His sudden move silenced the other two.

"I am no one's paw. And I am certainly no longer a child,

to have my decisions made for me. My choice is clear: to cross Lord Agni's stronghold if I am able, or to add my bones to His collection, if I am not." Darn spoke with a growing fury, and both of his companions stood dumb with surprise. "Wish me well, or curse me for a fool. But stand not and think to decide my fate, for my life and will are my own!"

Elias blinked slowly, for once unsure of his response.

"But the Trial of the Robe requires at least a full turn of the seasons for preparation. You have no maps, no supplies. No knowledge even of where it is you travel! The desert will consume you like a sweetmeat, a ripened fig easily plucked from the tree! I cannot allow …"

"Thou cannot forbid either, my Master. I have read the ancient texts: any Disciple who feels worthy may attempt the Trial, at any time." Darn squared his shoulders, and tried to force a note of bravery into his voice, though in truth the taste of fear was sour in his mouth. But his decision was made, and he would stand by it. "I cannot allow my presence to wreak havoc among our Order, or bring suffering among the people we are sworn to protect. Besides," he added, with a sarcastic grin, "it pleases me to think that those who would see me hang can now dread their own sleep, worrying about where I may be hiding." Jehred and Elias both grinned in return, despite their opposition.

Elias made several more abortive attempts at winning their argument. But each time, Darn's determination won out, and the Flame Master quickly realized the futility of his position. Understanding that the matter was already settled, Jehred left the pair alone on the wind-scoured parapet to return to the abandoned guard station, there to scrounge for whatever food and drink might be found.

Two Sons of Agni stood silently side by side, looking out at the desert, each lost in his own thoughts of death and loss, life and triumph. Elias felt a brief flash of burning pain as a remembrance of his own Trial swept through his mind. But those thoughts were swiftly chased away by an overwhelming sense of pride. For Darn was, indeed, his most prized student: unlike Elias in so many ways – in truth, in all the right ways. The boy was honorable to a fault – which at times had vexed Elias to no end. But the lad was keen as a blade, iron-willed, and fast – *Lords*, the boy was fast! But above and beyond all else, he possessed a soulfire so bright it was almost painful to look at, at times. None of the other Masters would venture to guess as to why the boy burned so brightly. But Elias knew the answer was simple: Lord Agni Himself had laid His Hand on the boy.

This one may well die in the attempt, Elias thought. *But if he falls, he will ride by Agni's side. And then I will ride the winds of revenge from one end of this city to the other!* The Flame Master's scarred and callused hand unconsciously reached for the boy's shoulder. And for the briefest of moments, Master Elias, Warmark of Agni's Disciples, fearsome warrior and abandoned whore's son, understood a father's love.

Though fear continued to sidle around his ankles like a companionable hound, Darn looked eagerly out into the vast wasteland which lay before him. The words rushed out of him in a hurried whisper, and neither knew if he spoke to Elias as well, or only to himself.

"Herein lies my destiny. To prove my worth or perish in

the attempt. Perhaps it is just the Trial of the Robe which calls to me. Or perhaps I go to put an end to my pain, or simply to punish myself for the loss of Loon and Eillena. My thoughts are all a mist now. All I know is that I must go."

Elias nodded slowly in mute answer, for he too realized that fate was calling his student to the unknown future, a future that waited for him under the burning sky, out among the dunes.

Jehred returned with a trio of water skins and a net bag of dried meat and fruits slung from his shoulder. "I liberated these from th' watch station in th' tower," he remarked, as he handed the scavenged booty to Darn. "Will have t' do fer ya, I suppose. Ya may be able t' find more out there, if yer willin' t' eat whate'er ya can catch. Wouldn't count on it, though, so stretch ev'ry bit as long as ya can." Then he handed Darn a light, hooded traveling cloak.

Elias found his voice, and once again the edge of confidence led his words, by tone alone refusing to entertain any thoughts of failure. "'Tis five days travel by bundhar from here to the Red Mountains in the west. A man on foot may make it in twice that, if he travels hard at night and finds some bolt hole to hide in during the day. None but those of our Order have ever survived such a journey though, and many have failed in the attempt." He paused and tapped at his lips with a forefinger, giving his words weight, then turned and motioned for the others to follow him. He moved towards a narrow, twisting set of stairs that led downward.

"Make a straight line for the second highest peak north of the setting sun, Elias continued. "In that direction – if Lord Agni wishes it – you will find an oasis with a safe spring to drink, and perhaps some game as well. The tents of the Scarab Folk are often pitched there, but trust them not. They can be generous hosts, but they are a crafty and devious people. Be sure that should they perceive you as weak or unprotected, they will strip you bare and leave your bones for the vultures." Elias instructed his student quietly as the three followed the winding staircase down through the coarse sandstone. "Further westward, a few small unmapped springs lie, though none but the desert people can find them with any certainty. Beyond the oasis, aim for a handspan *south* of the point where Lord Agni's chariot falls from the sky, and look for a stretch of crags which are called the Sleeping Dragon: it will be clear when you see it. At the end of the Dragon's tail lies the Scarlet Keep, where this first journey of yours comes to completion. Our brethren there will see to your needs. And from there, a new journey will unfold – one of unimagined challenges, I am sure."

Darn felt a dawning shock as the full implication of his decision settled upon him. Elias' words – which spoke of failure as well as triumph – seethed within Darn's mind. It was all he could do to nod in answer to Elias' instructions, and try to remember each one as if his life depended upon it.

The men reached the end of their descent and stepped into a large, cool antechamber. The room was enclosed by coarse unadorned sandstone walls, and capped by a thickly buttressed ceiling of the same material, magnificent in its quiet solid strength. At the other end of the chamber stood a pair of massive doors, barred shut by the trunk of a goldenoak tree wrapped about with dark bands of iron. Though originally titled after some forgotten chancellor or dignitary, this entrance to Shiningrock's sheltered highlands had for centuries born only one name: the Gate of Bones. Here, to pay for their crimes, were brought enemies of the Shiningrock Council, infamous or particularly loathsome prisoners, and even a few unfortunate losers of ugly partisan elections. Oh, of certain, these prisoners were not killed outright or even harmed in any way, and by this means the members of the Council kept their hands lawfully free of any bloodshed. Those under sentence were simply set outside the forbidding portal, and its massive doors closed against them: a final and inalterable fate for most. The Fortress of the Gate was carved from the very cliffs themselves, which stretched for leagues both north and south. Once beyond the Gate, there was no returning without the aid of wings. There was a spot – an overhang called Mercy's Point – where families of the condemned could lower food and skins of water down the cliffs on long ropes. But it was three days' walk north from the Gate, and few of those sentenced ever made it that far. There were worse things than just sand and sun in the desert.

Seldom were such sentences rescinded, though the Chancellor and his council often stayed for a time to listen to the condemned weep and wail and beg for forgiveness. On rare occasions mercy was granted and the doors reopened, though such mercy was generally found only through the proper application of substantial political contributions. Beyond that chance lay only the desert, which howled and moaned at night like a great hidden beast, wanting for fresh and succulent prey.

Jehred disappeared into the shadows cast by the flickering torchlight, walking off to the right of the doors. Darn and Elias head the brief jingle of keys, then the heavy snick of an iron lock. Moments later, chains began to rattle and strain in their traces, and slowly, the tremendous bole which held the portal shut lifted from its rests.

One great door rocked on its hinges, and Jehred walked back quickly to catch at a ring set in its face before it swung too far. Still, a small whirling dust devil leapt through the open door and spun for a brief heartbeat across the chamber, then died with a slight whistling cry, leaving its bones of sand on the floor. Darn saw the two older warriors tense, and Jehred's sword appeared in his hand as if by magic. Both the men relaxed once the yellow whirlwind had spun itself to nothingness.

"Ya ne'er know what may be birthin' such a cloud: could be th' wind, could be sumthin' else," Jehred mumbled, as if embarrassed for his reactions. He strained to pull the heavy door back an armspan or two, then stepped forward to stare cautiously out over the desert's stronghold.

Elias turned to look at his young apprentice – look *up* at, actually, the small-statured master noticed with no small amount of chagrin. Darn started to speak, but Elias chose to exercise the rights of his station and trampled over the boy's words. The Flame Master knew that Darn would die rather than back down at this point. He also knew that without proper appreciation of the dangers that lay in wait, along with the courage to face them all, the boy would die all the same.

"Today, you face the truest trial of your life," Elias said, calm, quiet and serious, a tone which Darn had perhaps never heard the master use before. "The trial you faced in the Circle; the matches and 'games' and endless training under my tutelage; your boyhood adventures; even the justice enacted upon the passing of our delightful friend Loon." Elias waved out into nothing, nothing but glaring sunlight and the steady hiss of windblown sand. "It all pales in comparison with the task laid now at your feet. For if ever Death glanced in your eye and winked in passage, She now lays dressed and perfumed in the lee of a dune, waiting for you only to find her bower and fall lovingly into her dark embrace."

Elias stood quietly for a moment, then laughed loudly and suddenly, as he slapped Darn across one shoulder, startling the boy despite his training. "Ha! By Agni's Holy Sunburned Arse!" Elias said jovially. "'Tis not as if none have tread this path before and lived to tell the tale. I myself have passed this way twice in my life so far: once for the robe I wear, and once in pursuit of a Scarab bandit who thought to escape me across the sands after cheating me of forty trachams in a crooked game of Whore's Gambit. Foolish man." A jaded wrinkle of a smile, Elias' most typical expression, had wormed its way back onto his face. As his laughter faded, he hooked an arm around Darn's shoulder, and gently guided the young man forward the last hand of steps to where the sand began.

The two robed figures stepped outside the doors, one white as the ravenous sun of midday, the second crimson as the blood of the sated, dying sun of evening. They joined Jehred as he stood guard just outside the forbidding portal. The captain remained alert, with sword in hand and a tiny dune already cresting over the toes of his hobnailed boots.

"What see ye, Jehred?" Elias questioned.

"Naught but sand 'n scrub – an' a bleedin' lot more sand, as always," the soldier replied. He shook his head slightly once in either dread or disbelief – he wasn't sure which. *Only fools and the damned go this way,* Jehred thought, even though he himself had crossed the desert a hand of times escorting Imperial caravans. But running guard on a fully-stocked caravan was a far, far cry from walking across on your bleeding feet! The Captain's eyes continued to scan the horizon, then check in both directions along the cliff's foot, inspecting every rolling ball of wire grass, every dust devil and cactus and pile of rocks in sight. Then he spoke over his shoulder without turning.

"Darn, ya canno' trust a bedamned thing in this thrice-cursed valley of desolation. Th' well ya hope t' find may be an illusion, or worse yet, dry er poisoned. Th' sand itself might not e'en be sand, but th' coarse-grained back offa sandtrapper. Th' mountains an' landmarks are always twice 's far away 's ya thought, a'first. Th' wind is more than wind, th' men may be far less than men, an' th' desert itself is far more than jest flat sand. Trust nothin' out there – nothin' a'tall!"

Elias grinned at Jehred's back and rolled his eyes comically as he turned to face Darn. One callused and scarred hand disappeared into the folds of the master's robe, then returned a moment later holding a pair of crimson-hilted daggers. The knives were identical, both having flattened, triangular blades of brightest steel inlaid with silver letters of an unfamiliar, spidery script. The handles were of red-heart cedar, and the pommels ended in short stiff points of blackened iron. The edges had never known a whetstone's face since they were drawn from the dwarven forge that birthed them, nor would they ever need one. The blades were the Flame Master's weapon of choice, and he had carried them a score of years – gifts from a dwarven clan chieftain whom a much-younger Flame Master had rescued in a skirmish along the edge of the Klemish empire. Elias handed the daggers to Darn, then closed the astonished boy's fingers around their handles. The knives were the only personal item the master was ever known to cherish.

"Trust these blades, Darn," Elias said solemnly, "as they have always struck deep and true. Trust the directions I have given, for they are my own, and twice they have brought me through to the Scarlet Keep. Trust what Jehred had to say as well – even if he does worry like an old woman." The master reached out to grab his student by the arm, and the intensity of his gaze was echoed in a grip which threatened to sink to the bone. "Most of all – *most of all* – trust yourself, your training, and above all else the soulfire that burns within you. For even the sun itself may be blinded by the Flames of one who has discovered his bonds and surpassed them!" Elias relaxed his hold then, and patted the boy lightly, carefully on the arm.

"They will send word from the Keep when you arrive. I will know of your victory, and Jehred and I will drink many pints in your honor. But I shall still be proud even if the word never comes, for more courage is spent in the beginning of a great trial such as this than at its ending." For the first time in their acquaintance, Elias took Darn's hand in a warrior's clasp, hands gripping forearms tightly: a grip of equals, and of kinsmen.

"Fare well, young Spark," the master continued. "And bring back a trinket of Camdian blue jade when you return, for I am acquainted with a certain young damsel in town who pays dearly for such stones – and pays in a most delectable mint of coinage, I might add! Now be off, for Jehred and I have plans to quarrel over and misdirections to lay."

Jehred stepped back beside the pair, still alert for any danger from the windswept wasteland. "I'll make sure that no one mounts th' watch-wall b'fore midday. By that time, should they even guess where ya've gone, none will be foolish enough t' try an' follow." The captain at last switched his sword to his left hand, so that he also could clasp hands with they boy. He spoke through gritted teeth, and his eyes held an odd mixture of tears and cold blazing fury.

"I shall ne'er forget whatcha did fer Loon, Darn. Ya treated him good all th' time, like a real person an' a true friend. An' ya did whot needed t' be done fer th' vermin that took 'im away from us." Jehred leaned in closer, and Darn thought he could smell the taint of blood on the soldier's breath. "Come back t' us, boy. Walk yer path quickly an' come back, fer there's much vengeance yet t' be reaped."

Darn looked steadily into the captain's eyes, eyes that had seen too much pain and death and suffering, eyes that had forever lost their joy. And in there, Darn saw his own reflection, and he did not care for the future it foretold. He gently disengaged his arm from Jehred's grip, and shook his head in resignation as he backed a pair of steps away.

"My vengeance is done, good Captain," Darn answered, ignoring his companions' furrowed brows. "Any else deserving of retribution must be judged and punished by another, for my hands and heart are bloodied enough. I am certain, though, that my esteemed Master here would be gracious enough to act in my stead."

Jehred stared back, uncomprehending for several silent moments. Then shades of his own past came back for a brief haunting, and he felt his face soften slightly at the boy's plight. Jehred ducked his head in a slight nod of acceptance. No farewells left, the grizzled soldier spun on his heel and tramped back inside, pausing only to knock the sand from his boots.

Elias chuckled, and Darn turned his attention back to the crimson-robed master.

"Vengeance is never quite done, my good lad," Elias laughed, somewhat disturbing in his good humor. "Interesting how that works." He paused long enough to pick a grain of sand from his teeth. "I will indeed be more than happy to judge and exact punishment in your place. Though be assured that there will still be vengeance burning for answer upon your return." He laughed again as he turned and walked to the gap in the great doorway, then he paused before stepping through.

"Ahh. Near to have forgotten," Elias said. "A final item I plucked from your room, which you may find use for along the way." He reached into another hidden pocket, and moments later a small embroidered skin pouch sailed through the air to land at Darn's feet with a muted clash. Darn retrieved it from the sand with a smile and tucked it under his sash without a further look; he knew that the small sack held a handful of smooth stones, along with a worn leather sling. It brought him great comfort to feel the weight of it at his side again.

Darn stepped forward, his back to the sandstone cliffs which loomed over him like the mighty walls of a titan's castle. He gazed across the vast waste of desert land that stretched into the west, and stared for several moments of the jagged teeth of the Red Mountains which wavered far in the distance. Then he settled the net bag of dried goods and his water skins into comfortable positions over his shoulders, and slipped Elias' daggers safely into the folds of his sash. The traveling cloak, Darn noted, matched the yellow-white of the sand perfectly, and he fastened it round his neck and drew up the hood.

Behind him, the stout doors drew shut with a deep and resolute thud. Now alone on the sand, Darn forbade himself to turn back for a last look – perhaps afraid that the sight would break his courage. He took a moment to fix upon the second tallest peak to the north, made sure that he could distinguish it from any other landmark, then began to walk with a steady easy rhythm, his shadow going before him. The rising sun peered over his shoulder, watching closely and hungrily as the young man moved deeper, step by step, into the land where only the glaring orb held sway.

Darn knew that before him lay his destiny, beyond uncounted leagues of burning desert and scrubland. Therefore, he never once looked back at the sandstone cliffs and forbidding doors behind him. In choosing so, he did not see the huddled piles of moldering rags and sun-bleached bones that lay half-covered with sand at the cliff's base, didn't see the scratches and scrabble marks around the edges of the great doors. He saw only the sand and the sun, which taunted and laughed at him and dared him to enter into their domain. And so the young Flame Dancer stepped forward, accepting their challenge.

Chapter Sixteen
The Daughter of
the Desert

The sun rose like a bloody eye above the rim of the desert canyon, gazing down upon a barren wasteland, the fruit of its own relentless labor. No birdsong rose to greet the morning; nothing praised its coming. The last few living creatures abroad scurried frantically in search of a dark cool bolt-hole. A horny-faced sand viper raised its head and tasted the air as the sand trembled beneath it. As the vibrations split into the sound of a tread, the snake worried itself quickly beneath a flat stone.

A lone figure trudged across the desert landscape, companioned only by a shifting mirage of shadows that danced before him. Darn raised his head only long enough to correct his course, and to check the surrounding scrub on the odd chance that it might hold something to eat. He raised his water skin, allowed himself a single, furtive swallow, then dropped the near-empty skin back to his side. The sun, the heat, even the lack of food he could endure. But Darn knew that if he didn't find more water soon, he would be providing fodder for the rest of the desert's denizens. And as he'd come to realize, the Escarp Desert kept its water to itself, doling it out in tiny measures only.

For three days now Darn had wandered through the sand and scrub, his only companions the black vultures that circled high above him in the mornings and evenings, ever hopeful for an easy meal. Their boldness had provided Darn with his dinner the night before, when one of the feathered scavengers had flown within sling range. The bird was tough and stringy, with an aroma and flavor that one would expect from an animal that considered a four-day dead, sun-bloated bundhar to be an emperor's feast. But its addition to his menu did stretch the rest of his food supplies, and even provided the boy with some badly-needed moisture. So Darn had paused to give his thanks to the Lady, along with a word for the buzzard, and tried not to grimace as he chewed a long wingbone.

By Elias' words, Darn should have reached the first oasis by now. But he was unsure of how far he might have drifted south in the early hours of dawn. Walking in the night was excellent advice, Darn agreed: unless impotent clouds deigned to cover the moon and the Guiding Star, that is. After a second night of stumbling in the darkness, Darn had accepted the inevitability of traveling mostly during the day. That way, despite the heat, at least he would be able to ensure that we wasn't walking in circles, and wouldn't end back up at the Gate of Bones by accident. He tried to estimate how far he might have wandered off course, then took a new fix on a peak still far, far in the distance, and walked on.

One exceedingly uncooperative dune did its best to prevent Darn from gaining its summit. Its crusted surface would sometimes support him for two or even three steps. But then it would collapse unexpectedly, dropping him waist-deep in sand as fine as flour, or sending him tumbling back down to the bottom of the dune in an avalanche of dust and debris and sand. Darn imagined he heard a rumbling from deep within the dune each time he fell, like sand-choked laughter. In turn, Darn cursed the ancestry of the dune, naming it the dusty remains of the West Wind's flatulence, destined for neither inclusion in a princess's playbox nor incorporation in the mortar for a magnificent temple, nor even to stand in silent grandeur as did the sandstone cliffs that bordered the desert's western limits. He pronounced it the dunghill of sand dunes, a lumpish pile of windblown debris fit only for the litter-boxes of the city ratter's feline workers.

The sand dune was cowed into gritty shame by Darn's words. The pain at its ignominy almost made the dune give one great heave – which was all the movement that its kind were allowed, and only once a millennium at that – and drown its tormentor in a sea of dust. But sand dunes were ever the most indecisive of entities, and so it gave up playing its games with the boy and sulkily returned to polishing the treasured collection of bones it kept hidden away in the unlit vaults of its granular depths. Darn refused at first to trust his senses when the surface of the dune seemed to become fixed somehow, and the pebbles no longer rolled beneath his feet. Then he smiled and accepted his victory, and marched steadily up the side and over the top with no further delays.

At first, Darn discarded the splash of color as some trick of his eyes, played in an unconscious effort to add some definition to this mind-numbing, unending sameness that surrounded him. He looked dully at the emerald-green fronds, and continued marching. Then a unique smell – one he never remembered having smelled before – worked its way into his brain, and every fiber of his body screamed out together in the same desperate voice: WATER!

The oasis was small – smaller than Elias had painted it, in fact. But the handful of tall palms and the carpet of lush, verdant grass that surrounded it bespoke of the spring's potency. The aquamarine surface of the pool glistened like the crown jewel of some desert giantess' tiara, polished until smooth and unblemished. It beckoned to Darn as few forces in his life ever had, and its call was not one to be disregarded. He stumbled forward like a broken puppet, and threw himself gracelessly into the spring's chilling embrace.

Darn drank again and again, till only the need for breath pushed his head back above water. His body seemed to draw in the precious liquid through his very skin. His face, slack with bliss, suddenly screwed up in pain as his stomach cramped violently. Darn waded quickly to the bank, bent over, and retched up all he'd just drunk. He trembled uncontrollably for a while, but finally turned and sat carefully on the bank. Then Darn cupped his hand and slowly began dipping water up to his mouth. And for a long shifting of the shadows, he knew no greater pleasure in the world.

***

Darn awoke with a start, though his body never betrayed him. Lovely, cool water still swirled around his ankles as he lay on the bank of the oasis pool. But some change in the sounds around him, some uncertain lacking that hadn't been there before, had pulled him from his sleep. Darn cracked one eye open, searched the shadows for a moment, then sat bolt upright. A number of striped, tented pavilions were set up all around the edges of the little sanctuary. The dingy brown, humpbacked forms of resting bundhars could be seen in the shade on the far side of the pool, though Darn was surprised that he hadn't smelt the malodorous beasts before now. He moved slowly to his feet, turned to step, and almost ran into the purple-and-gold fabric of a tent staked just behind him. An unpleasant prickling began at the base of Darn's skull, like fire ants wandering about searching for a place to bite. Despite the silence of his other senses, Darn slid a long step across the sand before spinning about. The source of his uneasiness stood there quietly, and smiled at the rags of confusion and surprise – aye, and a scrap of fear, as well – that fluttered before the boy's face.

The Scarab Headwoman seemed an embodiment of her people: tall and regal, skin burnt almost black by the fierce sun under which they lived. The blousy, white pantaloons she wore fluttered and snapped in the breeze, though the brilliant skeins of multi-colored silk that wrapped and braided her jet hair kept her face clear, reinforcing the air of untouchability that surrounded her. The chains of hammered silver that she wore about her neck signified her position as head of her clan, even though that title generally belonged to the eldest male. Where her wind-whipped garments outlined her body, it looked hard and strong, a match to the grizzled Scarab warriors that Darn had seen on occasion in the city. Her nose was long and sharp as a knife's blade: patrician, they'd have called her looks back in Shiningrock. But it was the woman's eyes – piercing, depthless, ancient somehow – that took Darn's attention by the throat and held it in an unbreakable grasp. The smile on her face, pearls set against her blackened skin, cast a net of calm over the boy. Even so, a voice from some far corner of his mind reminded him that Scarab folk had never been known for their kindness towards strangers.

She raised her hand in greeting, and said a few words in a coughing, consonant-filled language that Darn could not understand, though their meaning was clear enough. Darn returned the gesture and greeted her in common-Eldorn, hoping that the message would at least convey his respect, if not his actual words. The Headwoman hesitated, as if tasting Darn's words to extract their true flavor. Then a spark of understanding blossomed in her eyes, and she replied in halting, high-Eldorn.

"Greetings, young traveler. The rains have fallen many times since I have seen other than the Children-of-the-Sand." Her voice was soft, low and raspy. She bowed slightly, and Darn returned the greeting without taking his eyes off of her. "My name is S'skyla," she continued, "and all of this ..." she waved an arm vaguely, encompassing the camp, the oasis, even the desert beyond, " ... is my own to command. But come, for your journey must certainly have exacted its toll upon you. Please allow the hospitality of my humble camp to provide for all of our needs." She lifted aside the flap to her tent and motioned extravagantly for Darn to enter. He did not follow immediately, as courtesy would have, for the call of the spring-fed pool tugged at him still. But the Headwoman permitted no delay, taking Darn's arm in an astonishingly strong grip and leading him into the dark interior of her pavilion.

After four straight days beneath the desert sun, Darn's eyes refused to adjust to the tent's dim interior. Vague murky shapes hinted at chests and tables, a sleeping pedestal crowded with pillows and hung with ribbons, and other less discernable objects. The musk of some heavy incense hung in the air, almost overpowering, clouding his senses. Darn's clearest thought seemed to be that even in the heavy shade of the tent, it barely felt any cooler than it had a moment ago standing in the sun. Of course, his mind insisted that it had to be cooler within the tent than without. Perhaps his body had been broiled for so long that he had simply become numb to either pain or relief. The Scarab woman's voice broke through Darn's thoughts, as he saw her lift a pitcher from a low table.

"Before all else, your thirst must be slaked," she said, as she filled a heavy ornamented goblet. She took a sip from it herself to demonstrate its safety, then passed the remainder to Darn. Just the sound of pouring water made Darn's throat seem to swell tight. He gulped greedily, the taste sweet as nectar on his tongue; as soon as he had drained the vessel, he held it out unabashedly for a second helping. The Headwoman smiled and brushed aside his rudeness, filling the goblet again and handing it back.

Darn drained the cup a second time, and still his thirst seemed as powerful as it had when he walked the sands. If anything, his throat seemed dustier now than it had earlier. He knew the worth of water in this land though, and the value of the gift that had been offered to him; he handed the goblet back and politely refused a third cupful, even though his body cried for more. Once I return to the pool, he reminded himself, I shall immerse myself up to my eyeballs if I care to. Until then he would act as if he possessed some measure of self control.

His hostess set aside the pitcher and cup and moved to sit on the edge of the pillowed and be-ribboned bower, motioning for Darn to join her.

"And now to satisfy my own desires," she remarked huskily. Her attempt to sound seductive seemed more like the raucous cawing of a crow settling down to feed.

Though she was attractive enough in a rugged sort of way, Darn felt that bedroom favors in return for a few drinks of water was a bit of a hard bargain – particularly since he could drink from the oasis pool without charge. And something about the woman caused an unconscious clenching in his guts, though he could not name the source. Still, she had been courteous to him when many others would have met him with drawn swords. Darn shrugged in resignation and sat down. *The Scarab menfolk certainly must be lacking, if a dusty and bedraggled wanderer such as myself seems a tempting morsel,* he thought.

Darn's mind whirled, searching for some topic to delay the evidently inevitable payment for his accommodations. A curious note from earlier drifted back up to the surface of his thoughts, and he gratefully seized upon it.

"Where … uh .. where lie the rest of thy people?" Darn asked quickly, almost spitting the words out as the Headwoman stretched across the bower and reached for his arm. "I neither saw nor heard aught of them on my approach, not even a guardsman. And even an ignorant fool such as myself knows of the Scarab folk's legendary watchfulness." Darn itched at a streamlet of sweat that tracked its way down his ribs.

S'skyla withdrew somewhat and a frown of irritation creased her forehead, only to be erased a moment later by the milky glow of her smile.

"The guards you did not see, simply for they did not wish to be seen," she answered smoothly. "They signaled of your approach in the morning hours, long before we set up our encampment." S'skyla pulled nonchalantly at a cord knotted at her throat, and the muslin blouse she wore fell magically aside, leaving her dusky bare torso to gleam dully in the gloom of the tent. She picked a round fuzzy fruit from a nearby platter and offered it to Darn after taking a bite herself. "You would have been slain out of hand, had the sentries not known of my certain .. ah … taste for men from the

city. Boys, in particular, I find almost maddening in their sweetness."
She laughed lightly, but Darn felt no inclination to join her. "As for
the rest of my clan," she continued, gesturing out towards the rest
of the camp, "they are simply waiting out the heat of the day. We
know the desert far too well to tempt Her when She is strongest ...
unlike the fools and caravaneers from the city."

The muted sound of clanging pots drifted in from outside,
and now Darn could hear indistinct voices and even the noise of
children playing. Strange that he'd heard nothing earlier; still, he
supposed they could have been sleeping or perhaps hiding until
their clan leader had dealt with the newcomer. Darn mulled the
thought over for a moment or two, and unmindfully bit into the
fruit S'skyla had handed him.

A thick cloying sweetness, almost rotten in its intensity,
forced Darn to gag, though he hid it behind his hand. He longed
to spit out the rancid slimy pulp, but he knew that refusal of food or
drink was a serious slight to the desert nomads, people who fought
so hard to draw sustenance from the land around them. With grim
determination, Darn swallowed both the nauseating mouthful of
fruit and his own revulsion, then passed the offering back to his
hostess with a weak smile.

S'skyla's hand shot out to bat the fruit aside, and she grasped
Darn's wrist in a remarkably powerful grip. Caught off guard, Darn
found himself drug roughly across the bower, and for a brief instant
the pillows seemed less than soft, and the silks less than smooth.
The headwoman's face now loomed close to Darn's own, near enough
to smell the dusty clove-like scent of her breath, and feel the heat
of it washing against his skin. Her free hand gripped his robe at

the neck, and in a single motion she ripped it aside, easily tearing the strong silk fabric.

Darn wasn't exactly frightened, but he was far, far from comfortable. The situation certainly was not proceeding as he had anticipated. It wasn't as if he were unfamiliar with the arts of the boudoir, for after Katrïnn had provided his introduction, Darn had eagerly accepted the invitations of several of the younger working girls along the wharves. He'd also had a brief dalliance with the lovely daughter of a visiting Bandaran prince, who would have had his head and other miscellaneous parts in payment had the incident been discovered. But the Scarab woman was coarse and harsh, not smooth and soft as he'd been accustomed to. What if he offended this chieftain, and she called five hands of warriors to avenger her honor? Frantically, the young flame dancer searched for any conversational barrier to delay the proceedings. The only thought that came to mind was flimsy at best, but he was desperate.

"Bundhars!" he nearly shouted in his haste. "I struggle to remember when I have heard a group of bundhar so silent, for the ones ye have tied seemed to have forsworn the constant bellowing, coughing, grunting and snorting of their kind. Why, I haven't even heard one break wind yet, and as Sandali the merchant would often say, 'Bundhar don't exhale – they just fart out each breath.' They are ever the most cantankerous of beasts, and never have I known one to be silent for more than a moment." A sudden insight bloomed from deep within his memory, and for an instant his puzzlement pushed aside all else.

"Bundhars?" Darn questioned. "I thought that thy people disdained the use of bundhars for all but the largest caravans. As

I recall it, I have ever only seen Scarab menfolk astride their fleet-footed droes, the thick-tailed ones that are bred by no one else."

At this interruption, S'skyla's face grew angry, her lips pulled back from her teeth in a snarl of frustration, and her eyes blazed for a moment like burning embers. She slashed her hand back towards the oasis, and sounds of the vocal and intestinal discord normally associated with the unpleasant pack animals broke forth as if on cue.

"We train the bundhar to be silent when staked, in order to ensure the security of our camps," she fairly spat in explanation. "The droes are being ridden by our patrols, or are shaded under an overhang near here." The headwoman was obviously aggravated now, and when Darn opened his mouth to pose another question, her free hand clamped around his throat so suddenly that Darn nearly struck her in unthinking response.

"What!? What now!?" S'skyla shouted into Darn's face, and she shook him with such force that his teeth snapped together. "Will you ask next why our privies do not smell? Why there is no smoke from our cook-fires? Why we do not raise a banner upon the highest hill and proclaim our location to any that may care to descend upon us?"

For a moment, a single instant that stretched out long and thin, the interior of the tent lightened perceptively. Darn felt the searing rays of the sun once again biting into the raw red flesh of his neck. An eddy of wind-blown dust scurried across the floor, seeking refuge from its tormentor. The mournful howl of the wind was once again the only sound to be heard, with no interruption by man or beast. And the hands that clamped onto his arm and throat were suddenly unyielding and sharp-edged.

But as quickly as they had arrived, the sensations were whisked away, leaving only a queasy unbalance of Darn's senses in their wake. S'skyla's dark brown face stared intently at him from the length of two noses, and Darn could feel the silky softness of her breasts as she rubbed sinuously against him. Her anger from moments before seemed to have dissipated, and she cooed to him in a throaty growl, thick with undisguised lust.

"Come, my fine alabaster morsel. Do not tempt my anger with such idiocies."

She released her hold on Darn's throat and began to stroke his face in an attempt at tenderness. But Darn could feel the tension in her touch, and noticed also that her hand never strayed far from his neck. He imagined he could already feel the flesh there bruising from her rough handling.

"Another drink, perhaps," S'skyla soothed, and she poured Darn another bubbling goblet full of water. "To quench your thirst, before we discuss the quenching of my own."

Darn's distrust had grown steadily since he'd entered the Scarab folk's compound, and Captain Jehred's words of caution echoed in his head. But despite his misgivings, Darn's thirst demanded that the offer of water be accepted. Reluctantly, he put the cup to his lips again. He could feel the cool liquid slide down his throat, could smell the salty metallic tang of it, and could taste the minerals in it. He was completely immersed in the welcome relief of much-needed refreshment, when he felt a sharp stabbing inside his mouth. Something crunched between his teeth as Darn brought them together, and a moment later he spit the offending mystery into his palm for further examination.

S'skyla moved quickly to dash Darn's discovery onto the floor, but not before Darn could make out a tiny arachnid form, legs still waving about in a posthumous attempt to right itself. Clarity flooded into Darn's mind just ahead of a wave of revulsion, and for the barest of moments, Darn no longer held a golden goblet but a battered tin cup in his hand, full of dust and spider webs and their tiny industrious spinners.

Darn glanced back at S'skyla's feral smile, and forced the shifting in his sight. S'skyla's lips seemed to melt from her face, taking the rest of her flesh with it, and the ghostly shade of twisted fangs floated dimly behind the gleam of her faltering smile. Then her hand was back on his throat, this time pressing in with determined intent, and Darn's vision faded to its former murkiness.

"The deliriums of the desert have come upon you. I can see it in your eyes," S'skyla answered to his unspoken question. "You must lie down for now, to allow your body and mind to rest and accept my offerings." With an unbreakable grip she pressed him firmly down into the perfumed sheets of the sleeping bower. "Fear not, my little dove," she cooed, "for I shall lay here beside you until you have no more need of me."

Darn resisted his host's suggestion, but found to his chagrin that her hold on him was all but unbreakable. His captured arm felt as if it were caught in a steel vise, and his other arm seemed hopelessly ensnared in the twisted silk bed sheets. S'skyla's legs had somehow managed to pin his own legs between them. And the hand at his throat had forgotten the tender strokes from moments ago, resorting instead to heavy-handed pawing that dug deep into his flesh. Darn strained only once against his captor's grip, then tried to relax and martial his thoughts. He knew from painful training lessons not to waste energy struggling against a stronger foe. So instead, Darn fell back upon a reliable weapon that had proved difficult to disarm, nearly impossible to parry, and one that cut to the bone quicker than any sword blade: his sharp-edged tongue. It had gotten him into more trouble than he cared to remember, but it had also extricated him a few times as well. Darn gathered his strength and voice, then lashed out.

"Lay with ye?" Darn laughed, trying to sound confident and disdainful at the same time. "Rather would I lay with one of yon bundhar, 'fore I would touch a flea-infested drudge as thyself! E'en the embrace of a greater snot-beast could bear no less welcome a touch!"

S'skyla's face went slack in momentary disbelief at the barb, and her hold loosened somewhat. The coal-black eyes of the Headwoman grew so wide that they seemed to teeter on the edge of their lids, ready to drop out onto the rug. Her face darkened perceptively as her fury reached explosive dimensions. And as Darn had hoped – had bet his life on, in fact – the dim light within the tent once again began to grow, and the forms of the bed and other furnishings began to melt and change. Indeed, S'skyla herself began to waver, as if another form inside of her was straining to burst free.

Refusing to pause for an examination of his surroundings or to reflect on the results of his taunts, Darn continued his verbal assault. He worked frantically to free his arm from the bedclothes that held it captive. , knowing that he must be prepared when S'skyla's rage found its release.

"Better dugs have I seen on a sway-backed hound dragging

a litter of pups. And I must confess that thy breath reminds me of nothing other than the charnel house back in Shiningrock. Could ye turn aside before killing me? For even there the breeze changes direction once a day, bringing a brief respite from the foul stench." S'skyla shrieked then, so keen and high-pitched that Darn felt something burst in one of his ears – indeed, for the rest of his days he would be partially deaf on that side.

"Insipid mortal fool!" she howled. "I would have gifted you with pleasures beyond your imagination, sensations such as only the gods may enjoy. All in exchange only for the useless husk of your flesh at the end." Full sunlight struck Darn in the face, blinding him somewhat from seeing the details of S'skyla's transformation. Her skin seemed to slough off of her face, dripping away like hot candle wax. And the hand which still pinned Darn's arm lost the soft padding of its flesh, leaving behind only hard angles and sharp edges. Some small calm portion of Darn's mind noticed that the camp sounds from outside had vanished, and that the sun beat down on him again, for above him fluttered only a tattered strip of ragged canvas held aloft by a few thin poles. The less-than-calm portion of his mind pointed out that breathing was no longer a possibility, due to S'skyla's grip on his throat. To this last observation, the young Flame Dancer's body answered with immediate and abrupt action.

With the entrapping bed clothes revealed to be scraps of rotten rags, Darn tore his arm free and struck. His first two blows took S'skyla high on the side under the arm, a blow which often left the living with broken ribs or punctured lungs. But S'skyla seemed to take little notice. In fact, she grinned at the blows, chuckling dryly through twisted fangs of quartz.

"Please, struggle as much as you wish," S'skyla responded, laughing at Darn's attempts to dislodge her from atop him. Her voice was now harsh and grating, like a blade's edge drawn across a slate. "Beat your delicate flesh-bound arms to a soft pasty pulp against the beauty of my bones – many have done so before. Exhaust yourself now, so it will take far less time for you to succumb to the sun once I have staked your body out among the rocks." A withered worm of a tongue snaked out to run over her pointed teeth in a horrible parody of seduction. "And once your flesh has been dried to perfection, I will sit down to a feast such as I have not known in ages."

The flesh and clothing that S'skyla had worn earlier were now only vaguely-colored mists, a leftover from the creature's conjurings. Darn could see geometric shapes dimly glowing beneath the bones of her rib cage, and her eyes now showed no iris or pupil, but only gleaming faceted crimson stone. She tightened her grip on his throat, and Darn could feel hot splinters of crystal begin to pierce his skin.

"Perhaps you would like to scream for me," she said. "The sand-grubbing Scarab wastrels that are left out to appease me are so stoic about the whole matter. Besides, they're usually near death by the time I find them. Such a song you could sing for me, hmm? Perhaps if I pulled out each of your eyes, then left them to hang on your cheeks for the flies and sand chiggers to devour?" A dry grating echoed from within her chest, and Darn realized that she was laughing even as she released his other hand and reached for his face.

The instant they were free, Darn's arms were moving, scissoring up and across his body. His palms crossed paths at the skeletal limb which clutched his throat, one striking directly above the elbow joint, one directly below. Upon later circumspection of the event, Darn felt justified in admitting that the results of the blow were rather spectacular.

Whatever construct or forces held S'skyla's arm together, they were no match for the Flame Dancer's blow, and her elbow disintegrated in an explosive cloud of bone and mineral dust. Her hand and attendant forearm flew off and shattered against a small boulder that stood where a chest had once sat in the tent-that-no-longer-was. The upper portion of her arm waved uselessly in the air.

At that point, S'skyla ceased to laugh, and Darn began. The soulfire crackled greedily in his belly, and his limbs surged with newfound strength and speed. He laughed because Death had come calling, and he, simple Darn of Warden Woods, had dealt the first blow. Regardless of how it ended, Darn knew that Elias would be proud.

Darn recoiled with a backhand strike that took the creature across the jaw line. He paid in blood for his action, though, as a serrated fang slashed across his forearm. But the rewarding *crack* of splintering bone brought S'skyla down and off to one side. Darn rolled away quickly and tried to stand, but something slipped and crumbled under his feet, forcing him to scramble away on all fours. Sharp pebbles dug vicious furrows in his knees, and he tore the wound on his arm even wider on a ragged edge of splintered bone. He reached the edge of the sleeping platform and tumbled over the side, then spun to face the atrocity scrabbling for purchase behind him. But Darn ignored the distractions, for his host stood up upon her bower. And the view of his almost-lover and her boudoir were more than Darn would ever care to recall.

The creature's lair lay in dappled shadow cast by the ragged canopy stretched above it. The orange hue of a rough sandstone mound peeked from between the white and yellow globes that pillowed its surface. S'skyla took a step forward, and an orb shattered under her foot. One of its companions fell off the edge of the bower to land at Darn's feet and leer up at him: it was a human skull, its dome carefully pried off and its contents thoroughly pilfered.

Darn's stomach simply collapsed, having no time for slowly rising gorges and the like. Darn bent over and a vile black slime slid from between his teeth, littered with the mangled corpses of hundreds of tiny spiders and the remains of something that he did not wish to examine more closely.

"Oh, don't stop now," a voice hissed lightly, like blowing sand, like the quiet malignant progress of a sidewinder. "Beg please continue. Soil yourself as well – it adds such a subtle piquant under-flavor to your fear." She took another step forward to loom over him.

"I had forgotten the significance of the sash. It has been so very long a time. But now it returns to me: the warriors of the greatcity, those that worship my Father and preach their invincibility. I have savored the sun-sweetened remains of four of your predecessors, and found their scarlet sashes to be attractive additions to my wardrobe. Indeed, this is an unanticipated delight: perhaps it is my birthday! In any manner, I shall perform a special sacrifice with your skull, offering a portion to the wind and the sand and the sun before sitting down to my feast!"

Darn spit one last time in a futile effort to rid himself of the foul taste, and wiped backhandedly at his mouth as he looked up at the speaker. His stomach flopped once more at the sight, then lay spent. Perhaps the sudden flare of his soulfire branded his stomach into obedience, or perhaps his rising anger trod his revulsion down. In either case, a second review of his earlier meal was precluded. But nothing could force back the disbelieving horror that scratched at his eyes, now that he could see his foe fully.

S'skyla's illusions had all faded now, and the harsh rays of the sun accented every grotesquerie of her true form. Darn could see much of the skeleton that made up her frame: obviously female from the set of the hips. The face of her skull was varnished with an amber patina of age, and one leg bore the deep scars of a hyena's teeth. But what held Darn's gaze in a loathsome but fascinating grasp was the panoply of crystals and rocky growths that covered her like clothing, pelt, and adornments all at once. Her skull was encrusted with fine white crystal needles, mocking the wild black mane which had once grown there. And bangles of garnets and opals swung gaily from the side of her skull as her earrings once had. Jagged spines of stone grew haphazardly from her back. Razor-edged blades of quartz graced her fingers and toes with formidable claws, and filled the maw which even now drew closer to Darn's face. He noticed with an odd detachment that the heavy necklace of hammered silver medallions still hung about her neck, the only feature to survive S'skyla's remarkable transformation.

"I am the Daughter of the Desert, whom the tribes pray to for deliverance and forbearance," S'skyla intoned dramatically, pausing in her advance to proclaim her own self-importance. "I am She who was born twice: once of the womb, and once of the sand." She raised her arms wide-spread, as if to glorify their parched and empty embrace. "All the magic of the desert is bound in amongst my bones. To the Desert Herself, I am the only begotten Daughter. To the denizens of my domain, I am a force of nature, as much as the wind and the sun. To those who still bear the flaccid burden of their flesh, I am known only as Death."

The creature lowered her arms and stood expectantly for a moment, waiting for Darn's cowering reply. She was slightly disappointed.

"To myself," Darn replied, as he reached down towards his feet, "ye are known as the most pompous pile of moldering carrion scraps as I have ever had the unpleasant distinction of laying eyes upon!" Darn straightened suddenly and whipped his arm forward. The skull he threw flew straight and true, though S'skyla contemptuously moved to bat it aside. But unfortunately for her, the limb that she swung no longer had a forearm or hand attached. Her useless stump swept through the air a span too low, and the thrown skull took her full in the face.

Though the missile shattered harmlessly against her, the insult was more than the desert-spawned demon had endured in over a hundred years. S'skyla began to howl madly and hungrily, like the bone-sucking cold of the East Wind that danced over the desert dunes in winter, feasting on all who dared to brave its onslaught. And like that same wind, she leapt at Darn mindlessly, seeking only his death.

Darn's heart caught in his throat as he realized he'd been caught flat-footed, for he hadn't expected his taunts to take effect so quickly and effectively. Four razor-sharp talons whisked past his face, so close he could feel the hot wind of their passing. He began to congratulate himself on performing a well-executed dodge, when the claws of S'skyla's trailing leg slashed into his calf as she finished her pass. A troubling amount of blood sprayed out as the adamantine nail bit into Darn's flesh, painting S'skyla's own leg with a deep crimson veneer as well.

S'skyla spun about as soon as she landed, kicking up a plume of sand. Darn knew that she'd be prepared for his dodge this time. He tried to look for a weapon of some sort without taking his eyes off the monster. Her second charge took longer than he'd expected though, so Darn took the extra time to clamber back atop the bower of skulls, granting him at least the advantage of a higher position. He remembered Elias' daggers at last and began to slip the silver blades from his waistband. Then he considered S'skyla's present form, and thrust the knives back into their sheaths while he cursed his own foolishness. As he took a fighting stance, Darn began to gulp huge draughts of the burning desert air, using it to stoke the soulfire already blazing in his crucible. Had he not far worse to fear at the moment, Darn would have worried that the soulfire would simply consume his frail flesh in one fierce explosion. But with no other option apparent, Darn simply brought up his hands and steeled himself to receive S'skyla's attack.

Strangely, S'skyla seemed too preoccupied to attack. She was busy cursing to herself and using handfuls of sand to furiously scrub the blood off of her leg. Darn stared in marked confusion, unable to decipher why such gore should bother a creature who planned to dine upon him later. Then he recalled her earlier words of feasting on his *desiccated* corpse. A tiny seed of an idea took root in the depths of his brain, sprouting the barest greenery of hope upon the flimsy hopeless stalk of a plan.

Finished with her gruesome toiletry, S'skyla straightened and fixed the glittering orbs of her eyes on Darn. When she spoke this time, all traces of sarcasm and even humorous disdain had evaporated. Her voice now held only the deadly crystalline certainty of the mid-summer desert.

"You could have died softly and quietly. This much I would have granted you, for my illusions would even have allowed me to remember the pleasures of the flesh. And had you pleased me enough, I may even have been swayed to place a piece of my own crystal heart within your chest, and raise you up to reign over this realm by my side." S'skyla stepped forward slowly, the reflecting sunlight turning her life-stealing talons into handfuls of diamonds. "But you have rejected my gift, and insulted my mastery," she continued. "Death for you will be a unreachable treasure: one for which you would sell your own mother. For I will crucify you and drink of your soul for a thousand years." As the grating hiss of the last word passed the splendid dreadfulness of her crystal lips, S'skyla leapt towards Darn, the darkest angel of this desert hell.

A stony claw swept downward, bringing Darn's death in its grasp. Instead, it met a half-empty leather water bag swinging upward. The dagger-sharp points pierced the water skin without slowing, releasing the precious liquid it carried in a crystal spray. The water splashed full over the encrusted skull that S'skyla wore for a face, and wherever it touched, bone and mineral began dissolving away.

It was the desert's oldest nemesis, over which a never-ending war was fought again and again. Water. Life. Here in this land, they were one and the same. Though the desert held unchallenged mastery from the Rendrac peaks in the east to the sloping Crimson Hills in the west, still the tiny oases remained, dotting the great beast's hide like so many blue-green boils. And what was painful to the desert itself, was devastating to its chief avatar.

S'skyla fell backwards into the sand, screaming through the remains of her ruined visage. Frantically, she rolled over and tried to halt the dissolution of her face by rubbing it in the sand, all the while calling upon the power of the Desert, the mother of which she was born, to aid her. To Darn's growing horror, granules of sand began to stick, fusing themselves into the bone and crystal that made up her form. S'skyla loosened a cry of salvation at the discovery, and ground her face even harder into the desert sand.

Darn's reasoning mind screamed for escape. But his training was anchored at a deeper level. Without conscious direction he ran in behind the creature and leapt high, then landed with a twin stomp on the back of S'skyla's ankles. In living creatures, such a blow normally tore the tendons attached there, leaving their owner with a pair of crippled feet. In skeletal manifestations, the results were less spectacular, if equally damaging. The brittle bones simply crumbled to dust under the impact, leaving S'skyla with two legs that ended in splintered stumps.

The bloodless apparition gained a standing pose once after that, but the contest was over all the same. Darn's taunts and a well-timed lunging attack drew a desperate clawing swipe in return that stole what little remained of S'skyla's balance and took her back down to the sand. Darn darted in for a crushing kick that shattered most of her ribs on one side. As several glowing crystalline structures set within her chest exploded beneath the blow, S'skyla let loose a dry and terrible howl of despair.

Darn retreated a few steps, to gain some safe distance. He stood swaying, ready to resume his attack, as he watched S'skyla's demise and savored his narrow victory. Once again, though, Darn found himself terribly disappointed. The Desert answered Her child with a tremendous sigh of wind, and a whirling cloud of fine white dust blew up from nowhere, settling about the site of the battle. As Darn watched with dread, S'skyla's injuries began to knit at an astounding rate, regrown and reconstituted from the very body and soul of her patron goddess.

Darn glanced anxiously down towards the beckoning water of the oasis. It alone had been the only thing not cloaked in illusion when he'd arrived at S'skyla's camp, the only thing left unchanged. But without another skin or vessel to carry the waters of salvation back and complete S'skyla's dissolution, the unholy bitch would continue to regrow all the cutlery needed to make Darn's life dreadfully short and painful. He could just wade out into the oasis pool and wait out her assault, Darn supposed. But then the monster could hold siege against him as surely as an attacking army, for he had to eat at some time. And Lord and Lady! How would he sleep, standing waist deep in water?

Darn felt an odd sensation then, like the heavy hand of his lost friend Loon laid companionably on his shoulder. And as he thought of Loon, the answer to his dilemma dropped upon him. And Darn could do no more than smile like an fool and think of how loud Loon would have laughed. He stepped up to where S'skyla knelt in the sand, hoisted his robe, pulled his loincloth to one side, and took careful aim. After that, Darn could almost hear Loon's laughter as he watched the "Daughter of the Desert" melt back into the sand and stone and malignant elemental forces that spawned her.

Chapter Seventeen
Trial of the Scarab People

Darn rested at the oasis for two days after his struggle with the sand demon. First, though, he constructed a low sleeping platform out of branches and palm fronds, and mounted it on weathered poles that he scavenged from S'skyla's pavilion. Then he set the platform several paces out in the waters of the shallow lagoon. He didn't think that S'skyla was capable of reconstituting herself after the thorough dissolution that he had visited upon her. But Darn would take no further chances with the desert's trickery. Only the inviolate safety of the oasis water would allow Darn to sleep and shield him from nightmares of being staked out on the sands, slowly turning into a sizable haunch of jerky for a crystalline monstrosity to later dine upon.

Darn awoke slowly on the third day, and at first his eyes refused his summons to open. After suffering under the relentless sun, then battling the desert's high priestess, the cool shaded surface of the oasis pool held Darn as tightly as did a toquil-addict's twisted smoke. It demanded that he simply lay quietly and luxuriate in its blessing. When finally he pried his eyes apart, Darn allowed himself a full two heartbeats to curse his foolishness, as he counted the number of lance heads and arrow points aimed at his heart from the edge of the pool an arms-length away.

Darn almost laughed when he thought of how ridiculous he must look, lying on his little platform out in knee-deep water. But from the looks on their faces, the Scarab warriors that surrounded him saw no humor whatsoever in the situation. Each of the men seemed as taut as the bow-strings they held, ready to release and deliver Darn's death at any time. None spoke or motioned in any way, but merely stood guard.

After a long moment, several of the warriors stepped aside to apparently allow the passage of some person of authority. Their eyes never left Darn though, and their weapons never wavered. Darn slowly moved from his pallet to stand in the water, feeling foolish, but fearing to offend the clan leader by failing to rise at his approach. But as the last intervening warriors stepped aside, recognition drew the sour taste of bile into Darn's throat, and a surge of soulfire's fury poured into his *crucible*. He stepped forward out of the pool, disregarding the blades and darts of the surrounding fighters, even swatting at several to clear them from his path. At last only two dour-looking warriors remained, with faces like burnt leather and eyes like falcons', stationed on either side of the object of Darn's anger. Darn gave the pair as little notice as he did the surrounding sand.

The woman stared calmly as Darn approached. Ignoring the stray locks of hair that the wind whipped across her face, she rubbed a finger over the flat necklace of silver she wore, but offered no words. She looked much the same as she had when Darn first met her, though she seemed to have dreamt up new clothes for herself. But there was no mistaking the pale white streak through the middle of her raven mane, the strong, clean limbs, the piercing black eyes.

"Hail, Queen of Dust!" Darn called out as he made a mock bow. "I see that ye have returned, conjured once again out of the rat turds and dirt from which ye were spawned. Have ye not yet drunk enough from my fountain? Then I shall be more gracious with my serving this time!" Saying so, Darn pulled his tunic up and his loincloth aside, took his member in hand, and took careful aim at the apparition.

One of the clanswoman's bodyguards uttered a short hard curse, and swung a wickedly-curved scimitar down towards Darn's busy hands. Though he knew it to be another of S'skyla's illusions, Darn could not ignore the glinting edge that sliced towards his family parts like a headsman's axe. Neither could his body deny its innate response to shirk aside at the last instant.

Darn froze in shock as he felt the thin deadly blade slice through the air a fingers-breadth from his hands and their precious content. A corner of his sleeve parted in the blade's passing and floated slowly to the ground. The stream that Darn had already released splashed over the Scarab warrior's hand and arm, and painted a dark dwindling trail down the man's pantaloons as its source withered and dried up.

This cannot be! The thought danced in Darn's mind like a chattering monkey. *Shadows do not bear live blades. Nor do their clothes stain wet from my water!*

Darn's self-introspection nearly cost him his head as the scimitar returned for a high backhanded stroke. But even without his conscious direction, Darn's body knew how to perform under attack. He ducked the blade and spun, lashing out with a low reaping kick to knock the warrior's legs from under him and drop him squarely onto his turban-ensconced head. Darn hoped fleetingly that the silken headgear had provided the Scarab guardsman with little protection from his fall.

Darn could hear laughter swelling up from the surrounding Scarab warriors as the swordsman regained his feet. But the Flame Dancer was too busy dodging silvery death to appreciate the humor of the situation. The warrior's scimitar flashed from all sides as he circled in. Darn slipped and danced aside as best he could, fighting to resettle his clothing and avoid being filleted both.

With each unsuccessful attack, the Scarab clansman, Teshret K'malli, felt his rage grow and grow, until finally he lost all semblance of control and swung wildly, murderously, like an enraged child might. Even as Teshret berated himself for allowing the boy to surprise him, the infidel youth somehow bewitched the warrior's limbs again. He moved as if stuck in amber, so slow that the boy was able to dart in and pull the turban down over his eyes. Teshret cursed a thousand tortures upon the city dweller, promising him a slow and demeaning death for such dreadful affronts. But when the warrior cleared his vision, he thought that the outsider had disappeared – that is, until his right leg suddenly buckled and he found himself foolishly astride his knees, sword unblooded – a terrible dishonor. Almost thankfully, the following blow took Teshret at the base of his skull, and darkness carried him away from his shame.

Melbessi Q'nari snickered as his cousin dropped face first into the sand, felled by an unarmed boy from one of the eastern towns.

The insults that I shall pile upon K'malli will tower higher than the Mountains of Blood, Q'nari thought, as he grinned and stepped forward to retrieve the crazed city youth's head. *At last, this day shall place me high above that fool,* he congratulated himself. *And my Lady will be forced to recognize me as the only swordsman worthy to stand by her side.*

Q'nari whirled his scimitar through an elaborate and acrobatic pattern, weaving a curtain of steel death before the tattered foreigner. He allowed himself the briefest glance to where his clan's headwoman stood, to be sure that she would be able to fully observe and appreciate the proficiency with which he would dispatch the pale-haired intruder.

A sudden explosion of pain in his groin tore the grin from Melbessi Q'nari's face. But far worse, he felt the sword ripped from his hand. He spent an eternal moment registering the look of disappointment on his clanswoman's face, then a breaching wave of agony washed over him, sending him tumbling in pursuit of his cousin's disgrace. As he fell, a second kick caught Q'nari just behind the ear, and his eyes were rolled back in their sockets even before the sand came rushing up to meet him. It mercifully denied him the sight of his broken sword clattering down in pieces to join him on the ground.

Darn snapped back his foot and allowed the Scarab warrior to crumple ungracefully to the sand. With both bodyguards dispatched, Darn found himself only a few paces away from the woman he had taken to be S'skyla. Darn took a single step forward, and instantly heard the ominous hiss of an arrow, deadly as any adder. He spun and reached out to almost lazily pluck the dart from the air, then continued the spin to return full circle, and had the steel point of the arrow pressed to the headwoman's throat before a gasp of surprise had fully passed her lips.

Darn stepped behind the Scarab leader, using her as a shield. "I wish ye no harm," Darn growled in her ear, "but I wish even less to

be target practice for thy warriors. Bid them set their weapons aside
... *NOW!*" He pressed inward with the arrow, emphasizing his point,
and hoped that his meaning was clear even if his words were not.

The Scarab headwoman spoke calmly to her clan in their
own throat-wrenching language; the archers among them lowered
their bows, but their arrows remained notched to the strings. The
spearmen couched their weapons, but no one relaxed, least of all
Darn. Then the raven-haired woman spoke back over her shoulder
in remarkably clear Eldorn.

"My men will not attack unless you harm me, though I
doubt that you need the arrow for that. Pray allow me to face you
and speak as equals."

Darn dropped his hand and the barbed shaft to his side,
struck silent. For some reason he did not fully understand, he
released the Scarab clan leader and took a step back from her, though
he remained within easy striking distance. The desert woman turned
to stare intensely at Darn, and as he looked back, he realized that
indeed, this was not S'skyla as he had first supposed. This woman
bore the same hatchet-sharp nose, the same lustrous mane of jet
hair, and fine firm sun-darkened limbs. But her eyes were deep and
luminous, like black pearls rather than the soulless chips of flint or
the faceted crimson gems that S'skyla had born in her sockets. And
though her face was quite similar to the one that S'skyla had worn,
the net of fine laugh lines that etched the corners of her mouth and
a old knife scar along one jaw line lent her features an individual,
lived-in reality.

The Scarab clanswoman looked hard at the necklace of
flat-plated silver that hung around Darn's neck, while fingering its

twin at her throat.

"The headwomen of our clan are buried with their *talum*," she said coldly. "The necklaces which speak the tale of our heritage. That one," she pointed at Darn's neck, "bears the stamp of the Tegetti family, who have been the smiths of our clan for many generations."

She said nothing else: no accusation, no questions. But the word almost burned in the air between them: *grave robber*!

Darn had little hope that his tale would be believed, for he hardly believed it himself. Yet the Flame of Honor would allow him no lies. He sketched the tale of his encounter with S'skyla, of how she had placed shadows in his mind and sought his death, and of how he had brought about her demise. This, he explained, was why he had gifted the clan with such an unusual gesture of welcoming. Even as he spoke, Darn heard how ridiculous his story sounded. He braced himself for the headwoman's scorn and for a renewed attack by her warriors.

The regal desert leader stood quietly, then nodded in acceptance of Darn's story, and much of the tension seemed to drain from her limbs and face.

"When we were small, my mother used to tell us the story of the Daughter of the Desert. They used it to scare the young ones into silence." She shook her head, and when she looked back up, Darn thought he could detect a glimpse of shame on her face. "Most of us believed it was only a tale, no matter that some of our scouts returned with strange stories full of desert madness. But there were always those among us who truly believed. And though my mother forbade it, my grandmother would sometimes whisper to me that S'skyla was her grandmother's grandmother. The Queen of Sand, she was called, who spilled her own blood onto the dunes as an offering, and was granted a return to life by the GreatMother Desert. Many of the old ones in our clan still disappear out into the sands when their time of ending approaches, seeking Her out and adding themselves to Her power."

After a long silence, the clanswoman returned from her thoughts and turned to speak to her tribe. Though Darn was unable to follow her words, she seemed to be recounting his recent history to them, pointing repeatedly to the silver *talum* that he still wore. The surrounding warriors looked astonished, shocked, some painting open disbelief on their faces, while others cautiously approached to obtain a better view of the talisman. As they spoke and whispered among themselves, the clanswoman turned back to face Darn.

"I am Dal'q n'Ritti, the headwoman of this clan. For your bravery, you have our honor and our promise to suffer you no harm, as long as you are within our company."

In a strange but somehow graceful gesture, Dal'q spit on her fingertips and held her hand outstretched. Darn had seen two Scarab traders use a similar gesture during a bartering session in the bazaar at Shiningrock once. Praying to the White Lady that he guess rightly, Darn spat on his own fingers in kind, and reached out to mingle the moisture with that on his host's hand.

"I am Darn of the Pyre, adherent and disciple of the Three Sacred Flames," Darn replied in turn. He began to withdraw his hand, but saw his host's face tighten and felt her people tense. Quickly, he added: "I most sorrowfully regret the pain I have wrought, and pledge to bring no further harm to thee or thy people." Darn thought for a moment, then lifted the *talum* over his head. He bowed slightly and held out his hands. "This, then, belongs to you by all rights. Please accept its return as my gift."

Dal'q smiled genuinely, and accepted the *talum* with reverence, then held it up for her people to see. Many pressed forward to touch the sacred metal, and ask for its blessing. Some others, though, muttered darkly and made hidden warding gestures.

A groan from one side signaled the return of Melbessi Q'nari to consciousness. The fallen Scarab warrior managed to struggle up to his knees, one hand still cupping his groin protectively, when his eyes chanced upon the remains of his shattered sword. A cry broke from within him at the sight, and he snatched up the pieces and held them to his chest, sobbing deeply. Through obvious pain and effort Q'nari gained his feet, then slowly turned until he faced Darn and his clan leader. He screamed an unintelligible curse, grabbed a handful of his own beard, and ripped it from his face in a rage.

"Carbuncle on a bundhar's arse! Deceitful unbeliever! Son of carrion eaters!" Q'nari shouted in his native tongue. "For this affront you shall die a thousand times! The sword of my father's father ..."

"... would still be whole, had you either held your hand or paid more attention to your task," Dal'q interrupted, using a quiet but forceful tone that cut through Q'nari's tantrum like a sword through smoke. "Who did you seek to impress, attacking an unarmed boy?" The disdain in her voice was evident even to Darn, who understood not a word of the conversation. "Now put away your broken blade, and drop that handful of hair. You looked foolish enough cupping your jewels. Besides, you are no match for this Son of Agni."

"I have been more than a match for those of the crimson sash in the past!" Q'nari blustered. But even as he cursed, he tried to discretely toss the remnants of his beard behind him, and worry the splintered haft of his scimitar back into its sheath. At his words, the headwoman shot him a withering glare, and Q'nari ducked his head to avoid her gaze. Then he quietly began to comb the sand for the remaining shards of his broken blade and shattered ego.

Dal'q returned her attention to Darn, and for the first time some crude attempt at a smile stitched its way across her face. "Please forgive my warriors," she began again in Eldorn. "They often allow their personal desires and petty rivalries to overrule their brains." She gave the unconscious K'malli a delicate prod with her toe, then motioned for her retainers to remove him from his embarrassment. That accomplished, she clapped her hands twice, and immediately the entire clan began to set up camp, raising silken tents and broadcloth pavilions with amazing speed.

"Please honor us, and abide as our guest," Dal'q said to Darn, formally, though still cordially. "For it is our custom to celebrate Lord Agni's children when we meet them, and to play whatever role in their trial that Father Sun deems."

Darn wondered briefly at the twisted wording of the Scarab headwoman. But as she ushered him inside a huge cobalt-blue canopy, and he laid eyes on a feast that was even now being made ready, his belly argued for leniency. The first cup of wine he was offered, Darn eyed suspiciously, taking his time to sniff it as well, even rubbing a bit on his tunic to see that it wetted. After the last vintage he'd shared, Darn would take no chances.

In a short matter of time, the Scarab clan had erected their entire camp, complete with a banquet hall, sleeping quarters, a smithy, privies, and an audience chamber for their leader. Food and drink flowed in greater quantities than Darn would have believed possible, particularly given that they sat somewhere in the center of the most inhospitable desert in the land. Dal'q was as good as her word, and Darn was treated like an honored guest throughout the evening.

The two older warriors whom Darn had encountered earlier, Melbessi Q'nari and Teshret K'malli, approached late in the evening, a slim young woman in their company. In halting Eldorn, the woman introduced herself as K'deeda t'Mal, a niece or some such relation to both of the men. As best she could, K'deeda explained that her uncles were bound by honor to accept their defeat. As ransom for their lives, they would accept Darn's bloodline into their clan. To this effect, she, K'deeda, had been given the honor of spending the night with Darn, in hopes that she would bear his child.

Teshret looked at Darn directly, and uttered a few words, then bowed slightly.

"He says, 'Son of Agni understands Honor.' " the young woman translated.

Already feeling the effects of the powerful Elibran wine that had flowed liberally throughout the evening, Darn was thoroughly rocked in his seat by the girl's unexpected offer. He tried to politely refuse, but K'deeda seemed unable – or unwilling – to understand his reasoning. Darn looked to Dal'q for rescue from the situation, but she only nodded slightly and remarked that the custom was not uncommon among her people.

"They must raise the child as their own," Dal'q said commandingly, glaring at the two older men until they both dropped their gaze. "It is the only way for them to regain their honor in the eyes of the tribe," she added firmly

Not wishing to offend the girl's hard-faced uncles any further, Darn shrugged sheepishly and took the hand that K'deeda offered. As he followed the young woman from the tent, Darn could feel Dal'q's eyes upon him. He glanced back once, but the clanswoman's face looked carved from stone, and her eyes were like dark pools that reflected everything but kept their secrets deeply hidden. Darn shrugged again, and followed K'deeda out into the cool desert night.

***

Darn awoke from a nightmare of being burnt alive, only to find that reality was just as certain a death, if not as quick. The morning sun had risen high enough to finally touch him where he lay in the shade of a dune. Darn sat up quickly and tried to wipe the sleep from his eyes, then looked around in stunned silence.

The nearby ground still showed the imprints where K'deeda's tent had stood around him the night before. Other than those marks, there remained no sign of the caravan's existence: no footprints, no tent pegs, no manure, no charcoal from their fires, no bits of litter or trash, not even a trail to mark their leaving. It was as if they had been plucked from the desert sand by Lord Agni's Left Hand.

Darn took a quick inventory of his possessions, and found that most of them had apparently departed together with the Scarab folk. In fact, Darn seemed to be left in the company of exactly two water skins – one whole, and the other leaking slowly through his patchwork repair – and the garments that he wore. Everything else that he had carried was gone: the meager store of food, his sling, and of course, Elias' daggers. All disappeared into the sandy wasteland, along with his companions from the evening before.

"I see – this is how they keep their promise to suffer me no harm," Darn said viciously to no one, pounding his fists into the sand in anger. "They have no courage to kill me outright. Only enough to leave me here with nothing, to starve and go mad, or step back out and face the Desert again even poorer than before. Much thanks!"

As he filled his waterskins from the oasis pool, Darn pondered his next course of action. Should he try to locate his hosts from the night before and liberate his belongings? Or should he consider the encounter an expensive lesson, and continue on his way? Discretion, logic, and good common sense dictated that Darn simply accept his losses and set out for the Scarlet Keep that much less burdened. Pride, Anger, and their bastard child Vengeance demanded the return of Elias' daggers at the very least. Aye, and perhaps a score of broken bones and a few cracked crowns as well would help to further ease the debt of honor which Darn was owed. It was a battle often fought in the minds of men, one which nearly always contained the same outcome.

As Darn contemplated his situation, his hand strayed to his waist. It took several moments for a certain absence to register itself on his thoughts. Then, face raised to the burning sky, he raged incoherently as the true depths of his loss pulled him under: his sash was missing. His crimson sash. The personal gift of Master Tobani that marked Darn as surely as the brands on his chest. Darn's scream brought his soulfire coursing into his *crucible*, out of control like a firestorm. He spun a kick at a nearby palm tree, his shin landing with a bruising *thud*, digging deeply into the bark of the tree. Darn kicked again and again, powerful crushing blows, and he shouted loudly with each strike in hopes the Scarab Folk would hear his rage and tremble. But when both the tree and his leg began to show strain from the battle, Darn gave a last shout and a kick, then tamped down his soulfire enough to break its control over him, allow him a bit of rational thought as he planned his pursuit. His choices had now been pared to only one: the theft of his sash was an offense which the Flame of Honor simply would not accept. He would retrieve his sash and his honor, and the Scarab Folk would pay for such disrespect with their bones and blood, or Darn would perish in the attempt.

Darn circled the oasis until he located what he felt must surely be the well-hidden trail of the caravan. After marking the spot and its relation to the rising sun, Darn stepped to the center of his personal emerald sanctuary, and doused himself in the cool, life-giving waters of the oasis pool one last time. He gave thanks for the gift of the water, then drank his fill and more, till his stomach would surely burst. After a final, long look at the pool, he stepped back to the trail he had marked, where the endless sea of sand and stone lapped at the edges of the oasis.

Rolling waves of heat shimmered and danced above the desert's surface. Every measure of sanity within the young man cried for him to continue on to the mountains, to forget the trinkets and wares he had lost. Darn considered the idea for less than a heartbeat, then tossed it carelessly aside. After all, hadn't Elias said that Darn must leave all sanity behind at the Gate of Bones? With his decision firm in his bones, Darn cinched his robe tight, settled his waterskins, and followed a faint path back into the beating, burning heart of the desert.

***

As the eighth day of his journey dawned, Darn came to the realization that he would soon be dying. The water he'd carried from the oasis three days before was nearly gone. His only undamaged water skin had split open when Darn took a tumble over some unseen rocks in the night. He had scrambled to save what water remained in the torn skin, and had desperately lapped up every drop he could find that clung to the hateful stones. Still, he had lost nearly all of it, and for some gray period of time Darn knew he had raged and cursed unintelligibly at the sun, the sand, the Order, the rocks, and most of all, at himself.

When his mind returned, Darn forced himself to sit quietly and examine his situation. He carried one leaking quarter-full patchwork water skin, and the hooded robe that he wore over his tunic. Nothing else. Nothing but the growing paranoia that a dark specter followed several hundred paces back over his left shoulder. He'd caught glances of fleeting shadows that melted back into the sand when he tried to look more closely. He suspected more of S'skyla's trickery. He also suspected that his brain was simply frying under the desert sun, like an auric's egg cracked onto a hot stone. He hadn't recovered a single piece of his gear or goods from the sand. Not so much as a broken knife blade or a stale crust of bread. His sling had been taken along with the rest of his supplies, denying Darn the ability to do anything more than curse the buzzards that dogged his steps from dawn to dusk, their moving shadows haunting him even while he stared at his feet and trudged onward. The desert remained empty, as it had since he'd lost sight of the oasis, with nothing to blemish the flawless face of its desolation. Darn was left alone with only his shadows and the death that stalked him.

Once, Darn had felt sure that he'd discovered the caravan's tracks leading over several long sloping dune faces. But after following it for most of the afternoon, the faint path had just faded into the drifting sand. Darn was left without even a guess as to whether the track had been real or a deliberate falsehood, or if the desert had swallowed it up simply to torment him further.

Darn drifted back for a while into that gray shadowed land of the insane and the dying. When the bone-sucking cold of the evening shocked him back to the waking world, Darn found himself heading roughly southwest, stumbling over rocks and stunted black bushes. Just knowing that he was traveling in roughly the proper direction, and that the terrain had changed from an endless sea of sand, were reason enough for a weak smile of hope. Darn didn't care if it was a false hope or not – at this point, it was the most powerful tool at his disposal.

He'd chanced upon one small barrel cactus as he'd stumbled along. It had charged him a handful of invisible barbs for the mouthfuls of liquid that its crushed pulp had relinquished: a small price to pay, Darn thought. Two blue-striped tail-breakers, nosing about for a snack, had wormed their way up Darn's sleeve while he slept. Though the small lizards barely made a mouthful each, their discovery and subsequent devouring had lifted Darn's spirits quite a bit, and provided some measure of moisture besides. A scampering dung beetle, late returning to its daytime den, followed as dessert.

Dessert in the desert! Darn tried to laugh, but the feeble croak that he retched out sounded like a dying carrion bird, and felt like a branch of blister-thorn being pulled from his throat. He did not laugh again.

434

Darn struggled to reach the top of a windswept dune, slipping back at least a pace for every two that he gained. But at last he made the summit, higher than any he'd seen so far. His efforts were rewarded with an unending vista of windblown rock, scraggly patch-thorn, and an ocean's worth of sand: nothing else. Could his body have spared the moisture, the boy would have wept a sea of tears at the sight. Instead, his chest hitched in dry sobs.

Darn tried to take a sighting through the shimmering waves of heat that the sun sucked up out of the parched earth. He aimed at some distant smear of color low on the walls of the sky, and began to pick his way down the side of dune. On his third step, the thong of one of his sandals broke again, and Darn walked on without it. When darkness fell, Darn huddled in a crevice split in a large boulder, hoping to draw on the warmth that the stones held from the day. And sometime that night, or early the next morning, Darn drank the last of his water while still fast asleep, and he dreamt of pools and rivers and cool creek bottoms.

***

The brooding morning sun sent a lash deep into the narrow crevice, whipping cruelly across the shins of the young man hidden there. Darn woke with a start at the touch of the sun's brand. As he scrambled to his feet, the flat barren slap of the empty water skin against his hip told him that his dreams of the night before had proven costly. Then he was backhanded by the thought that he had slept away the cool predawn hours. Truly now, the Grey Stalker followed only a single tenuous step behind him.

Darn looked at the rising sun, stared straight at it for a painful moment, then decided against wasting his strength to curse it. It was Lord Agni's abode, after all. Whatever trials He should see fit to set before him, Darn should accept proudly and pursue with all of his heart.

Yes, and perhaps flying treemunks should drop from the skies and shit me a pile of golden chestnuts! he chided himself in anger. *I was such a fool to lap it all up their dogma.*

As if in answer to his heretical thoughts, or in an unprecedented gesture of pity, the angry orb overhead gifted Darn with a single moment of respite, an atonement perhaps for the unnumbered days of misery and torture it had bestowed upon him. As it crept up over a spiny set of crags, the sun stretched out crimson arms to cradle a rise of stones in the long distance, stones that looked like nothing more than the head and withers of a great somnolent beast. Darn could quite clearly make out the saurian-beaked snout nestled atop rounded hilltops of forepaws, and the snaking ridge of its tail curling away between two flat-topped peaks to the south. The Sleeping Dragon, Elias had said, would lead Darn to the end of his journey. And there it lay dozing, waiting for him to arrive.

Darn turned to laugh at the fleeting shade that had followed him from the Gate of Bones. An oft-glimpsed ghost, it lurked at the corner of his eye and danced in the moon-shadows at night. Darn knew that it was his own Death, staying close so as to be ready for the final moment. But Darn had no fear of his Death, for at the end of the Dragon's tail sat the Scarlet Keep. And there lay the end of his journey … and the award of his robes. No such trivial impediment as death could douse his indomitable spirit and prevent him from completing his trial. He never paused to consider the distance at which the mountainous beast crouched. He only hurried out into the erupting rays of the sun with a dangerous drunken stagger to his step. Something small and black and quick dashed out from under Darn's foot just as he left the crevice. He shuffle-stomped onto the little monstrosity and stuffed it into his mouth with no concern for its taxonomy.

Darn stepped out into the wasteland with no water, no shoes – only a lizard or bug or something squirming its last between his teeth. That, and the unalterable goal of reaching the Scarlet Keep.

***

Darn fell once again onto the hot sand. Though his legs continued to churn for some time, the dying young man hadn't the strength to lift his face up out of the sand, much less regain his feet once more. He clawed feebly for purchase, scrabbling uselessly at the sand. Then one hand gained grip on a small outcropping of rock, and Darn was able to pull himself a scant handspan forward. Exhausted beyond words, beyond thought, Darn knew he could go no further. Neither Agni's Honor, nor his own soulfire, nor the thirst for vengeance in his heart, could stir him from his sandy grave. But still, his hand refused to relinquish its grasp upon the stone, the only solid foundation left in his world.

Darn drifted past sleep, on into a realm that borders both the world of the sun and the world of the spirits. Darn's mother spoke to him for a while, as did both Peg and Loon. And though he knew it not, Death cradled Darn in its bony arms and whispered quiet thoughts in his ear of peace and surrender. Much of Darn's soul listened to those words and breathed them in, yearning for the peace they promised. But one small corner of his mind noticed an irritation, an insistent tugging at the tenuous cord that still bound him to the world of the living.

A distant drumming sound beat at the edges of Darn's skull until he could no longer ignore it, and he was forced to draw back from the endless slumber that called to him. Darn looked inside himself and saw the feeble flickering of life-spark, of soulfire. He sucked in a stuttering sand-laden breath, and drew air deep into his *crucible*, feeding the flames there. He could move neither his arms nor legs, and his eyes opened only onto pain and darkness. But he could still feel sharp edges of stone biting into the fingers of one hand, so he desperately held onto that pain, his single connection to the world of the living.

***

The two Scarab warriors pulled sharply on the braided reins in their hands, and their mounts – sleek droes, blowing green foam from their nostrils and pitching their eyes wildly – abruptly raised their long sinewy necks and braced their bowed legs, sliding to a surprisingly smooth stop. The brothers had ridden hard for two nights and a day, changing mounts only once when they chanced upon another clan at an unmarked oasis. But no amount of cajoling could convince the two to pause in their journey and enjoy their cousins' hospitality. They had commands to follow, and no wish to anger the one who had issued them. So with a quick farewell and an few extra bags of goods, the two leapt back aboard their fresh-rested droes and sped off across the endless desert sands, crouched along the outstretched necks of their mounts. The droes ran like the scorching wind, their long muscular legs and widely splayed feet kicking up great gouts of dust with each stride, and their tails – heavy with stored fat for long desert journeys – held straight out behind them for balance and speed.

Keshmel slipped from his saddle and dropped lightly to the sand, while his brother Qu'jat clucked lightly to his droe, trying to calm it as it danced nervously from foot to foot. Both of the nomads were young, with Qu'jat just recently come into his manhood and still awkwardly adjusting to the unaccustomed turban and other trappings. But they had both proven themselves to be fierce fighters, skilled hunters, and among the swiftest riders of their clan. And although it was less than three turns of the seasons since they both wore the braided locks of boys, the pair had accepted their clan-mother's assignment without comment or question – unlike Melbessi Q'nari, their uncle and until recently one of the clan's most respected warriors, who had paled and trembled when the appointing hand had moved towards him.

Nonetheless, both of the young men were nervous – scared almost witless, actually, though neither would have admitted it under threat of the Death of a Thousand Cuts.

"How sure can you be, that this is the spot that was spoken of?" Qu'jat asked in a voice that still cracked on occasion.

Keshmel nodded westward into the growing twilight, towards a distinctively spine-backed ridge of mountain peaks.

"The Dreaming Render lies a day's ride to the west," he answered, stroking the new silkiness of his moustache, which was finally – *Great Mother be Praised!* – beginning to curl at the ends. "Here is the edge of the Stone Sea. And here are the twin stones of which we were told," he said, patting one of the large boulders that sat nearby. "But beyond those truths," he added, in that knowledgeable older-brother voice which frequently earned him Qu'jat's ire, "something speaks to me, and tells me that this is the appointed spot. So here it is that we shall wait, until we receive a sign." Keshmel nodded to himself as if satisfied with his explanation, then began to follow the rest of the peculiar instructions he'd been given. He removed a clay fire-keeper from one saddle bag along with some tinder, and soon had a small fire burning. Then he pulled a pair of desert hares from the other bag – he'd brought them down with a sling stone when they'd stopped at midday – skinned them, and placed them on a spit over the fire.

Qu'jat glanced about uneasily. His brother's reasoning brought him no balm to ease the twisted feeling in his guts. The rocky hilltop where they rested had been swept mostly clean of sand by the last storm, providing an excellent vantage point and a fairly comfortable place to spend the night. But still, Qu'jat chewed nervously on a thumbnail, bright white teeth glowing in the twilight gloom, and he shifted about anxiously in his saddle until his droe snorted and stamped her feet in annoyance. Qu'jat patted his mount's long neck and spoke gently to her, until finally she quieted and began nibbling at some withered blood thorn that fought for life among the stones and sand. But when he turned his attention back to his brother, the crack in Qu'jat's voice revealed both his youth and his unease.

"What if the sign does not come?" Qu'jat worried aloud for them both. He tried to scan the surrounding desert without spooking his mount again. "How long must we wait?"

A quavering high-pitched howl stabbed out from somewhere among the distant dunes, amidst the growing pools of shadow. Both of the droes perked their ears to the sound, and the male stretched to his full height and answered with a belching grunt, stamping his great splay-toed feet in agitation. Keshmel whirled, and his scimitar leapt into his hand with such fluid speed that even Uncle Raj would have been impressed. But for once the gleaming crescent of steel brought the young Scarab warrior no comfort. His scalp crawled, alive in answer to the chilling call.

A thump and rattle sounded directly behind him, and Keshmel spun and slashed in one flowing movement, only to wound nothing but the wind. A net bag of flatbread and jerky sat heaped on the ground, and a pair of odd-shaped daggers lay crossed on top of it. He looked up to find his brother cursing and jerking at a pair of water skins that stubbornly remained tied to his saddle.

"Our charge is fulfilled," Qu'jat shouted, as he tore the skins free and tossed them down to land beside the other supplies. "You said yourself that this is the appointed place!" The mournful howl rent the air again, seeming to come from two or three different directions at once. Qu'jat spun in his saddle, and his droe stomped in nervous agitation. The boy's eyes were as wide as those of his mare, pools of black-brown surrounded by rings of stark white terror. He jerked his mount's reins and kicked frantically to get her moving. He no longer made any pretense of hiding his fear.

"We have heard the demon's voice!" he shouted, voice cracking in his panic. "It has plagued our steps since we left our people, and nothing else could match the speed of our mounts!" He twisted about in his saddle, trying to peer through the growing gloom that crept up on them from all sides. "We must flee this place now, and leave that which it demanded!"

Keshmel forced a frown onto his face, pushing aside the

look of fearful surprise that had sprouted when the howl sounded. After all, he was the older of the pair by a full cycle of the moons. *Shaa!* He would be picking his first wife soon: he would not allow childish fears to prevent him from completing the task laid upon him. Angrily, he thrust his sword back into its scabbard and set his fists on his hips.

"Qu'jat, are you still a nursling, to quiver by your mother's knee at the howl of a jackal or the scream of a miercat?" Keshmel walked to where the desert sand lapped at the edges of the rocky outcropping, and waved a hand out towards the dry endless sea. "I have seen no demon – and we have seen no sign! We were commanded by our clan-mother to bring *these* items to *this* place and await a signal of some kind! Do as you wish," he looked back to scowl at his brother, "but I shall not leave this hillock until I receive the sign of which we were told." He drummed one fist against his chest in a gesture of inarguable finality, then turned to walk away.

Keshmel lost his balance as his foot caught on something, and he flopped unceremoniously onto his rear, raising a small cloud of dust. He cursed himself for a moment, looking up at the stars as they began to poke through the darkening sky. Then he sat up, and angrily kicked with his free foot at the bramble or bush that seemed to have snared him. Then he paused – froze actually, though the word would have meant nothing to him – when he saw what held him fast: a blood-encrusted hand, reaching up from the sand.

Keshmel closed his eyes, and wished the phantom vision away. Then the hand shifted a bit and tugged the young man forward. Keshmel's disbelief vanished like spilt water, and he kicked at the bloody apparition to free himself. As he tried to draw back his foot, an arm appeared behind the grasping hand. Then a figure began to rise up out of the sand, moaning dryly. Keshmel's pantaloon's darkened with a growing stain, then he twisted away and stood and ran in a flash, forgetting the sword by his side, forgetting even to give voice to his terror. Fear stripped the young warrior of his newly-won manhood, revealing the little boy who still shook at night, reliving his grandmother's tales of the desiccated hunger of sand demons.

Qu'jat was either less or more scared than his brother. For when he made out what clutched at his brother's leg, his voice ignored his terror and took wing into the night sky.

"Aieeeeeee!" Qu'jat raked his heels down his droe's ribs and the beast leapt forward with comical grace. "That is sign enough for myself, older brother!" he shouted over his shoulder as he and his mount fled the hilltop. "Stay if you wish – we will remember you in song!"

Keshmel wasted no time in answering. He was beside his droe in a instant, his knife flashing to cut free several sacks and a wadded tangle of crimson silk from his saddle. He was mounted before the sacks hit the ground, and racing after his brother's back a moment later. A wrenching yowl split the air again, reaching in from all sides to stroke the young men's souls with an icy touch. The two brothers laid low along the necks of their droes, never glancing back, and fought to prove once again that they were the fastest riders in the desert.

***

Heavily-booted feet climbed slowly out of the desert sand and crossed the stony hilltop, an odd broken set of small steps

443

following closely behind. They paused when they reached the far side of the clearing, where the sand once again held dominion – paused before the bloody broken-nailed hand that reared up there, clutching feebly at nothing. A thick-fingered hand reached down from above to grip the sand-encrusted wrist, then slowly and steadily drew a desiccated white-robed figure from the clutches of the dune, as if born from the Desert Herself.

Chapter Eighteen
The Return of the Lost

For the second time in less than a moon, Darn could not decide if he was dead, alive, or drifting in some in-between nether region. Then slowly his senses began to return, one after the other.

Darn became aware, first, of something cool and wet being wiped repeatedly across one side of his face. An odd mixture of sounds insinuated themselves into the dark space he occupied: the crackle of dry twigs giving up their lives in a fire; a not-quite familiar tune being hummed deep and quietly; and an abrupt, fluttering *Brrrrrppttt!* from somewhere nearby that added an exclamation to the tune. Then a scent drifted to Darn's nose, the faint musky odor of some type of beast, mixed with the smoky tang of seared flesh. Darn could feel the soft comfort of a blanket insulating him from the hard ground. He opened his eyes, and the familiar stars of the Dragon and the Hunter glimmered against the sable night sky. But the most blessed sensation of all, he realized, was the feeling of being *quenched*, of having been dipped in the coolest, most holy pool in the world. His body no longer screamed for water, and the thick veneer of dust that seemed to have coated his throat since he'd passed the Gate of Bones was finally washed away. He opened his lips, and a deep whispering sigh of contentment slipped from between them.

A pop from the fire brought caused Darn to weakly roll his head to stare in that direction. Though half-blinded by the flames, he could still make out a cowled figure seated on the far side. No one else appeared within the circle of firelight, though some ancient part of Darn's brain buzzed with the sensation of being watched from the darkness. The stranger held a long spit over the fire, slowly turning the sizzling carcasses of a pair of desert hares. Darn felt his stomach knot painfully, almost excruciating in its emptiness, and saliva filled his mouth in a jaw-aching flood. Had he the strength, he would have crawled through the fire's darting flames to beg for the slightest morsel.

Darn swallowed hard, unsure of how to proceed. He hesitantly cleared his throat; discovering that it brought only a small measure of discomfort, Darn moved to address his mysterious savior.

"My thanks, kind stranger. Ye must be responsible for my salvation from the desert's grasp." Darn waited through several long moments, an appropriate length of time for a reply. Receiving none, he repeated his statement in halting Chak'ran, then tried a few phrases in broken Elibran. In desperation, he even sang a few measures of the elvish language-song, the *Sidhest*. Still failing to wrest a response from his host. Darn struggled to a half-sitting position, touched both hands to his forehead, then spread his arms wide: the universal sign of thanks. The silent figure nodded in answer, and Darn slumped back to lay on his side, for he found he was still exhausted.

Darn's inscrutable companion stood slowly, making no sound, like some desert ghoul rising from its grave. The figure was tall, towering over Darn, and the width of his cloaked shoulders blotted out a wide swath of stars from the sky. His deep cowl continued to hide the stranger's face, allowing no more than twin reflections of the fire to escape its shadow. The man – at least Darn assumed it was a man, though from the size he reasoned his savior could even be a smallish troll – the man walked around the fire towards Darn in complete silence, boots gliding silently over the sand. He stepped between Darn and the fire and became a featureless black outline, destroying Darn's hope for even a glimpse of the man's features.

The spit that skewered the still-sizzling hares stabbed into the sand within Darn's easy reach. The stranger hunkered down as if to share the meal, or to raise questions of Darn's adventures. But still, he never uttered a word, only motioned vaguely for Darn to begin eating. The man also produced a water skin from somewhere, and it landed with a slosh on the sand between them.

After an uncertain pause, Darn reached out and gingerly tore a hindquarter loose, juggling it between his hands and blowing on it till it ceased to burn his fingers. And when he bit into the crispy flesh Darn was absolutely sure, to the roots of his soul, that the roasted hare was the finest repast he had ever sat to. Darn fought his hunger's ravenous demand that he shove the entire haunch into his mouth, so he forced himself to eat slowly, chewing small pieces until they disappeared, then washing each one down with a swallow from the waterskin. He glanced at his host several times, hoping to elicit some comment or catch a glance of the man's face within the deep cowl of his cloak. But the stranger never moved or uttered a word, only watched silently like a stone sentinel.

As Darn tore the last scrap of flesh from a long thigh bone, he finally took notice of a sound that his mind had simply melded into the rest of the desert's night noises: a quiet mewling whine that sounded now and again from somewhere behind him. While still trying to keep one eye on his mysterious benefactor, Darn rolled over to peer into the gloom. And for the space of two heartbeats, he stared directly into a pair of glowing green eyes that hung a handspan or less away from his own.

From the nearby darkness, a staccato cry stabbed at Darn's ears. And on the heels of this dissonance followed its maker: a furred knot of wriggling flesh that leapt straight into Darn's face, flashing ivory fangs that came within a finger's breadth of his nose and releasing count after count of the painfully shrill noises.

Darn yelped in surprise, even as he realized that his exhausted limbs would never respond in time to keep the black monstrosity from his throat. All he could do was lower his head to protect his neck and try to wrap his arms around the beast, not allowing it room to move and launch another attack. But the creature seemed to slip through his grasp like smoke, lunging again and again at his face. In a sudden inspiration Darn tried to roll towards the fire, hoping to at least dislodge the creature, if not set it ablaze. But after a single turn, his rolling stopped abruptly as he fetched up against two ironwood trunks rising from a pair of heavy hob-nailed boots.

Darn looked up past the writhing bundle of fur and fangs that he held clamped to his chest, and glared at the stranger standing over him. Even though the man's face was still hidden in shadow, Darn could discern the gleam of teeth bared in the darkness, smiling down at him while the black beast fought to reach Darn's throat.

"Call back thy beast!" Darn yelled in fury and terror, for now he could feel the beast driving some sort of hard stinger again and again against his stomach. "Call it back and bring battle against me thyself, have ye the stones for it!" he shouted up at the silent figure.

Few things in the world could have convinced Darn to

relinquish his hold on the nightmare familiar that continued to struggle and snap at his throat, eager for his life's blood. But the sound that reached the Flame Dancer's ears drained all strength from his limbs, loosening his grasp and allowing the creature he held to lunge for his face.

It was the sound of laughter: a raucous roaring that grew in volume and depth until it seemed to echo from the roof of the midnight sky; a howl to shame all other denizens of the desert into silence with its power. It was a laugh that any primeval god of storms and battlefields would have given his sword hand to posses. And it swept across the desert like an elemental force of nature, leaving all who heard it swirling and tumbling in its wake. At the sound of it, Darn could feel an idiotic grin spread across his face and tears spring from the corners of his eyes, even though he knew it meant his mind must surely be broken.

"Ya shouldna call 'er such names, ya know," a deep voice answered from above. "Ya ne'er know what price ya might hav'ta pay fer it!" As if in agreement, a cold wet tongue drew a glistening track up one side of Darn's neck and across his face.

Darn looked down. Somehow, the slavering demon that had hungered for his flesh only moments before had been transformed into a small, curly-haired, dirty black dog, one that wiggled and barked incessantly and jerked at his sleeve for further attention. His mind might refuse to accept what his eyes told him was true, but in his heart Darn knew the frolicking beast's name as well as his own.

"P-Peg?" Darn asked in a cracked voice, and the little dog danced a crooked circle or two in delight, revealing the tiny pegleg and harness she wore in lieu of her own left hind leg. Darn reached out to pet the ragged-coated mutt, but her substance seemed to melt and waver somehow under his touch. The little dog whined as she squirmed out from under his hand, but then turned back quickly to lick at his fingers, as if to show that no slight was intended. The tongue on his hand wasn't exactly wet: it was light and smooth, but then gone, leaving only a remembrance of dampness.

Darn knew that he was either mad or dreaming. Or dead, of course – he could be dead, he considered. Either way, it mattered little at the moment, for Darn had turned back to find the dark-cloaked stranger now crouched at his side, and lit by the light of the fire.

Golden curls tumbled down to the young man's thickly-muscled shoulders, and a light patchy beard fought to cover his cheeks. The trace of a scar was etched across his chin, a trophy that Darn had watched him acquire in a bout with Big Meg, a mug-wielding serving wench twice his size. Piercing blue eyes gazed out from beneath shaggy brows, with a guileless intensity that had often forced Darn to examine the integrity of his own soul. And anchoring it all was a grin so broad it threatened to split the top half of the young man's face from the lower.

Darn reached up a disbelieving hand, shaking in both fear and wonder, and laid it aside his dear friend's face. Again, not quite substance, but a remembrance of skin and bone. There, and yet not completely there.

"Loon," Darn whispered. "By the White Lady, it cannot be!"

"Well o' course it can be," Loon answered with complete sincerity. "Me an' Peg, we're both growed up now, an' we can go where we likes ta go. 'Sides, weren't nobody t' tell us we couldna go." Loon nodded hugely, congratulating himself, and Peg yipped and wagged her raggedy tail in agreement. "An' who else didja 'spect t' come stompin' out through this buzzard garden ta look fer ya? No one else dumb enough fer that nonsense but silly ol' Loon, that's who! An' ol' Peg, we knew she could find ya, if anyone could!"

Darn shook his head, unable to believe or to disbelieve in his friend's manifestation. He struggled with his next words, but could no more deny them than he could deny the feeling of Loon's hand resting on his shoulder.

"B-but Loon...P-Peg is...is dead. And ye..."

"Oh noooo!" Loon started to wail. He looked about frantically for his little dog, who had wandered behind a boulder in search of something to interest her. "Me ol' Peg is dead? But she was jest here! Me poor, poor Peg!" As if in answer, Peg came scampering from the darkness and sat at her master's feet, her tiny head cocked in puzzlement as she watched him cry and wail. After an unsatisfying wait, she set her teeth into the hem of Loon's trousers to gain his attention, and gave it a good shake. Darn could almost believe he heard a small voice say:

Here I am! Now what is it, Boy? For I was tracking a particularly juicy beetle, and I don't have time for such foolishness!

Loon ceased his blubbering and looked down in surprise. Then, with a whoop of joy he snatched the tiny mutt from the ground and pressed her tight to the hollow of his neck, rocking her back and forth and muttering her name. Peg was having none of it, though she kicked and squirmed to no avail.

"Darn! Ol' Peg ain't dead! Here she is, right here!" Loon looked sideways at his friend, a mischievous glint in his eyes. "Why'd ya tell ol' Loon a fibber like that? Are ya tryin' to play a joke on us?"

He snapped his teeth back at Peg in answer to her own mock attacks, then set her back on the sand to continue her canine investigations.

Darn sat upright. "It is the truth, Loon. Ye and Peg are both very, very dead." He could no longer smile at his friend's antics. For either Loon must accept that, indeed, they had passed on to another plane of existence, or Darn must accept that the desert had pushed him over the edge of sanity, into the chaos of madness.

Loon looked hard at Darn's face, as if waiting for a punch line. Then his smile dropped away. "Are ya sure?" he asked in honest surprise. "I sure don' feel dead. An' see ol' Peg – she don' look dead." Loon held out a hand to his furry companion, and his unquenchable smile returned at the sight. The curly-haired mongrel trotted up and proudly dropped a dead scorpion at Loon's feet. She looked up and whined, growled and muttered a few times, then barked sharply twice. Frown lines formed across Loon's brow for a fleeting moment, then vanished as quickly as they'd come.

"Why, Peg, she says we is jest travelin' light, that's all," Loon interpreted. "Says she does it all the time: leaves the meat part behind, an' wanders about a while b'fore goin' back."

"But Loon," Darn answered slowly, "thy body ... they burned it. And Peg's as well. Ye cannot ... cannot go back." Darn lowered his head, unable to meet his friend's eyes, tears spilling down his cheeks. "Peg is dead. I held her myself while she died. As I ... as I held you, my friend." Salty drops ran streaming through the dust on Darn's face. "Loon, look at me – understand me: ye have died and passed on. Jehred told me himself that he lit thy funeral pyre."

Loon sobered at the sight of his friend's tears, and for a space of time both the humor and the smile with which his infirmity gifted him seemed stolen away. He stood quietly for a moment, chewing on the truth that Darn had offered him. Then he frowned sternly and looked down at Peg.

"Ya fergot t' mention that part, Peg," he admonished, wagging a sausage-sized finger at her. Peg looked cowed for a moment, then brightened and rattled off a staccato of barks, snapping playfully at his finger before hobbling back off to her hunt.

Loon straightened and sighed, a long breath of sadness and acceptance. Then he turned back to Darn and grinned – a grin that held a taste of pain.

"As she says, what's done is done. I canno' argue with 'er there. But ya know, t' tell th' truth, I'm feelin' pretty good right now! Ain't been very hungry as late, an' I noticed I ain't had t' drain m' lizard since we came out after ya. Other than that, I feel just fine! Still," he slapped a hand against his broad stomach, "it won' be easy, knowin' I've got no belly t' fill!"

Loon looked away to the desert, and his face seemed to dim. When he spoke again, his voice was quiet, bereft of the golden sunshine of his laughter. At the sound of it, Darn thought his heart would break.

"Course, I knew somethin' seemed a lil funny. Cause I kin remember in parts that greasy whoreson Black Kirt whackin' off m' leg. But then I thought mebbe I dreamed it, cause I got two legs now – see!" Loon's face darkened suddenly, as the recollection drew others along behind it, scavengers struggling for a moment's remembrance. "Dirty bastard 'ad taken m' dear ol' Peg," Loon snarled. He looked fiercely to Darn. "But I knew ya'd find 'er! Knew ya'd save 'er!"

Darn bowed his head at Loon's words, and he fought to push the barbed reply from his throat.

"But Loon, I ... I could not save Peg. For they wounded her badly, and she was far beyond my skills to heal." Darn hung his head even lower, and he felt a fresh scar tear back open inside him. "On my word, I would have given my life to save her!"

Loon patted Darn's shoulder awkwardly, the touches somehow soft but still painfully forceful. " S'all right, friend Darn, s'all right. Peg tol' me thatcha saved 'er from a whole bucket o' pain. An' that's more 'n anyone else coulda done." A hard smile settled on Loon's face, a great dollop of vengeance souring its normal sweetness. "An' in what kinda coin did good citizen Smithson havta pay fer 'is crimes?" he asked quietly.

Darn bared his teeth as he answered. "Paid in full," he said, lifting his right hand, the fingers curled into a claw. "With screams, and blood, and the roots of his soul."

"An' still, he weren't worth m' good ol' Peg," Loon added. "He weren't worth a plate o' piss, as Jehred always says."

They all three sat silently for a passage, even Peg apparently lost in thought. Then a gentle breeze stepped through their camp, scattering embers and half-eaten food, sending the three running in chase and stealing away the shadowed mood that had befallen them. Once the food was again in hand, Loon's track of conversation bent back once again, and Darn leapt to follow him.

"Darn," Loon pondered. "Whadda ya s'pose they did wi' m' leg?"

"The one they cut off?"

"Well o' course *that* one! I know where th' other one is!"

"Well, I believe that it was burned on thy pyre, as well," Darn answered, perplexed. "Why? Should we have treated it otherwise?"

"Well, mayhaps," Loon replied, rather sheepishly. "I guess that Jehred oughta had taken that greenstone outta m' boot a'fore they burned it." He seemed deaf to Darn's astonished reply, and dismissed the past events with a simple shrug. "At least Smithson didna get it."

"I don' remember much after they took m' leg. Mebbe jest talkin' t' ya a bit, but I ain't sure." Loon stopped and scratched his head, working hard for his words. "Then, me an' Peg, we was somewhere ... somewhere else. Someplace I never been b'fore, though I might o' dreamed about it a time er two. An' I had m' leg back – wasn't hurtin' er nothin'! It was really nice an' sunshiny kinda place, with lots o' trees an' soft grass. Seems like we was there a long time, but mebbe only a lil while. It was hard ta tell, but it was real, real nice." Loon smiled dreamily. But then his eyes opened wide.

"But then th' White Lady, She was ... She was *with us*, Darn! She was lovely an' wise an' all bright! An' I was so scairt, cause I ain't always been good all th' time, ya know? But th' Lady, She took m' hand an' She stood me up an' tol' me not t' fear. An' She said I should be proud o' th' man I'd been. An' it made me feel so good, ya know, an' it took all my scairtness away." Loon's smile returned, but his eyes darkened seriously. "But then, the Lady said that we had rested enough fer now. She tol' us that ya needed our help. That we was the only ones that could save ya. So we ... uh ... we *came*. I ain't sure how, really. We was *there*, an' then we was jest *here*. In the desert."

Unfamiliar lines of concentration and concern creased

Loon's brow, as he struggled to understand the mechanics of his existence. But after a moment or three, as was his particular gift, such difficulties fell from him as he simply accepted what *was*. Regaining his cherubic smile of gigantic proportions, Loon continued his tale, arms waving extravagantly to build on his words.

"Dint know how t' find ya at first. Then Peg, She said as I should look fer yer fire, yer fire inside. An' ya know, when I closed my eyes, there it was - burnin' way off crost th' sand like a shinin' red star. So we found ya quick as that. But ya couldna see us. An' we couldna touch ya. An' ya never seemed t' hear what I said, 'cept fer once in a while." Loon paused for a moment, and laid a heavy if insubstantial hand on his friend's shoulder. "It's all right, ya can cry if ya want. I won' tell nobody. I blubbered like a baby when we first seen ya, me an' Peg both. We really missed ya, even when we was in that sunshiny woods an' it was so nice t' be there." Peg sat at Loon's feet, looking from her master to Darn and back, nodding after each part as if testing to make sure that Loon had the story correct.

"So we came, an' finally found ya at that little green waterin' hole. An' weren't that a pretty little place, what with all them frond trees an' ferns an' all, out there in the middle of all that sand. Like a lonely pickle at the bottom o' th' barrel, jest waitin' fer someone t' chance upon it. Hmmm." Loon rubbed his belly absent-mindedly, and smiled in satisfaction and embarrassment at the accompanying rumble that echoed forth. "Mebbe I'm hungry after all," he said with surprise. Then a frown twisted down the corners of his mouth, as another memory laid a sour taste on his tongue.

"We saw what them rott'n Scarab fellers did t' ya, stealin' yer stuff an' all. What a rotten thing t' do! Didya know that that girl ya

456

laid with put somethin in yer wine? She weren't even very sneaky about it, but ya ne'er noticed, what with all the blood gone from yer thinkin' end an' all." Loon leaned over and slapped Darn's leg to highlight the point. It was like being hit with a wet loaf of bread. Darn's blush went unnoticed as Loon warmed to his own tale.

"Well, e'en a potato-head like ol' Loon knew ya wouldna do too good without yer water an' food an' gear an' all. Ol' Peg said that she could find them Scarfies, then find our way back here t' ya. So we went after 'em like heroes, jest th' two of us! Like ... uh ... what was that story Ol' Gedwolf tol' me?" Loon scratched his head mightily and squinted hard for extra thinking power. Peg barked twice sharply, and Loon nodded. "Oh, oh yeah, I 'member: like Prince Varsok d'Kontor an' his dire wolf Fangblade."

"Peg told you, Loon?" Darn almost leapt to cut off Loon's rambling tale. "Can Peg speak now as well?"

Loon snorted in amusement. "Darn, don' be a goose, now. Ol' Peg, she talks and talks all the time. It's hard t' get her t' hush up sometimes, like when she's in her season, an' that big ol' bull-n-bear dog o' Kiplin th' Sailmaker comes a sniffin' around. Jehred don' hear her, but I think he jest don' take th' time t' listen well."

"Fine, Loon, fine." Darn cut in. "We can discuss Peg's dialogue and paramours later." Darn rolled his eyes. "Pray continue: the Scarab folk and my belongings ...?"

"Oh yeah. Well Peg, she set off after that Scarab clan inna flash, an' we caught 'em in no time at all, it seemed. They had yer stuff – had it inna trunk wi' some other red sashes like yers. An' they was *laughin'* over what they done t' ya. Well, th' menfolk was laughin', but th' lady with all th' silver, she wasn't laughin' none.

Neither was that girl ya pillowed with. Well anyways, I tried t' steal yer stuff back, but I couldna pick any of it up. Couldn't even wallop none o' them laughin' Beardies right in their fancy lil mustaches either, though I surely wanted ta. Loooooonnnn! We'd o' knocked every one o' their heads together, if we coulda, wouldn't we, Peg?

Peg added a throaty growl, thinking of what fun it'd been to grab hold of one those pointed beards and shake mightily.

"Well, ol Peg, she got so mad that she set t' wailin' whilst she was sittin' there in th' middle o' their camp, but they couldna hear her. She was jest so mad, she kept yellin' louder an' louder, an' then all th' sudden, they *could* hear her! Anyways, most of th' bundhars an' all o' them floppy-footed droes o' theirs, well they was all terribly upset by Peg's howlin', an' they took off in ev'ry direction ya could think of. So Peg, she let loose even louder, an' now them Scarab folks, they could hear her too. An' let me tell ya, they didna think no more highly offit than did their livestock!" Loon rocked back on his heels as he laughed, and he scratched the fur behind Peg's tattered ears.

"Well, Peg, she hollered like that fer a day anna night, followin' ev'ry time they'd move their camp, then cuttin' loose with her bayin' agin jest as soon as they had their pretty tents set back up. Now that was a whole lot of fun an' all, but it didn't get yer stuff back. Then I had th' great thought that if Peg could make herself heard, then mebbe I could jest as well! So I sent a few words o' prayer t' the White Lady, an' thought a lot 'bout how bad off ya were. Then I felt somethin' in me middle – somethin' hot an' funny – an' I jest knew they'd sure as hell hear me if I got mad enough. So I stalked right inta th' middle o' their clan meeting, an' loud as I could – which is pretty loud, ya know – I called them stinkin' Beardies ev'ry bad name I ever heard, an' I even made up a few new ones on th' spot! Then I told 'em what I thought of 'em, stealin' yer stuff an' leavin' ya out in th' desert like that with no food an' only that little bit o water."

"Well, they thought I was a ghost er demon er somethin', since they could hear me, but they couldna see me."

"Loon," Darn broke in. "That is what I have tried to explain: ye *are* a ghost, ye and Peg both!"

"Hhmph! Loon ain't stupid, Darn! Ghosts only come out at night!"

"Loon," Darn gestured broadly, but said softly, "it is night, my friend."

"Oh," Loon looked about in bewilderment, "yer right. But we been here during the day too. You jest ain't been able t' see er hear us." The matter settled as far as he was concerned, Loon caught up the ragged tails of his story.

"Anyways, we told them Scarab riders that if they didna bring ya back all th' stuff they stole, *plus* plenty o' food an' water, an' all them other sashes too, that I was gonna haunt them! Well, it was really more Peg than it was me, with her howlin an' all, but I dint let them know that cause they might not been so scared if they'd knowed it was jest a mean little dog making all that racket, not some marrow-sucking demon".

"Anyways, I tol' 'em if they didna do ma biddin', I was gonna be sharin' their camp all th' time. Mebbe start comin' ta visit 'em whilst they was sleepin' er squattin' o'er a trench. That spooked 'em a bit, though they was still arguin' bout what ta do. So then I tol' 'em that I'd also be comin' 'round ta slice off a knuckle-width of each man's pride-an-joy ev'ry night. Well, ya ne'er seen any pack o' fellas move so fast ta pack up some bags an' get 'em hung b'hind a pair o' fast riders!" Loon laughed deeply, obviously enjoying his witty charade. Darn just sat and smiled, drinking in the sight of his impossible friend and the sound of the young man's laughter as if he'd never drink again.

"Me and Peg, we ran them two boys th' whole way here!" Loon jumped up and started jogging in place. "Lords o' Fire, can me an' her run fast these days! No matter how fast they rode their beasts, me an' Peg jest trotted along aside 'em. We only eased up when we saw that them poor droes was 'bout ta drop. We couldna hurt them fuzzy ol' droes, ya know, what with them big funny feet an' sad eyes an' all, an' bein' so sweet ta pet. Not like them nasty ol' bundhars, that'd spit on ya er take a chunk outta yer shoulder 's soon 's look atcha ..."

"The riders, Loon?" Darn gently redirected his friend's wayward recounting.

"Yah – riders, that's right. So Peg found ya agin, an' I herded them boys here. Got me a fair imitation of Peg's howl...wanna hear it? Oh, okay, mebbe later then. Well, we had 'em drop yer stuff here. Peg said ya still smelled alive, e'en though ya was buried in th' sand. So I prayed an' prayed t' th' Lady once more. An' I thought real hard 'bout what I needed to do. Then I jest reached down an' grabbed hold an' jerked ya up outta th' sand." Loon dusted off his hand, as if spiritual manifestation was just a simple matter.

"But Loon," Darn asked, shaking his head, "how is that possible? Shades have no substance, but ye – and Peg – are both whole and real. Well, mostly."

"I dunno, Darn," Loon answered, shaking his head and smiling, though his eyes were sad. "It feels sorta funny when I touch somethin', like I got big fuzzy mittens on m' hands. An' it hurts a bit ta be this way – kinda like thinkin' too hard, er holdin' yer breath too long. But th' Lady, She promised we could do whate'er we needed ta save ya."

Loon's smile turned true as happier matters moved in to occupy his mind. He stood and stretched upwards, blocking out half the stars in the night sky. "Ha! Ol' Peg an' me, we sure surprised ya, didn't we?" Loon bellowed out a laugh and snatched at Peg's tail, reason enough for a savage canine counterattack. "Bet ya ne'er expected t' see *us* out here, didja?"

"No, Loon," Darn said weakly, smiling even though his lip cracked in two spots. "I expected to encounter many strange things in Lord Agni's domain, but none as strange as the pair before me!" He continued, in mock anger. "Still, ye could have spoken to me, rather than leave me to believe that this beastie was to have my entrails for a midnight snack!" Darn scrubbed Peg behind one ear, to which she answered with a series of satisfied grunts.

Loon nodded in exaggerated agreement, and reached around to scratch at his rump, an act he had always enjoyed before. This time, though, it brought no relief for the itching, and Loon frowned at the thought, but only for a moment.

"Well, I been a'talkin' to ya all day t'day...last night too," Loon answered, quite seriously. "I jest ran outta things ta say, I guess. I feared ya might not open yer eyes e'er agin. Ya slept fer a night an' a day!" Loon held on to a stern expression as long as he was able - at least the span of a heartbeat or two - before the foolish grin that

461

granted him his name slid back into its accustomed place on his face.

"An' b'sides – oh Lord an' Lady, Darn! It was *so* pow'fully funny, watchin' ya lyin' there, an' ya not knowin' who I was, an' bein' scairt of ol' Peg an' all! Loooooooooonnnnn! I was sure I'd wet m' britches, not tryin' ta laugh an' all. But ya looked so funny, rasslin' all crazy with ol' Peg an' callin' 'er names an' such!" The image was too much for Loon's meager control, and once again the waves of his laughter rolled across the barren seabed of the desert. Darn's own laughter felt fine coming out, though it added to the din no more than an extra drop in the ocean.

As the sound of their laughter faded, Darn found himself staring into the darkness, simply enjoying once again the simple pleasure of Loon and Peg's company. Then slowly he realized that the sky behind Loon was painted with a faint wash of scarlet: Lord Agni's chariot was riding to bring dawn to His domain. Darn turned around and squinted hard, trying to discern any pathways among the crags to the west.

"Loon," Darn asked, "have ye any thought where we may be? I have been lost in this forsaken land for so long I no longer trust right from left."

Loon thought carefully before answering. "No, Darn, I ain't got so much as a clue. In th' middle offa whole, *whole* lotta sand, best I can tell. I ne'er been here b'fore, ya know."

Darn clenched his teeth and looked down at the sand, and remembered that this too was part of Loon's unquenchable charm. Even Peg seemed to be tested, though, shaking her little head at her master's foolishness.

"But ya know," Loon added, "mebbe we can walk up an' ask

th' folks whot live innat place up there." As he pointed a nail-bitten finger, the sun broke over the eastern horizon and flames lit the mountains to the west. A few degrees south of the newly lit peaks, a series of descending ridges appeared out of the dying shadows. And where the ridges ended, on the edge of a long high plain, sat a walled manor-place that shone a deep ruby red in the morning light.

For a long moment, Darn had no words. When he found his voice, it was hardly more than a whisper.

"The Scarlet Keep! I came this close, and still almost failed!"

"Look's like a nice kinda place too! Awf'lly pretty, ain't it?" Loon said with simple sincerity, and Peg added her assent.

A narrow winding path led up from the desert floor, carved into the bare sandstone of the cliff face. The keep at the trail's end held a tall single tower within its walls, all formed from blocks of ruby-colored stone that were dug from the cliff itself. In truth it was a rather lonely looking, forlorn place. But compared to the desolation of the desert, it looked only to Darn like blessed sanctuary. Though the climb up the cliff-side path would be a trial in and of itself, still Darn was sure that he could make the journey in less than a day. And there, within the walls of the Scarlet Keep, an unknown future lay in wait for him, promising further pain and heartache perhaps, but adventure and triumph as well. Darn had never felt so strongly drawn to any place in his entire life.

Darn leapt to his feet with a jubilant cry, and started grabbing at the satchels of gear and food and drink. "Let us be off, Loon!" he said in a frantic rush. "With thy help, we shall be within those walls before nightfall, for a *cold* bath and a *cold* drink, and then much time to talk and laugh. I know not how long I must linger within the Keep after I don my robes. But after that, we three shall be off to travel to ..." Darn words dried up as he saw his mountainous friend shaking his head slowly.

"We canno' go with ya, m' dear friend Darn," Loon said quietly, and a fat lonely tear rolled down the broad expanse of his face, washing away the smile that normally rode there. "Th' Lady – She said we can't stay. We...we gotta go off som'ere else. I, uh, I ain't really sure where. Peg tells me she can hear sumun cryin' a long piece off, an' I think it might be Jehred. Bein' my brother an' all, he prob'ly worries about me alot, since he can't really take care o' me no more an' make sure I don' do stupid taterhead things." Loon wiped a sleeve across his face, leaving more mess in its wake than it took away. Then he snorted and blinked hugely as a wonderfully simple thought flared to life within his mind, and it brought his smile back from where he'd had it conveniently pocketed.

"Course, once I talk t' Jehred, an' tell 'im we're okay an' all, well me an' Peg, we might jest havta pay ol' Sott a visit." Loon scooped Peg up so he could talk to her eye to eye. "Whaddaya think Peg? Think ol' Sott would like it if we sang 'im a lil tune one night whilst he's sittin' on th' pot?" Peg yipped furiously, and her tail blurred in a fit of wagging.

Darn smiled at Loon's lunatic plan, for only his remarkable friend could ponder such foolishness given the situation he was in – namely, dead. *Like as ask a sand leopard to drop his spots*, Darn thought, *as to ask Loon not to scheme and play and laugh*. But Darn could not loose himself from the gnawing pain of loneliness that had begun afresh.

"But Loon, must ye leave *now*?" Darn asked in vain, though

he knew in his heart he was to lose his friend a second time. "I've missed ye pair of fools so badly. And I know not what will be asked of me when I leave the Keep. What if I have need of thy help, and Peg's?"

"Well then, Darn," Loon answered slowly, as if explaining something to himself, "if ya really need us, then jest holler real, *real* loud fer us, cause we might be a long ways away. But Peg'll hear ya, an' she'll tell me, an' we'll come t' help jest like we always done fer each other, as fast an' furious as a bunch o' Border Knights, dontcha worry." He laid a large hand on Darn's shoulder, where it sat light as thought. "But, I don' think you'll be needin' our help that much, frien' Darn." Loon's face grew serious for a moment, and the veil of simplicity that he normally wore dropped away.

"What e'er yer task, I know ya will meet it with courage an' honor an' grace. An' ya shall follow yer true heart, an' do whots right, jest like ya done fer me an' Peg. Ya will bring goodness ta a lot o' folks, Darn - ol' Loon knows that plain an' simple." Darn started to shake his head, but Loon would have none of it. "An' dontcha be settin' yer mind agin yerself, m' good frien' Darn. I seen yer fire b'fore: ain't no one t' stand against it once ya got yer hackles up. So ya just go on over t' that keep up there, an' ya tell them masters t' hand over a set o' red robes fer th' finest Flame Master whot e'er crossed that bedamned desert!"

Loon yawned hugely, and when he was finished, his smiling grace had returned. "So yer gonna be jest fine. If it makes ya feel any less weepy, though, me an' Peg, we'll be missing' ya awfully bad too, won't we Peg?"

Peg whined in agreement and seemed to nod. Then she

broke off abruptly and cocked her head towards the east – back across the desert – as if listening for a lost sound. She jumped up and began running around in a circle, barking hurriedly. Loon looked at her intently for a moment, listening to her yaps, then he straightened up and hitched his shoulders.

"Sorry, Darn. We got to go *now*, Peg says."

Darn stepped forward and lost himself in Loon's mammoth embrace. His immense blond friend certainly didn't feel like a ghost, but he didn't feel quite all the way *there*, either. Part of Darn knew that in the days and years to come he would question his friend's appearance, and might one day consider the whole thing to be only a drought-induced hallucination. But for now, his heart told him what was real: Loon's arms on his shoulders, Peg's ear-piercing yapping, and the tears pouring unashamedly down his own face. That, and the renewed pain of a wound that had only just begun to heal, tempered by one final conversation with his friend.

The two broke apart awkwardly, both wiping furiously at their faces.

"Go then," Darn said, and he waved back towards the east. "Time waits not, e'en for the likes of Peg and Loon!" He tried desperately to laugh. "And give old Sott a kick in the arse for me, as well."

Loon's smile threatened to outshine the dawning sun. "Oh, we will, I 'spect, be spendin' some powf'lly funny times at Sott's Inn sometime here soon. Be ya sure 'bout that!"

Darn bent over and snatched up a wriggling Peg. It seemed impossible to hold her, what with all her curly hair and a definite uncertainness about her form. Still, the little mutt fought furiously to reach every spot on Darn's face with her tongue.

"Ye must watch out and guard over him now, Peg," Darn said to her sternly, before sputtering to a stop as she slipped him a quick sloppy dog kiss. When he reopened his eyes, Darn found the little mongrel staring intensely back at him.

"*Well, have I not always done so?*" a tiny, bright voice questioned in the back of Darn's mind.

He looked over at Loon in sudden astonishment, but his friend was staring off into the eastern distance. And when Darn brought his gaze back to Peg, she was once again only a happy, frantic, slightly-tattered little dog squirming in his arms. Darn set her carefully back on her feet, then stood up, feeling a little stunned, until Loon's voice broke through to him.

"... be off now. I'll pass 'long word t' Elias thatcha made it here alright. He'll be mighty pleased t' hear it; got himself a fortune o' silver bet on ya 'gainst some o' th' other masters an' half th' gamers crost th' city!" Loon walked to the edge of the rocky crest, and Peg hobbled over to stand beside him.

"Look fer us at dusk, some ev'nins when yer out an' alone," Loon said, smiling over his shoulder. "Dontcha worry none; we'll find ya." He turned abruptly then, and the first rays of the rising sun struck him full in the face.

"Come now, Peg," Loon boomed. " We got us a fair piece o' walkin' t' do."

The pair stepped out onto the sand, and Darn could see that they left no footprints. And he was fairly certain he could see outlines of the dunes and rocks on the other side of Loon showing through.

"How 'bout a song, ol' Peg? Wha? No, not *that* one! Oh,

so be it. But I pick next time 'round!'"

Darn could hear the pair arguing as they crested the top of the next dune, and he watched as their outlines began to shimmer and fade. Shortly after, he could see nothing more of them, though for a while he could hear a song drifting upon the wind:

> *Oh, Capon th' Lucky had a hole in 'is heart,*
> *fer a maid'n who lived in th' sea.*
> *An' Left-handed Loric, 'e lusted fer pearls,*
> *an' whate'er oth'r treasures there'd be.*
> *So off they set, inna boat often patched,*
> *an' they vowed as they nailed down a board:*
> *"We'll not return till we're loaded with loot,*
> *an' we've plumbed th' depths of 'er hoard!*

After a while, Darn lost the sound of the tune and found himself humming alone, accompanied only by the wind. He turned his back to the burning eye of the sun, and slowly picked up his gear and supplies from where they lay, sadness and purpose both draped around him. But as Darn stepped out onto the sand for the last leg of his first journey, a faint call, a parting gift, drifted back across the dunes, riding the shoulders of the desert wind. And it drew a smile back to the young man's face.

"Loooo-oooo-oooo-oooonnnn!!!"

Chapter Nineteen
The First Step

Darn paused in his wanderings to pull open one of the Keep's upper windows and stare into the east, out into the barren corpse of the Great Escarp Desert. He could almost hear Her call to him, beckoning, daring him to step back within Her grasp, to challenge the heat and despair and deadly monotony once more.

Wager again, Her voice rasped in the wind, *double or naught!*

A shudder passed through his bones as Darn listened to the deceitful challenge, and he felt no shame to admit his relief that the crossing he'd made need never again be attempted. Then he thought of the reception he had received upon reaching the doors of the Keep, and pride bubbled up from his chest like a cold mountain spring. He remembered the Keepers' amazement when they admitted to seeing his campfire within a few candlemarks' trek of the Keep's walls. By the Order's strictures, they were forbidden from coming to his aid, even had he fallen a single step from walls.

Several of the red-robed masters had been waiting for Darn at dawn's light, standing at the bottom of the stone stairs that led from the desert floor up to the Scarlet Keep. The three Flame Masters – Remmy, Goeterum, and Salvic – were young, newly come to their robes themselves. All three had been present at Darn's victory in the Circle of Judgment. And all three had reluctantly opened their ranks to accommodate the new Adept student. They hadn't exactly been friends before they left on their own sojourns across the Escarp a hand of years earlier. But all of them knew Darn and grudgingly respected his abilities. Still, they were confounded when a lone

Flame Dancer showed up at their doorstep unannounced, with no prior message from the Pyre, no preparations, nothing – just a bag full of foodstuffs, four extra sashes, and half a roasted hare on a stick. And they could not help but show their awe at Darn's determination and courage. To camp within sight of the Keep for the night and dare the desert's entrapments one last time, rather than sleep within the safety of the Keep's stone walls, was either the measure of a fool or a true Child of Agni.

Darn closed the shutters against the windblown sand, and continued on his way down the rough-carved hallway. The satchel and bedroll that hung from his shoulder bumped softly against his knee as he walked, counterpointing the whispering treads of his steps. The Keep's Steward had been most generous – or so he had said – in stocking Darn's supplies for his upcoming departure. Then again, as the bandy-legged and tight-fisted accountant had pointed out, Darn hardly had need of further foodstocks or gear, given the amount he had brought back with him from the depth of the desert's maw. Darn simply smiled and nodded his head, as he did in answer to all questions of his journey, for the Strictures allowed that any who made the desert passage had the right to keep the details of their trip to themselves. To Darn, the tale of his journey was not one to be offered lightly or freely.

The twisting passageway emptied into a large, plainly-dressed hall without furniture or obvious function. On one long wall hung an intricate tapestry that told the tale of Firstmaster Tyrin's rebirth in the desert. The opposite wall was divided into three sections, filled with row upon row of brass plaques and plates, each imprinted with a representation of the Three Sacred Flames.

Hectar l'Donal, read the first plaque that Darn examined: *slain in the 3rd Klemish Invasion during the reign of King Tetwald II.* These then were the markers of Flame Masters who had fulfilled their duties, and had given their lives in service to the Order. The columns of plaques stretched towards the darkened corners of the ceiling, hundreds, or perhaps even thousands of them, the topmost being so tarnished with age as to be unreadable. Darn glanced at several others, and a chill shivered him as he noticed that none he could see told of a natural or peaceful death: ... *died in the Great Troll War ... poisoned aboard a Parthinian galley ... lost to the Desert ... slain in personal combat.* And so many others simply stated: *killed in pursuance of the Three Holy Flames.* Darn closed his eyes and stepped to the next group of plaques.

Each of the plates in the second section held only a name, and perhaps a line or two of title, being markers of all the living Flame Masters. Darn couldn't help but notice the blank space left at the bottom of each plaque, waiting patiently for the scribing of an epitaph. After a few moments of searching, Darn located several names that he recognized: Era and Tobani and even Master Elias. At the very top, Grandmaster Saura's name was inscribed on a slightly more elaborate plaque, already brown with age. At the bottom were plaques so new they shone like mirrors. The last of these said simply: *Darn of Warden Woods.*

The third section of wall was covered with rows of small brass rectangles stood on end, each with a name inscribed upon it. A short hook stood out from the end of each marker, and upon some of these hung scarlet sashes: the last surviving remains of Flame Dancers who had succumbed on their journey through the desert or had otherwise perished along their path. The masters of the Keep explained to Darn that oft times peaceful tribes of Scarab Folk would pause in their wanderings to barter and trade, and the masters paid a reward for any sashes that the desert people recovered from corpses sleeping in the sands. Darn had expected his recovery of several stolen sashes – including his own – to cause an uproar among the masters. But the Elder of the Keep, Master Donawd Terraget, had shrugged his shoulders wearily, and offered only a plain sour comment in answer.

"Should've worn 'em tighter about their middles, then," he said.

Darn searched for the four sashes that he himself had hung upon the brass hooks. Reminders, each and every one, of how close he had come to shaming his teachers and joining them with his own memento hung on this wall of failure and oblivion. He found himself unconsciously rubbing a hand along the sash that wrapped around his hips, the sash that now bore Darn's name embroidered beneath that of Master Tobani. After one more long look, Darn took a deep breath, sighed and offered a quick prayer, then turned and walked from the room.

The corridor ended at a small, thick-walled guard room. Murder holes in the ceiling above peered down with pupiless stares, and Darn realized suddenly that he was quite anxious to quit this forlorn place. A stout door of bloodwood squatted along one wall, bound with iron straps and barred with a thick beam of the same rough-cast metal. Darn smiled and nodded to the fat guardsman on duty, who in turn made quite a show of puffing and grunting as he lifted his opulent rear from his station-post stool and cranked the windlass that raised the bar from the door.

The small portal swung open slowly, as if reluctant to admit any sunlight into the gloomy chamber. But Darn showed no hesitation as he stepped through, out into the blazing breath of the sun once again. For a moment, Darn's senses lied to him, swearing that he had returned to the Land of Ashes. Then his eyes became accustomed to the glare, and he could see the tough wiry grasses and thorn bushes that fought for holds upon the rocky hills, along with the hardy brittlecone pines that hung tenaciously wherever their roots could find cracks to delve inside. Though harsh, the land atop the plateau did indeed support life, and promised more welcome lands beyond.

Darn pulled a scrap of parchment from his robe, and re-read Master Elias' words. The message had been sent from the Pyre, tied to the leg of a homing swift. To no one's understanding, it had been waiting for Darn at the Keep's aviary *before* he arrived. The note contained Elias's congratulations on Darn's safe passage. It also held a map that showed the way to the hold of one Baron Umbeck in the Wresnian Provinces. It appeared the Baron had need of an arbitrator in a rather nasty clan feud, and he could not trust his own people's impartiality. When the request had been brought before him, Master Elias replied that he knew the perfect candidate for a job requiring a sharp mind and a sharp tongue besides.

The master's letter rambled for a bit more, telling of a rash of mysterious disappearances and brutal kneecappings that had been visited upon certain well-known Shiningrock political and business leaders as of late. Strangely enough, neither Captain Jehred's garrison soldiers or Elias' Flame Dancers seemed to have been able to catch a single perpetrator of these heinous acts. Darn could hear Elias' boisterous laughter behind the words as surely as if the black-humored master stood beside him.

The letter ended on a strange note: Elias mentioned that he had known of Darn's arrival at the Scarlet Keep long before he received word from the masters stationed there. A visitor in a dream had told Elias that his prized student had honored him, enduring trials that had gifted many others with failure. The news brought Elias great joy; it also allowed him a chance to double most of his bets and even triple a few, before Darn's fate was revealed to the rest of the masters.

The statement made Darn wonder about a vision of his own, gathered while wandering lost in the barren desert, a vision of lost friends and healed hurts. Such thoughts quickly brought pain on its heels. But the sense of loss was no longer so great or so bitter, and in a way that was comforting.

Darn carefully placed the letter and map back inside his robe, then settled his load of foodstuffs and gear around him. The Keepers had said it was a dayturn's journey to the closest town of any size – Greenholm – but it was an easy walk, if a long one. The name of the place, and the path to get there, seemed to suit Darn finely. He adjusted the set of the twin daggers that were thrust beneath his sash, and snugged the sash down tight. Then he stepped out onto the rutted cart path that led westward, away from the Keep, away from the desert, away from Shiningrock and Warden Woods and all that he had ever known.

The scarlet silk of the young Flame Master's new robes caught the sun's rays in its folds and drenched them in fire and blood. With excitement and fear, caution and exhilaration all roiling in his guts, Darn could spare thought for little else other than the steps that waited before him. For a moment, a sudden fear raced up his spine – fear of facing his future alone. Then a faint breeze whispered in his ear, in what almost seemed like a silly little tune. And whatever the zephyr's song, it brought a smile to the young man's face as he stepped out onto his path.

Perhaps Darn never noticed – or perhaps his mind just chose to ignore – that as he walked, he cast three shadows: one of middle height, flowing and robed; one exceptionally tall and broad, that stepped with an easy unencumbered grace; and one very small, that moved with a hobbling gate and occasionally danced in circles around its larger companions.

Glossary

Gods

Agni, Lord Agni- God of fire; rider of the sun; patron of the Disciples of the Flames.

Bes- Mother Bes; fertility goddess.

Elandril- The White Lady, goddess of healing and nature. Patron goddess of many of the elvish tribes, and some of the more rustic human communities.

Eshatti- Goddess of pleasure and dance.

Gorah- Death god of the Crimian steppes.

Shara- Goddess of beauty and wisdom.

Tattargi- Father Terror; god of storms.

Volar- The Great Destroyer; god of battle, and patron of soldiers.

Places

Bandarin Isles- A group of volcanic islands in the center of the southern sea. With no overall system of governance, its many ports thrive on a steady trade of piracy, goods, and slaves. Natives of the isles are deeply feared for their ferocity and cannibalistic tendencies.

Barony of Wresnia- The western-most lands held by the human king, though the Baron of Leige traditionally ruled his lands as he saw fit. Trade with the rest of the Eldorn kingdom had to travel through the high passes of the Skräal mountains then down the great river D'or.

Carpath Peaks- Frozen, ancient mountains in the far north; inhospitable to any but the great stone trolls who reside there.

Chak'ran Isles- Large island chain in the far eastern sea; known for its spice and slave trade.

Courdeless- The city-state of the Sidhe elf king.

Dagarr's Keep- Ancient watchtower guarding Shiningrock's northern approach.

Dawnwoods- Ancient forest hidden in the Rendrac mountains; ancestral home of the Sylvan elves; hidden to non-elvish eyes.

Eldor- The human kingdom, stretching from Jerrholm in the north to the Crimian Steppes in the south – or as far as the king's campaigners can extend his hold.

HeshuiIsland- Nation in the cold northern seas. The people of this mountainous island are fiercely proud, and renown for their fiery tempers.

Hovill- Northern town renown for its rich grain fields and excellent breweries.

Greenheart Forest- Thick forest covering much of the land between Shiningrock and Lorring. Most humans stay to the coastal road to avoid the deep woods.

Jungles of Yot- Impenetrable, sweltering jungles of the far south, inhabited by aggressive natives who wield the darkest of death magics.

Khalthmus Mountains- Home to the mountain dwarves, who fiercely defend their ancestral lands. These now-desolate hills to the north and west of the elven lands contain deeply-mined sources of gold, mithril, gems and other treasures.

Kingdom of Klemire- The traditional enemy of the Eldorn Kingdom, the Klemish armies long ago conquered most of the Eastern Lands. Only the wide Sarretto Sea and the relative weakness of the Klemish navy keep the hordes at a distance.

Lorring- The Eldorn king's seat of power. The immense walled city and heavily-fortified castle have withstood four major Klemish sieges.

Perthan Peninsula- The greatest croplands and vineyards of the southern kingdom, the Perthan Peninsula feeds much of the world. It is ringed and ruled by the Five Cities and governed by the Sons of D'Quoralot, who grudgingly pay homage to the Eldorn King in Lorring.

Rendrac Mountains- The long north-south spine of this range separates Shiningrock's highlands and the Endless Marshes from the Escarp Desert.

Shiningrock- A great port city of questionable renown. All races, kingdoms, and people are to be found in this major trade center. The commercial heart of the Eldorn Kingdom.

Skräal Mountains- The barren, southern range that rises from the Crimian Steppes.

Tharian Confederacy- Loose collection of city states in the far east, known for producing the finest sword steel – and the finest swordsmen – in any land. The Confederacy traditionally has played off the Klemish and the Eldorn kingdoms against each other. Lack of unity between the states is all that prevents them from being a major political force.

Warden Woods- Small rural village on the edge of Greenheart Forest. Birthplace and early home of Darn.

Time and Measure

Candlemark (mark)- The amount a candle would burn between sounding of the city bell, commonly taken as a thumb-length.

Dayturn- A full turn of the days: Moonday, Marketday, Weaversday, Butchersday, Walkingday, Harvestday, Solace.

Hand- Common method of counting five. Often called a full hand to indicate ten.

Moons Months: Icebeard, Hunger, Sowing, Blossom, Birthing, Fishers, Midsummer, Dog, Frost, Harvest, Hunter's, Midwinter

Common Terms

Bint'rong- A large, slow-witted and long-tailed fruit eater, often called a bear-cat. These docile creatures live in the forest canopy, though they grow to half the size of a man.

Bundhar- Ill-tempered beast of burden, bred for use in the desert and the arid steppes. Notorious for their bad smells and bad attitudes.

Droe- Tall, bipedal riding beast bred exclusively by the Scarab folk for travel in the desert. The creature's large splayed feet and comical appearance belie its tireless speed running across the sands.

DromaCommon- bronze coin, worth a full hand of coppers

Fenlock- Large, slow-witted game animal common to the highlands, prized for its tender flesh.

Green Robe- A True Healer and follower of the White Lady. They have the ability to absorb another's injury or illness, and mend it using the Healer's innate power.

Kritt viper- Small snake from the Endless Marshes, whose addictive venom brings euphoria, madness, and eventually death to its partakers.

Las'ona- In the Sidhest, a soul cloud, the embodiment of energies radiated by all living creatures.

Nania- Wooly beasts kept for their fine fleece; common herd animals for common folk.

Passaratt- In the Sidhe tongue, a blood oath that will be defended with the maker's life.

Sandtrapper- Type of giant, desert-dwelling mollusk that lies hidden in the sand waiting for prey to walk nearby, which it then enfolds and consumes.

Shisha- Dried resin of a certain Crimian plant that has euphoric and hallucinogenic properties.

Sidhe- Those people of the Elven race that live west of the Rendrac mountains. Often called the High Elves, more for their love of cities and aristocratic society than for any real differences from their cousins. The ancient Sidhe kings led all the Elven people in the Great Troll Wars.

Sidhest- The ancestral high tongue of all the Elven people.

Solari- A gold coin of considerable value, worth the daily wages for perhaps twenty men.

Soulfire (soulflame)- The internal life-spark which all are born with; the human fire that drives the base emotions of fear, passion, and anger.

Sweetleaf- Common herb used for smoking.

Sylvan- Elven folk who remain east of the Rendracs, choosing to live in traditional tree-homes. Most of these tribes reside in the Dawnwoods, or scattered throughout Greenheart Forest.

T'aacha- A minor Sidhe aristocratic title, usually given to a distant cousin of the king.

Talum- Silver torc often worn by the Scarab folk to identify their clan.

Thungari- Large, semi-intelligent beastmen from the Jungles of Yot, nearly twice the size of a man, with heavy talons and incredible strength. The shaggy creatures are able to follow a few words of human speech, and are often used as expendable guards.

Treemunks (treerats) - Small furred vermin that frequent the tree-tops, they are known to spread disease.

Tsaa- Common curse word, referring to dung, used to express displeasure.

Warmark- Military leader

www.ingramcontent.com/pod-product-compliance
Lightning Source LLC
Chambersburg PA
CBHW071216250626
47163CB00001B/13